When Love Takes Over

Caroline Grace-Cassidy

POOLBEG

This novel is entirely a work of fiction. The names, characters and incidents portrayed in it are the work of the author's imagination. Any resemblance to actual persons, living or dead, events or localities is entirely coincidental.

Published 2012
by Poolbeg Press Ltd
123 Grange Hill, Baldoyle
Dublin 13, Ireland
E-mail: poolbeg@poolbeg.com
www.poolbeg.com

1

A catalogue record for this book is available from the British Library.

ISBN 978-1-84223-494-5

Typeset by Patricia Hope in Sabon 11.5/16
Printed and bound by CPI Group (UK) Ltd, Croydon CR0 4YY

www.poolbeg.com

When Love Takes Over

About the author

Caroline Grace-Cassidy lives in Knocklyon, Dublin, with her husband Kevin and two daughters Grace and Maggie. She has been a film and television actress for the past ten years. Caroline does not enjoy housework but she does enjoy a glass or two of wine and a good old singsong. This is her first novel.

Acknowledgements

Firstly I would like to offer my most sincere and heartfelt thanks to all at Poolbeg Press, especially Paula Campbell for believing in my work. Paula, you have been amazing during this process and I look forward to our journey together.

Gaye Shortland – thank you for your fantastic edit but most of all for your wonderful encouraging words. They mean so much to me.

My love for reading was nurtured from a very early age by my mother Noeleen Grace. Mam, you always instilled in me the joy that books can bring. This book would never have been written without your passion. Thank you for your constant love and support.

For my dad, Robert Grace aka Robbie Box. You are my rock star . . . thanks for always being there for me.

For Samantha & Keith for sharing my growing-up years . . . how fun were they?

For Margaret Kilroy – always in my thoughts.

For my Maro – Marina Rafter – you define the word *friend*. Hurry up and have those babies so we can hit Kehoe's again!

For Tara, Amy, Honor & Chris - thank you for taking such great care of Grace.

For my husband Kevin – your support in both my acting and writing careers has been unwavering. When I have really felt like throwing in the towel, you were always there to pick me up. Thank you for being the most incredible dad in the world. Your patience, understanding, selflessness and kindness amaze me every single day. Thanks for making our home such a happy one. You are also very easy on the eye. I love you.

Thanks to all the wonderful actors I share the scene with! And to all the casting directors who call me in!

Finally, thank you so much for reading this book. I really hope you enjoy the story and I would be delighted to hear from you through my site **www.carolinegracecassidy.com.**

Love, Caroline x

With all my love

For Kevin, Grace & Maggie Cassidy

1

Dublin, October 2010

I'd known that the supermarket wine had been open in the fridge for over a week, that it was dirt-cheap and didn't smell great, but I sank it anyhow. Now my head was splitting in two. It felt like a woodpecker was drilling and scraping his claws on the inside of my brain to get out. I tried to lift my head off the pillow but the pain pierced me between my heavy sticky eyes and I flopped back down. I reached for the comfort of my much-loved Debenham's goose-feathered duvet but instead found a rather smelly hairy brown throw. Where the hell was I? I tried to move again and now realised I was naked. Stark naked. White breasts flopping from side to side as I tried in vain to catch them. Turning as fast as was humanly possible with the head I was nursing, I saw the bed was empty apart from my awful nakedness. The room was still out of focus as I squinted against the alcoholic poison swirling through my brain. Then I spotted my Trinny & Susannah wonder knickers, my Olympic champion of hold-in knickers, the one and only no-flesh-is-escaping-from-these-babies – on the floor. In all their shabbiness – once jet-black, now after a million washes merely dirty-carpet grey. Oh, the humiliation I felt that I'd actually worn them! What was wrong with me? Think, woman, think! No need – the lucky man was entering the bedroom. The light flicked on and hurt my eyes.

The shock was audible, I'm afraid, as I said rather too loudly: "Oh fuck! Christ! What?"

Paul smiled at me, though if it had been the other way round I'd have been mortally offended. "So was it as good for you as it was for me then, Mia?" asked the builder who had been putting an extension on Carla's house for the last two weeks.

Carla. I knew there was something else nagging me – we were going breast-shopping today! I was due to meet her in town at ten o'clock to help her try on the new boobs.

"Shit!" I sat up, my old boobs fell out, not the best look with the rolls of flesh on my white stomach clambering up to meet them. I threw myself back down. "PP Paul – I mean Paul –" (we called him PP Paul as he was never out of the bloody toilet) "please can I have a moment to get myself together?"

"Sure, Mee-Mee Mia!" He grabbed his white T-shirt off the edge of the chair and left the room.

I noticed he had a small tattoo on his left shoulder that looked like Gargamel from *The Smurfs*, but surely not? He was in good enough shape, if fairly hairy all over. Oh man, I sighed again, why do I do these things? I couldn't remember a damn thing but I knew as the day progressed every last little embarrassing detail would come flooding into my mind. Playing on widescreen HD. Voice-over by that man who voices all the big cinema movies, with the too-slow, booming voice. I found my bra and jeans under the bed but where was my top? Just as I was about to wear a Liverpool jersey I spotted in his very messy, overcrowded wardrobe, he knocked gently on the door and then called, "Just found this in the van, Mia!" I opened the door a smidgen and slid my hand out as he dropped my priceless, loved-and-treated-with-kid-gloves, black silk Karen Millen hides-a-multitude top.

In his van. It was in his van. Oh, Mia.

I looked at myself in the mirror. I was a fright. An absolute fright. I mean, I wouldn't answer the door to a blind postman looking like this. I was so pale, yet had red blotches all over my face. Brown hair like an eagle's nest. Bloodshot panda eyes. Beard-rash. Chapped lips – the severe dehydration I was suffering from certainly didn't help. I bashed down my hair with the back of my hand. Licked my fingers to try and rub away most of the black eyeliner and mascara from under my glazed green eyes. I pulled myself up straight, my five-foot-eight-inches straight. Apparently I carried my weight well (I often got told this like it was a great compliment). The silk top slid over my bulging stomach. I was in need of a trip to the gym, if only I had a membership somewhere. No skinny jeans for me, I'm afraid – my Next 'boyfriend' jeans were my 'It' jeans. Okay, okay, so they were from the men's department, but who could tell? And they fitted so much better. I rummaged around again for my high-heel Office FMB's. Under the bed I found a dog-eared copy of *Catcher in the Rye* and an old shoebox, but no boots. A yellow Doc Martens shoebox. I slowly pulled it out and my boots were revealed behind it.

"Cuppa?" He was holding out a chipped, yellow, stained Liverpool FC mug as I shoved the box back under.

"Emm, no thanks, I actually have to run – I have to meet Carla in town."

I stood up slowly and finished dressing as he stood there slurping his tea and staring at me. Perfect, white, straight teeth – funny I'd never noticed him this way before.

Should I thank him? Apologise? Shake his hand? It was embarrassing as we said our goodbyes and I breathed a sigh of relief as I made my way out onto the busy streets of Rathmines.

My whole being told everyone who passed me: 'I didn't go home last night – I'm a dirty stop-out whore!' (Well, maybe the whore bit was a bit strong but you know the feeling?) I felt dirty, not because I'd had sex with a stranger (well, he wasn't exactly a stranger) – oh no, I'd done that plenty of times before – but dirty and hung-over and slightly used. Call me a snob but the filthy student-type flat didn't help matters. It made me itchy. I stopped at Insomnia and ordered a latte and a double-choc-chip muffin and took my mobile from my bag as I wriggled onto a ridiculously high stool.

"Carla," I muttered through a mouthful of cake, some falling out of my mouth as I tried to stuff in as much as was humanly possible at once. I am on my way."

Two Skinnies, obviously just finished their morning Pilates, stood sipping their green teas and staring at me. Why didn't they sit? Did you burn more calories by standing? I made eye contact with one of them and they both looked away.

"Where the hell were you last night? I left the plastic on the latch all night!" Carla's breath was raspy as she walked briskly, no doubt holding her mobile well away from her precious ear. Carla was a walker. Yes, you know the type before I even tell you. She actually *liked* to walk. *Preferred* it to a car or bus, she said. She was a stunner too, of course (goes with the actually-enjoying-walking bit, I think).

Carla O'Leary had joined our small auctioneer's office, Clovers Auctioneers, two years ago, and had become the top seller straight away. Boy, could she sell a house! She was all blonde hair, black Armani suits with blinding white shirts. Owned a red Mini Cooper that never left the driveway. I couldn't have met her at a better time. Things in Number 31, Coolpak Park had been getting very tetchy between my mam and Samantha and me. Samantha was my much prettier, much thinner, much more successful, mother's Number One, younger sister – yeah, blah, blah, blah! She always was and always would be the smarter and the prettier one. She worked in IT (whatever that meant – I had no idea and, to be brutally honest, little or no interest to ask) but it seemed to earn plenty of money so I couldn't understand why she still lived at home. Dad left home years ago. In fact, I couldn't remember him ever living with us really. He shacked up with an Aer Lingus air-stewardess in Dun Laoghaire – Angela. She was once the Face of Dublin Airport – I think that bothered Mam more than her stealing her husband and our father. Dad met her at a funeral and that was that. He was gone the next week. So, to get back to Carla, when I heard she was looking for a flatmate for her newly owned first home – a massive renovation project in Ranelagh – I jumped at the chance and moved in.

"So meet me in the Collins Banks Clinic as soon as you get into town." Carla rang off.

Oh, did I mention she was also the nicest, kindest, most generous person I had ever met? I'd been waiting for a friend like her literally all my life.

I polished off the muffin and drained the latte, and was still wiping the froth from my mouth as I hailed a cab. These FMB's were not walking boots by any means and I wished I was as organised as Carla and had a squashed-up pair of flats in my bag – the type of shoes I saw on *Off the Rails*, a 'must have' item for every woman's bag, except I didn't have any. I didn't really have any 'must have' items to be honest. I wasn't a 'must have' kind of girl. I gave the taximan my destination and sat back and closed my eyes.

I remembered drinking wine in the house in Ranelagh (I couldn't call Ranelagh home, as home was still Coolpak Park – except that it wasn't home either), watching MTV, singing aloud to Girls Aloud live at Wembley. This involved screeching into the mirror above the TV, pouting and pointing my finger seductively. With Carla at an engagement dinner at the Unicorn Restaurant, I was all alone. There was something about a Girls Aloud concert on the telly with a few drinks on me that made me feel sexy. As though I was Cheryl Cole (she really should have gone back to Tweedy, though), up there grinding my perfect body to my perfect pop song. I ground my hips and swigged from my wine bottle as I roared the cheesy lyrics. Oh, I loved the clothes and the body – and the hair-envy I felt with a few drinks on me was depressing.

I was thoroughly enjoying having the place to myself and then I heard the doorbell – well, the plastic sheet with a bell attached by a piece of string that covered a gaping hole where a back door should be. It was PP Paul. He looked good and smelled great.

"I left my mobile here today," he explained to me, hands thrust deep into the pockets of his blue jeans.

He was about six foot one, I supposed, and was wearing a brown sweater and brown boots. He had black sort of messy, spiky hair, and was good-looking in an if-you-like-that-kind-of-look way. I didn't. I went for guys who were not so attractive. Less competition out there.

"Yes, yes, a drink in town sounds great!" I enthused when he suggested it.

Yes, it was all coming back now. Into his messy white van. Getting halfway up the road and then diving on him. Pulling my top over my head and him upping the never-used fifth gear to reach his flat in Rathmines in record time.

"Here ya are, love!" The taximan grinned cheekily at me in the rear-view mirror and pulled up outside the shiny medical centre.

I paid as he laughed quietly and hummed Dolly Parton's "Jolene" (smart arse) as I slowly counted out my change and got out – it was obviously a popular destination these days. I ran up the steps into the immaculate foyer and saw Carla at the reception.

Oh, what I wouldn't have given for two soluble Solpadeine at that point!

Big smile. "Hi there!" I managed brightly.

She was perched on the edge of a chaise longue. Wearing white jeans, black belt and a black shirt, with black wedges. Her sunglasses perched on top of her voluminous blonde hair. So much hair, all smooth and shaped and bouncy. She didn't have Girls Aloud envy, that was for sure. I caught sight of my reflection – well, it was hard not to in a small area covered in head-to-toe mirrors. Pasty, blotchy skin from sleeping in last night's make-up and stubble-rash.

The glowing, big-busted, luminous-toothed receptionist fussed around Carla. Just as well, as the look Carla was giving me was just about to become fifty questions.

"So, Carla, what size are you thinking of going?" the tiny brunette asked with her beautiful gold notebook and matching gold pen in her hands. Her perfectly manicured long red talons glinted in the light thrown from the chandelier overhead.

"That's exactly why I needed to bring my friend along, you see – I just can't decide. Yours look great, what size are yours?" Carla wasn't one for wasting time – she was direct and straight to the point. So was James for that matter, her well-to-do gentleman of a boyfriend. Old money, he called it. Old money bought him a huge house, The Tindles, on Killiney Hill, with tennis courts and apparently no need for a day job. Well, that wasn't altogether fair – he was a writer – although what he wrote was beyond me. No one had ever seen his work. As far as I was concerned, he was a lazy, spoiled, ill-mannered brat who didn't deserve Carla. Whereas Carla's straight-to-the-point was honesty, his was rudeness.

"Thanks so much, I'm a generous 36C," she beamed back and her teeth blinded me.

"Would you mind," asked Carla, "if I took a closer look?"

The receptionist duly obliged and obediently stuck out her chest in her pale-pink cardigan for Carla to gaze at.

"Miss O'Leary?" the doctor said, breaking up this very weird scenario.

We followed him down the corridor and into his disinfectant-smelling, yet weirdly trendy office.

I was well and truly bored. I know that's a bit selfish but, as far as I'm concerned, if you've seen one pair of jelly sticky-out boobies you've seen them all. I found a paper cup and drank lots from the water cooler as I oohhed and aahhed at Carla. I had told her a million times that I thought she was crazy to do this. She had beautiful small breasts but she was insistent. She'd be the first one to say that my opinion really mattered to her, but her heart was set on this so there was no more I could say.

She was naked now from the waist up and the doctor was doodling on her chest with a big smelly marker. Drawing arrows this way and that, and dots around her breasts, and I found this was mildly erotic. Suddenly I got a flashback of PP Paul bearing down on top of me, his hot mouth wrapped around mine as he explored my body with his tongue.

"Okay, I think we are happy with this then?" He reached into his desk drawer and pulled another lumpy plastic wobbly silicone booby-implant out.

Carla stood up and said quietly, "Excellent – a generous 36C it is then, and sure if I change my mind I can always come back." She smiled at the doctor.

"Don't forget to hold onto your receipt. This does not affect your statutory rights," I said in a low man's voice with my chin stuck into my neck, and as I laughed out loud they both gave me an uncomfortable look.

"And for you? You are considering . . ." He paused, looking down at a clipboard, then back up at me. I shook my head and he looked back down at his clipboard. "Liposuction then?" He tried to find his notes on me, flipping furiously through the pages on his clipboard, and then went crimson from the neck up when he realised his error.

I pulled myself up and stood tall. "Not today, doctor. I am perfect just the way I am, thank you!" I flicked my hair, turned and walked straight into his glass door.

"Are you on that computer again!" my mother screeched at me from the kitchen.

"It's an iPhone, Mam!" I shouted back. Hangover progressively getting worse and only shower and sleep would save me now.

Saturday-evening dinners were compulsory in 31 Coolpak Park and I was fed up with having my Saturdays taken up. I just couldn't seem to ever get out of the rut.

"It's from my boss Dominic so I have to reply, okay?"

Dominic was my boss and owner of Clovers Auctioneers, 26A South Frederick Street, Dublin 2. He owned the entire old building and he rented the other office spaces in there. He drove a brand-new BMW convertible (so ridiculous with teenage twin boys to ferry around to tennis, Gaelic football, rugby, soccer, wrestling). Dominic was what you would call . . . let me see . . . a nice way of putting this . . . a bit of a prat. He always wore black trousers, always – as a tribute to his idol Johnny Cash. He had a balding head but took great care of the five strands of hair that remained at the front (we suspected he wrapped them in tin foil getting into bed every night) – he wore bright, colourful shirts and stupid cartoon ties and crazy outdoor shoes (wacky, he called them – in fact, he called himself wacky). I know what I always want to do to wacky people – whack them! Hard! Snap them out of it. He would try and make us laugh all day every day and it was completely and utterly draining. How he ran such a successful business we couldn't work out. There were four of us in the office: himself, myself, Carla and his long-suffering wife Debbie who came in three days a week to take care of all the accounts. Debbie kept to herself really and didn't leave Dominic's small back office to come out into our main one very often.

He was emailing me now to *remind* me to be at Foxrock at ten o'clock in the morning for a private viewing of Number 34, Torquay Road. He often did this on a Sunday. It drove me insane. I asked on Friday evening before we went to the Palace if I was needed over the weekend and he said, "No . . . unless you want to work? Ha, ha . . . sure I know you – you'll be falling down drunk somewhere – like myself I might add!" Then he proceeded to lie on the floor World-Cup-celebrations-Gazza-style and mimic himself lowering pints (you get the picture). I especially hated the way he used the word *remind* as if he were doing me a favour. Then the iPhone email updated the page and it read, 'PS: Mia, please come and see me early on Monday morning before Carla and Debbie get in. I have something urgent I need to discuss with you. Did you hear me? Ha! I bet you said yeah. Dominic.' I pushed the stupid cursed iPhone (Dominic had bought Carla and myself one each) deep into my fake red Chloé handbag and made my way into the kitchen for the dreaded corned beef and cabbage. Oh, even the smell!

My world felt odd today. I certainly didn't *adore* my job but I adored not living at home and I was the wrong side of thirty and had never done anything else. The Irish economy had never been so bad and, while the entire country talked politics, I didn't. I didn't want to know. I wasn't stupid by any means but I couldn't get as heated about it all as some people. I had enough gloom in my life without all that. We all knew the recession was hitting Clovers – sure it was hitting every business but especially the property market. However, Dominic kept saying we were doing okay. Holding our own. Our jobs were safe. People were still buying houses, people still had to live. Yes, at much lower prices, but the market was still moving. Clovers also had properties on the books that we rented and renting was on the up and up. I had worked for Clovers since I left college. As sad as that may sound to others I actually felt a tinge of pride about it, don't ask me why. I know I wasn't exactly Employee of the Year, what with my favourite websites eBay and Perez Hilton and TMZ.com and all those distractions and the odd (well, not that odd) early exit to the Palace when Dominic was away from the office – but I was doing okay. I was interested in property – genuinely, really interested – and I wanted to own my own home someday. A sprawling old mansion somewhere in Roundwood in Wicklow near Daniel Day Lewis would be nice. We could sit by the open fire in the local Roundwood Hotel, sipping pints of Guinness and reading poetry. I could get some of those early days NHS John-Lennon-type glasses and sit at his knee. He could stroke my hair. Traditional Irish music piping away in the background . . .

Anyway I wasn't interested in working anywhere else, put

it that way. Well, unless Daniel needed a PA, in which case I could dress in a skintight chequered pencil skirt (à la Joan in *Mad Men*) and a skintight low-cut white blouse, and walk elegantly and pain-free on six-inch stilettos (my body can be any size in Dreamland – no point in trying to seduce Daniel Day Lewis otherwise, the state my real body is in). He would gaze at me over our matching round-rimmed as I took notes, until one day it would be all too much for him and he'd drop his well-chewed pencil onto the old oak desk, stand up and take me into his strong method arms and say, "I can't contain myself any longer, Mia! It's you, it's been you for so long my body aches!" – all this is in the voice of Bill the Butcher for some reason. Scary to most women but sexy as hell to me. Ah, that would be nice. But hey, if that job wasn't on offer, as far as I was concerned work was there to pay the bills and not to be enjoyed. Although I did really enjoy it most of the time. Carla said she *loved* the job, that she couldn't wait to get into work every day and see what deals she could close. She would own her own business one day, I was sure of it.

I took my seat at the dinner table and picked at what I could. Samantha was in flowing form with IT this and promotion that and Niall this and Niall that (he was a long-term man on the scene). I didn't pay any attention but I nodded. Her voice droned. Two women could not be further apart in their lives than we were and I was slightly sad about this. But again only slightly. I did not lose any sleep over it, I assure you, didn't even feel guilty that I didn't lose sleep (if that makes sense?). We were terribly civil to each other. An outsider wouldn't even notice.

My mind was on PP Paul and the night was fast-forwarding in my memory. He was full-on passion. He had me naked in a matter of minutes – well, he would have done, except my jeans got tangled up in my boots and I had to reef the lot off with superhuman power myself. He explored my body with all his might. The wine had shed me of any inhibitions about my body and I duly gave as good as I got. I remembered his arms so tight around my neck it started to hurt but in a sexy way. A small shiver went down my spine.

"Did you fart again?" my mother barked at me.

"No, Mam," I muttered.

"Well, stop moving your arse around on that chair like you are trying to let a fart and pass me the butter."

2

The house was freezing when I got in. Carla had lowered my rent while all this renovation work was going on, even though I said she didn't have to. I resealed the plastic back door and went into the living room where she and His Majesty (James) were watching recession *Property Snakes and Ladders*.

"So how was the dinner?" Carla looked at me through sympathetic eyes as she snuggled up again. James never bothered to look up, let alone say hello to me.

"The exact same. I'm hitting the shower – eh, bath – and then bed," I said (I kept forgetting the shower was no longer in use – nothing to do with the renovation work, it was just broken). I went back into the kitchen. Rolls of felt and tiles and presses were stacked against the wall and somehow I liked the look of them this evening. PP Paul would be back on Monday, I thought, as I reached into the fridge for a bottle of Sparkling Ballygowan. I stuck my head further into the empty space and dug out my two remaining chocolate digestives. I loved my chocolate really cold. It drove Carla mad that I kept the biscuits in the fridge and my fizzy jellies in the freezer. I crunched on a bickie as I made my way upstairs and ran myself a really hot, soapy bath (courtesy of Carla's Jo Malone stash). The nice Jo Malone promised me that all my stresses would just fade away – that was why she could charge a small fortune for such a small bottle of bubble bath. I peeled off my stinking clothes and was grateful the steam had fogged the full-length mirror so I didn't have to look at myself. I gently crept into the bath and actually let out an audible gasp as my shoulders submerged into the warm bubbles, then my whole head went under. I found I could think very clearly underwater. I immediately thought about PP Paul. I resurfaced, wondering did he fancy me? I mean, I know he had sex with me but what did that mean? He was a man. Didn't men have sex with any woman who was offering it? Was I tarring them all with the same brush? I supposed I was really. But, let's be honest, I offered it up for free, big-time!

I added more hot water with my big toe, a skill that I had taken years to master but was now an expert at since the shower no longer functioned. I had never had a serious boyfriend. There were men. There were Alan and Noel, a couple of months each and both relationships finished by them. I got the 'I'm just not ready to settle down' from Alan (almost forty and who I really had liked a lot) and 'This is just going way too fast' from Noel (still living at home with his mammy at thirty-seven and I didn't really care all that much for him if I'm brutally honest). Carla said I must have been giving off a desperate vibe but I honestly didn't think I was. I had regular snogs, don't get me wrong. The Palace off South Frederick Street could be a pick-up joint on Friday nights (if you were looking for it) but as many times as I wrote out my much-asked-for mobile number on the back of beer-mats – going over each number like a maths professor to make sure each one was well rounded so there could be no mistaking a 5 for a 3 – they never called. A few weeks ago I actually tried asking this guy for *his* number. He turned a whiter shade of pale and said, "I don't need this, you stalker" – after three slow dances and a particularly grinding last dance to Beyoncé's "Halo". (There was no dance floor in the Palace – you just danced on the tiles outside the toilets if you wanted to.) I wanted a man (I won't lie to you) but I wanted one I really liked. I couldn't settle for marriage and babies with just any man. He didn't have to be Brad Pitt or even Brad Pitt's uglier, less-talented younger brother but I *had* to fancy him. I wasn't money-orientated and I didn't have a list that a man needed to tick boxes on. I just needed chemistry. I fancied a lot of men but none seemed to want to carry it on further.

I put my head under the water again. Was my biological clock running away? Was it ticking like Lisa's in *My Cousin Vinny*? I mimicked her as I scrubbed my legs with Carla's Elle McPherson's Fruit & Honey Exfoliator. "My biological clock is *ticking like this* and the way this case is going, I ain't never getting married!" I laughed. I loved Marisa Tomei in that movie. Should I just get out there and get anyone? I put my head back under and quickly came back up to feel the cold air on my face. I wiped away the foam from my eyes. I was thirty-six years old. The wrong side of thirty, as I said (and as my mother so frequently told me). But I took great comfort from all my forty-something idols who were just beginning motherhood, like Nicole Kidman and Halle Berry. I thought John Travolta's wife was pushing it having a son at forty-nine, but only slightly. The world had changed, at least the Western world – very few women were having babies and getting married before they were thirty. I wasn't saying it was the way for every woman, but I thought it was bloody great to be able to do it all. Of course, I really wanted a baby, didn't every woman? On the other hand, I wondered, how do you know you want a baby if you've never had one? All I knew was I thought about it a lot. I looked at babies in buggies. I sometimes went into Mothercare and picked up the tiny white Babygros and little booties. (I would never admit to that though. Even I knew it was a little too Rebecca De Mornay.) But it was like saying of course I wanted a husband – I never had one before so how did I know? I grabbed for my razor and slid it down my legs. It would be better if I was ten years younger. The pressure of life as a thirty-something was sometimes, to be perfectly honest, a royal pain in the ass.

What would Carla think about me having sex (really great sex) with PP Paul? She was very strict with him and called him Mr Hewson (I know, that's Bono's real name – Paul said he gets it every time). She was a professional; she wanted the job done well. This renovation was costing her a lot of money and she had borrowed up to the hilt. She was under pressure but never let it get to her. Paul said she was lucky – it would have cost her three times the amount this time last year for him. Anyway it was just sex, secret sex. It was nice, really bloody nice, but that was it. It was a lovely feeling to know you were fancied, no matter what. I'm sure PP Paul won't be able to look me in the eye when I get home from work on Monday. I thought. Work . . . my mind darted away from PP Paul's massive erection and on to Dominic.

I felt slightly sick, not sure if it was still the hangover or because of having a dirty thought and then Dominic appearing in my mind's eye. I wondered what he wanted. What on earth would I do if I lost this job? I couldn't share my life with corned beef and cabbage again. I'd better really try to close this sale tomorrow before our meeting on Monday. I pulled the chain of the plug with my wrinkled big toe and second toe and let the water drain away.

3

Sunday morning arrived bright but with that biting first-day-of-November cold. I dipped one foot out of my cosy bed and the floorboards tried to bite me. The house was so, so cold. The wind blew through all the windows and gaping holes downstairs and seemed to blow right up into my bedroom.

"Get up, Mia!" I shouted at myself and was pleasantly surprised when I obeyed.

I dressed in my Oasis navy suit and pumps but rummaged for a clean, ironed shirt. I'd have to sneak into Carla's room and steal one of her largest, loosest ones. All her shirts were kept in the plastic from the dry cleaner's and hung from what she called her BMW system (Black, Mixed, Whites). I eased the handle of her bedroom door down and opened the door just a crack, very slowly.

I froze. *Woh!* There, spreadeagled and tied to the bedpost with pink fluffy handcuffs was His Majesty James in all his morning glory! I covered my mouth with my hand. I was rooted to the spot. It was like seeing a car crash. I couldn't take my eyes away, much as I wanted to. Carla was nestled into his chest, a picture of innocence in super-comfy red pyjamas with giraffes printed on them and her blonde hair tied in a high ponytail. James obviously dyed his hair if his ginger nether regions were anything to go by. I tried to close the door quietly again but it banged at the last second in the draught. I stood there frozen, my mouth still wide open from the shock. Then I crept away.

I swallowed hard, feeling queasy. No wonder she kept on asking PP Paul if he could fix the lock for her bedroom door whenever he got a spare minute. I supposed I should mention I had looked in, or it would be a sort of secret between us and we didn't have any secrets. Or maybe some things should be kept private. I stifled a giggle. I never would have I imagined in a hundred thousand years that Carla was into that sort of thing.

I threw on my trusty Mango white shirt that could well use an iron but buttoned up my jacket to cover it. I knew I read somewhere that eating breakfast helps you lose weight, or kickstarts your metabolism, but when I didn't feel I had to eat I really tried not to and the morning seemed to be the only time my stomach felt this way. I grabbed the car keys of my trusty red Ford Ka and headed to Torquay Road in Foxrock to close the deal on Number 34.

She was all "Oh I want it, daaaaling!" in her Burberry mac and *he* was all "Oh, I don't know, daaaaaaaaaaaaling!". I hadn't worked in the business all these years not to know I was onto a winner if it was the woman who liked it and we just needed to persuade the man. Mr & Mrs Smythe-Byrne. The house was great. A four-bed detached on the main street and minutes away from the Golf Club. It was a superbly planned house. It had been recently refurbished with a state-of-the-art, in-demand German kitchen. The worktops were in polished granite with tiled splashbacks and a tiled floor. This all looked out onto a large landscaped garden. There were two living rooms, both with fitted cream-wool carpets and the large hallway had solid French Oak flooring through-out. All very contemporary. And three bathrooms. It was at the higher end of the market at seven hundred and ninety-five thousand and had been reduced by twenty-five thousand over the last three months. I had shown this one a lot. A couple of years ago I would have had people fighting over it, camped outside (I'm not joking) but now I needed this well-off couple to bite.

"If you need me at all I'll be in the kitchen, just doing some shopping on eBay – there's a magnificent Burberry jacket I'm trying to get my hands on," I called in to them and smiled inwardly.

"Oh!" Mrs Smythe-Byrne looked me up and down as if she might have misheard me, and patted her mac. "This is the latest Burberry mac, not available in Ireland until December," she said, rubbing the buttons.

"Really?" I feigned massive interest. "It's like totally fabulous." I spoke her language – personal contact made. "So, Mrs Smythe-Byrne, are you a model?"

"Oh no!" she laughed and fanned her face with her spindly hands. "I'm an interior designer actually." I nodded my approval. "So you must be impressed by the Sinead Kelly design in this house then?" I gazed adoringly at her silly, overly made-up, Botoxed face. She hadn't a clue about interior design.

"Is that who it is? I really didn't know." She was shocked, I think, but it was hard to tell. "Yes, it's wonderful!"

I sat down at the glass table and put on my seller's face. "It's such a wonderful property. My dream home, if I'm honest with you . . ." I looked wistfully out to the back garden and away, "maybe someday . . ."

She looked dutifully sorry for me. "Please call me Stephanie-Jessica."

Wow, a four-barrelled name!

"Yes, I love the house," she assured me, "I just need to persuade Marcus now. I may have to apply some pressure."

Inside my head I was shouting: *'What do I say next? You have her – think, Mia – play it cool!'*

"Have you ever tried tying him up with pink fluffy handcuffs, Stephanie-Jessica?" The words were out before I could take them back. I broke out in a sweat.

"Excuse me?" SJ looked extremely shocked.

"Yes?" I replied, curling my hair behind my ears.

"I'm sorry? I didn't quite catch what you said?" She stared quizzically at me.

I rubbed my eye. "Who said what, please?" It was an old trick I used in school but never in this situation.

Stephanie-Jessica took a step back. If only she was capable of expression I might have gauged what she was thinking.

"Thank you . . . em . . ."

"Mia," I offered.

"Yes, Mia, we'll discuss it and get back to you." She gracefully glided away on her six-inch heels – Manolos, I guessed.

I locked up the house and headed straight for the Palace. Sunday morning drinking – nothing quite like it.

Tim was polishing a large bottle of Jack Daniels as I sat up at the dark bar.

"Don't usually see you this early on a Sunday?" he quipped as he pushed a black and white *Guinness Is Good For You* beer-mat in front of me and turned it the right way around.

"I know, Tim. I need a drink. Bottle of really cold Budweiser, please, from the very back of the fridge."

Tim was from Galway and was full of banter. With his floppy blond hair and baby face he looked like a teenager although he assured me he was thirty. A genuinely decent bloke. The Palace was one of those pubs that was always full of bearded men (and occasionally bearded women). Souls sitting alone nursing G&T's in the dark corners. I loved it. I had even got Carla to fall in love with it. It wasn't pretentious like some of those bars on Dawson Street with overpriced drink and desperate women dressed in the kind of nothing that cost a fortune. Okay, yeah, women that made me feel bad about myself and drink that price made my purse upset. Real people drank in the Palace. There were even toasted ham-and-cheese sandwiches all night if you needed to sober up a bit. Made with thick doorstep bread. White. People who wanted to get drunk and flirt and forget about it the next day came here. It was dark and boasted twelve bar stools and five tables, a toilet and a cigarette machine. No one came here to find the love of their life really.

"Desperate weather, isn't it? Brass monkeys," Tim said, plopping the bottle onto the beer-mat.

"Yep, desperate, Tim." I smiled at him and watched a dribble of froth make its way slowly down the long neck of the bottle.

He ran his hands through his blond hair.

I took a long slow drink by the neck. "Ahhh, Sunday drinking! Nothing like it!" I said out loud to myself this time (you could totally talk to yourself in the Palace – it was widely accepted and even encouraged). I sat there and people-watched as Tim worked and made toasted sandwiches for the regulars who knew to ask for them. It wasn't advertised, you see. It was like an opium den except for the ham-and-cheese toasties.

My mobile rang in my bag. I rummaged and ended up with everything on the counter just as I got to my phone on the last ring. "Hello?" I almost shouted in relief.

"It's me." Carla was walking. "Where are you?"

"I'm not in the Palace anyway." I paused. "Okay, hard morning," I added by way of explanation, clasping the phone under my ear as I stuffed lip gloss, pens, tissues, Aloe Vera Vaseline (without lid) and loose change back into my bag.

"Oh, that sounds good – I'm on my way. Is Tim on?"

"Yes." I tried to keep the phone to my mouth.

"Will you ask him to make me that Baileys minty thing he did for your birthday last year?"

"Okay." I flipped the cover and put my iPhone back into my bag.

That's not like Carla, I thought, as I ordered for her. She doesn't usually do alcohol this early. Alcohol gives you wrinkles.

"So, Tim, what's new?" I pulled out the old Vaseline again and applied it to my dry lips after I picked the fluff out of it.

"Not much, just looking into some college courses actually." His blond floppy hair covered his left eye.

"Lucky you," I said. "What kind of courses?"

"Well, I've always wanted to do sound engineering so looking into that. What's up with you?"

"Pretty boring –" I began as the door opened and newspapers blew off the counter.

A pale-looking Carla entered the Palace. Her greeny-looking creamy drink was waiting for her. "Hey!" She took off her white Nike sports jacket and pulled herself up on the stool. "Hey, Tim!" She smiled and waved at him as he dealt with another customer at the far end of the oak bar. He gave her a huge smile and waved back. "Well, what's going on then?" she asked me, sipping daintily from a red straw that was oversized for the glass.

"Just had to work, that's all."

"No, I mean what's going on with PP Paul?"

I was shocked. I mean, I was expecting she'd pick up on a bit of awkwardness between me and him in the house (she knew me well enough by now) but how could she guess already? "Why, what do you mean?"

She tilted her head to one side as though she had something in her left ear she was trying to shake out. "Well, he called around this morning looking for you. Why would he do that?"

I could feel the redness creeping up from my toes to the tips of my ears.

"Oh, Mia, you didn't!" She actually looked like she was going to throw up. She was making that face where you blow air into your cheeks and your eyes pop wide open.

"What? So what?" I pursed my lips a little defiantly.

"What? He's my builder. I need him to do a professional job. This is such a scary time for me financially, you know that? I don't want some lovesick puppy moping around my half a shell of an overpriced house!"

I straightened myself on the uncomfortable bar stool. What was it with these bloody stools everywhere? What was wrong with backs on stools? Soft comfy cushions? A chair you could melt into? "Now, since when has any man moped around me like a lovelorn puppy?" I opened my eyes wide. "So what did he say?" I was strangely excited. My mouth was dry, palms sweaty and my heart was starting to race. He had come looking for me. I couldn't remember the last person I had been intimate with who had ever wanted to see me again, let alone come looking for me!

"He asked for your mobile but I didn't give it. I said he could talk to you tomorrow." She paused, staring me in the eyes. "You don't fancy him, do you?" Carla threw her blonde hair over her head and scooped it up into a thin black hair bobbin. Simple move, yet it looked like she'd been in the salon for hours to achieve the look.

"No . . . yeah . . . yeah. I dunno, he's . . . nice."

"Nice?" Carla's perfect blacklined eyes bulged.

"Yeah, nice, so what?" I picked up my bottle and nodded at Tim to bring another.

"Okay, enough said." Carla drank her drink.

"So, where's lover boy?" I asked, trying hard to push the picture of his naked body out of my mind. She looked uncomfortable . . . oh no, she must know I'd peeked into the room this morning.

"He's gone horse-riding with his friend Max." She tightened the bobbin on her hair.

"So I didn't close the Foxrock deal," I said, changing the subject as quickly as I could. The atmosphere was odd.

She shrugged.

My mind went blank. Silence engulfed us.

"Have I told you that I eat crap a lot and don't ever tell you?" I said. "No? Well, I do, and right now all I want is fish and chips with loads of vinegar, a huge cuppa tea and my bed."

"You're on."

We finished our drinks, flicking through the Sunday papers. Then, saying goodbye to a now-busy Tim, we headed down to Leo Burdock's. Carla was quiet and I just didn't feel like asking her why. I'd messed up this morning, my tactics had backfired and I hadn't sold the property. I could have but I didn't. We stood in line outside the door of Leo Burdock's in Christchurch in the freezing cold before eventually getting indoors and placing orders. I wanted a smoked cod, large chips and a portion of curry sauce. Carla got a small bag of chips which she didn't salt and ate on the walk back to my car. She had said she'd take a lift due to the cold and her lack of SPF 15. I really wanted to eat my chips but on the other hand I really wanted to keep everything for my cuppa tea and my bed and book.

I knew deep down that I couldn't wait for it to be morning so I could see PP Paul.

Paul, I decided as I drove home way too fast, he was just Paul from now on.

4

He was lying under the kitchen sink when I tottered into the kitchen. By 'tottered' I mean I was wearing ridiculously high heels that I never wore to work. I coughed. It was only seven in the morning and he was already in full work mode. He slid out and pulled himself up. He was wearing his dark-blue work overalls and pale-brown Timberland boots.

"Cuppa tea, Paul?" I asked very casually, delighted with myself. He was attractive, no doubt about that.

"Please." He wiped his greasy hands down the sides of his filthy trousers. "I'll just pop to the loo to wash my hands."

I watched him go and felt the butterflies swim around my stomach. This is crazy, I thought. I shook my head as I filled the kettle and took two I LOVE NYC cups from the makeshift press. I dropped two teabags in and waited for the kettle to boil. He returned to the kitchen and the smell of Palmolive Almond Milk soap flooded my nostrils. I liked a man who washed his hands well.

"So . . ." He pulled up a chair and began setting the boxes upright so we could use them as a table. "Off to work then?"

I smiled. "No. I just got up and dressed this early on a Monday morning for the craic."

"Huh?" He looked confused.

Oh, Mia, you stupid cow, be normal! I bit the inside of my lip and could feel my face going red. "No. Joke. That was a joke. Yeah, I am. I am indeed. Working. Going in to work. Now, actually. In fact, I don't have time for tea – I'm late – so see you later." I turned and grabbed my denim jacket and headed for the plastic. The cold air was welcoming on my bright red face.

"What on earth was that?" I asked out loud and a woman walking her dog by looked to see what I was talking about. She was checking the road to see if the dog had done a secret shit that she hadn't witnessed, her empty plastic pooh bag begging to be filled. I raised my hand to her and she nodded slowly. She understood I was having a moment.

I tried to calm myself by taking deep breaths. I got in my car and drove to South Frederick Street where I parked behind the office in one of our four free car-park spaces.

I opened the old red Georgian door with my keys, trudged up the stairs and sat at my desk.

"Oh, well done!" Dominic breathed last night's garlic all over me. "You remembered to be early." Shit. I hadn't remembered at all. In fact, I had completely forgotten about the meeting.

"Come into my boudoir . . ." He pointed the way to his office as though I had never been there before. I followed him in.

"Take a seat!" He picked up the chair and ran to the door with it. "Ha! Not literally!"

I plastered a weak smile onto my face.

"So, recession." He clicked his tongue on the roof of his mouth. "*Ressseessioonnn* . . ." He dragged the word out long and slowly while wiping the screen of his computer with the back of his hand. "It's all scary out there, eh, Mia?"

"Yes," I managed. What was going on here? Was he about to let me go?

"I am the boss, I have responsibilities. I cannot let Mr Recession wreck the lives of *my* staff, can I? Shoo, Mr Recession, shoo away!" He ushered his imaginary recession out his glass door.

"No, Dominic." I crossed my legs. He looked at them. I uncrossed them. I may not have had skinny toned legs but they were long and covered in a tight black skirt to over the knee. My legs from the calf down were okay actually and in their six-inch heels I was showing them off to my very best ability.

"Okay, let's get one thing straight here. You. Are. Going. Nowhere. *Yet!*"

My eyes narrowed – conversations with Dominic were so difficult at times.

He straightened his tie with Homer Simpson on it. "However, your work has not been good by any standard lately, Mia, so I am moving you around. You are going to become a team player. I have taken professional advice on this. In recessional times the people who pull together pull the deals. It will now be a pair. Two heads are better than one. Like Ant and Dec. Like Brucey and Tess. Carla is doing fine on her own so I am bringing in my niece Anita to work with you. Obviously I have to cut your wages somewhat but, the more sales you close, the more commission you will make, so it will all even out in the end." He sat back and straightened his tie again, awaiting my reaction.

Homer mocked me in his white briefs. What could I say? I had no choice.

"How much will you cut my wages, Dominic?"

"It will be a fifty-per-cent cut, I'm afraid."

I stood up and then sat down again. I needed this job. I had to have money to live on. I could not go back home ever again – Saturday evenings were hard enough.

"It's not as bad as it sounds, Mia – with two of you selling there should be no problem whatsoever getting big commissions. This is how they do it in the States."

The smell of last night's garlic was just too overwhelming and I had to leave the office.

"Fine," I stood up.

He looked at my shoes.

"When does she start?" I quietly asked.

"This morning."

I left the room.

At nine I was just getting a coffee from the small kitchen off our office when a small woman appeared at the door. (I say kitchen but it was a kettle and a very old, noisy fridge.)

"Can I help you?" I asked.

"Yes, I'm Anita, Dominic's niece, and I'm due to start work here today."

She was petite, with a well-lived-in face. She couldn't have been more that thirty-five or thirty-six. Shy-looking with her black hair scraped back in a long plait running down her back. In her blue suit and light-blue shirt, she could almost have passed for a prison officer.

"Oh hi, sure. Let's get Dominic – he's in his office."

I walked out to join her just as we heard the roar of "Anita!" – Dominic was out of his office, making a pretend run in slow motion, his arms out wide. He ran past Anita just as she opened her arms to embrace him. I could have killed him.

"Sit down, Anita." I pulled out a chair for her.

She looked thankfully at me and sat, dropping her shoulder-bag and a carry-bag on the floor beside her.

Dominic introduced us again and went on a roll of outlining

our work for the week as Carla and Debbie came in. There were several viewings coming up and I wrote down the details by hand as I always did. Anita looked at him with her big blue eyes and I thought her face was pretty but that she looked so sad. Dominic went about setting up her laptop and pulling a chair over to my desk. So we were sharing a job and a desk. I shook my head. I would have to start looking around for another job. I could manage now because the rent on Carla's was so low but once the renovation work was done the rent was going up. There was no one hiring that I knew of. Anyway, I was sure it wouldn't be too long before Carla moved in with His Majesty in his Killiney palace and rented out her house to a professional family. That was the way it was looking and it made perfect sense.

I bent down and took off my shoe to rub my sore foot. Dominic's eyes were on it like a hare on a rabbit. I quickly put my shoe back on. The morning passed with me showing Anita the ropes. We had no viewings today but two tomorrow. At lunchtime she took a Tupperware from her bag and a flask of tea. She removed the tin foil to reveal half a sandwich with what smelled like chocolate spread. "My kids needed the bread for their lunches, so this was all that was left," she explained with a smile. "My daughter is on a tour to Dublin Zoo today so I allowed chocolate-spread sambos."

"How many kids do you have?" I asked as I got up to put on the kettle. Carla was out again on a cushy sales conference (Dominic always sent *her*) and Debbie was in Dominic's office.

"Just two. A boy and a girl." She bit into her sandwich.

She was oddly familiar to me – must be Dominic's mannerisms, I guessed. Unfortunate, but genes will be genes.

"Stevie is seventeen and Katie is three."

My mouth fell open and she giggled, a giggle that might have come from a naughty child. "Seventeen?"

"Yes, I had him when I was very young and then we were years trying for Katie – ironic, I know."

"You must have married really young?"

She nodded and bit into her lunch again.

"That's really brilliant. So you're Dominic's brother's daughter then?"

"Yes, I'm an only child. Dad is older than Dominic. To be honest," she looked over her shoulder and whispered, "they don't get on at all. Family stuff."

I understood her father totally.

"I need this job, Mia. I need it badly. I was working for the Focused Theatre for twelve years and have been let go. Cutbacks. I must have sent hundreds of CV's over the last few months but nothing. Then I knocked on Dominic's door by pure chance – I had no idea where he lived, we're not a close family by any means. Anyway, I was selling door-to-door encyclopaedias and he offered me this job. I think he was impressed with the way I wouldn't take no for an answer. Well, I had to sell some books – I'd had to borrow the money to buy Stevie's tickets for his Debs. They're two hundred euro a pop – what a joke! He bought the encyclopaedias in the end." She let out a sigh that I can only describe as one of huge relief.

I wondered what her husband did. I imagined, if she was talking like this, he must be another one who had lost his job. I wasn't going to pry. I drank my coffee and didn't bother with lunch after all those chips yesterday. The fish, however, I had no guilt about.

Paul was loading his white van as I struggled up the driveway against the beating wind. I'd had to park on the road miles down so as not to block him in. Not a good look, I noted, as my hair stuck to my MAC lip gloss (newly applied just in case he was still there).

"How's it going?" He pushed a roll of lead into the back of the van and slammed the double doors shut.

"Fine!" I scraped my hair back. "How's it all going?"

"Grand, getting there, should be done on time if I'm lucky."

He wiped his hands on his overalls and I noticed the muscles tensing in his upper biceps. I did fancy him. I realised it like a bolt of lightning. I really fancied him. I wanted to jump his bones right there on the makeshift porch. How had this happened? Even I knew this was ridiculous. But right now I wanted to wrap my naked body in the plastic and devour him alive.

"Good," I managed and stood mute.

"Well, better get going and sit on the M50 reading the *Sun* for a few hours!"

He smiled and I went weak at the knees. I managed to block the *Sun* comment from my reasonably intelligent mind.

"Okay," I smiled.

He kept smiling. The wind blew again and by the time I fixed my hair he had closed the van door on the driver's side and was revving the engine.

"Shit!" I shouted at the wind. "Piss off!"

I dragged myself into the house and headed straight to my room. I flopped onto the bed and kicked off my shoes. Why didn't he ask for my number there? He had the chance. Or why didn't I just say: "I heard you were after my number." Casually. Breezy. Sexily. I scratched my head and wiped away the gooey gloss with the back of my hand. Staring at the ceiling, I lay there and planned out the rest of my week. I liked to do this on a Monday – it was better than writing a diary. Work hard all week is my Number One priority. *Paul.* Clean the room. *Paul.* Try and be nice to Mam on Saturday and tell her in the nicest possible way I hate cabbage. *Paul.* Ask Anita for a drink to the Palace after work on Friday. *Paul.* Buy hair magazines and be brave and go for a new style. *Paul.* Cut out all carbs and yes, Mia, white Vienna roll is a carb! "Oh, go away, Paul!" I shouted.

I looked around my bedroom. It could do with a tidy but wasn't too bad. I loved it with its old bay window and window seat. I had papered it in Laura Ashley light red and white and had my fantastic old bed from Arnotts that I'd taken from Coolpak Park. There was a mirror, wardrobe, beside table and lamp. There was no carpet on the floor which I hated but I couldn't afford to put a carpet in someone else's house.

"Mmmm, Paul," I muttered as I bit my pillow hard.

Anita was already at our desk when I arrived in. "Morning," she smiled at me. She looked tired. Black rims under her eyes.

I took off my coat and started up my computer.

"We have a viewing in Knocklyon," she told me. "Four o'clock, it's a three-bed semi, it's –"

I raised my hand to stop her mid-flow. "Anita, I'll look at the brief, don't feel you have to tell me." She looked embarrassed.

"Sorry, I don't mean to sound narky," I said. "It's just that I take a while to warm into the day – I need to have a cuppa and then read my mails, okay? Sorry." I smiled at her warmly.

She looked like she was about to burst into tears.

"Are you okay?" I lowered my voice as Dominic approached, clapping his hands. "Ladies, morning all, let's close today like we never before closed! Let's close closely, closely close! Okay then!" He turned on his heel and left.

A lone tear dropped down Anita's face.

"Bathroom – now." I stood up and she followed me. "What's the matter?" I handed her a lump of the cheap, harsh, grey toilet paper.

"I'm so, so sorry about this!" she sobbed and waved her hand in front of her wet eyes.

I watched her, puzzled and really curious.

"Oh, my life . . . I cannot believe I'm doing this on my second day here!"

I just smiled at her.

"Sorry, well, it's Stevie's dad, Katie's dad, my husband – ah, we're fighting, again, a bad one this time and he's walked out, again."

"Oh no, Anita!" I was shocked. "That's awful, what was it about?"

"Oh, he's not happy. He's never happy. He tells me all the time. I suffocate him, he says. He's never at home lately, he never helps with the kids, he goes to work and sometimes doesn't come back for days. The other day he told me he leaves the house in the morning supposedly to go to work but really just sits in the library. Says there is no work. That's why I have to work, we need the money. But I know he has money. He buys stuff for himself and hides it." She blew her nose hard. "He always has new clothes, new runners. So I tried to talk to him last night, adult to adult, but he just lost the head with me and went into the spare room saying I was wrecking his head and slammed the door."

I got more tissue for her. "Here, blow again." I smiled limply at her. "Oh listen, Anita, that's just awful, it really is. I mean, if you really can't talk to him you need to ask him to try marriage counselling or something. Are you still in love with him?"

Her head moved violently up and down. "Oh God, yes, totally!" She continued to nod and blew again, this time disposing of the sodden tissue in the bin. "But I don't know if he still loves me. Sometimes he says he does and after the rows calm down he is usually all apologetic but, well, he had an affair before and I found out about it." She scratched her head now and let out a sigh. "He says I can't get over it, but that's not true. I can and I have. It eats me up, no question, but for the sake of our family I have buried it deep in me. He's hot and cold all the time with me. We had to get married because I was expecting Stevie but we were really in love. As I said, we were trying for years for Katie and well, that really upset him, but he wouldn't go for any tests. So we just thought it would never happen. Then I found out I was pregnant and at the same time found out about the affair. He said he was so sorry and would never leave me. I told him I never wanted him to leave ever, but I told him the affair had to stop. He agreed and said he was sorry and I believed him. I know he loves us deep down but he's a bit of a sod. He has a bit of a temper, you see –"

The knock made us both jump.

"*Ladieeessss*, what's keeping you two? If it's girl-on-girl talk in there I want in – if it's about periods then I don't!" Dominic snorted with laughter and made pretend vomit noises.

I ushered Anita into the cubicle and opened the door. "Sorry, Dominic. Periods. Heavy ones." I pulled a sour face as I exited and then made my way back to my desk. I felt dreadful for Anita. Men could be so cruel. What an absolute asshole her husband sounded. I knew what I would do – throw him out on his arse! If he'd fallen out of love with her, he should talk to her. Not leave her in the dark guessing. Communicate. And affairs – no way!

Anita emerged and sat back down, red-eyed and forlorn. She whispered over the computer tops, "Mia, I am dreadfully sorry. I don't know what came over me. Please forget everything I said. I have enough of my friends demented over the last year with my personal life. I want this job, us, to be professional, just to be colleagues."

"Of course, Anita, whatever you want – but if you ever

need an ear, I am here and I'm a good listener." I reached over and took her hand for a nanosecond before she pulled it away.

"Thank you, Mia, but I would really appreciate it if we never mentioned it again. I just want to get on with things."

"Deal," I said and we smiled at each other.

Knocklyon was a really pretty area, I thought as I looked around. Full of greenery and young families. The house was a perfectly nice three-bed semi in Hunterswood. But there was no way this couple was going to bite. I could tell from the moment they entered the house. Don't ask me how I can tell immediately – I just can. I suppose it's the lack of questions. They were just looking in every room and *oohing* and *aawing*. I got the sense of "someday this will suit us" (I get that vibe a lot). A serious buyer wants to know about local schools, shops, what the traffic is like in the mornings (I never lie about that one, ever) – they are the important questions, not will the acrylic IKEA rug be staying?

Anita was doing her best, but I just sat back. It was all pointless. The couple were either looking for ideas or, as I said, looking way into the future. We were in and out in minutes.

On the drive back to the office, the atmosphere was a little tense in the car.

"So, what do you think?" Anita asked me. "Do you think they'll put in an offer?"

"Not a chance!" I indicated left at Superquinn shopping centre to head back down onto the Knocklyon Road and checked my rear-view mirror.

"Well, why? I mean, I tried my best – but you were very quiet, if you don't mind me saying so – you didn't exactly speak up."

"Look, Anita, no offence, but I am doing this job a lot longer than you. I know it better." I kept my eyes on the road.

"But surely it's about selling, and I have been in sales for years. I have sold things, tickets, to people who actually already had tickets!" Her voice was raised now and she was beginning to annoy me.

"Anita, I'm sure you are an excellent salesperson but it's not about selling a theatre seat – what we are doing is we are selling a lifestyle. It has to be craved. It has to be wanted so badly that they are willing to mortgage themselves to the hilt to live there. Do you understand the times we're living in? They have to want to live there much more than you want them to buy it. Then, when that is part of the deal, then and only then can you sell them that house."

She shook her head. "I just don't agree with you."

I took a deep breath. It had been a long day. I chose to put an end to the conversation and as we drove in silence my mind immediately rushed back to Paul. I wanted to get back to see him before he finished today. My heart started to pound now as I thought of him. It was a brilliant out-of-body experience, fancying someone. Every song on the radio meant more – your senses were more alive. He had asked Carla for my number. He had come all the way over to see me – I wasn't there so he asked for my number. That was fact. I was going to talk to him tonight. I wasn't going to play any games – just sit down, ask him if he wanted to go for a pint with me on Friday night.

"Goodnight, Dominic! Night, Debbie!" I shouted into the back office when we got back.

Carla had been out all day again. I envied her all these conferences, free lunches, cosy hotel rooms. "Coming, Anita?" I said as I gathered up my things.

She smiled faintly at me. "Em, no, I just want a quiet word with Dominic before I go." She looked away quickly.

"Oh right, see you tomorrow so." I pursed my lips and left.

What did she want to see him for? Was she going to tell him I didn't work hard enough this afternoon? How dare she! Two days in and going to the boss! I had a good mind to wait outside for her and ask her what exactly she had said, but I knew it would be childish and ridiculous and would make me look like a total lunatic.

I got into my car, started the engine and blared some Lily Allen. I wanted to get home, fast.

5

Carla was in front of the TV when I got in. There was no sign of Paul or his white van.

"Yo there!" I flopped down beside her. "What a day!"

She paused the live feed on RTÉ news and Anne Doyle was stuck in a very odd pose. "So what's Anita like then?"

"Grand," was all I could offer. She didn't push for more. "How was the conference?"

"Grand," she answered and I didn't push for more. However, she went on. "That new Gibson Hotel on the docks, opposite the O2, is just out of this world. We have to go there for cocktails before Christmas. It's stunning." She stood up. "Dinner?"

"No thanks, Carla, I'm going to have an early night. I'm feeling really tired – totally wrecked, in fact." I made for the door. The bloody Gibson Hotel! I had read all about it – Harry Crosbie's newest venture – why didn't Dominic ever send me on those courses? I had one foot on the bottom stair.

"Oh here, Mia!" She had followed me out and handed me a torn-off piece of paper. "Sorry, I almost forgot!" She grinned wickedly at me.

It was Paul's name and a mobile number. "What's this?" I said stupidly, looking at her.

"Well, Mr Hewson asked me to give it to you as he had to rush off early, collect someone, or something like that. I'm assuming it's his mobile since it has his name above it?"

I held it in both hands like it was a precious code to unlock the jocks of Mr Indiana Jones himself.

She headed into the kitchen and I followed her.

"I'm going into surgery in the morning," Carla bent down as she opened the oven, her tiny booty in the air, "so I have asked Paul to leave the work for a week and he is happy to do so – I need peace and quiet to recuperate."

I looked at her. She straightened up, looking worried. "Carla, why are you doing this? There is just no need to put yourself through this, you know!"

She turned to me, her eyes suddenly blazing. "You know why I'm doing it, Mia, you fucking know why! Because I know you looked into my room last weekend – and yes, so what, James is kinky! He likes kinky sex – in fact, it's a huge, huge deal to him, and quite frankly he doesn't like my little tits, they don't do it for him, they are not what he needs to turn himself on. So if I don't get bigger tits there is every chance he will leave me. Happy? Are you happy now? Isn't that what you've been trying to get out of me for weeks now?" She spat the last words at me and even spat on her own chin which was just so unlike her.

I was dumbstruck. "What the heck, Carla? I hadn't a clue! I thought this was all for you! I mean, yes, I saw James in the furry handcuffs, but to be honest I presumed it was your idea."

She opened the fridge and pulled out a bottle of wine. Without thinking, I glanced again at the piece of paper in my hand.

"Oh, just go call your builder!" She spat the words at me and stormed out of the kitchen.

I followed her into the living room. "Carla, I love you, I love you to bits, more than my own family sometimes. I just honestly don't know what to say, well, I do, but you won't want to hear it. I think you're the most beautiful creature in the world, inside and out, so I just can't understand why you would want to do this to your beautiful, perfect body just for a man! I know it's not because of the money he has because, well, I just know you too well . . . and, honesty, Carla, I don't like him."

There it was, out in the big wide open.

She poured a large glass from the bottle and kept her eyes down. "I know you don't. You're never yourself around him – it's a dead giveaway. But I am in love with him, Mia, and you are my best friend in the world – I have told you everything about me and my life and opened up to you like no one else I have ever met. You are precious to me too. But I want to do this for him – so, okay, yeah, a part of me knows it's totally crazy but I'm going ahead with it. And you are right, I couldn't care less about his money or if he will ever have his successful writing career, but he makes me feel so loved – that's all I can say. He gets me."

Her big open eyes stared into my little pudgy ones. I took her glass from her hand, sipped it and gave it back.

"So okay, I don't know what else to say to you then," I sighed. "Sex is obviously a huge part of any relationship but it's not the ultimate. If you don't want to have this boob job, please don't do it."

"Will he stay with me," she whispered, "if I don't get it done?" Her head was down again.

I sat beside her and draped my arm around her. I couldn't believe this from her. "Then let him go, Carla! Men are always throwing themselves at you. You won't be single for long, I can promise you that." I wrapped my arm tighter now around her thin shoulders.

"I love him, Mia, I really love him. I honestly can't stand the idea of not having him. I am doing this for him."

I checked my words before they left my mouth for once. I needed to be here for her now. "Okay, Carla, you are a strong woman, and you are so right. This is your decision and I'll support you all the way."

Her face relaxed and she beamed at me before throwing her arms around me. "Ah, thanks, darling, I knew you'd understand!"

I hugged her tightly. I didn't understand. I understood that James was a total fucking prick. I understood that alright but if I said so now I would lose her.

"Hi, Paul, it's me, Mia!" I addressed my mirror in a voice I didn't recognise as my own. Too bright. "Hey, Paul, Mia here." I brought my voice down and just ended up sounding like Dustin Hoffman in *Tootsie*. "Paul, Mia, hey, hi!" Too weird.

I looked at the iPhone in my hand. It was already after ten o'clock now as my chat with Carla had evolved into a shared vegetarian pizza and two bottles of wine. One red and one white. So I knew I would have a headache in the morning. I was confident and slightly tipsy. I stared at myself in the mirror. I lifted my hair up and dropped it again. Drink always gave me a better reflection.

I looked at the iPhone again. Never drink and dial, I told myself. Then I whispered it to my reflection. Too late – I was dialling. After the fifth ring (are you supposed to hang up after four? Is five just that one ring too many?), he answered.

"Paul, hey, I'm Mia, it's me here, em Mia, so, well, I heard you gave Carla your number to give to me? Or not heard – I didn't hear – I have the piece of paper – thank you . . ." I squeezed my eyes closed. My head was already starting to pound in time with my heart beating and I found it hard to swallow my mouth was so dry. What was I saying?

"Hi, Mia," his voice was very low. "Em, I can't right talk now, I'm busy – so can we talk tomorrow?"

"Sure, righty oh, yes, lovely jubbly!" Again I squeezed my eyes tight and made a face at myself in the mirror. I was mortified. Was that a brush-off?

"Great, speak to you in the morning then," he added really warmly, then he hung up.

I dropped the phone onto my bed and pulled off my clothes. I didn't think it was a brush-off, not the way his voice sounded when he'd said, "Great, speak to you in the morning then." His voice was so sexy. Had I made a fool of myself? Oh, what did I care? It was all about nothing. I was really getting carried away here, this wasn't like me. I pulled on my old David Bowie T-shirt and leggings and began the nightly routine of taking off my make-up. (Did women really do all this in the morning too? Why? There was no make-up on then. I never got that one.) As I watched the white cotton wool turn dark brown, I thought about Carla. Who'd have thought that she could be so insecure? That's what I put all this fake-boobie business down to. Oh, how I'd love to give Kinky James a piece of my mind! I rubbed at the war paint and pulled the gunk out from the sides of my eyes. I wasn't going to judge her, I was just going to be there for her, there to pick up the pieces when all this shattered. And it would, I knew that much. What was next? She should tell him his dick was too small and see how fast he ran to get a dick transplant or whatever it is they do with dicks these days.

I piled on the expensive moisturiser that promised me the prize of youthful glowing skin and got into bed.

I needed to close tomorrow. There was a second viewing on the house in Foxrock – not my double-barrelled Smythe-Byrne friends but another lovely family, the Conroys. I needed this commission. I turned off my side lamp. The house was quiet apart from the wind whistling around downstairs. I dreamt of Paul. And willy transplants.

It seemed like only five minutes ago I was taking this off my face, now the routine started all over again. Putting it all back on, that was, not cleansing it again. I could hear Paul downstairs, obviously collecting what tools he needed for his week away. Carla was in the bath, ready to welcome her new assets. I wondered if her old boobies were aware? I dressed in dark navy trousers and a white navy pinstriped shirt. I was shaking as I brushed my hair. This was ridiculous. I knew nothing about this man other than that he was pretty good in bed (well, from what I could remember) and that he could build me a house if push came to shove. I liked the excitement of it all. I especially liked the fact that he liked me. I think that was what it was all about – I knew he wanted to see me again and that felt good. I couldn't remember the last time I felt like this. Stop thinking and just go down, I told myself.

He was bent over, nail perched in his mouth, hammer in one hand, when I said mightily cheerily, "Good morning, Paul!"

He removed the nail and smiled at me and my heart raced. "Hey, Mia, sorry about last night, bit of business I needed to attend to." He ran his hands through his hair and I flicked on the kettle.

"No worries at all," I smiled, a nice flirty smile, and opened the new teabag packet by stabbing the knife into the plastic. I hoped the action wasn't too masculine.

"Anyway . . ." he came closer, I could smell the coffee off his breath and I actually liked it, "I was really glad you called – I was hoping –"

"Good morning, Mr Hewson, how is it all going today?" Carla burst in. "I hope that you don't mind keeping the project on the long finger for the rest of the week?"

"No, that's grand. I'm just in to batten down a few hatches for you until I can restart."

Carla was very pale.

I smiled at her. "How are you getting to – to the clinic?" I asked.

"Walking," she said and pulled her small Louis V wheelie-case from under the table.

"With a suitcase?" I was amazed.

"Yes." She zipped up her jacket and stared hard at me. Then she left through the plastic.

The sudden silence was electric. He was inches from me. I moved closer and looked into his eyes. We were alone again. His presence seemed to take over the entire kitchen.

"Sorry, you were saying?" His coffee breath was warm on my neck.

The plastic rustled. I didn't turn round.

"Actually, Mia, could you come with me?" Pale-faced Carla was back.

"N-n-now?" I stammered.

"Yes, now – we can hail a cab on the way – I know how you hate to exercise in the morning."

She was right. I did hate it. I swallowed hard. I had never been this horny in my entire life. I looked at her. I held my breath to steady my voice. "Of course – I'll call Dominic on the way." I bent down and rummaged in my bag for my phone and when I stood back up Paul was hammering again. I felt slightly dizzy. I let out a long, slow breath.

"Come on!" Carla said. "I have to get a move on."

"Yes, sure." I waited for Paul to turn around but he didn't. "So, em, see you next week then, Paul?" I managed.

He turned, expressionless. "Yeah, girls, see you both next week so. Have a good one!"

I pushed the plastic out of my face with force and headed into the cold grey morning for Medical Mystery Land.

With Carla prepped for the op, I headed for the wonderful world of the clinic's vending machines. I was suddenly starving and the sight of the machines stuffed with drinks and crisps and chocolates and me with a fistful of change was all too much to ignore. I punched in the codes and out fell a Kit Kat Chunky and a packet of King crisps, not the regular ones but the pub ones in the black packet if you don't mind. Extra, extra cheesy in my humble opinion. Extra crispy too. Extra good. Coffee and the Kit Kat first and then the crisps.

I flicked through *VIP* because that's all one can do with *VIP* – I mean you can't actually be seen to be reading it. It's supposed to fill a gap. How long did new boobs take, I wondered, as I glanced at the clock on my iPhone. Dominic would be freaking out and what about Anita and the Foxrock viewing with the Conroys? We had two other viewings today as well and she didn't drive. Oh, how did I get myself into these situations? I should have told Carla I could drop her but then I had to go.

As I was licking my fingers to the bare bone, the taloned temptress receptionist presented her beauty in front of me. She recoiled from the obvious delicious crispy smell and actually made a face. It was an Oscar-winning performance, I had to admit, or was she really that repulsed? It was the face you make when something smells really bad but you need the social manners to hide it. Like a nurse dealing with an alcoholic homeless person who's peed and vomited on themselves. It's not their fault, they are ill but it's not pleasant either. *I* was ill.

I loved cheese and onion crisps and sometimes, even though I knew it was so wrong to eat them, I couldn't help myself.

She now draped the red talons across her mouth and nose and closed and opened her eyes several times. "Em, excuse me, but Carla won't be ready to see you for a few hours. There's the surgery and then she has to come around from the anaesthetic. There really is no point in waiting."

"Oh!" It was at this point I admitted to myself that I was hoping Carla would change her mind at the last moment and come flying out to me in her theatre gown, the surgeon in hot pursuit. "Right." I stood up. "I'll be back so. Later. I'll phone to check."

She gave me a blinding smile and I exited with as much dignity as I could muster.

There was no point in going in to work. I'd probably have to leave again almost as soon as I arrived. Nothing for it. I headed for the shops and the eateries.

Carla did not look good. In our entire time knowing each other I had never seen her look so bad. Even when she had the worst bout of gastroenteritis I had ever witnessed or when she had the adult chicken pox for that matter.

"Hi," I whispered as I approached the bed.

Her eyes filled with tears.

"Oh, Carla!" I held her hand gently.

"It's just so sore, Mia," she whispered. "I never imagined it would be this painful."

"What happened?" I asked her as I pulled my chair closer to her bed.

She looked worn out. Carla never looked worn out.

"Well," she tried to move in the bed, "when you left me I had to undress, put on a gown and these absolutely vile white compression socks, then I had to scrub my chest with anti-bacterial soap." She winced again with pain. "Then the surgeon came around and asked me more bloody questions, confirmed what size I wanted, and took 'before' photos. Which I'm sure are fabulous." She tried to smile. "He drew those 'cut here' lines on my chest with that big purple marker again. I think then I waited for a while but I was in another world. It wasn't real to me. I started to really wonder what the hell I was doing here, Mia, and where the hell was James anyway?" She paused now, obviously not wanting to tell me the next bit. "He didn't answer his phone this morning. I called six times and left three messages."

I squeezed her hand but didn't know what to say.

"I was really calm, Mia, and I wasn't panicking or anything but honestly I was just about to get up and leave when I was wheeled down to theatre. I started to feel weird again like I was sinking underwater or something. I remember lying there and seeing the nurses hovering above me, reassuring me. I thought I peed in my pants but I wouldn't have, would I?" She looked horrified.

I shook my head but secretly thought she might have. It was like women poohing during childbirth. We all knew it happened but we decided as the female race that it was really best for us all just not to acknowledge it.

"I saw the anaesthetist stick a very large needle in my lower arm and I waited to fall into oblivion. Last thing I remember is a purple oxygen-mask thing being lowered over my face and thinking, 'Why am I still awake?' I felt a bit drowsy, then sweet nothingness. Of course I don't remember the sweet nothingness part. The next thing I know I'm back in my bed with an IV drip in my arm and an oxygen tube up my nostrils, moaning with severe pain, with a splitting headache and shivering like crazy. The girl in the next bed, who was just going home after her nose job, said when they wheeled me back to the ward I was roaring crying going, 'Owww, it hurts, it hurts, it so fucking hurts!' She said I put her right off the idea of having her boobs done. She had a new nose and that was enough." She tried to move and yelped with the pain.

I got two large pillows and propped them behind her back as gently as I could. I would have loved to strangle James. "Okay, just rest now – stop talking." I couldn't listen any more, it was too painful to watch her struggling to tell me all this.

She shook her head. "I just have this awful, throbbing pain in my nipples, Mia, and I am absolutely freezing. I think I slept or maybe I actually passed out with the pain for a while there. A nurse came over and propped me up. I can't use my arms at all – it's way too painful – and she gave me water."

"So when can we see them?" I asked. I really had no desire to see them whatsoever – once she was okay and was happy with them that was all I cared about. In fact, the whole idea made me horribly queasy.

Carla shook her head. "I have to keep the bandaging on for ten days post-op, so, all going well, after that." She winced again. "So anyway, the next few hours and days won't be much fun. I have to sleep basically sitting up so the implants don't end up in the wrong place, and for circulation to flow to the wounds. Pass me those painkillers the nurse just left in that white plastic cup, will you?"

I held the water for her as she gulped down the absolutely massive white tablets.

"I won't be able to walk upright or dress myself for days," she said. "Remember I got my implants placed under the muscle, which is more painful so they tell me now and with a longer recovery time."

I nodded as if I did remember. I really hadn't been paying attention that day. I was squirming in my seat and silently caressing my boobies – I was sorry they had to hear all that. I put my hands over my nipples as if they were tiny ears I was shielding from this information.

I sighed. "So where the heck is James? Carla, I'm sorry, I hate to do this to you but I really have to get to work." I stood up.

"He's most probably on his way as we speak – you know the way he gets caught up in his writing. You go."

I had no choice, my job was teetering as it was and to use the excuse that I was nursing a friend through her boob-job just didn't wash, even with me. I kissed her gently and made my way back home to get my car.

Why do I always get the sneezers beside me on the bus? He sniffled and snuffled and groaned the entire rocky journey. He examined what he had just deposited into his tissue over and over again. A seat became free further up the bus but I really didn't want to insult him by moving. I willed every light to stay green but just as we approached them on newly amber, oh so slowly the obedient driver slowed down some more to allow them to turn red. He also let out every car at junctions as though no one had to be anywhere. I was getting more and more wound up and the journey took forever.

"Well, well, well!" Dominic rubbed his eyes again and again, making the point that he could not quite believe what he was seeing.

"Yes, sorry, Dominic," I said and slid into my seat without making eye contact. "Stomach cramps all morning. Running to the loo every minute. Better now."

To my relief he let it go and retreated to his office. My head was spinning. I needed chocolate and I needed it now. I slid open my drawer and, as discreetly as you can snap a square of Cadburys Whole Nut, I did it and stuffed it into my mouth.

"So with Carla off sick we have a lot to do today. I was hoping we could get on the road as soon as you're ready?" Anita's eyes burrowed into me. "It's just that I have my VHI overdue for renewal – it's thousands and I haven't got the money to pay for it so I need to be working. The Conroys viewed again – I grabbed a cab – but I'm not sure they can afford it, Mia. Mrs Conroy said that they wanted to think about it and would get back to us early next week."

Oh for fuck's sake, it was like having a hungry puppy following me around all the time! "Right!" I chewed and swallowed the lump of chocolate whole instead of going through the soft sucky motions I loved, and grabbed my keys.

We drove past the old Boland's Mill and down into Ringsend to Number 121, Ringsend Villa Cottages. Cute but small and in a superb location and it was right beside Ringsend Park too. This area had been a goldmine for properties before it all went belly-up. Prices had now dropped dramatically. Anita went on and on at me. I could feel my temper rising and I didn't really know why. We passed Ringsend library and turned left at the church onto the road. I pulled in outside the house and undid my seat belt.

"Listen, Anita, I totally understand your situation but I have a busy life too and I can't handle this pressure hanging over me all the time. I feel that you are constantly pushing me and it's added stress I just don't need. I think you are a great person, I really like you but . . ."

She glared at me. "How dare you! You have absolutely no idea what my life is like. You swan around as though the world owes you a living. Drinking and smoking. Constantly complaining. Dominic pays your petrol money and your tax and insurance, so as far as I'm concerned you need to grow up!"

She got out of the car just as Mr O'Driscoll came into view

and what looked like his boyfriend but could easily have been his mate or his brother. I couldn't decide as they walked up. Cheeky cow, I don't even smoke! I gave up smoking years ago but whenever anyone mentioned smoking my over-whelming desire to light up returned. I checked my face in the rear-view mirror and got out. How dare she speak to me like that! I was fuming.

"It's just the current place we live in is not working out. There are some terribly homophobic people in the building and it's starting to really frighten us," Mr O'Driscoll informed us as he opened and closed the fridge as if he was daring the door to fall off. He was wearing a tight green-leather jacket, was of very thin build and had grey skinny jeans on with boots that weren't laced up though they had laces on them. He had a mop of curly black hair.

"Yes," said the newly confirmed boyfriend (though the touching and stroking had confirmed this for me already). "Last week they put a shit in our letterbox."

"A what?" I asked.

"A shit," he replied.

"A human shit," Mr O'Driscoll now offered by way of explanation.

"Jesus. That's awful," Anita said.

"Oh, that's not the worst of it! It's this particular apartment, three louts rent it – they have painted our hall door pink when we were in Ibiza, they order pizzas and Chinese food all the time to our address and last month they climbed the tree outside our apartment the night of our friend Donal's 30th, and videoed our themed party and put it up on YouTube. While that didn't bother me in the slightest, some of our friends there were desperately offended and frightened that people would see them and they'd be outed." He shook his head.

"What was the theme?" I was suddenly really curious to know.

"Less Is Definitely More." Mr O'Driscoll grinned cheekily and I loved his smile immediately.

"Cool!" I said, and the two of us giggled like teenagers.

"Anyway, time is pressing on and we do need to see other people today, Mr O'Driscoll , so if we could perhaps move on?" Anita eyed me again.

I really felt like taking that stupid clipboard and bashing her over the head with it. Oh, I was an awful bitch – she did need to earn money really badly and had a teenager and a toddler and her VHI and a horrible husband to support. If indeed the husband was still there? Maybe he had left them? I decided to cut her some slack there and then, and vowed to work my ass off for the rest of the week. Bygones and all that. I didn't hold grudges.

"Well, we are just looking at a few properties right now so not committing until we have seen more." Mr Cassidy looked at Anita quizzically as she headed upstairs before us. "I'm Peadar, by the way," he said and shook my hand as he made a face at Anita's back. Not a mean face but a face that said, 'Ooh, ah, she's a bit narky today eh?'.

There wasn't really much to see in the house and it did need an awful lot of work upstairs so the two men thanked us but told us they really didn't want anywhere that they couldn't move into straight away. We left the house and I locked the front door.

6

The weekend arrived with a welcome hug and on Saturday I went to collect Carla from the clinic. She had stayed a few nights in the clinic's adjoining hotel and spa, Cloud, where her recovery was monitored as recommended by her surgeon. Another money-making recommendation, I thought, but she insisted she wanted to go, despite my saying I would nurse her at home and take a few days off work. Paul had not been back all week as Carla requested nor had he called me. I missed him around the house in the mornings but even more I missed the fact we hadn't spoken or made any arrangements to see each other again. I had spent a lot of time all week in the evening in the back garden with my mobile in my hand, just in case the coverage inside was crap. But he never called. I decided to have a wine-free week so I wouldn't drink and dial. I couldn't get him out of my mind though, and the weird thing was I actually looked forward to going to bed early so I could close my eyes and picture him and smell him and feel his arms around me. I had it bad. Even I knew it was quite ridiculous.

Across the road from the clinic I bought Carla *Vogue* for

€6.56 and vowed there and then never to buy that magazine again. What a rip-off for a magazine full of ads! They should be paying us to read it! She was sitting in the gleaming reception but somehow now the place seemed even faker than before. It seemed to promise one thing and – looking at my dear friend here – deliver the exact opposite. The receptionist had other fodder now and was totally ignoring Carla. I wondered how much of her was real? Was her nose real? Were her ears pinned back? Was she unrecognisable as the girl she had once been? I smiled at her without speaking as we left.

"So where's James?" I asked as I indicated to pull out – she couldn't put her seatbelt on so I was extra cautious.

"Oh, what is it with you and James? He's writing – he can't be disturbed. Mia, he's an artist – he needs his space."

Jesus, I couldn't do right for doing wrong these days and I had to face my mother and sister for the rest of the day. I was keeping my mouth shut. No one bloody asked about me – how *I* was. Carla never even mentioned Paul.

"Are you on that bloody phone again? You'll get brain-fry!" my mother screeched up the stairs.

"I am on the toilet – is that okay with you, Mam?" I shouted through the bathroom door.

"Well, I hope you aren't throwing up because that is not the solution to your weight problem – exercise and eat less, that's what Kelly Osbourne says. The corned beef is up – it's getting cold! Hurry up!"

Dinner conversation was strained to say the least, with Samantha banging on and on about her work with IT this and IT that and asked me had I ever disabled cookies? "I once bit the legs off a gingerbread man," I told her, but she didn't laugh. That was about the height of it. She told us they brought Niall's dad John everywhere as he was fierce lonely since his wife Esther had passed on. I tried to lighten the mood with some showbiz stories – Charlie Sheen's boozing, Lindsay Lohan's jail time – but they seemed less than entertained. I got all my gossip from E! News. It was a bit like a drug – I needed to know what was happening in Celeb World. That was why I had no time for *VIP* magazine – I craved information on the *real* celebs of the world. The Angelina Jolies of the world as opposed to the so-called Irish celebs, the Irish models who stood in bikinis on a freezing cold Grafton Street dressed as Pints of Guinness or jumping over fences to promote Paddy Powers. Then there was that breed of loud, fake, OTT reality TV stars with their ridiculously over-bleached white teeth and desperation in their eyes for fame – they were all just plain silly.

I didn't mention Carla's boob job. I didn't think they would understand.

I tried to picture Samantha and Niall having sex, please don't ask me why but I did, and I couldn't.

I imagined it went like this:

Interior, night, Niall's house.

Niall: "Good evening to you, Samantha."

Samantha: "Indeed, and a very good evening to you, Niall."

Niall: "Ehem, would you care for me to push your buttons this evening at all?"

Samantha: "Why, Niall, I think that would be very appropriate."

Samantha closes curtains.

Cut to Niall smoking a pipe and Samantha sipping a Spritzer.

We all ate in relative silence, with me just pushing the food around the plate as much as I could.

"So, Mia, what are your plans for Christmas?" Mam asked as she scooped up the end of the gravy from the metal gravy boat with a piece of bread – the heel of the loaf, her favourite.

"I'm not sure, Mam, I think I may just take it easy and chill in my own place in Ranelagh." Please, *please* say 'Ah sure, that's okay, love!'.

"Over my dead body. This is a family home. I want you here with us for Christmas, isn't that right, Samantha?"

"Well, actually, Mam, I've been invited to Niall's for dinner and I have accepted," said Samantha. Mam's face dropped.

Oh, this was even worse than I could ever have imagined! Christmas dinner, just the two of us! Not even sisterly love to break the tension.

"But, Mam, he says that you are more than welcome to come. We'd love to have you." Samantha eyed our mother closely.

Ah, fantastic, I thought. But then I heard the sniffle. The 'I am put out and hurt' sniffle.

"Thank you, but no, my place is here with my other daughter." Sniff again and Samantha looked genuinely hurt.

"Ah, but Mam, it will be great! You know his dad's a widower so we're all pitching in to make the dinner. He has a beautiful home, I keep telling you about it – you'd love it!"

Sniffle. "I'm sure." Even the fake phone voice was on now. "Thank them from me profuselidy but I have a spinster daughter to think of. I have responsibilities here."

So that was that. It was me and her and a big massive turkey. I'd prefer to be the turkey. I looked at my sister and gave her a weak smile. She gave me a weak smile back.

7

I was pacing the bedroom now. Carla and His Majesty were in the front room. Why he spent so much time here when he had a mansion on Killiney Hill I had no idea. I hadn't asked Carla where he'd been or when he'd turned up. My bedroom was closing in on me. I needed a drink. I needed it now. I padded downstairs and opened the fridge – the kitchen actually smelled of Paul. If I could just wait a matter of hours I would see him face to face. That way I would appear breezy and not at all bothered. A free spirit. Isn't that what all men wanted – free spirits but in very short skirts and high-heel shoes (not the hippy, 'haven't washed these stinkin' dreadlocks for a few months' types).

I poured a large glass of white wine and padded back up. Sit on the bed and by the time you have drunk the wine he will have called you . . . that way you can say 'Phew, that was close – I nearly called him first'. I wondered if I should give in and go on Facebook just to see if he was on it? But I had made a solemn promise with Carla that neither of us would go there:

Facebook was not a part of our lives. I have to admit though I was secretly jealous of all those Facebookers who didn't seem in the slightest bit embarrassed that they spent hour after hour nosing into each other's lives . . . sounded quite good to me if I was really honest but I knew I would become addicted. I put some Sting on the CD player and sat back and sipped my wine. Sip. Sip. Sip. Then: *Glug. Glug. Glug.* I moved to my dressing-table and started to apply my make-up. "An Englishman in New York" inspired me to experiment with some green eye shadow and eyeliner and I loved the look. Definitely not for daytime but nice for night. I brushed my hair and opened my wardrobe.

I was going out.

Without verbalising it or indeed planning it, my body had taken over and it wanted to go out. But with who? On my own. I would head to the Palace, pull up a seat at the bar (it was never, never jam-packed) and have a drink. I might even have one with an umbrella in it. But what does one wear when drinking alone? I rummaged. How about a very short purple Vera Moda skirt that I hadn't dared wear in years? I drained the large glass. Yes, indeed. Teamed with a low-cut black top, black tights and my knee-high boots. I stood in front of the mirror. Damn, my reflection looked mighty good and that wine was strong. I don't suppose you were meant to fill the glass to the brim. Keys, lippy, purse. Padded back down. Quietly peeled the plastic off the makeshift back door and escaped.

As I thought, the Palace had some people in it but wasn't full to the door. Saturday nights were like that. Tim was working – oh yay of yays – I could stay for as many as I wanted now and have some great company. He was chatting up a couple of American tourists when I pulled myself up onto the bar stool.

"Excuse me, sir, a cocktail of your making, if you please!"

He beamed at me. "Howrya, Mia girl – wow, don't you look brilliant – where are ya off to?" He removed a silver shaker from the shelf and proceeded to pour different concoctions into it.

"Nowhere," I didn't mind admitting it to him. "Nowhere to go and I was just going stir crazy at home and wanted to get out for a while."

"How did Carla get on?"

I narrowed my eyes and looked at him. "Huh?"

He leaned on his elbows on the bar. "The bloody boob job? How did it go for her, like?" He tossed his blond hair. "I was thinking about her all week, didn't see her at all."

Carla never ceased to astonish me. She wouldn't breathe a word about her boob job to anyone, yet she tells the local barman in the Palace all about it.

"She told you?" I had to double-check.

"Yeah, we are friends, you know . . . we . . . sometimes go for a drink."

"Wow, okay." I shook my head. I was just accepting a delicious-looking apple-type-tini thing from Tim when the door opened and a well-on, noisy bunch stumbled into the bar.

"Ah, here we go! Always when I'm on my own!" Tim stood up straight and tied his black folded apron tighter around his waist. "Lads, one at a time now, what can I get yous?"

As orders were shouted at him over my back I stared straight ahead. I didn't want any crappy drunken conversation. I didn't want to be picked up. I just wanted to have a few drinks, get a Chinese on the way home and go to sleep. All the while not ringing or texting Paul. I sipped again. Would I go for prawns in black bean sauce and fried rice or the ever-so-sinful three-in-one tray?

"Eight sambucas, please!" A hand rested on my shoulder. "Sorry, love, just trying to squeeze in there to get me drinks if ya don't mind."

I froze. I knew before he spoke again. I knew the smell. The weight of the hand on me. I knew it was him. Heart racing, palms sweating, I turned around slowly.

He smiled at me through drunken eyes and then, as sharp as you like, he sobered up. Just like that. "Ho-ho-how . . . hi . . . Mia, wow . . . shit . . . hi!"

I curled my toes up tight in my boots to settle my nerves. "Howyra, Paul?" I smiled at him. A big, breezy smile. It felt fucking great. I hadn't been desperately ringing him when he was on a night out with the lads. He hadn't been on a date or sitting home in his flat forgetting all about me. He had been out, he was busy. And I looked good.

"Grand, yeah. It's my mate Dean's stag do – been a weekend of it – well, we started on Thursday night actually. You look . . . hang on, let me give out these drinks . . ." He held them over his head and made his way to the large group.

Aghh, I looked what? I wanted to hear what word he would have used: great, sexy, cute, amazing, the same, fat? Spit it out, man!

He was back. "Want to sit over there for a sec?" He pointed to the window seat, my favourite seat in the Palace.

"All okay there, Mia?" Tim shouted at me as he pulled pint after pint and wiped the sweat off his forehead.

"Oh yeah, fine, we're – friends!" I shouted back to him, giving the thumbs-up for some reason. "Boyfriend?" Paul indicated Tim.

"No!" I was taken aback by that comment – why on earth would he think I had a boyfriend?

"So what's up?" He knocked back his sambuca in one go.

"Em, not much, to be honest." I twirled my little umbrella by the stick.

"So are you one of those girls that sit at the bar waiting to be bought expensive cocktails all night?" He must have meant it as a joke, I knew that, but the boyfriend comment still had me riled.

"In the Palace? I don't think so. It's not the type of bar a girl comes to meet that type of man." I wasn't smiling.

"Rich men?" he almost growled at me.

"Well, yeah, that's what you said – you just asked do I come here to be bought expensive cocktails." I shifted uncomfortably now.

He looked at me sourly. "So what you really want is to be sitting in the Four Seasons with some rich bastard plying you with cocktails and then taking you for a ride in his shiny Bentley?"

I was stunned. That was nothing short of insulting. Was he joking? What on earth was going on here? My blood was beginning to boil. "Listen, Paul, I'm just in here for a quiet drink and to talk to my friend. I don't really need this."

His face dropped just as two very drunken and very sweaty friends approached.

"What are ya up to now, dickhead?"

One gentleman extended his hand to me which I took and which was extremely sticky. Our hands squelched apart. "Ooops, sorry about that, darlin'!" He licked his hand. "That's the sambuca, sticky ole shite!"

"So who is she, Pauly man?" the other slurred.

That was enough. Paul jumped up. Scalded cat. "Alright so, see you on Monday!" he threw in my direction – and he was gone. Lost in the crowd of Deano's drunken stag.

I picked up my bag. "Tim, I'm heading off."

He smiled at me. "See you next Friday maybe?" he said as

he wiped down the now drenched bar with his off-colour white cloth. "Tell Carla I was asking after her, won't ya?"

I stood outside and breathed the cold fresh air. What had just happened? Had that really happened? I started to walk. Appetite completely gone now. Why had he been such a prick to me? Or had he? Was he just fooling around and had I got on my high horse and taken it all too seriously? But he had sprinted from me as soon as he got the chance.

"Oh, Mia! Mia!" I stamped my foot hard on the pavement and shouted and a girl at a bus stop across the street answered, "Wha'?" I'd told Mam the name was far too common these days.

I hailed a taxi. Town was heaving and the taxi sailed along, narrowly missing falling people as we went up Dame Street.

The light was still on in the front room and I crept up to bed. I didn't even take off my make-up. I never skip that. Not even when I am totally hammered at five o'clock in the morning – I'll at least grab and wipe. I curled up in the bed in my short skirt and low-cut top and cried myself to sleep with sheer frustration.

I woke suddenly. I could definitely hear a noise. I turned over to look at my alarm clock and the green flashing figures told me it was 4.26 a.m. There it was again. A gentle knocking. What was it? I sat up. It was coming from my bedroom door. I walked over, heart thumping. I put my ear to the door. There it was, so faint a mouse wouldn't hear it.

"Mia, Mia, Mia . . . let me in . . . Mia, Mia, Mia . . ."

I opened the door. "Jesus Christ, Paul, what are you doing?" I hissed as I pulled him in. I leaned him against the wall as I locked the door.

"Listen, I'm really sorry, I don't know what came over me." His attempt at whispering was so bad – you know the drunken silent voice?

"*Shhhuusshhh!*" I pleaded with him. If Carla thought he had broken into her house she would have him arrested, I knew that for sure. That wasn't the kind of thing that amused Carla.

"I just got mad jealous when I saw that barman looking out for you. So stupid, I am so bloody stupid!" He rolled down the wall and hit the floor with a thud.

I slid down beside him. "I don't have a boyfriend, I mean if I did and we were . . . carrying on like this . . . that wouldn't make me a very nice girl, now would it?"

He shook his head and stared at me. "I wish I was as nice as you. I wish I could change everything, well, not everything but . . ." He rubbed his hand down my cheek. "Have I blown it here then?" He turned away from me. He was so drunk. His jacket was obviously lost – he was shivering in a light orange Penguin T-shirt and faded denims with his red Adidas runners.

"No, not at all!" I smiled. "I just have no idea how the conversation ended with me being rogered in the back of a shiny Bentley at The Four Seasons by a bald fat bloke."

"I never said that!" he snorted. Then he snorted louder and went into a fit of laughter. He actually rolled around the floor clutching his stomach.

I wasn't laughing. Carla would slay me. I tried to keep my hand over his mouth as I pulled him up half onto the bed. I thought I heard the floorboards creak but must have imagined it.

"I am such a fuck-up," he mumbled. "I am a funny lunatic though. All my mates say that I'm a born lunatic."

"*Shush*," I repeated, both because I didn't want him to say anything in this state that he'd regret (I'd been there before many a time) and also because I was totally shitting myself that Carla would wake and come in.

"How did I get here?" he mumbled. "How is it I'm here? Oh, sorry, Mia, I'm fucked!"

And with that the man of my dreams passed out on my pillow. He knees were on the ground and his upper body and head flopped over my bed. I dragged the rest of his body up to join him. As I lay beside him, I wondered what he had meant. His drunken talk was worrying. Why did he think he was a fuck-up?

"You know what, Mia," I whispered to myself in the dark, "he'll tell you when he is ready."

I spooned him and fell asleep.

I stood over the kettle, willing it to boil faster. "Come on, come on!" I hissed at it, jumping up and down in my bare feet. It was freezing in the kitchen. The two cups with large spoonfuls of coffee peered back at me, daring Carla to come and judge for herself just what was going on. At last the kettle clicked off and I poured the boiling water in.

I gently nudged my Sleeping Beauty. He tried to open one eye and failed.

"Take your time – coffee."

He groaned. Then he pulled the covers over his head. "Oh no, it's all coming back. Shit, what time is it?"

"Yep, been there, many a time. What I say is forget about it, drink your coffee and let's go for breakfast before Carla gets up. It's just after nine."

I did feel bad. This really wasn't on in her home but what could I have done? Thrown him out in the state he was in? 'Yes!' I imagined Carla shouting in my ear.

His face went whiter. "Oh shit, I really should go, I . . ." He shut his eyes tight. "Oh no, doubly shitty, Carla would fire me if she knew I broke in here like that, wouldn't she? What was I thinking? What a gobshite I am!" He was genuinely pissed-off big-time with himself.

But I understood. "It's fine, she won't ever find out. Now let's get out and get some grub into you."

He sat up, leaned out of the bed to where I was crouched down at the bedside locker and kissed me on the mouth. Now I won't say he had the freshest breath ever but it was a lovely kiss. I stood up and went and dressed in the bathroom and, as luck would have it, last night's make-up just needed a little touching up – the eyeliner was all over the place from my tears but the foundation was almost perfect. I redid my eyes and away we went. What a shame it was bad for your skin to sleep in your make-up – or was that just another big marketing ploy by the cosmetic companies to make us keep buying more? My mother had never taken her make-up off her entire life and her skin looked fine to me. She slapped a bit of Astral face cream on now and then – that was it – her skincare routine, she called it.

He was sitting up at my dressing-table when I got back, obviously sending a text message. "Great coffee, lifesaver." He looked slightly better, bit more colour in his mush. He pushed his phone deep down into his pocket and we crept downstairs and I pointed for him to step over the creaky step at the very bottom. He duly obliged.

We were relieved to hit the fresh air.

I wanted to hold his hand or at least link arms but it didn't seem the right thing to do. I was always looking at couples who held hands or linked arms. I loved the way it looked. It was so comfortable. I wanted to feel it for a while.

"Where's your car?" I asked.

"It's at home." He thrust his hands deep into his pockets and shivered with no coat. "Hey, why don't we take your car to . . . I dunno . . ." he paused and scratched his head, "say Glendalough . . . and spend the day there?"

I happily agreed and we got my car and drove in effortless companionship mostly, listening to music, commenting on the scenery and my unspoken passion in the car was at times so hot I had to open the windows. What on earth was wrong with me? Was I going through the change my mother so often spoke of? I would have gladly pulled over and done it there and then in the car, in a bush, public toilet on the side of the road, hard shoulder, anywhere. I was normally never like this. His phone rang often but not once did he even attempt to take it out of his pocket. Great manners, I thought, as I put my foot down on my little Ka's accelerator a little harder. We talked about the exchange we'd had in the Palace again and I told him all about Tim and my Friday-night sessions there. Ironically he had never been there before. Could this be fate? My mind was rushing away with me as he swapped Kings of Leon for Massive Attack. I mean, what were the chances of him being the builder Carla picked and then him being in my local? Okay, there was every chance. I forgot the fate bit as quickly as I had thought of it. I told him about Carla's boob job and didn't feel I was cheating her by doing so. I told him about my Christmas plans and he just listened.

By the time we had parked and were seated in the cosy hotel bar in Glendalough I had pretty much told him my entire life story. He had told me zilch. He ordered a Guinness, hair of the dog he explained, no other cure would come close, so I ordered a glass of Shiraz. For some reason I'm not that comfortable eating on dates or even all that hungry for that matter.

Paul obviously didn't feel the same. He ordered sweet and spicy chicken wings for starters and fish pie with extra chunky chips for main. I went for chicken and vegetable soup and a vegetable quiche. Something I would never in a million years normally order. It's not easy to fancy someone, no matter how much you try, when they are eating chicken wings, I noted, as I sipped my wine, and he tore at the meat on the small bones, sticky sweet sauce sitting all around his mouth. There was a fingerbowl but I'm not sure that he noticed. I smiled regardless. He started to talk a little as I asked him some questions about his work and friends, but not much about family, and I didn't want to be too nosy so I just listened. He loved his job, it seemed, but was very strapped for cash. "Low funds," was a phrase he used a lot. I couldn't understand this. I knew what he was charging Carla and it was a sizeable amount. Surely his little bedsit and van couldn't cost that much?

After another two pints, and two glasses for me, we took to the outside for a walk. It was a typical cold day and, even though he had no coat, he insisted. It was bright and exciting as we walked the famous grounds of this old monastic site founded by St Kevin. There were many walks around the two lakes but we just sauntered easily. The area had been preserved, being part of the Wicklow National Park, and it was still possible to enjoy the haunting solitude of it all. I imagined how far St Kevin must have felt from civilisation here. We watched the tourists taking photos and eating ice creams in the cold. I was slightly merry. We paused behind a large stone wall so as not to interrupt a spoken tour that was going on.

Suddenly his arms were creeping up inside my jacket, his hands freezing cold on my bare back, and I gasped. I hoped he hadn't noticed the love handles too much as he skimmed over them. There was no sucking those babies in no matter how hard I tried. Then, as I still had the image of my love handles in my mind, his mouth was on mine and I devoured him back. My hands were all over him. Oh, it felt so good! He was very hairy and his skin was taut.

"Mia," he leaned back, "would you think I was way out of line if I asked you to get a room with me here?" His breath was heavy on my face.

"No, let's do it!" I was already halfway back to the hotel.

"May I help you?" The receptionist had taken her time in asking.

"A room, please, double, for one night," I said without the slightest hint of embarrassment, tapping my nails impatiently on the shiny wooden reception desk with its gold-plated surround.

"Certainly, madam, if you can just fill out these forms." The receptionist pushed her logoed pen toward me.

"Ah, come on, really?" I asked her, completely exasperated.

She looked at me as though I was nuts. "Well, yes, it's hotel policy, I'm afraid, so if you can give us your credit-card details here . . ." She tapped-tapped away while I filled out the form, my body a raging mess of hormones. "Now breakfast will be served –" She held our key card in her left hand. I tried to make a grab for it but she was too quick for me – experience, I guess. "Breakfast will be served in the dining room from seven thirty to ten thirty. As you will see, these times are coloured-coded, seven thirty to eight thirty being green, a nice quiet time – eight thirty to nine thirty orange, heating up and getting busier – and then nine thirty to ten thirty is red alert, red alert, red alert." She suddenly turned herself into a robot and spun around three times in quick succession as I looked on in amazement.

I lunged for the room card and again she was too quick.

"One final thing. Anything you drink from the minibar will be charged at minibar prices. So no point in replacing with cheaper products. That's all, enjoy your stay, Miss Doyle." She slid the card across the counter and winked at me.

I leaned in to read her name badge. "Bridget," I whispered, "you're so not funny!" I turned away and went back to where I had left Paul.

"I have to go." His face was ashen as he sat rooted to the oversized, comfy, red-leather couch under the window. He was shivering now in the warmth.

"I don't understand," I said, the room-card gripped tightly in my hand.

He was staring at his mobile. "It's a – family emergency. I can't go into the detail but I have to get back right now. All those calls earlier that I ignored – it was about that. Please, Mia, I need to go right now." He stood up.

"Of course!" I grabbed my bag off my shoulder and rummaged around for my keys. I went and dropped the room-card back on the desk as Bridget, who had obviously heard it all, looked at me in surprise.

We walked out to the car. "What was –"

"Stop, please!" He put his head in his hands. "I will explain when I can. If you can't accept that, then we'll have to just leave this!" He threw his hands in the air and looked so stressed I didn't feel I could ask another thing.

I drove back the hour's journey in silence and dropped him at Tara Street station.

"Sorry, Mia," was all he could mumble as he slammed the door shut.

I drove home and Carla was in the kitchen. She looked a lot better.

"So where have you been?" she asked as she winced and turned to face me at the half-finished counter top.

I draped myself over the counter, suddenly exhausted. "Ahhh, out and about, you know!"

"No, I don't," she smiled. "So where were you?"

"With Paul," I sighed and she didn't comment. She knew not to.

She moved into the front room in her Uggs (oh, how I wished I could wear Uggs and not look like a crazy granny who had been waiting for hours for a bus in the cold!). I followed her and she upped the TV volume to my huge relief. I lost myself in the *EastEnders Omnibus*, only getting up once to make us both a coffee, and alone I devoured a full packet of Chocolate Hobnobs.

8

"*It's the final countdown!*" Dominic was on his knees playing air guitar, a long scarf draped over his head.

Oh God, it was really too much to take on a rainy Monday morning when I had been splashed from head to foot by a driver who flew straight into a massive puddle as I tried to cross the road into the office. She knew she did it – I saw her look in her rear-view mirror as I screamed. I wondered how she felt? Did she feel awful? Did she think it was hilarious? Who knew? I hated her.

Anita was at her desk, tapping away. Ashen-faced again. Dressed today in a black dress with a black cardigan, thick black tights and black pumps. Cheery, I thought as I took off my dripping coat and flung it over the radiator. One good thing about our office was that Dominic didn't skimp on the heating and it was always lovely and warm.

Anita had the right idea, though, as far as Dominic was concerned. She didn't look up at him so she wasn't forced to laugh and get more wrinkles like me. Lately I was trying to fake-laugh with my mouth closed tight so as not to invite more lines. They were creeping into my face and quite frankly they had no right.

"So," Dominic continued, "Mia, Anita, please. Carla had a client, Mr Gordon McHale, interested in Number 2, Shrewsbury Road – he wants to look again this morning." He rubbed his hands together and hopped up and down.

Anita spoke quietly. "We can do it."

My mouth fell open. "No, surely that's Carla's commission – she rang every client and told them to call her mobile directly if they wanted a second viewing." But poor Carla was still in too much pain to come back to work. I knew all about the multi-millionaire property tycoon Gordon McHale from her.

"No, no, no!" Dominic removed the scarf from his head that was, I presumed, acting as Joey Tempest's long hair. He rolled it up. "Carla was supposed to be back today – she's phoned in sick again. Mr McHale rang the office to say her mobile was powered off – he's only in Dublin for a few very busy days so it's you two he has agreed to see now. He wants this property, Mia – it's there for you."

I couldn't believe this. Carla had been on this for a few months – she knew he had the money – he just needed to sort out some geographical stuff, she'd told me. It was just a question of where he would be living. I picked up my phone and sent her a quick text.

"Shall we?" Anita had her black coat, black scarf and black bag all ready to go.

"Fine." I smiled the biggest one I could rustle up and we headed for the most expensive road in Dublin.

"So what's up with Carla anyway, is she okay?" she asked as I made a left onto the Merrion Road. "Virus." I twiddled the knob and Billy Idol blared out "Rebel Yell". I sat back into my seat, still damp, but ah just what I needed – some comfort rock to make me feel better. It wasn't up to me to tell Carla's operation details to Anita – that was up to Carla if and when she decided to share with the office.

"Sorry but could you turn that down, please?" She held her hand to her head. "I've had a very tough weekend."

I glanced at her and then back to the road, turning the music down to almost inaudible. I'll be honest, I wasn't best pleased. Being told what to do annoyed me at the best of times, but in my own car?

"My son, Stevie – he had an accident," she offered.

Now I felt awful. "Oh shit, is he okay?" I indicated again and checked my mirror. "What happened?"

"He was wearing a ring, a ring I gave him for his Debs, a Claddagh ring. He was mucking around with some friends on an abandoned building site – he jumped off a dumper but there was a bit of metal sticking out – it caught the ring and pulled off his finger."

I nearly crashed the car. I actually swerved into the middle of the road. I felt like throwing up. I was dizzy. "Shit. Fuck. Could they sew the finger back on?"

She was rolling down the window now. "No," she said.

My mouth was hanging open but I didn't have another word to say. Nothing would come out. She continued to look out the window as we approached the house. What could I say? This poor woman, she really was having a run of bad luck. I reached my hand across and patted her leg, I don't really know why it felt like a good idea at the time but it turned out to be slightly embarrassing.

We parked and I got out first, and there parked up in his silver Mercedes waiting for us was Mr Gordon McHale himself and, boy oh boy, was he hot! I felt terrible for even thinking this after what I had just heard about Anita's poor son but I couldn't help it. I was in awe of his beauty. No wonder Carla was keeping this gem to herself. As the door opened and he got out,

I saw upon closer inspection that he was a George Clooney lookalike, with the slightest speckles of grey through his brown hair, but with the fantastic eyes of Gerard Butler. He was in short a complete and utter ride-me-sideways bloke!

"Hello." He approached me and extended a manicured hand from the sleeve of his dark-blue suit and sparkling white shirt, tieless and open to the second button. He was tall, over six foot, and with a build I wanted to eat there and then. He was simply magnetic.

I couldn't breathe. "Yes, indeed," I managed in a highpitched voice and took his hand. I think I actually rubbed it slightly.

"Still no Carla then?" He peered in at poor Anita.

"No, she's still under . . . the weather." I managed to get my voice back to the correct octave. Wish I was under *you* right now, I thought, and immediately Paul poured back into my head. I felt for my mobile in my pocket in case he rang or texted. It was deadly silent.

Anita emerged with her million files under her arm.

He beeped the locks shut on his car. We introduced ourselves as we crunched our way on the gravel up to the huge redbrick. We climbed the steps to the old red Georgian door. I pushed it open as I removed the key and stood in to turn off the alarm. I looked up. As I stood in the entrance hall with its Travertine marble-flagged floors I was overwhelmed. It was simply stunning. I gaped in awe as Anita took over and went into her well over-rehearsed spiel.

"Mr McHale, as I'm sure you know Shrewsbury Road is widely regarded as the city's premier residential road. This house has been extended and refurbished over the last few years and as you know this property is an excellent choice for those seeking a quality residence which is ready for immediate occupation on this much-sought-after tree-lined road in the heart of Dublin's Embassy belt."

I hoped she would take a breath here and indeed she did.

"Can we perhaps move into the living room and sit?"

He was smirking at us, I was sure of it.

We followed him into what I would have called the drawing room with its incredible bay windows, rare decorative cornicing and white marble fireplace. It was all brick-inset with a slate hearth and coal-effect gas fire. Gordon sat on the white couch as Anita continued. I stood and stared at the magnificence of it all.

"Number 2 is situated towards the Merrion Road end of Shrewsbury Road and this house enjoys one of Dublin's most convenient and sought-after locations, Mr McHale, with the majority of the city's amenities within easy reach. Just some of these notable features include the excellent restaurants, boutiques, shops, hotels and sports clubs located in Ballsbridge and Donnybrook. Also within walking distance are the RDS, Herbert Park and the Lansdowne Road Football Stadium."

"Aviva," he interrupted her.

She was startled. "Sorry?" She looked over her shoulder as though he was greeting someone who had just arrived.

"Aviva," he smiled at her. "That's the new name of the football stadium."

"Indeed." She nodded again and again, then continued.

He glanced at me, now obviously very amused, but I pretended not to notice.

"Many of Dublin's premier schools are also close by, including St Michael's College, the Teresian School, Gonzaga College, Mount Annville, Alexandra College, to name but a few." Here she turned the page over on top of her clipboard. "This is a unique and exciting opportunity to purchase one of Dublin's finest residences on Dublin's most-sought-after residential road."

God, she was boring me to tears. I glanced over at gorgeous

Gordon and he had a look of complete and utter bemusement on his face now. As he caught my eye this time he held my gaze for a few seconds. Carla would have a hernia after all her work if one of us didn't benefit from this man's need to buy a massive house on the most expensive road in Dublin. I had to do something.

"Isn't this just incredible, Gordon?" I extended my arm. "I mean, come on, who in their right mind wouldn't want to live here? It's the ultimate dream house in the ultimate dream location." Beckoning to Gordon, I walked through into the bright kitchen with its circular island and double glass doors, looking onto the large landscaped gardens, and they both followed me. "Imagine a barbeque out there on a summer's day – must be to die for!" I looked up. "And those ceilings!" They were so high and gleaming white. He leaned back on the white kitchen counter and draped his arm over the edge of the sink, turning on and off the tap. "Suits you," I grinned at him. "It's a piece of history, it's so interesting, and means so much more than the bricks and cement that holds it up. It's so uniquely Irish, this road. It's the best house I have ever been in my life and career and that's just the truth." I really meant it. "Can't you just feel the presence of this house?"

"*Sold!*" he grinned and pointed behind me as though he was looking down the barrel of a gun. "To the lady in the mirror!"

I turned on my heel to see who it was and it was me. My reflection stared back at me, complete with muddy ear that I hadn't noticed in my tiny rear-view mirror. I rubbed it away. My make-up was on but my hair was a damp mess still. I patted it down. Ha! Holy smoke. I had sold this house. This magnificent, wondrous, stunning, fair-priced, recession-cowering building had been sold by yours truly. It could hold its head up high again. I had sold a house on Shrewsbury Road.

He stood up and rubbed his immaculate hands together.

"Let's sign!" Anita butted in, thrusting her large pen into his face.

"How about a cup of coffee?" I jumped in now. "Insomniac is down the road. We could chat while going over the paperwork?" I gently removed the pen and pushed Anita's hand down slowly.

"How about a drink? Kiely's is down the road – we could chat while going over the paperwork," he suggested.

"As Sir wishes," I said, a little too tongue-in-cheek but I felt he was enjoying it. I called it as I saw it with people.

"Well, in that case I could go on to Inchicore in a taxi and meet Mrs Kilroy and her son there?" Anita suggested.

"Great idea," I said as I drew her aside. I lowered my voice. "Please tell her I am really, really sorry not to get to see her today but will be in touch with her this afternoon. It's a done deal but she really just needs to have one last look around with the engineer. She adores the house and she knows the area like the back of her hand – so it's almost done. Go easy on her though, don't push."

Anita left and I breathed in the smell of this building one last time. I knew I would probably never set foot in a house like this again. It was spellbinding. We headed for the door of this newly sold mansion before I'd even got to see the swimming pool (of course there was a swimming pool, it goes without saying).

"So what'll it be?" he asked as we strolled into the pub.

He had been on the phone since we left the house to walk to Kiely's. I didn't mind. I was enjoying the stroll beside him and the glances from every car as every woman turned her head to look at him and then me. To size me up. Was I worthy in their eyes? Clearly not, as I could tell from their expressions.

Especially the ones who lifted their shades to look at us. They were the worst culprits.

"Em, I don't know, Mr McHale, it's only early in the afternoon. What are you having?" I pulled at my grey skirt and matching jacket and wished I'd made more of an effort. At least they were dry and mud-free, I supposed, and the shirt was newly opened this morning (I wasn't one of those people who washed brand-new shirts – I wore them. Same with new duvet covers – they went straight on). Usually on Mondays of late I would be glammed up to the nines but with Paul still off work at the house I didn't feel the need.

"Heineken for me and whatever you want, but I insist it's alcoholic – and call me Gordon, please?" He undid the button on his suit jacket as he relaxed.

"What if I didn't drink?" I quizzed him.

"Oh, you drink," he leaned in closer to me, "I just know you do."

I stared back at him, praying all the muck was gone from my face.

"Can I get you anything?"

We both looked up at the waitress who nearly dropped her Guinness tray and glass tip-jar full of copper coins and looked at me as though she'd like to slit my throat. As though I'd wronged her in some awful way.

"Two bottles of Heineken, please."

He removed his jacket completely now and both myself and the waitress gave a little sigh that only other women and cats could hear.

"So, congratulations!" I removed my folder and placed it on the wooden table. I manoeuvred some beer-mats and the plastic tomato-ketchups to make room.

"Yeah, I'm pretty happy. I've been after it for years really but my business was going to take me to China so I had to hold off. However, I'm happy to say I'm fully based in Europe for the foreseeable future." He had the most gorgeous smile.

"And is Mrs McHale happy?" I had to find out.

He gave me a lopsided grin, before nodding. "She is, thank you, she's extremely happy."

I knew it, too good to be true. He had no wedding ring on but none of them do nowadays, do they? I felt more relaxed for some reason when I knew he was married. Don't ask me why but he became less threatening to me.

The drinks arrived and we sipped them. As always when I drink during the day, I felt drunk after the first sip.

"My lawyers and my inspectors will be in touch with you now, if that's okay, Mia?"

I took down the essential details and emailed them to Dominic via my iPhone. We discussed the down payment, the paperwork, insurance, solicitors and every other boring detail that came with selling houses, the plans for this and plans for that. He knew it all already.

"Another?" he asked after I drained the bottle.

"No, God, I shouldn't really," I managed meekly.

"Two Heineken, please." He motioned to the waitress again by holding up one empty bottle. She was on it in a flash.

"So are you married, Mia?"

"Me? No, why do you ask?" Seriously I was a little drunk after the first bottle and no-food scenario.

"Just wondering. So is the lovely Carla in a serious relationship then?"

Ha! Bingo! Bull's-eye! This was the one and only reason I was sitting in this pub with this ride of a man.

"Dunno." I rubbed my hand against the phone in my skirt pocket. What was wrong with me? I was pretty crazy about Paul, wasn't I? Yet here I was, openly fancying this stranger. But Paul's a stranger too, I chastised myself – what do you know about him?

"So, any other questions I can answer for you, Mr McHale?" I stared at him and he smiled.

"No, I don't think so, not for the moment anyway."

I was starting to tear up the beer-mats.

"Well, actually there is something." He put his drink down and leaned towards me again. "Carla mentioned staying with her boyfriend who owned a property on Killiney Hill. I asked her what house and she told me The Tindles. I was pretty shocked as," he picked up his Heineken again and took a long, slow drink, "I own that house but employ a housesitter as I don't want to rent it. Mrs McHale stays there when she comes to Dublin. He, James, is my housesitter, so I suppose I can't understand why, if she's in a serious relationship with this guy, she doesn't know this?"

For the second time that day my jaw fell open. "James? Are you saying James doesn't own The Tindles? That you own it and he minds it for you?" I stared at him.

"Yes, my lovely Mia, that's exactly what I am saying about Mr James. I didn't know what to say to Carla as I was landed totally on the spot but I thought maybe you should know. I don't really want James pretending he's the Lord of the Manor, if you know what I mean, so obviously I need to address the problem as soon as possible. Drink?"

"Are you joking? I'll be locked! Oh my God, Carla will never believe this. But his writing study is there, his stuff is all there!"

"Well, actually my study is there and, yes, his stuff is there because as I said he does live there. He maintains the house for me and I pay him a good wage to do that."

I shook my head in utter disbelief. "So he's not minted gentry then?" I asked, afraid of the answer.

"No, Mia, I can safely say he's not minted. So, drink?"

I shook my head again. "I can't believe this, I can't believe you. I'm sorry, I'm not calling you a liar, Mr Mc– . . . Gordon, but Carla's not some stupid bimbo. Surely after a year she would have copped this? Does James never talk about the sort of stuff that homeowners talk to each other about?"

He just shook his head. "Obviously not. The Tindles was the first big property I ever bought so it's very special to me. When Carla said she was spending the night in The Tindles, her boyfriend's house, it stopped me dead in my tracks. Honestly, I would have told her today if she wasn't ill, but when Dominic mentioned you I thought that would be even better."

I couldn't comprehend it.

"To be honest, Mia, he seems to me like a slippery little eel."

I nodded, still a bit stunned.

"Okay, then, drink tonight?"

He really was the most gorgeous man I had ever seen. This must be what it's like to have George gazing into your eyes – oh, Stacy, you lucky cow – what was going on here?

"Or do you have a special someone in your life?" He sipped eloquently from the end of his bottle, not a big slug yet not a girly sip either – it was perfect.

He was taking the piss out of me, wasn't he? I caught my reflection in the mirror again and agreed with my inner voice. "Well, you see, Gordon, I am seeing someone actually," I said proudly. "Listen, I have to go."

I fumbled for my sleeve and he gently took my arm and placed it inside. "There you go!" He opened his leather wallet and dropped a fifty-euro note on the table, then stood up and began to walk away.

"Are you not waiting for your change?" I asked.

"No, I'm not. I used to be a lounge boy. I relied on tips." He held the door open for me.

"So, Mr Gordon," I really was a bit pissed now and the sunlight was hurting my eyes, "I'll be in touch when we have finalised all the details."

"Over dinner?" he asked.

I ignored this, wondering was I okay to drive after two bottles. I shouldn't really.

"I'll be away for a while so I'll see you when I return. The deposit is secured with my solicitors at MGP on Leeson Street."

He leaned on his car door when we reached the house. We both stared up at it and then he said, "Are you going to tell Carla? Because I really have to speak to James? I can't have this."

"I don't know yet. I have to think about this. Give me a few days, can you?" I stepped back. "Can I call you about it?"

"Okay, Mia, no problem." He folded himself into his car.

I bent down and said, "I'll call you." Then I turned on my heel and walked towards my Ford Ka.

Man oh man, what a man that was! What a dreamboat! I had never used that phrase before in my life but it was appropriate now. What an unbelievable turn of events about James! And I knew it was true, I just knew. What should I do? He beeped at me as I checked all my mirrors several times due to the two bottles of Heineken, and I beeped back as he drove away.

When I was safely parked at the office, I got my phone out to check the time. Three missed calls. Paul. I dialled my voicemail as quickly as was humanly possible. No messages. Shit. How did I miss all three calls? I leaned my head against the window and closed my eyes. I reeked of drink and had no chewing gum. I couldn't call him yet – there was too much stuff spinning around in my mind. I dropped my head on the steering wheel now. I had to work out what was going on with James. Was he taking Carla for a complete ride? What a guy Gordon was! But he was married so a bit of a player, no doubt. What had Paul wanted today?

As I was getting out of the car I dialled his number.

"Hello, Mia?" he answered after the first ring.

"Paul, hi, sorry I missed you. I was with a client. I hope everything's okay?"

"Yeah, it is, I suppose it's okay, as okay as it's going to be. Sorry I had to rush off like that, I really am." He did sound sorry.

"Don't worry," I said. Why couldn't I ask what the emergency was? I didn't want to scare him away, I supposed.

"So Carla was on to me – I'm back into the house tomorrow."

"Okay, great," I said. "Be good to get some actual doors on at last." I slammed the door of my car with my foot as I was carrying my files.

"What do you mean?" His voice had changed again.

"I mean, doors, you know, it's kinda breezy without them." I squeezed my eyes tight.

"Well, it's not my problem your friend went to get her boobs done and threw me out mid-job, is it?"

"Hey, that's supposed to be private!" I snapped at him.

"Why did you tell me then?" He rang off.

For fuck's sake! What was this? What was going on here? Was this guy for real? I slammed the numbers of his phone into mine again and it went straight to answerphone. I did this three times. Then I hung up.

I returned late to the office at the exact same time as Dominic. He had been out all morning getting his car serviced and, as soon as he saw me, he broke into song. "*Money, money, money, always funny, i-in Dominic's world!*" He took me by the hands and spun me around the path, nearly knocking a woman over in the process. She muttered "arsehole" under her breath and I totally agreed with her. I untangled myself and opened the main door. Dominic put his two hands on my shoulders in the doorway, bad breath stronger than ever and sweat patches under his arms.

"That's my girl, Mia! I got your text earlier and Gordon McHale was just on the phone, my mobile phone – he loved you – you sold it to him!"

"Great." I managed to drop my shoulders and his hands fell away. "That's fantastic, Dominic, I'm delighted!"

"And hang on . . ." He made sniffy noises in the air then came right down to my face and almost met my lips. "Is that a little drinky winky breathy I smelly? Getting him drunk, were you? Wanted to have your wicked way with the millionaire?"

"No, I had a beer with him to sign the deal, that's all."

I rolled my head around my neck, and let out a long slow breath. We made our way into the office with him whistling a happy tune, and he disappeared into his own office. I removed my coat. Anita was bent over her computer and didn't look up.

"How did you get on with Mrs Kilroy, Anita?" I unpacked my folders onto the desk while pressing 'get mail'.

"No joy. Deal's off," she snapped back.

"What?" I stood up. "No way! That's a done deal. She's absolutely mad after the place."

"I told her she was wasting our time if she doesn't meet the seller's price."

What! I took a deep breath. "I know, Anita, but there's room there, loads of room, for them to come down. Did you even ask?" My palms were beginning to sweat.

"No need because I have another couple about to go in at the asking price, I think. I showed it to them today too." She smiled, she actually smiled, and even though it was at the worst possible time a part of me noticed how her face lit up and her eyes actually twinkled.

"No." I had to make a stand.

Mrs Kilroy was a fantastic old woman. She had grown up in Inchicore on that road and had to emigrate to London when she was a teenager. Now she wanted to come back. Her children and grandchildren were back here now and this was her dream house. She had known the family who lived there before she left and the last man standing had passed away a few months ago. He had one son that he left it to and it was to be sold. I had been onto his son's solicitors and we were working something out. I had to get this house for her. It was more than a sale, it was someone's life's dream. Her son-in-law, Mick, a chef, had told me in strictest confidence that he would match the seller's price if we couldn't get the price down. I was starting to feel really angry now. It would be my fault if they lost this house, with me wasting time playing the diminishing market.

"Did you sign anything, Anita?" I almost shouted at her.

She was taken aback and pushed back her chair. "I really don't like your tone of voice, Mia."

"I really don't care because I am angry, Anita. This was my gig. I have been on this for ages and you knew that."

"You can't get personal in this job, Mia – it's about making the sale, closing the deal, not about what person wants the house more. I'm surprised you don't know more about business!" she spat back at me.

"Listen, Anita," I closed in on her now, "an auctioneer's basic goal is simple. They must make as much money as possible for the client who hired them. To accomplish this, it is important for an auctioneer to have a good feel for the value of the item or items, still with me?" I was almost hissing at her. "More importantly, Anita, the auctioneer must know the market that will be most likely to buy the items and how to advertise most effectively to entice them to the sale. The auctioneer must also have a thorough understanding of any laws that govern the sale of a particular item. I can reel off speeches too,

Anita. I know what my job description is alright. But we work both ways in this office, because that's how Dominic operates Clovers. It's not all by the book. It's not the same as an ordinary auctioneer's. One day you could be meeting students at the bottom of Dorset Street and showing them threadbare flats, another selling Shrewsbury Road. I'm sorry your son had a terrible accident, I really am, but you know what? I don't think I can work with you!" My head was spinning again. Had she sold this house from under my nose in an afternoon?

"Now, now, ladies," Dominic was walking out of his office, reading that morning's reports, "come on now, we are all a team here!" He drummed his fingers on our desk and dropped the report on it. He would have seen Anita's comments about her morning's work.

"*She's* not a team player!" I hissed.

"No, because I have a life with real commitments, real problems and real everyday shit – *you don't*!" she hissed back.

"Listen, you don't know anything about me," I said. "Nothing!" I tried to calm down.

"I know you are lazy –" She stopped, knowing she'd said too much.

"Oh really, I'm lazy, am I? How?" I knew she was sort of right but she didn't have the right or the knowledge to say that about me. How very dare she!

"Okay, enough!" Dominic clapped his hands hard as Debbie emerged from his office, no doubt to see what the carry-on was about.

"I am busy in here," the mild-mannered woman said, trying to put a stop to us.

"And so am I." Dominic was looking concerned now. "I don't want to hear another word, girls, please. Sort it out. This really isn't on." He looked from me to Anita and then went back in to join Debbie in his office.

I took a deep breath as my phone rang. It was Paul, of course. I grabbed it and my coat and went outside.

"Yes, Paul?" I leaned against the cold stone wall. I wished I was a smoker again as I did most days when stress was involved in my life.

"Sorry, Mia, I'm a bit on edge right now," he apologised.

"Yes, okay, so am I." I couldn't believe what had just gone down in there.

"Do you want to meet tonight?" he asked.

"Okay."

"Is everything okay with you?"

"Yeah, fine, just work shit, that's all. See you later. Maybe we could meet up in the Palace straight after work? Because, Paul, I really need a drink."

We made our arrangements and I headed back in.

"Listen, Mia, I didn't mean what I said about you being lazy. I had no right. It was all that came to my mind. Believe it or not, I'm not very good at arguments." She had a wry smile on her face.

"Anita," I got down on my hunkers beside her "I was really hurt by your words, seriously – and in front of my boss – I thought that was pretty low. But I know you're in a hard place in your life. The Mrs Kilroy deal is a big thing for me and, yes, I am an emotional person and I really want to help her get this house – but that doesn't mean I'm not good at my job."

I went back to my seat.

The rest of the afternoon was awkward and dragged by, as we sat in silence but needing to communicate. Dominic emerged from his office with a stack of files under his arm and planted himself at Carla's desk, no doubt so that he could keep a close eye on the pair of us. I sent a few emails to Carla about some viewings toward the end of the week. I would have to call Mrs Kilroy's son-in-law Mick as soon as I left the office, to see if I could salvage anything. No point in calling him now with Dominic all over me. I hated when he listened into my phone conversations in heated moments. He wasn't saying anything about Anita's news on Mrs Kilroy as I think he thought I could fix it. He knew how well I'd been getting on with Mick. Sometimes, just sometimes, he knew when to shut up and bide his time. This industry was all about second chances, sleeping on decisions, deciding on one thing and then immediately changing your mind. He was giving me space and time to fix it.

Debbie came out and handed Dominic a piece of paper.

"Okay, great, Debs." He stood up and addressed myself and Anita. "Right, it's all arranged."

We stared at him and waited to be enlightened.

"A team-building trip to County Clare – Lahinch to be precise. Exact times TBC but it will be at the weekend. So, it will be you two, Carla and myself – Debbie's not coming. It will be great for all of us. Team spirit. Team-building. One for all and all for one. I will not take no for an answer."

"I will need to organise something, Dominic," Anita mumbled under her breath, frantically flipping through her diary and colouring in the entire weekend in bright luminous yellow pen.

I glanced at the clock. "Home time!" I bolted for the toilet.

Team-building! Christ, how was I going to get through this? I reapplied some MAC foundation and pencilled in my eyes. I sprayed some Dove deodorant and flung a brush through my hair. At least I would have Carla there for moral support, I supposed. I headed out of the office for the loving arms of the Palace and the largest G&T I could get my hands on.

"So basically this woman is just a freak." I sat back after briefly explaining the day's antics and took a long grateful drink from my good friend Mr G&T. I had left out the part about having daytime beers with my George Clooney look-alike.

"Shit, she sounds like a nightmare!" Paul was a bit distracted and quiet in himself. With a little overnight stubble, in jeans and shirt. He drank his pint of Heineken.

"Oh she is, she is!" I was just about to go into the whole finger accident when Tim came over. "How's Carla?" he asked.

"Hey, there. She's okay, thanks."

Tim collected the empty glasses from the tables, expertly carrying about six pint glasses at once, his hand like an electronic claw scooping them all up in one go. "Would you ask her to give me a buzz whenever she can?" he said.

"Sure I will," I said.

"Thanks." Tim grinned and went back to the bar.

I turned back to Paul.

"Okay, I have to head off," he said.

I laughed.

"No, really," he said as he drained the remainder of his pint in one go. He stood up.

"What?" I was bewildered. "Where to?"

"Home. See you in the morning."

"Is this because Tim just came over to me?" I couldn't believe him.

He glared at me. "Ah, don't flatter yourself, Mia," he said coldly and left with a chilly breeze in his wake.

I sat for another while after he closed the door behind him but couldn't understand him or us. What was it we had going on? I honestly hadn't a clue.

"Another G&T!" I called up to Tim who was fiddling with the Sky controls to get some football match on for two older men sitting at the bar. I had so much on my mind. I had to tell Carla what was going on with James, I had to. But she was so vulnerable right now. Maybe I needed to tell James I knew and let him come clean himself. Why me? Why did I have to know all this? I also had to get that house for Mrs Kilroy. I drained my glass and sucked on the ice cube, lost in thought.

"Hi there!" Carla was cooking pasta and draining it as I came in.

"Hey, how are you feeling? Are you alone?" I fixed the plastic back down.

"No, James is here, do you want to eat with us?" she was still wincing slightly as she held the colander and I took it from her.

We stood back as the steam engulfed us both for a second, then I evenly distributed the whole-wheat pasta onto the plates. I was a stickler for this – exact amount on each plate – as my mother used to definitely give Samantha more spaghetti on her plate on the rare occasions she cooked "that Italian shite" as she so eloquently put it.

"I'll be really glad to get back to work tomorrow." Carla smiled at me.

She had taken the news that I had closed the deal with Gordon McHale exceptionally well when I'd called her earlier. Typical. Carla gets on with things, she's just not a moaner (I was a bit, I suppose, but I was working on it). She doesn't dwell. She always looked forward never back. I think she felt truly guilty for having all this time off for a self-inflicted illness. She wasn't one to take a sickie.

"Yeah, and you know, Carla, I'll split that Shrewsbury Road commission with you. My share, not Anita's obviously."

"You absolutely will not!" She pulled at her ponytail to tighten it. "It's my own fault I lost that deal. All's fair in love and war, Mia!" she laughed.

"It will be so great to have you back in work. I hate it there without you now. Seriously, one minute I really like Anita and feel really sorry for her, the next minute I want to choke her. It's just not like me."

"You have a lot going on at the minute – you're living in a building site, you're still tied to your mother's apron strings and you're seeing someone I think you really like but who you'd like to see more of? Am I right?" She quickly finished mixing her large bowl of tuna with a walnut and ricotta pesto sauce and piled it on top of the pasta.

I picked up the pesto jar and studied it. Where would someone even buy this? It smelled nice but didn't look so appetising.

"And speaking of Bob the Builder, Paul will be back in the morning." She winked at me.

"Carla!" James yelled.

"He says I won't make a good wife," she whispered to me. "It's ready, love!" she yelled back at him. I lifted the two plates onto our Paul Costelloe personally signed tray (I had it signed by him in Cornelscourt last year as a present to us. We loved it. He was a true gentleman, Paul Costelloe).

"What's keeping you – gossiping in there?" called James from the front room. "Seriously, doll, I am totally starving, I can't wait another single minute!"

"Oops!" she laughed but it wasn't her real laugh, it was an embarrassed laugh.

"Carla," I put my hand on her arm, "I have something I need to tell you but I don't quite know how to say this." I dropped my eyes to the floor.

She inhaled deeply. "Then don't." She flicked her ponytail and slowly carried the tray inside.

I would have carried it but I got the feeling she wanted away from me as quickly as possible. So what was I to do? I popped two slices of Carla's brown 'linseed-poppy-and-God-knows-what-else' bread in the toaster. Did she already know?

Was it really any of my business? Was it even that big a deal? Well, of course it was – he was deceiving her, she didn't know who he really was. I plopped a trusty Lyons Gold teabag into my mug. But I knew Gordon would tell her if I didn't. He had to. I stood there listening to the silence coming from the other room, the smell of toasting bread wafting around me. I hadn't heard him thank her, or *oohh* and *aahh* and tell her it was a delicious meal. I really felt sorry for Carla and I hated it.

My mobile rang and I reached into my pocket for the vibrating phone.

"Hi, Mia, it's Mick Kilroy here – what's goin' on with me ma's house? I thought we had an understanding?" He sounded angry.

"Oh hey, Mick, we did, we do. Let me make a few calls and I will get straight back to you. I'm sorry – it was something that happened when I was out of the office, you see. I'll sort it."

"Mia, she's eighty – it will break her heart if we lose this gaff."

"I hear you, Mick."

I had to ring Anita. My toast popped up. I still didn't know exactly what had happened today with the Inchicore property and I had to find out. I felt it was better to let the afternoon pass and not get into another argument with Anita. However, I couldn't leave it any longer. I searched for her number in my phone and hit call.

"Hello," she answered meekly.

"Hi, Anita, it's me, Mia – from the office – Mia Doyle." As if she didn't know – I'm sure she hated the very sound of my name. "I was wondering if we could talk?" I could hear voices in the background.

"Well, no, not really. I'm at the hospital – it's not very convenient for me."

"Okay, sorry, but I really need to find out about Mrs Kilroy and what way you left things with the Inchicore property? What was said to the other viewers?"

"Can you hang on another few minutes?" she asked someone. "I really need to take this outside."

I heard a mumbled conversation in the distance and then footsteps as she made her way outside. "Sorry, I have to be quick. Stevie's dad has just got here and I don't want to leave him alone."

I felt awful. "Of course, if there's anything I can do?"

"Well, I have no VHI, it had just expired, the story of my life."

I really wanted to tell her to go back in to her poor son but Mrs Kilroy was waiting and I couldn't let her down either. "What I didn't explain to you, Anita, was that I had a deal with Mick, Mrs Kilroy's son. I was able to offer the full amount if it came to the crunch. I was biding my time. I was playing the market at its own game."

"Oh. Well, I have it sort of sold to that gay couple we met last week, Mr O'Driscoll and his partner. I thought it would be perfect for them so I called them and they came right over."

I felt angry again. Why had she messed this up all so badly? "For crying out loud! They could have bought anywhere, Anita – we had them on our books to show them any property we thought suitable for them over the next few weeks!"

"Well, they loved it immediately when they saw the view there was of the newly opened Grattan Crescent Park. They both got very excited. They were nodding at each other eagerly, so it's sold in principle only, I would say. They really loved that view of the park. I mean it's not a done deal or anything, just a handshake and a 'let's talk next week'. But I feel it's a deal I can do unless you are set on asking them to back out. They know an engineer they wanted to take a look at it before they called their solicitor."

I flicked down the button on the kettle again to reboil (Carla hated the way I always did this – I'd burn out the element, she kept telling me, but I never did).

"Listen, Mia, I need the mon–"

I stopped her. "I know, I know, Anita, you need the money."

"Now if you don't mind, my husband has to leave soon so I'm quite busy here." She hung up.

"Shit." I threw the phone onto the counter and it bounced into the sink and bashed off the dirty dishes.

"You okay in there?" Carla shouted in.

"Yeah, sorry, dropped my phone."

I spread some strawberry jam on my now cool toast. I'd have to go to Mr O'Driscoll 's apartment now and try and sort this out. I checked my emails on my iPhone as I munched and found his details. It wasn't too far thankfully, just off Ballsbridge. I drank my tea quickly, washing down the rest of my sweet toast, grabbed my coat and headed out the plastic door. As I drove the short distance, I thought about what Carla had said. I agreed with it all but my mother's apron strings was a bit much. I mean, I didn't live at home, I barely went around to visit. I liked to be as far away from my little family as possible. Why had she said that?

9

There were big black security gates on the apartment block (funny, I thought, the place presented such a safe façade and yet this couple were terrified inside) but I was lucky someone was coming out as I got there so I slipped in. I rapped three times on the door.

"Go away, leave us alone!" came the frightened call.

"Mr O'Driscoll! It's me, Mia Doyle from Clovers Auctioneers – we met last week in Ringsend!"

Then I heard various chains and locks being undone and the door slowly opened. There, peeking his head first and then the rest of him complete in his white robe and pink fluffy slippers stood Peadar O'Driscoll, glass in hand. He pulled the door fully back now.

"Come in, darling!"

So I stepped in.

The apartment was beautiful. So wonderfully furnished, cosy yet modern and personal. I loved it. It was obviously a much-loved home.

"Oh, this place is fantastic!" I ran my hand over the glossy red kitchen counter, caught sight of my unkempt nails and pulled them away again.

"We love it," Peadar said.

It wasn't big but they had made the most of the space. Dark grey tiles ran the length of the kitchen-cum-dining area, thick white curtains covered the open door onto the small balcony. The wallpaper was almost fully covered as there were literally hundreds of pictures on the walls, even in the kitchen and, as I later discovered, in the bathroom. All seemed like holiday snaps of the two men. Obviously very much in love. Sun, skiing, horse-riding, even sleeping – it was all there captured on film.

"Damien is still out at work. What can I do for you? But let me get you a drink and something to nibble on."

"Oh no, I'm fine!" I protested.

"I insist," he said. "Curl up there with a glass of wine while I baste the chicken." He pulled the heavy curtains closed and pointed to the couch.

So I sat. I kicked off my shoes and curled up on their marvellous, soft, worn, leather couch and he gave me a huge glass of red wine. He plonked a bowl full of pretzels and nachos on a small glass table beside the couch. As I sipped the wine – it was perfect – lovely warm temperature and rich velvet taste – he returned to the kitchen then came back with a cheese dip.

"So, Mia, what do you want to talk to us about?" he called from the kitchen.

The smells were incredible.

"It's a bit complicated, I'm afraid." I sat up and waited for him to come back into the room.

He peeped his head around the sliding door, wiping his hands on his pinstriped blue-and-white apron and looking at me enquiringly.

When he saw me looking so solemn he came back in, carrying a glass of wine, and took a seat.

"You see, Peadar, I had more or less promised that house in Inchicore to an older lady. She's in her eighties and relocating back home after a lifetime in London. All her family are here, in that area. It was my deal and Anita more or less went behind my back and took over and offered to show you guys the house when she really shouldn't have."

"Oh really?" He sipped his wine.

"Yes, and I'm terribly guilt-ridden that I didn't go with Anita. I didn't know she had called you guys so I thought it was in the bag, so to speak, for Mrs Kilroy."

"Damien loved it. He works in town so the location was great for him. It's him that really matters, you see." Peadar looked down and then back up at a picture of himself and Damien framed in a bright-orange rubber frame. It appeared they were celebrating something in the photo, glasses raised in a toast, both dressed in smart suits with matching ties. "I don't work any more, you see, so where we live locationwise doesn't matter to me. To be honest, the only place I want to live is right here in our home but I can't – it's too stressful for us." He swirled the red liquid around his enormous wineglass.

It was so unfair. Who were these absolute bullies who were literally pushing this lovely couple out of their own home? Peadar made his way over to me now and filled up my glass again.

"Is there no way you can deal with this bullying?" I asked.

"Ah, we've exhausted every option, Mia. We've been to the Guards several times – apparently they got a warning but that's it. We just don't have the . . ." he paused, "well, the time really for a long court battle so we can't afford to get our lawyers involved and, to be honest, we're too scared to threaten them."

The door banged and a voice called out. "Peadar, I'm home! Oh, what smells divine?"

Damien looked startled when he saw me sitting there.

"Oh, hello again," he smiled and extended his left hand.

Peadar filled him in as he took his dark overcoat and brown leather briefcase from him and brought him a glass of apple juice.

"Doesn't drink," he told me by way of explaining the apple juice and threw his eyes to the heavens in mock horror as he went back into the kitchen.

Damien seemed so strait-laced in his black striped suit. There wasn't a camp bone in his whole body and I marvelled at the wisdom of the saying '*Never judge a book by its cover*'. I needed to remember it more often.

"Oh dear," Damien said, sitting down, "that's awful. Obviously I would never stand in the way of someone if it meant that much to them. Please go ahead, Mia, and consider our interest off the table."

I let out a long sigh of relief and reached into my bag on the tiled floor for my phone. I seriously needed to clean this bag out, I thought as I fished through pieces of paper, unpaid bills, make-up and loose change.

"Dinner!" called Peadar.

"Oh, I'll leave you guys to it." I closed my bag again.

"Indeed you will not!" said Peadar. "It's all served."

"Come along," said Damien.

I obediently followed him into the kitchen. I was so relieved they had been so accommodating. I sat and excused myself while I belted out a text to Mick Kilroy who responded immediately with a happy face.

The dinner was the most amazing spread. I learned that Damien worked in banking while Peadar was in charge of the household chores. He used to work full time for the ISPCA but finished last year. Two nicer people I could never hope to meet. They were fantastic, easy company. The roast chicken dinner was melt-in-the-mouth (is there anything better?): roast potatoes, stuffing with sage and parsley, carrots, green beans and the most divine home-made chicken-stock gravy. How strange that this was one of the most enjoyable meals I had ever had and I had only met this couple once before this. They were so happy and so in love. I wanted that for me, I thought as I helped myself to more delicious roasties. The tongs couldn't quite grasp the slippery spud and Peadar said, "Pick it up, I always do!" and with that he leaned over and picked out another roastie for himself although his plate was still more or less full. I did the same, cut the roastie open and dropped a large knob of butter on top.

The two men were trying to unblock the salt cellar with a toothpick and my mind wandered. Could Paul be the one for me? Could we be a Peadar and Damien? I thought not. I knew I was blind to him and what was going on with him and us. But what *was* going on, I asked myself as I swallowed the buttery potato. I was having a bit of a thing with the builder – that was about it, after all. In my silly (and obviously desperate, my inner voice added) mind I had made it out to be more. I wasn't sure what was going on any more. I wanted it to be more, I wanted him to like me, to follow through, probably more for my self-esteem that anything else. I wanted to be part of something, something like this.

I sipped some of the sparkling water I was now drinking because I was driving, in a very comfortable silence. Michael Bublé hummed softly at us in the background and the candles on the table seemed to sway to his voice.

"Peadar, this meal is seriously divine." I raised my glass to him and the three of us clinked.

"Chin-chin!" Peadar said in the old *Withnail and I* tribute toast.

"Oh, I love to cook, don't I, Damien?"

Damien held his hand. "I am spoiled. I get this every night, Mia, can you believe that?"

"If only I could get him to drink a glass of this wonderful wine with me!" Peadar laughed.

"Nope, I just don't like the taste of alcohol," Damien smiled back at him, "but I enjoy watching you enjoy it and how it makes you a bit sparkly!"

"Damien!" Peadar slapped his hand and they laughed.

"So, guys, again thanks you for your understanding. I am going to work my butt off to get you the house of your dreams, so tell me everything – locations, type of property, what you are really looking for." I sat back, stuffed and content.

They looked at each other and I felt a sense of sadness descend over the table and about both their eyes.

"Well, Mia dear, you are a total pet. We are going to the Canaries for a sun break before Christmas and will need that property as soon as we get back really. Ideally a two-bedroom near to Damien's office on Westland Row."

"No!" Damien raised his hand. "No, this property should be near a park, like we discussed, and we should be able to see the park from the bedroom window. That's what I – what *we* really want!" Again I felt a strange tension as the two men looked at one another.

Suddenly I felt it was time to leave.

"Okay, I'm on it! I'll start my search next week." I stood up and lifted my plate.

"Sit down!" boomed Peadar. "Where do you think you are going, my girl? I have chocolate puddings in the oven and fresh home-made vanilla ice cream!"

"Is he joking?" I asked a now-smiling Damien and the tension was lifted.

"I'm afraid not!" he laughed and patted his slightly rounded tummy. "I honestly don't know how I'm not twenty stone!"

There wasn't a pick on Peadar, I noted.

"Please take your drinks in to the couch. I will clear. Mia, coffee or tea with your dessert?"

"Oh, tea would be great, please, Peadar. Are you sure I can't help?"

He flicked me away as though I was an annoying fly.

I sat with Damien on the couch and he flicked on the television. He went straight to Sky Sports. "Seriously?" I had to ask.

"Oh, yeah, I'm a massive sports buff, well, a massive Man United fan."

"Obsessed!" came the singing voice from the kitchen.

"Does that shock you a bit?" he asked as he removed his shoes and wiggled his stocking feet.

"Honestly, Damien, it does a little – I mean you're so . . ." I'd started this now so I had to finish.

"So?" He was laughing.

"Hetero!" I laughed.

Peals of laughter from the kitchen. "He is, isn't he, Mia?" Peadar was in stitches. "I say that to him all the time but he just doesn't see it!"

"Despite the fact that I don't wear fluffy dressing-gowns and Fusion pink furry slippers," (see, I'd never have known they were Fusion), "or carry a small dog in my briefcase, speak with jazz hands or cry when every episode of *Glee* finishes, I assure you both I am one hundred per cent gay and proud of it – proud of me and my life as a gay man!"

"Hurray!" Peadar danced around the living room while licking the back of a large spoon.

The sight was so comical, I laughed hard.

"So where did you guys meet?" I was intrigued by them now.

"Well . . ." Peadar went to sit but Damien caught him just as his bum hit the seat and hooched him back up again.

"Desserts? You always do this when we have guests, then complain to me for the rest of the night that I made you sit and chat and I ruined all your hard work of making the desserts."

"Oh, quite right!" Peadar pecked the other man on the cheek, left the room and returned with (and I'm not joking here) a dessert trolley, just like they had in *Hello, Dolly*, a silver masterpiece of one, stocked now with three incredible-looking warm chocolate puddings and home-made ice cream, a pot of tea, a pot of coffee, cups and sugar bowl complete with miniature spoon.

We each took a dessert on our lap and with the first bite I thought I had died and gone to heaven. It was melt-in-the-mouth. Cut into the pudding and the hot chocolate sauce ran all over the ice cream. "Oh, Peadar!" Damien was now licking the back of his spoon. "This is incredible! Thank you, darling!"

"So . . ." Peadar continued, "we were both in An Óige – do you remember that organisation, a type of walking thing? I liked walking – to be honest. I had heard it was a great way to meet people. On my first walk I saw Damien. I nearly fainted. People don't believe this story, do they, Dames, but honestly I had palpitations and couldn't speak. It had never happened to me before in my life, and I had seen a lot of men." He winked now and licked his spoon seductively as I laughed and Damien cut in.

"I asked him was it his first day as he looked nervous – he ignored me."

"Because I physically couldn't speak." Peadar was now pulling at my arm as I tried desperately to get another chocolatey mouthful in before he tugged again.

"I thought he was rude so I walked off," Damien offered, delight on his face at the retelling of this story.

"So, after the walk, there was tea and digestive biscuits at the clubhouse," said Peadar. "I walked straight over to

Damien who was mid-dunk, introduced myself, pulled him into a quiet corner of the hall and told him that I thought he was the most exquisite man I had ever seen in my life and could I possibly make dinner for him that night?"

Damien playfully put his hand over Peadar's mouth. "He didn't even know I was gay! What a risk!" Peadar pulled his hand away. "And, Mia, that was it, he never went home that night after dinner or again for the next ten years!"

Suddenly Peadar's hand flew to his mouth and his breath came fast and furious until he literally burst into gulps of tears. They were hard tears, the hardest tears I had ever seen in my life. Damien dropped his plate on the tiled floor and it smashed into pieces. He rocked Peadar in his arms, both now crying. I didn't know what to do. I stood up and sat down again.

"Sorry, Mia." Peadar shook his head and wiped his nose with the back of his hand. "How awful of us!"

"No, please, I should go anyway. I'll see myself out." I felt I had to leave them alone. I shouldn't be there for a second longer. "Okay, I'll be in touch really soon. Thanks again," I said feebly as I grabbed my coat.

Damien kissed and kissed the top of Peadar's head.

"Thank you, Mia," Peadar whispered to me as I left, closing the door softly behind me.

What had all that been about? Was the bullying so bad that it had them in that state? What was going on there? I vowed to start searching on my laptop for properties for them to see as soon as I got home.

I was literally bursting out of my shirt, I saw, as I stood in front of the mirror to undress. I had to go on a diet and start taking some exercise. Tomorrow was Thursday, not a good day to start a diet, everyone knew it had to be a Monday. That was some kind of diet rule. So next Monday it was. I hadn't had any news of Paul all evening but he would be here in the morning.

Carla and James were tucked up in bed. I slipped on my nightdress and leggings and climbed into my cosy bed. Would he ask me out for a drink? If not, I would ask him, I had to. I had this unfinished feeling about me. I needed to place us properly in my head. How would I feel if it was just a breezy sex thing? Hurt. I plumped up my pillow. I turned to my bedside locker, grabbed my pen and pad and wrote a few notes to myself: *Paul. Mrs Kilroy contracts. Property for Peadar and Damien (near park) asap. Speak to Carla about James. Sit down with Anita for a chat. Try and get out of Christmas at Mam's. Ring Gordon McHale. Go on a diet!!!!!*

I drifted into a fitful sleep of houses and food and huge fake breasts.

I never thought I could be so aroused by the sound of banging. When Paul first started and I hadn't noticed him the sound used to drive me totally bonkers.

I jumped up and washed my hair with the shower hose over the bath.

As I was drying it Carla shouted into my room, "You who hated wet hair first thing in the morning, hey?" She was laughing in the doorway, dressed superbly in skintight black leggings, black high heels and long taupe shirt-dress. The shirt was loose so the new boobies weren't noticeable. Clever Carla, attention subtly drawn immediately to those fabulous toned legs and barely-there thighs. "See you downstairs!" She lifted one leg behind her as she vanished from the doorway.

I put on my new black laced top with jacket to match and tightish black trousers and teamed it with red heels. Not something I would normally wear to the office but, hey, a girl's gotta do what a girl's gotta do. I did my face and headed down.

Carla was at the new white kitchen table that Paul had put together from Stock off Grafton Street. It was pushed back against the wall to make room for his workbench. She was eating a bowl of muesli and drinking freshly squeezed orange juice. I grabbed for the coffee jar.

"Morning, Mia," Paul addressed me.

I looked at him. Stubble again, black working gear, obviously no immediate effort there to impress me at eight o'clock in the morning, I observed.

"Morning, how are you today?"

I saw him glance down and stare at the red heels: result.

"Yeah, mad busy, you know the way."

"I'm just going to finish this inside while I make some calls," my wonderfully subtle friend said, making her way out of the kitchen.

I leaned against the new table in what I hoped was a very seductive pose.

"Paul," I started as he came closer.

"Mia, I suppose we really need to talk." He rubbed his left hand around his chin stubble.

"Tonight, please?"

"Sure, after work, the Palace?"

I put my hand on his arm but it didn't feel natural so I pretended I saw a piece of something on his sleeve and flicked the imaginary imposter away.

"No, somewhere else, say my place in Rathmines. Do you remember where it was?"

I shook my head and then dropped it in shame. Filthy girl.

He went to his builder's supplies and scribbled the address down with a pencil on the back of an empty nail box. "See you after work so." He turned and began removing the makeshift plastic to finally erect our door.

As I watched him tangled up in plastic, I sipped my coffee. He was seriously attractive, but what else was there about him? I wasn't sure I could actually say. Was he a great guy? Killer personality? Honestly I couldn't say because I didn't know him. I drained my cup, rinsed it and left the kitchen.

"I'm going, Carla, do you want a lift?"

"Actually, yeah, it still hurts to walk a lot with the babies bouncing."

She cleared up her breakfast dishes and we left for work.

"So, to sum up, basically it's time for the team-building holiday and not the end of the week as I originally told ye. Get home, get packed and let's be off by two o'clock at the latest!" Dominic rubbed his hands and made an imaginary golf swing.

I dropped my head into my hands. This was all I needed. Paul was expecting me tonight and now I wouldn't get to see him. It was already eleven o'clock and I had a pile of work in front of me to catch up on. It was ridiculous.

"Oh Dominic!" Carla stood up slowly. "Is this really necessary?" She chewed the top of her pen.

"Absolutely-wootley, Carla Waro!" He grinned at her. "There will be two cars out front of my lovely wife's house at two sharp – mine and Mia's – if that's okay with you, Mia?" (Like I had a choice?) "As of now you are free to go and get ready. Get packed, ladies!"

I opened my to-do list in Outlook Express and immediately tapped Gordon McHale's number into the phone. He answered at the first ring.

"Gordon? Hi. Look, I'm really sorry but I'll have to cancel our two o'clock meeting tomorrow in the Shelbourne."

He remained silent.

"It's just that we have a surprise team-building trip to County Clare – we're leaving for it this afternoon – I can't get out of it so I have to go, really."

Carla winced at me.

"Gordon?" I thought he'd hung up.

"Yeah, well, Mia, I am a busy man too, you know, so do you want this deal closed or what?"

I couldn't believe my own boss was putting me in this ridiculously unprofessional situation. I tugged at the waist of my now way-too-tight trousers – I was uncomfortable so I opened the top button. Oh, I had known they were too tight that morning but would I listen to my bulging flesh? No, I would not. I'd had the drive and the will to suck it in hard earlier but it was gone now and so it all came spilling over the edge.

"I am so sorry, Gordon, but it's out of my hands."

"Well, can Carla do it?" He was obviously distracted as I heard him type away at a keyboard.

"No, she's coming too, I'm afraid."

"Okay, well, there's not much I can do about it then, is there? I'll be abroad now for a while after today . . . but, Mia, before you go . . . I was hoping to talk to you about the possibility of you coming to work for me full-time? I want you to take on some business for me and, if you have time now, can we discuss?"

I couldn't believe my ears. I heard him tap-tap away furiously. What a mulititasker! I couldn't type and talk, just didn't have it in me. I cleaned the dust off my desk-phone nervously. "Sure, fire away." I sat back, wildly curious, hugely flattered, and with my belly relieved to be free I heard him out.

"Well, Mia, I have a few properties I let out all over Dublin, quite a few to be honest with you. I am looking for someone to manage then. As I mentioned, your friend is sitting in one for me at the minute but he's on my Get Out list. Like I said, he's a dodgy little yoke if you ask me."

I laughed a nervous laugh and squeezed the receiver nearer my ear in case Carla could hear our conversation.

"Okay, sorry, I forgot Carla's in the office," he said. "So, anyway, I'm looking for a property manager, someone I can trust, who knows this business inside and out – and after sleeping on this one for ages I've decided that I want you to do it."

I opened my mouth to speak and closed it again.

"Okay again, you can't talk. However, I need an answer when I return from China. I've been doing this job myself but just can't time-manage it any more. I could get an agency but I want a more personal touch and I like your way of working. You are honest, professional and yet wonderfully human. Property is about people's lives, whether renting or buying, and I want the best clients for all my places. I have some undesirable tenants in places now that I want out but need the places rented before I do this. It's business at the end of the day but we are in a recession and, as most of my business is in property, I need to be clever or I could end up in a hole." *Tap, tap, tap.*

I heard the sound of a mobile phone ringing in the background.

"Okay, so enjoy your team-building and see you in a few weeks. Shrewsbury is in the very capable hands of my solicitors. I have signed along all the dotted lines so you will be hearing from them, probably by the end of the week, I'd imagine. See you, Mia. Hello, Gordon McHale here . . ." He hung up.

I was gobsmacked. This was a dream job he was offering me. He didn't talk money but I knew it wouldn't be an issue. It was so exciting. He was a hard worker and wanted the same from his employees.

I slid open the drawer and felt around for a square of something.

"Is he pissed off?" Carla asked, the new assets now clearly on display.

She had removed her loose shirt-dress to reveal a skintight taupe T-shirt tucked into the black leggings. I mean, who could do that? Who could tuck anything into leggings and get away with it? I was surprised she was showing the boobs off like this – it just wasn't her style.

"Hmmm . . ." My mouth was full. I gazed down at my own escaping flesh and quickly stuffed it back inside my trousers. "Em, yeah, he is a bit, I think." I swallowed, flicked off my computer and headed for the loo.

My hair was a mess, my skin pasty and flaky. "You are a knockout, Mia Doyle," I said sarcastically as I glared at my reflection in the mirror. I had lashed the moisturiser on all week but, whenever real winter hit, it played havoc with my bloody skin. I let my hair loose and ran a brush through it. I glanced at my watch. Paul could be back from the suppliers by now. I whipped out the Touché Éclat that every living woman raved about – anyway, nine out of ten or whatever it was couldn't be wrong – but as far as I was concerned it was too light and only served to highlight my eye-bags. I lashed the mascara on to give me some wide eyes and left the bathroom.

I headed out of the office. "See you at two!" I called back.

Carla called after me. "Hey, hang on, aren't you waiting for me?"

I had wanted some time with Paul back at the house on our own. Mean, I know. I could be very selfish, I realised. Ever since Gordon told me about James I couldn't really talk freely to her though. It was awkward. I was hiding something from her and I hated it.

"So!" She threw her black Prada Bag (yes, real), over her shoulder and we left the office. "This is a right royal pain in the arse, isn't it, Mia?"

"You're tellin' me!"

We reached my car and set off.

"Poor Anita, did you see the look of total panic on her face? I mean, she has two children to think of! Does Dominic not think of that?" She sighed. "I mean, James and I were going to be spending the next week at his in Killiney. He's decided to take a work holiday from his writing and wanted me to stay with him and just chill out. I adore that house but I never get to spend any time in it. He doesn't like spending too much time there as he says it's like his office so I suppose you can't blame him."

"Hmmmm," I managed as I twirled the volume button left and right.

"You know, Mia, he's so talented. He showed me some of his writing last week and it's great. I mean, it's profound and I really think he can make it as a writer."

"So what's it about, his stuff, his writing stuff?" I asked as we pulled up at a red light.

"It's all about politics and courtrooms – all very John Grisham." She rolled down the window and the breeze cut me in two. Carla liked fresh air.

Probably *is* John Grisham, I thought. He's probably just rewritten a few chapters from *The Firm* or something to show her.

"He's going to be so mad I can't stay there with him now." She rolled up the window again, obviously due to my OTT teeth-chattering beside her.

"How does he like the new – you know?" I nodded at the girls and her face lit up a bit.

This amazing, clever, beautiful, woman's face actually lit up at the mention of her idiot boyfriend's reaction to silicone squashed into her beautiful, once-perfect breasts.

"*Oooh la la*, Mia, he loves them!" She was slightly pink in the face.

I felt queasy. For some reason, as a member of the female sex, I felt both disgusted and slightly cheated that a man could get so excited by this silicone, that he would want his partner to go through this for his pleasure. "That's good," was what I said back to her though.

"Are you okay? You're acting a bit weird lately? Is it because you really really want to tell me that you think James is a total and utter prick for putting me through the breast op but I wouldn't let you, in the kitchen last week?" She glared at me now, her blue eyes turning icy.

"Yes, Carla, it is." I glared back at her, willing myself not to shout the truth in her face.

"Well, get over it, Mia, it's my life – and you know what? I am actually sorry I trusted you with this now! If I had known you were going to react like this, I never would. James says you're jealous and, you know what, I think he might be right!" We had just pulled up to the house and she jumped out and slammed the door of my car hard.

"Jeez, love, you pissed her right off, didn't ya? Time of the month or wha'?" a rather strange man pushing his bicycle offered to me.

I nodded my head at him.

I could hear the clang-clang of hammer on metal as I approached the new white wooden back door with square glass panels. He was here. I licked my lips and sucked in.

"Hey." He looked up and wiped his hands on his top.

"Hey," I answered back. He looked tired.

"What are you two doing back so early? Carla's in a bit of a mood, isn't she?"

I shrugged my shoulders. "Fancy a coffee?" I asked.

"Great, yeah, love one." He smiled at me.

I filled the kettle and flicked it on. Carla was stomping around upstairs collecting her designer gear and no doubt folding it ever so carefully into her case. I leaned my head against the newly finished top cupboards. It had been ages since she and I had talked properly and this is what happened when we did. I knew she was also mad at herself. Our friendship suddenly felt to me like it was a million miles away. She was becoming someone I couldn't work out any more, someone I never thought she was or was capable of being. She was becoming the type of girl we both used to have a laugh over and thank out lucky stars we weren't like. How could she not see what she was becoming? Could I ever get her back? Not while James was in her life, that was for sure. I poured the water onto the coffee and the aroma rose. He thought I was jealous of them! Ha, what a laugh! And, you know what, even if he did really own the big house on Killiney Hill and was a top author, I swear to God I still wouldn't have been jealous of him. I wouldn't touch him or his life with a barge-pole.

Paul's phone rang and he answered it with a cheery hello as I scraped the bottom of the sugar bowl for the last grains that were clinging on there. I was hoping we could reschedule tonight's romantic Rathmines meeting now.

"Well, I can't!" He was speaking lower into the phone now.

I listened more, with my back still turned on him, knowing I shouldn't.

"It's not possible for me to get away right now. Ah, alright, get off my back!"

"Here you go . . ." I trailed off as I saw he was hurriedly putting on his coat.

"I have to go right now, Mia." He grabbed his green army bag and stuffed some bits in.

"What?" I shook my head.

"'Have to go right now' – is that not self-explanatory enough for you?"

"Oh, whatever, Paul!" I slammed the coffee down on the

counter and it splattered everywhere just as Carla entered the work area.

"Everyone okay?" She looked from me to Paul. "So, Mr Hewson . . ." She stopped when she saw him packing up. "I'm sorry, but are you going somewhere again?" she asked in a highly irritated voice.

"Yeah, have to run, I'm afraid, Carla." He stared at her.

I could see her face and she was really angry. This wasn't a good time for either of them and I braced myself.

"Well, I won't be paying you for this whole day and I want you here as many hours as you can put in during the next four days."

She had opened her mouth to continue when he said, "I can't be here – at all – for the next four days." He stood up straight.

"What?" She was nearly shouting now.

"I can't do it. I can't be here. I have to be somewhere else. My hands are tied." He moved towards the new door and rubbed his hand up and down the edges.

"Seriously, Mr Hewson, you need to be here. It's getting colder and colder and you promised you would have this done!" She stared him out of it.

I was mortified at the severe tone of voice she was using to speak to him and even more so that I just couldn't stand up for him. It was business and it was none of my business. They looked at each other for what seemed like an age.

"I just said I can't do it, Carla. My hands are tied," he repeated.

"Is this some kind of pathetic lovers' tiff? Because this is what I warned you about, Mia, this is my home – it's not a –"

"Carla, it's got nothing to do with me whatsoever," I told her.

"Well, you're fired so, Mr Hewson," she said plainly and clearly.

The words hung heavy in the air.

"Carla, you can't fire him!" I couldn't believe my ears.

"No, you can't fire me without giving me what you owe me now!" His eyes were blazing.

"Carla –"

"Stay out of it, Mia, it's nothing to do with you! This is *my* home. *My* money."

I had never seen her so angry and I knew it was more to do with me than Paul. It was totally unfair of her.

The clock ticked loudly from its place on the kitchen floor.

"So you want me off the job, Carla?"

"Yes, please, now, and don't ever come into my house at four o'clock in the morning again or I will call the police."

He turned his head to me sharply.

"I didn't say anything!" This was a nightmare.

"No, you didn't, Mia, even though you know what a light sleeper I am. I was terrified. As James quite rightly says, how could you put me in this position and be so careless about me and my property? Letting anyone into your room at all hours!"

"Ha, how could I be so careless with your property? I didn't invite him back – he just came back – we'd had a row and he was drunk. And he's hardly just 'anyone' – I think that's so out of line! Jesus, Carla, I'm not twelve! And he's not going to rob you!" I was spitting now.

"How do I know that?" she raged.

"How dare you!" he yelled.

We all just stood very still now, breathing heavily. Then Paul threw his bag over his shoulder, slapped his keys onto the counter, turned on his heel and left.

"For fuck's sake, Carla, what's going on with you? Was there really any need for that?"

"Yes, Mia, there was. I'll see you at Dominic's house if

you're still coming – or are you going to run after Bob the Builder like a lovesick teenager?" She too turned on her heel.

I grabbed her jacket a bit too hard. "His name isn't Bob the Builder – don't be so rude, Carla!" Now I was really angry. I knew I could just spill the beans on James but I could see she was hurting and, as much as I hated her right this second, I couldn't do any more damage to her. "Carla, you know nothing about me and him. Nothing." I let her go and she went to get her unused Mini Cooper.

For some reason right then all I wanted to do was to head to Superquinn, buy a long, thick, crusty white bread roll, fill it with mayo, baked ham, cheese, coleslaw, a packet of cheese and onion on the side, make a massive cup of tea, sit on the couch and turn on Oprah or Ellen. I could do that. I sat on the couch now. I could just accept Gordon's job offer, move back in with my mother for a few months.

But I couldn't. I had to face the day or lose the best friend I had ever known. I could never do that. Paul would just have to wait.

10

We arrived after almost four bumpy hours to what looked like two deserted stonewashed houses in the back end of Lahinch, County Clare. The day was grey and forbidding as I eased my too-large body from Dominic's car. We had left my car behind since Carla decided to drive. He had rabbited on and on incessantly since we left the office – as Debbie hadn't come, I opted to travel with him instead of Carla or Anita who were now chatting in Carla's Mini Cooper and both actually laughing. I felt totally alone. A total outsider in my own life. For the first time since I had met Carla I felt like I had no real friends, I felt like no one understood me. It was a horrible lonely feeling. How had I got here in the space of a few short weeks? Was it all my fault I was standing here like a spare tit? Like the round peg in a square hole? I shivered as the sea breeze came behind the houses and nipped at my bare face.

"Which house?" I asked Dominic as I hauled my bag from the tiny boot.

"Well, I'm in Number 1 and you girlies are in Number 2, but I can still peep out the windows and keep an eye on you.

No broadband, no mobile coverage, total isolated bliss!" Dominic was taking long deep breaths in and out as though he were a top yoga instructor.

"No coverage!" I was aghast. I needed to speak to Paul, I needed to speak to Gordon's solicitors again before five o'clock, to Mrs Kilroy, to Mick Kilroy, to Peadar and Damien and even to my mother. I had people depending on me! God, why could Dominic not see what a shite businessman he was? He could be running his own business into the ground just by having us all here. People like him had it all too easy. Life was not a box of chocolates and it was about time someone told Dominic Gump that!

"I know what you're thinking, Mia!" He raised his hands and shrieked like a girl. "How will I survive in the wilderness, how will my clients not back out of the deals, how will I check my Facebook? Well, don't worry – Debbie, as we speak, is on to every client explaining our absence. It's late Thursday afternoon now and we'll be back in the office on Monday morning, all bright eyes and bushy tails!" Yes, he ran around with his left arm extended behind him, waving it as though it was a squirrel-tail. I gritted my teeth. The other two were now out and watching this scene in confusion.

We made our way to our houses and I have to say the sight that greeted me was not what I expected. We opened our door and were greeted by an open roaring turf fire and a newly erected Christmas tree (way too early in my humble opinion though the smell of pines and tinsel was beautiful to my nostrils). There was a timber floor, a large well-worn brown-leather couch with two armchairs, huge chunky cushions, a bookshelf packed with bestsellers and game boards, and the most unique display of candlesticks I had ever seen. Large candles, small candles, new candles, really old candles, smelly candles. The kitchen off the living room was small, with a slate-flagstone floor and natural stone walls, a cooker, microwave and small four-seater dining table. Upstairs there were three bedrooms and a huge bathroom with an old-fashioned bath that was so deep you could probably drown in it.

"Who wants what room?" Anita asked quietly, woolly hat pulled firmly down her face. Had Carla told her about our row, I wondered?

"One – two – three." Carla pointed to a room and then to each of us – she was never one to waste time on silly stuff like picking bedrooms.

I entered mine and gratefully closed the door behind me. I flopped on to the bed and kicked off my FitFlop boots. From the bed the window looked huge. It framed breathtaking scenery even on this greyest of days. The trees and mountains peered in at me. I have always been a bit in awe of nature. I never feel I give it the respect it deserves. That bothers me a little. I was never one of those walkers, with the weird-looking gear and carrying a branch. I'd quite like to be outdoorsy. But a beer garden on a hot summer's day is as outdoors as I get. My heart was racing and I realised I was nervous. It was the kind of feeling I had in school just before French where there were a couple of tough girls who gave me a hard time. I never skipped the class, wouldn't give them that satisfaction, but they did get to me. I remembered, as I tucked the soft pillow under my head, going to sit down and the redheaded one, Linda Hughes, pulling my chair from under me. The roars of laughter from them all. There was a lot of me to hit the floor, I supposed. Then there was the day they put Hubba Bubba Chocolate chewing gum in my hair and I didn't notice. Took me a week to get it out. Little things but bullies just the same. I never told my mother or Samantha, I don't know why really. I suppose I saw it as a sign of my own weakness and I didn't want them to think I was weak.

I jumped out of my skin as a knock came to my door.

"Eh, excuse me, Mia, but are you coming to dinner tonight?" Anita's voice asked quietly.

"Yeah, I'll be down in five."

I sat at the quaint old dressing-table with its small drawer and a bible. I checked my appearance in the mirror. For some reason since I had been seeing Paul I hadn't really been paying much attention to my appearance, as stupid as that sounded. Why was that? I noticed my eyebrows were way in need of a good plucking. My skin looked dull and needed a few nights of Carla's Elizabeth Arden eight-hour cream to sort it out. My hair needed a good trim – it was full of split ends. I tied it into a low ponytail and doused it in hairspray to keep the stray hairs in place. I put some red lipstick on for a change and some pink MAC blusher and grabbed my denim jacket off the bed.

"Hi." Carla looked up, half-smiling shyly at me as I reached the living room. She was curled up in front of the fire reading a dog-eared well-thumbed copy of *Gone With The Wind*. She was like a poster girl. All blonde and rosy-cheeked and beautiful.

"Hi." I smiled back at her.

Our eyes locked and we spoke to each other through them. My earlier anger towards her completely melted. Men were doing this to us. I wasn't having it.

"Are. We. Ready?" Dominic was rubbing his hands together as he stood at the front door.

All four of us made our way into the cold night and walked down into the town past a fabulous golf course and into the welcoming twinkling lights of Lahinch.

The town was really buzzing. There was muffled traditional music emanating from each door we passed and all I really wanted to do was to settle myself beside the fire in one of them and have a few pints of Guinness and a good ole sing-song. A ballad night.

Dominic had booked into a small Italian called Pepperso's and we took our seats. As we all looked at the menu, Anita asked which wine we were having. Oh great! I started to relax. There was going to be wine! We ordered a bottle of Faustino red and a bottle of white. As the waiter poured I almost grabbed the glass before he finished. I couldn't wait to feel the warm red liquid hit the back of my neck.

"So, my ladies," Dominic began.

Carla and I looked at each other with wry smiles. What was going to come out of his mouth?

"This isn't a joke, girls." For the first time in all my time knowing Dominic his blue eyes were deadly serious. He swirled his wine expertly around his glass. "I am honestly worried about the three of you. This is my business, my bread and butter, my family's bread and butter. These are exceptionally hard times. It's not a playground, or a ring for sparring matches. It's not a doss house. I have spent years, my lifetime, building up that client list that Clovers has. It's a unique company. Either you three all get on and can work together or I have to let the three of you go." He sipped his drink.

We were all dumbfounded. None of us spoke. I drained the glass and the waiter was on it like a shot. Great service. Silence engulfed the table.

"Okay, Dominic." Carla leaned towards him.

I noticed she was wearing gold eye shadow. If I attempted to wear gold eye shadow it would look demonic. Like the Tin Man in *The Wizard of Oz* rebelling against his tinned look or the dark-haired one from ABBA gone nuts. On Carla it was subtle and, although it was still really too early in my book, it was festive. Her skin was illuminated by the candlelight and I shook my head at her beauty. What on earth was she doing with an asshole like His Majesty?

"It's been a bit rough lately," she said, "but I'm quite sure the three of us can work it out. I really feel there's no need to even think that we can't."

She wasn't really making much sense.

"Seriously, Dominic," said Anita.

She was on the verge of tears and I didn't know why but I had little sympathy for her right now. I didn't want to lose my job either. I liked my job. But I wasn't begging for it. That's okay for you to say, you selfish cow, a little voice inside my head screamed at me, you have another job offer and you don't have two kids to support, with medical bills on top.

"I'm not here to make any of you grovel, and I know you wouldn't anyway. I just need to get this office back on its feet. I want it to work for us all. I want us to be a team. We *have* to work as a team. It was working so well. I made necessary changes when I took Anita on but it's the atmosphere and the personal goings-on that are affecting us all."

The waiter was back with prawn linguini for me, pepperoni pizza for a now very subdued Dominic (I noticed for the first time his tie was black with white piano keys down the side), lasagne for Anita and mussels with gnocchi for Carla.

I drank more wine as I twisted the creamy linguini around my fork, hoping that was the end of the conversation. The waiter dropped the Parmesan on the table and left. I reached for the Parmesan immediately; no one else stood a chance. I was the Parmesan Queen.

"I can't lose this job," Anita blurted out. "I'll do anything to prove to you I am the best worker you could hope for. I need it so much, Dominic, and I really like it. I really enjoy this job and the people – honestly – but I think it's –" she turned on me now and shook her tomatoey fork in my direction, "it's Mia, I think – she's the one with the problem with Carla and myself . . ."

The words literally tumbled out of her mouth. Fucking cow! So Carla had blabbed her mouth off to her.

"Excuse me?" Some linguini unintentionally hit her on the side of the face. "But how dare you! How dare you both discuss me behind my back! And, Anita, this isn't the boardroom of *The Apprentice* and Dominic isn't Lord Sugar so you don't need to sell your soul!" I stared at Carla, furious.

"Girls, shush!" Dominic leaned in and raised his finger to his mouth.

"I didn't say a word about you! Don't bring me into this, Anita – I don't agree with that." Carla dropped her fork.

I exhaled loudly. "Sorry, Carla."

"Well, it *is* you!" Anita's eyes were now watery as she talked back at me. "You don't like me, you don't want to work with me, you think I'm a snivelling little cow. Well, let me tell you something, Mia, I have it tough right now and a friendly female colleague wouldn't go astray!"

I knew she was welling up as she pushed her hair from her eyes and, oddly, ate a large chunk of her lasagne.

"Go on, Anita." Doctor Dominic nodded at her as he ripped a piece of pizza with his hands.

"You know I have personal problems –" She took a deep breath as Carla and Dominic nodded. I hadn't told Carla – it was none of my business to spread Anita's private conversation with me. "My husband and I, well, we have some issues, but we're working it out. He's not perfect by any means and we're struggling big-time, both with our relationship and our finances in this climate. I am, well, I'm not getting the support from him I should be while he's living away working where he can, and it made me wonder, you know, what if, what if one day he goes for good? Where will we be then? I have a teenager and a three-year-old to think about. College isn't cheap, you know." She paused and Carla handed her the glass of wine in front of her. "Oh, he's had an affair in the past, I know that – and why do I stay with him, why do I want him? Because I love him, I suppose – I love what we had and I miss it. He's selfish and vain and I hate myself for loving him." A solitary tear now dripped onto her cheek. "I have two children who love him too. I'm no good without him. He's stopped helping me with bills this last month, just stopped. Yes, I can take him to court but I don't think I have it in me. So I need this job, it's keeping our heads above water. It's security in my topsy-turvy life. It's keeping my kids safe and keeping them unaware of what our life could be like in the future." She sipped again and we all stared at her. "Then of course I had to get him to come home and mind the kids while I did this with you guys and, boy, was he pissed at me. The names he called me. I probably deserved them. I probably am a doormat." The tears came fast and furious now. The waiter hovered but quickly left. The fork that had been hanging in the air, loaded with lasagne, was now dropped onto the plate with a clatter.

Carla hurriedly pushed her seat back and went behind Dominic to put her arms around Anita. I just stayed quiet and let Dominic fill my glass.

Carla returned to her seat, opened her bag and passed Anita a fresh tissue.

"Sorry." Anita blew her nose. "Oh, what am I like? I don't even know me any more. Here I am, pouring my heart and life out to complete strangers practically." She pushed her lasagne plate away and picked up her glass, her eyes red-rimmed and sad. "Please forgive me, Mia. I honestly think I'm having a mini-breakdown. This has nothing to do with you and I am truly sorry. I can't believe I said that about you. I didn't mean that, Dominic, honestly I didn't."

"Okay." Dominic threw his napkin on his half-finished pizza. "I'm going now. Keep it up, keep at it. This is what's supposed to happen. It's none of my business as your boss – your personal lives, I mean. You three need to do this. In Debbie's words, you need to sit down and thrash it all out. They have my credit card, here's the pin . . ." He passed me his business card with four digits written in blue pen on the back. "I want you three to work through your problems and then have a great night. Tomorrow's all planned out for us so don't stay out too late."

With that he left us to it.

"Ah, girls, I'm so sorry," Anita said. "I had absolutely no right to say that it was your fault to Dominic, Mia, none whatsoever. I honestly don't blame you for hating working with me. If I were you, I'd hate me too. And I'm sorry, Carla, for dragging you into it – you've only ever been lovely to me."

"*I* haven't been lovely to you though, have I, Anita?" I asked in a soft voice. "I owe you an apology. My life is a bit chaotic right now too, believe it or not. So forgive me."

"Don't be silly, Mia – you've been great to me. I've been over-eager and overreacting to everything. I suppose all I want is to keep this job I actually like. It's the first proper job with a pension plan and security that I have ever had and that I think I could actually be good at."

"Anita," I put my hand on her shaking one, "I do like you. I honestly do and I'm truly sorry I haven't been more sensitive to you. I don't want any of us to lose these jobs, I honestly don't. I suppose we do need to pull together."

She nodded and smiled. Relief washed all over her face.

"Right, let's gets out of here and get well and truly drunk!" Carla slapped the table. We paid the bill and made our way past the bottles and bottles of wine on rustic racks and onto the street. As Anita walked ahead Carla tugged at the back of my coat.

"What?" I turned around.

Her face was strange, questioning, and her eyes wide open.

"It's okay," I said.

"You sure?" She held tight to my coat.

"Of course, Carla, we always will be okay."

"I know you want to talk to me, Mia. I know."

I nodded at her and she nodded back at me and then we hugged.

"How about Frawley's? It's supposed to be great fun?" Anita said as she pulled up her coat collar and wrapped her scarf tight around her neck.

"Great," I said and Carla nodded.

We crossed the road. Carla pulled on her cream leather gloves. The smell from the sea was intense. Seaweed and salt. We entered what I presumed was a joke on Anita's behalf and not a bar at all. It was like squashing into someone's living room on Christmas Day. I'd say there were twelve people in the entire pub and that was it – it was completely jammed. Behind the counter stood an old man. He was wearing a cream Aran jumper and had thick-rimmed black glasses with an eye-patch over his left eye. And behind him was his stock: loose tea, sweets, jam, teabags and cans of beer. Only Guinness on draught. As we ordered and stood against the wall, Carla struck up a conversation with the old man, Tom Frawley himself. He had been born in this exact room over ninety years ago. It had been a family-run pub and he had lived here and run it all his life. He had never been outside Lahinch except for one time when he was invited to the audience on *The Late Late Show* and he travelled up to Dublin. He wasn't mad about it. What a character!

As people came and went, we stayed. It was so small it was an excuse not to talk about any serious matters which I think we three appreciated. We were free just to have fun and were soon bantering and flirting with three Americans who had just arrived in.

"I'm Casey," the tall bloke introduced himself to me.

"Mia." My back was jammed against the wall to let two people out.

"Ain't this surreal?" he drawled, in his navy Boston-emblazoned hoody as he sipped his Guinness. "Great Guinness, guys!" he toasted his two friends who were busy chatting to Carla and Anita.

I hoped I didn't have food in my teeth – although I had barely touched the prawns at all, but that parsley garnish was a real bugger for sitting in between your teeth, its greenery staring at anyone who dared speak to you.

"So you girls all from Ireland then?" the American hunk asked.

For some reason I had absolutely no interest in talking to him. All I wanted to do was to get some coverage on my phone and check in with my life.

"Could you excuse me for a moment?" I asked him and motioned to Carla that I needed some air which she believed as it was so packed in there.

Outside was dark and calm and cold. I leaned back against the door and rummaged in my bag for my phone. Turned it on. As I waited for the signal, I watched a hen party stumble from one side of the road to the other. Complete with pink hats and feather boas and very short skirts. My phone beeped.

"Great!" I quickly dialled Gordon's mobile. It connected straight away. "Gordon?"

"Yes, hello, Mia."

"Listen, I just wanted to get in touch to apologise for my lack of communication on the phone today but as you quite rightly guessed I couldn't talk and –"

"Yes, I got the message, don't worry, it's fine. I didn't expect you to get back to me yet – you're too busy to think about my offer just now – and the paperwork can wait until you get back. So how's it all going there?"

I knew he was smiling, and for some reason I pictured him loosening his tie. "Oh, you know, Gordon, it's thrilling." I laughed.

"I bet."

"So, okay then, I'll think about your offer, and I just wanted to say thank you so much for thinking of me. I'm flattered. So okay, speak soon then. Safe trip." I rang off.

I knew who I was ringing next before I even dialled the number.

"Hi, it's me," I said quietly.

"Oh, hi. What's going on, Mia?" His voice was raised and sharp.

"What do you mean 'what's going on'?"

"I've called you about five times today and your phone was off. I was trying to tell you I wouldn't be home after all tonight – so it's your own problem if you arrived to an empty flat."

It took me a few minutes to catch up on what he was saying. "Oh, our arrangement, no, sorry, I didn't get the chance to fill you in but it's a –"

"Mia, come in here now!" Carla's eyes were dancing and she dragged me by the arm so I hung up immediately and stuffed my phone away.

One of the Americans was giving Anita a lap dance as she sat on the couch and old Tom Frawley was napping sitting upright on his stool.

"Isn't this hilarious!" Anita screamed and sang along to Ricky Martin's "La Vida Loca".

"That's Brett and that's Casey and the other one is Brendan," Carla shouted in my ear. "Gas, that, isn't it? He's American and called Brendan! Now this is fun!" She beamed. "So we're going to be okay?"

My beautiful friend was standing in front of me and I adored her. She was such a great listener and I felt more comfortable in her presence than any other person I knew. I felt like me all the time, I felt interesting and appreciated and I knew she felt the same. We were very different but so alike. We laughed in each other's company so much. We sparked off each other. I saw sides to Carla that no one else did and vice versa. We just got each other. I knew she laughed with James and that was why she liked him so much.

I held out my arms and she jumped into them. The boys wolf-whistled and we parted, to their grown-up chants of "Kiss! Kiss! Kiss!". I said to myself: okay, Mia, it's time to have some fun. I downed the brandy and Baileys with them all, then I got a lap dance from Brett and even gave one to Casey (poor Casey) and I didn't think of Paul or Gordon or Mrs Kilroy or my job or my family for the rest of the night.

"Rise and shine!" Dominic was bashing on the front door. "It's horse-riding at ten followed by a trip to the Cliffs of Moher, followed by a trip to the Aillwee Cave followed by a cosy night in by the fire, I think."

Jesus, my head was hopping and I dreaded to see what

Dominic was wearing on this excursion. I reached for the Solpadeine and the bottle of fizzy water I had bought from Tom Frawley to take home. What foresight! I stuffed the two tablets into my mouth, took a swig of water and swallowed hard. "Stay down!" I ordered them.

I heard one of the girls letting Dominic in. I had to put my head back down. I seriously needed to think about my drinking. What is it they said? If it affects your life or work in any way, you have a problem. Well, right now I couldn't move. That was surely a problem.

My old wooden door creaked open and Carla padded in, fully clothed.

"Ouch!" she said. One word – it said it all. She reached for my water. "Horse-riding?" She spat the words at me. "I can't go horse-riding unless I strap up my stupid boobs! It's too soon!" She lay back on my bed. The word *stupid* wasn't lost on me. "What time did we get home?" she whispered.

"I have no idea."

I realised suddenly how much I had missed her. Missed us. I hated this secret.

"Oh, Mia," she said as though reading my mind, "it's true what you said last night . . . about James . . . he can be a tosser at times."

I'd said that? Shit, what else had I said?

"But I have to figure out why I don't want to leave him. It's up to me to love him – *you* don't have to love him but I do, and I have to do some serious thinking, that's for sure."

We both stayed lying back on the bed, dreading any move.

I really should tell her now, I thought. I pulled myself up on my elbows.

"If you're both not down those stairs in five minutes, I'm coming up!" Dominic shouted.

"Alright, alright, we're coming!" Carla called.

We wearily left the comfort of my warm double bed.

As I held on for dear life to Happy Henry, as he was unfortunately called, given his obviously sour demeanour, my mind slowed down. The wonder that is Solpadeine was kicking in and my head was clearing. The girl in the chemist hadn't want to sell them to me so I had to play up the old bad back routine. In fact, despite my hangover, for the first time in weeks I felt my head was becoming strangely clear. If I was totally honest with myself, I thought as I bobbed up and down, I knew this thing with Paul wasn't exactly *Love Story*. I hadn't really wondered too much what it was until now. What was I expecting? One thing I did know for sure was that I was a good flirt and a good one-night stand – but was I good steady girlfriend material? Were we boyfriend and girlfriend material? I knew I attracted the freaks and weirdos for sure. And Paul was turning into a weirdo, I suddenly admitted to myself. The way he behaved at times was appalling. I needed to just end this as soon as I could. I wasn't standing for this crap, I was worth more. The nausea hadn't disappeared and for one horrible moment I thought I was going to throw up all over Happy Henry's neck. I swallowed hard and tried not to think about it. I took long slow cold air breaths deep into my lungs. Restart my love life, that was what I needed to do. Ha, that was a laugh.

I shifted my weight, apologising quietly to poor Henry for his heavy load. I had a super opportunity to go and work for Gordon but I would have to leave Clovers, after all these years, and this silly bonding trip had brought me closer to Carla, Anita and bloody Dominic. If I was going to be leaving anyway, why was I here? I mean, I'd be mad not to go and work for a millionaire property developer. I knew that much. I hadn't told Carla about the offer yet because, if I was really honest with myself, I felt it was her dream job and that maybe I'd snatched it from under her nose. But it was also niggling at me that Dominic said either we *all* sorted it out or we were *all* going. Surely, if I left, he wouldn't sack the other two? That wasn't fair and, to be honest, I didn't think it was his style. How could I sort this? The saddle was cutting me in two so I tried to stand up in the stirrups to give my bum a rest. I had to speak with Paul soon.

Anita trotted up beside me, in her hard hat. "Not so bad this, is it?" she laughed. "You know what, Mia, despite my throbbing head this is doing me the world of good, it really is!"

It had started to rain and I welcomed it. "Yeah, not really my cuppa tea with the size of my arse but I know what you mean."

She laughed. A proper free laugh. I had never heard it before. It was contagious and I laughed too.

"You know, I'm going to try and make a go of staying this happy," she said. "I want to enjoy Christmas and I really want the kids to enjoy it. I don't know whether that's going to happen with or without my husband, but I am making changes."

My stomach churned. Of all the things in the world I hated, it was women who didn't support other women. I was guilty of this with Anita and it hurt me. I didn't want to be that person. We walked the horses along the beach side by side, the rain gently falling, and the other two caught up with us, all four of us lost in our own little worlds. The sounds of the horses' heavy breathing was enough to cover any uncomfortable silence.

Jimmy the instructor hummed away to himself, obviously

aware that this was some kind of bonding thing thanks to Dominic who was sitting this one out back at the yard. I was relieved when he told me that as Dominic poured into jodhpurs would have been very hard for me to handle.

"Homeward stretch!" Jimmy called to the horses more than to us, and as though obeying his voice they took off at a trot again.

Oh, my arse was killing me – and poor Carla with those new boobs! I liked the musty smell coming off the horse and, in a weird way and apart from horrendous arse pain, I didn't want to get off. It was like we could put everything on hold while we went up and down this beautiful beach.

I knew I had to tell Carla the truth about James eventually but not until later. That was my decision. I was sticking to it. This was not the right time for it, not this moment. She was beginning to open up of her own accord and I needed not to influence her with the catastrophic information I had. It would be so much better if she realised he was a creep without all this. I needed to save all our friendships and of course jobs so that was what I intended to concentrate on.

We wobbled back into the yard and dismounted.

"I'm taking that up when I get home!" This new, bubbly, rosy-cheeked Anita beamed at me. "Seriously, my hangover has almost cleared! The throbbing pain has been reduced to a dull ache!"

"Good for you!"

I was handed a plastic cup with coffee in it and I gladly accepted it. It was without doubt the best coffee I had ever tasted in my life. I welcomed every warm drop as we got into Jimmy's jeep and he brought us to the wonder that are the Cliffs of Moher.

We walked up the steps and stared down onto the rough

sea, admiring the vast, wondrous cliffs. They really were breathtaking and made me feel very small and insignificant. The place was buzzing with tourists, all snapping away with their up-to-date digital cameras.

"*Rising slowly from Doolin they ascend to over seven hundred feet, stretching south for nearly five miles to Hag's Head*," Dominic read from his *Little Guide*.

I felt I'd love to sit down and paint it all if only I could paint.

"*Being almost vertical, their sheer drop into the heaving Atlantic Ocean is a haven for sea birds. One can see the Aran Islands, Galway Bay, as well as The Twelve Pins and the Maum Turk Mountains to the north in Connemara and Loop Head to the south*." He studied the view. "What I wouldn't give to see an Atlantic Puffin," he said wistfully.

"Wow, Dominic!" I said. "I never knew you were such a nature lover!"

"Look at this, Mia! Is it not the most beautiful sight in the world?" He cast his arm around me.

"It is, actually, Dominic, it really is!"

Soon we were off to the Aillwee Cave where we joined a tour. I trailed alongside Dominic as I was suddenly interested in what he had to say next. I never thought I would see the day. He studied his book religiously before the tour began.

"So, girls, gather round me! '*The cave was discovered in nineteen forty-four, when a farmer named Jacko McGann followed his dog who was chasing a rabbit. The farmer did not explore very far into the caves, and did not tell anyone of the find for nearly thirty years*.' Imagine that, thirty years?" He couldn't believe the man could keep something like that to himself – Dominic told Debbie every time he did a pooh. "'*He told cavers about the cave in nineteen seventy-three and that summer the cave was explored as far as a boulder choke. Show-cave development began quite soon after. The boulder choke was removed in seventy-seven and access was gained to the rest of the cave. The Marine Blast tunnel was completed in ninety-two to allow a circular trip.*'"

Wow! I slipped an Airwaves chewing gum into my mouth and was now really looking forward to the tour. Hangover gone. I was buying a horse.

During the tour of the cave, the guide informed us he was now going to turn out the lights and that, as absolutely no natural light could seep through, this was as dark as could possibly be.

He was right. It was haunting. Pitch. Everyone stood still and quiet and all I could hear was breathing and the ticking of watches. Again it reminded me of how shallow my little existence was. This was something I never dreamed I'd enjoy, being in a cave. Me, Mia Doyle? I hated lifts for crying out loud – but not enough to take the stairs, Carla used to remind me. The reality of that accusation actually made me laugh and I frightened the life out of whoever was beside me in the pitch dark, as they nearly jumped out of their skins – my laugh wasn't girly and light, it was more deep and hollow. There was so much I didn't know I liked doing. Maybe I was a brilliant tennis player or a fabulous golfer? How would I know? I had never tried either. I imagined myself gracefully swinging my racket at Wimbledon, clad in a beautiful short white tennis dress with cute headband to match. I glided through the air like Steffi Graf. In my box sat Mam and Samantha, proud as punch of me, and Elton John who was in London to create the set of his new reality show and was my biggest fan. There was one more space in the box but who did I want to fill that? My fantasy person. The cave smelled like I was under the sea and

I loved the escapism of it all. I couldn't believe who came into my head first.

"Mia!" Dominic was pulling me now, dragging me from my tennis fantasy. I must remember that one for a time when I couldn't sleep. "The tour has moved on! Do you want to be left behind?"

Horrors! No bloody way!

All too soon it was over and then back to the stables where we collected our cars. As Dominic went on and on about the cave not being all that dark and how he could make out shadows, all I could think about was food.

The turf fire had been lit again for us and we all flopped onto the leather couch as Carla put the kettle on. I kicked off my runners.

"So tonight, instead of the TV, I thought I'd book a Chinese meal for eight," Dominic announced. "I suggest, after the heads on the lot of you today, it's just a good meal you all need and then back home here for some bonding and board games."

Oh God, was he serious? Could we not just stay in and chill out and pig out? The thought of getting ready to go out again filled me with dread, the thought of putting make-up on too much to bear.

"So, ladies, get up those stairs and into yer best glad rags. I'll be back at seven so we can have a pint first!" Dominic was whistling as he left.

"That sounds really nice actually," Anita commented.

"Yes," Carla agreed as she put the teapot on the table.

"Bickies?" I begged and she obliged and came back with a full packet of Jaffa Cakes.

I tore the packet open.

"They were in the press, Mia, I don't know how long they've been there." Carla made a face at me.

"Carla, I don't care if they've been run over by a bin-truck, mauled by a leper. I am eating them!" I stuffed one into my mouth.

"Dominic seems nicer, doesn't he?" Carla poured the three teas.

"Totally," Anita nodded.

I had to hand it to him. It was a side of him I had never seen before – he was actually behaving like an adult and oh my God did it suit him!

The others went upstairs to have showers and I sat in front of the roaring fire, feet tucked under me. I loved the sound of the wood crackling and the smell of the turf burning. It was the ultimate in relaxing sounds. Someone should invent a CD of fire sounds. I'd buy it. I just wished I could get Paul out of my head. But he was always there since the second Carla had come into the Palace and told me he had come looking for me. Until then it was just a one-night stand in my mind, I knew that. If I was being really honest, I liked him more because he liked me. It was strange that I couldn't really figure out how I felt about him at all. Was I in love with him? Oh I was attracted to him, I was madly attracted to him! But I didn't quite know if I really liked him. I hadn't had a chance to find out. My head was spinning with my lack of understanding lately so it was hard to think straight. I hoped against hope that Mrs Kilroy would be signing for Inchicore next week – the wonderful boys were sticking to their gracious promise to back down – I had called Peadar's mobile and he had apologised again for his "Gwyneth Paltrow outburst" as he put it, but I shushed him and we both laughed. As for Gordon, well, I knew he wouldn't back out on me. I trusted him – didn't know why as I was long enough in this business to know that, unless you were actually handing over the keys, the deal was never done.

What would Carla do when I told her about James? She would dump him, I thought, as I uncurled my legs and stretched out now. She would, as she didn't suffer fools gladly and she absolutely hated liars. At least one good thing would come out of it all then, I decided. I wouldn't have to see that creep ever again. I headed up to my room, had a quick wash under the arms and in other major crevices, put on my jeans, a sparkly midnight-blue top that really no longer fitted me but was all I had. I was bursting under my armpits. I had those nice red high-heels with me though and they set it all off. God bless shoes. Well, God bless feet really – they just didn't agree with the rest of the body that too much food expands them. They were perfect body parts. I left my hair down and ran the straighteners through it. Maybe it was time for some hair change? I should escape this mousy brown mop and go platinum blonde. Exciting thought, but I knew I would never be that brave. I applied my make-up wearily and sprayed on Clinique Happy (oh, the irony was not lost on me!).

The Chinese restaurant was dimly lit and beautifully decorated in red and blacks. Lanterns burned dimly in every corner. We were quietly seated, menus placed in our hands, and then left in peace to consider our choices.

Anita, however, put down her menu and started off the evening by apologising to Dominic for pouring her life story out the previous night. But, she said, she felt the better for it. She felt stronger than she had in years. She had spoken to her kids earlier and they were having a great time with their dad in Airfield. Although Stevie kept saying he was too old to be hanging out with his dad and pot-bellied pigs, his voice told her a very different story. She smiled as she remembered the conversation. She looked so much prettier. Her hair was tied up loosely on top of her head, she had dark eyeliner on and dark-pink lipstick, and in slate-coloured jeans and a deep-rose shirt she looked great. She also looked about ten years younger.

"This is why we're here, ladies," Dominic couldn't resist pontificating. "It is important, this bonding – it's teamwork. We can close every deal in the world once we work together and watch each other's backs. Look at the Irish team in Italia '90! It was a case of David and Goliath. We didn't have the legs of the Argentines but we stuck together, watched each other's backs and we were great!"

I feigned interest in this comparison but all I wanted to do was to look down the menu and marvel at the amount of dishes on offer. I got extremely distracted whenever a menu was in front of me, I couldn't concentrate on anything else and just wanted to read it – I found it quite overwhelming – a strange thing but true.

Luckily, both Anita and Dominic stopped speechifying at this point and we all concentrated on the menu. I settled on a hot beef curry with fried rice and sat back. I had sipped a sparkling water in the pub before as I felt I should leave alcohol alone for the night. The others ordered a glass of wine each and I ordered a Coke.

We ordered our food, then chatted about work and properties. It was relaxing and actually helpful. I found out things about clients I hadn't known. Carla was talking about Gordon and how great he was. My ears were wide open now as she told us how he had come from a small council house in Firhouse, how he had to work a morning paper round as soon as he was old enough. He ended up doing three different paper rounds when other kids didn't turn up, starting his day at four in the morning before getting to school for nine. She said he ended up managing the newsagent's he worked for at seventeen, while working nights as a lounge boy, before eventually working his way up the ranks of the business world and becoming a property tycoon. Without attending college or for that matter ever sitting his Leaving Cert. Incredible, I thought as I watched a young couple kiss slowly in the candlelight at the table next to us, hands gripped tightly.

Dominic started to open up now as I watched him relax and tell us his story of how he came to this point in his life. For the first time I noticed he wasn't in his "wacky" gear – he was just wearing a blue jumper and jeans. He told us how his interest in property came when his family were evicted from their home in Limerick in the 1970's for not paying their rent. They found themselves in Colbert Station, the Limerick train station, with four large old suitcases and each other. Dominic's eyes were sad as he remembered his father begging friends and relatives for the train fare to Dublin so the parents and six kids could stay with an older relative. This old relative did indeed take them all in and eventually died and left the house to Dominic. His brothers and one sister never really spoke to him after, as they assumed he had been responsible for making the old man leave him the house in the will. "'Cunning', they called me," he told us. Dominic said all he ever did was made the old man laugh and sneak him whiskey and cigarettes because he truly loved the old codger. His parents stayed in that house until their deaths in the 1990's and it was not rented out. But with the mortgage behind him on that property, he began to buy old houses and do them up before finally opening his own auctioneering business under the family name Clovers.

He swore as a kid that his kids would have the best of everything and never want. I was both upset and relieved for him. I surprised myself that I cared about Dominic and his life at all.

My curry arrived and I gave in to temptation and ordered a nice glass of red with it. It was a mouth-watering curry, wonderfully spicy but not too hot and the soft fried rice melted in my mouth. Dominic's sizzling beef with red peppers looked incredible and I had a little taste of Anita's sweet and sour chicken and Carla's duck in orange sauce, both yummy. I ordered banana fritters and coffee for after – I couldn't resist and they didn't disappoint. The others all had coffee too but no desserts.

As the others finished their wine, the waitress arrived with four fortune cookies.

"Ah, this should be good!" Dominic laughed and we all chose one from the plate.

Dominic went first: "*A good time to keep your mouth shut is when you're in deep water*," he read and laughed out loud. "Well, that was well and truly written for me, eh, girls?" He knew we all thought so but none of us said we agreed with him. "Ah, sometimes I go on a bit!" He looked embarrassed now and I felt horrible.

"You don't!" I was appalled at my own barefaced lie.

"Ah, go on, I do. But it's just I came from such an unhappy, unsmiling, dark grim home, I wanted something different for my life. I wanted my home and work places to be bright and happy."

"Well, you certainly did that, Dominic." Carla smiled at him.

"That's very true, you did!" I laughed with him now as Anita went next.

"*Don't ask, don't say. Everything lies in silence.*" She smiled "Not sure what that means exactly but I'll think about it." She crumpled the piece of paper into her fist.

"Me, me!" Carla was excited. "*Ideas are like children; there are none so wonderful as your own.*" She gripped the paper to her chest. "Ah, one day, one day, I do hope!"

"Come on, Mia – your turn," said Dominic.

I broke the cookie and unwrapped the small piece of paper. "*The greatest danger could be your stupidity*," I read out loud. There was pause where I concentrated on sipping my wine without making any eye contact with any of the others.

"Ohhh," Dominic said.

"Ah, they're all a bit of a joke," Anita piped up.

"Aren't they though?" Carla laughed.

I made an excuse that I needed to grab a bit of air and left them staring after me. They all knew I was rattled but I didn't really care too much.

Away from the door of the restaurant, I dialled Paul's number.

"Paul, it's me, Mia."

"Oh! Hang on."

I waited.

"Yeah?"

"Eh, Paul, I'm just wondering something here – I'm wondering how you feel about me?" I flushed from top to toe but I had to ask.

There was no response for a moment and then I heard his breath near the receiver.

"I really like you, Mia, I think you're great," came the reply.

"Oh," I managed, not exactly overwhelmed with his response. "Well, what are we? Because honestly, Paul, right now all I feel is that this is some little fling we're both having with a bit of a destructive twist on top, and that I am being really, really stupid."

He was silent again for what felt likes minutes and I wasn't going to say another word to fill this silence.

"Mia, it's a bad time for me. I've lost my bloody job and they're not that easy to come by."

"Oh, I know, Paul, and I'll talk to her but –"

"There's no way on hell's earth I am working for that dumb blonde ever again!"

Here we go again, I sighed. I couldn't believe this was happening all the time. This was too much. "Excuse me, but she is my best friend, Paul, and I'd prefer you didn't speak about her like that. I'm not excusing what went on between the two of you but she is under a lot of pressure right now. Please don't call her a dumb blonde ever again." I kept my tone calm.

"What's that?" I heard him say. "Ah Jesus, I have to go, Mia. I'll call you back sometime, okay?" And he was once again gone. And yet again I was left feeling crap.

I had begun to dial my mother's number to let her know I was alive and was sorry I would be missing the corned beef and cabbage when the door opened and the three of them piled out, my coat over Carla's arm and two brown-paper-wrapped bottles under the other.

"Ah come on, let's go, Buzby!" she said to me.

I turned off the phone and dropped it into my bag. My phone was getting used to this abusive treatment, I thought, as I took my coat from Carla. I was glad of its warmth as I wrapped it around me. I had been so running on adrenaline that I hadn't even felt the cold outside. That fortune cookie had really got to me. Was I being terribly stupid? My heart was still pumping and I sighed loudly.

Carla raised her perfect eyebrows at me. I nodded at her.

We began the short walk back from Lahinch town to our cosy houses.

I loved the house. It felt like home already, it was so comforting to return to. Dominic and Anita were yapping away about Anita's father who I had completely forgotten about – he was Dominic's brother after all – but the two men still didn't talk. It was funny, I thought, how you could know people so well, work with them day in day out in such close proximity and yet not know them at all. For some reason my sister popped into my head. Did I give her a fair chance? Did I really know she was a pain in the arse? Well, yes, I think I did but when I got home I was going to make a bit more effort with her. Give her a chance, so to speak.

My heels were beginning to cut into me as we walked.

"Hello, lovely ladies!"

Our American friends jumped out in front of us and Carla and I screamed (Carla's was a proper frightened girly scream, mine similar to a caveman being tortured).

"Oh, I'm so sorry, Carla, I didn't mean to scare you," Brett, the dark and broody one, said.

"Oh, don't worry, Brett, I'm fine." She composed herself and flashed her pearly whites at him.

"So where's the party tonight, our beautiful Irish ladies?" Casey asked us.

"Well, no party, I'm afraid," I said. "It's a quiet night in."

"With those supplies?" He tapped the bottles lightly with his index fingers.

"I'll tell you what, gentlemen –" Carla, who always knew what to say in every situation I have ever known, got out her pen and paper, "do you have a cell we can call you on if we get this party started?" (See, she even knew to say 'cell' instead of 'mobile' – she even had a pen and paper.) "You could grab some beers and drop over to ours? As we mentioned last night, this is a working holiday and that's our boss Dominic Clover up ahead so we don't want to get into trouble, guys."

"Sure, totally understand," he said and raised his fabulous muscular thigh to lean on as he wrote a massive amount of numbers down on the piece of paper.

Good ole Carla, this night needed wine. Suddenly I knew that this was the perfect night to talk to her once and for all.

We decided to get into our pyjamas when Dominic said his goodbyes. We pulled the curtains and settled down around the fire. Anita told us she had promised Dominic she would speak to her father and try and arrange some kind of family truce. Dominic said life was too short and what he really wanted was for his two boys to have the chance to meet their extended family.

After a while Carla opened the wine and we sipped in comfortable silence. The house had a wonderful peace about it.

Until.

"So." Carla sat up, crossed her legs under her and simple as you like said, "Shoot, Mia!"

I jumped and spilled my wine on the floor. "What?" I said, grabbing for the kitchen roll on the table and stamping some sheets onto the wine.

"Shoot!" she repeated. "I mean, fire away, Mia, tell me what it is you have to tell me about my beloved James. I am ready for it. I know it's not going to be something very nice so don't worry." Her eyes were colder now.

"Shit." I sat back down like a scared rabbit. "What, now?" I asked, my eyes glancing over at Anita.

"Yes, now, in front of Anita. She's shared everything with us so I want to do the same. Go on, I'm ready."

"Only if you're sure, Carla?" Anita said. "I have no problem going up to my room and giving you two some privacy. There's a book I've been really waiting to get stuck into and I never get the chance to read at home any more."

Carla shook her head. "No, stay."

I took a drink. "Okay, Carla . . . well, this really isn't easy for me to say or for you to hear, but you have to and I have to, so it's best if I just come out with it."

She wasn't smiling at all now and I could see the whites of her knuckles as she held her glass too tightly.

"It's nothing like another woman, Carla, but it's to do with James' house, The Tindles, in Killiney. Well, it isn't his house. He only minds it – for Gordon McHale of all people."

The blood literally drained from her face. "Are you sure?" she managed.

"Yes, positive. Gordon copped it when you mentioned your boyfriend lived there. He wanted me to tell you. He's not happy with James spoofing you and really wants him out."

"Holy shit! He's a complete liar. A barefaced liar!" She stared into the fire, her legs curled up beneath her. "So where does he live then, Mia?" She wasn't quite grasping it.

"Oh, he lives there alright, unless Mrs McHale needs it and then he obviously stays with you. He minds the house, Carla. That's his job, he's a housesitter."

"Like Goldie Hawn in *HouseSitter*?" She scratched her head. "And what about his writing room? Where he does all his work?"

"Gordon's study."

She was stunned but so strong. She didn't throw herself on the ground and scream and shout. She sipped her drink, ashen-faced but in control.

"I'm so sorry, Carla, but maybe he has an excuse?"

She stared at me. "Mia, my love, he made me get a boob job that I really didn't want, he compromised my very being." She was still holding it together.

Anita piped up. "I think you're so brave, Carla. You did what you felt you had to do to please the man you loved. It's pretty much the same for me. I love my husband so I don't want to lose him but somewhere in that love you lose all respect for yourself because you let someone else be in charge of your wellbeing. I know I shouldn't be putting up with him and, like you, I should have been stronger but –"

"I do think I love him, you see," Carla cut in (for which I was grateful). "He gets me. He really gets me. But why would he lie to me like this and when was he going to tell me? What do I do now?" She was incredulous. "He does get me, girls. I feel comfortable with him. I'm afraid to be by myself. I'm afraid that I won't meet someone else who just gets me ever again. Until I met Mia I didn't really have a friend I could be myself with. Oh sure, in school I was popular, really popular, but it was only because of my looks. I never got past that. James . . ." she kind of half-laughed, "doesn't actually think I'm that attractive."

"I honestly understand where you're coming from," Anita whispered to Carla.

"But, you see, I'm not sure I do, Anita, and that's just being honest," Carla came back. "I'm not. I mean, how could I actually want to spend the rest of my life with a creep like this? That's just not me, Anita, it's not my style." She rubbed her eyes now. "Do you know, it was his snobbishness that was the only thing I wasn't sure about with him. I hated the airs and graces but I was willing to put up with them and that was his lie. I liked the fact he didn't paw over me, I suppose, as mad as that sounds." She threw a cushion across the room now and it hit the floor.

Aha, now it was hitting home and her eyes were blazing. That was what I needed from her. I thought he was a nasty piece of work, I always had, and I was glad he had been exposed. I wasn't glad I was the one who had to do it and I certainly wasn't glad that she was hurt, but I was glad that she wouldn't end up with him and I knew she'd meet someone much better in no time.

"Christ, Mia, how did you not tell me this immediately?" She unravelled her legs and dropped them onto the floor.

"I was too scared – you know me, I went into a blind panic," I mumbled.

"I thought you were going to tell me you knew about his fetishes, his tying me up, pouring candle-wax on me and all that crap I hated – but no, you had the bomb on him. You had the money shot." She sat back and suddenly without warning lifted her T-shirt to show us two, perfectly pert, bra-less, silicone boobies.

Anita's hand flew to her mouth and she was visibly shocked. I stifled a laugh (I always laugh when I'm uncomfortable).

"I hate them," she declared, still not looking down at them. "So I'll be rejoining the natural-boob race as soon as my surgeon can get this shit out." She fixed back her perfectly fitted, skin-tight, white pyjama top and tucked it into her perfectly fitted, skin-tight, white Lycra bottoms.

I got up and went over and hugged her.

"Oh, Mia, I always knew you didn't like him and that just bugged me so much as you like everyone. You give everyone a fair chance. And then when Tim in the Palace said he 'creeped' him out, well, that really disturbed me as Tim is just the sweetest, kindest guy I know. Do you know what, girls, wait till I tell you this!" She squeezed her elbows in tight against the boobies, pushing them together as though she was irritated by them now. "James insists on being in the toilet with me, when I go for a pooh."

"Jesus!" I shut my eyes tight, trying to block out that image forever. "What, Carla, are you serious?" I seriously couldn't think about that one too much.

"Yep, it turns him on." She shook her head.

"Wow!" Anita sat up. "That's pretty gross alright."

"Tim thought it was horrific and a violation of my privacy," she said.

"You told Tim this before me?" I was incredulous.

"Oh Mia, I was way too embarrassed to tell you. You of all people. You who leaves the taps running when she does a pooh so no one can hear the plop. You who sprays half a bottle of deodorant after you have –" she must have caught sight of my face now, "done your business. You were the last person on earth I would tell that to."

She was right. I wasn't great with bodily functions.

"Tim was asking for you the last few times I was in there," I told her.

"He was? Why didn't you say?" She picked up her glass.

"Had a few other things on my mind, love."

We all laughed.

"Are you going to ring him now?" I filled our glasses to the brim and licked the excess wine from my index finger and thumb.

"No, I'm not. I had planned my future with him, more or less, you know, in my head – we'd never discussed it though. You were bridesmaid, Mia, and you were invited to the afters, Anita – no offence but I didn't know you so well then."

"None taken." Anita raised her glass. "Gracious of you considering the way I'd been behaving."

"Not at all – of course you'd be invited." Carla turned to me.

"You know, Mia, you're the only one with a proper boyfriend now."

"Huh? Oh well, I really don't know about that – are you ready for another man saga?" I got comfy on the couch, ready to launch into the sorry tale – maybe they could steer me in the right direction.

"Oh yes, great," said Anita. "No offence but I didn't even know you had a boyfriend!"

"Well, I wouldn't exactly call him a steady boyfriend – he spits hotter and colder than a broken electric shower. But I think I like him, and I think that he likes me, but I dunno – we just seem to rub each other up the wrong way." I took a gulp of my wine.

"Start from the very beginning," Anita said. "Your turn to confess, ours to criticise!"

Carla grinned, looking like she was going to enjoy seeing me on hot coals for a change.

I had opened my mouth to speak when a loud bang came on the window and we all screamed in unison. (Yes, my scream was bear-like.)

"That'll be the lads!" Carla jumped up.

"What? How did they know where we lived?" I gasped at her.

"I texted them. Now let's have some fun, come on! I'm a big girl – yeah, I've been a fool, a stupid fool, and no, my feeling for James won't go away overnight but I know this is all for the best. I hate liars. I can deal with anything else but not lies. I can't be with someone who lies. No." She shook her head fiercely. "And you know what else? All that freaky sex, it's not for me. I love sex, I love sex as much as the next person, but I don't like being afraid of what's coming next every time I close my bedroom door. All those toys and gadgets!" She shuddered and then skipped in her bare feet to open the door to reveal the boys standing there armed to the hilt with trays of Heineken and Guinness.

I welcomed them now with open arms. Like long-lost friends after only two meetings. It was what we needed to break this horrible situation. Distractions. Nothing like a few hot Americans for a bit of old distraction. Anita put on a Christmas CD Dominic had left and we played Twister – I laughed harder than I had in so long. They were complete and utter gentlemen, just enjoying our company, and although I saw Carla and Brett share a long, lingering kiss under the mistletoe that's as far as it went. I sang "Fairytale of New York" with Casey into two wooden spoons (yes, Casey had a grandmother from County Clare) as the others danced around the room.

When I went into the kitchen to put on some frozen pizzas that the boys had also brought along, Carla followed me in and closed the door gently behind me. "What are you going to do, Mia, about Paul? Do you want me to give him his job back?" She sat on the kitchen table, legs swinging, as I lit the gas oven.

"I seriously haven't a clue. Help me out here, what do you think is right?"

"Well," she said, "I think he seems like a nice enough guy. I mean, I was awful to him and I didn't let him explain his situation. My God, I'm such a man's woman and here we are, man-bashing all night – it's just not like me! But I think he needs to make you happier than you seem to be when you're seeing him? What's all that about?"

I didn't answer.

"When we get back to work on Monday I'll call him and offer him the job back."

I noticed how all her toes were perfectly proportioned. My second toe was bigger than my big toe. It made flip-flop life very difficult. "He might tell you where to go?" I said now, dragging my eyes away from them.

"That's up to him but I'll apologise for overreacting. Where did he have to go anyway that was so important?"

"You know what, Carla, I haven't the faintest idea," I told her as I closed the oven door and sat up beside her. "Are you really okay?" I put my arm around her tiny frame.

"Well, no, but I sure as hell will be. Can you believe James? Can you believe I was so stupid I believed he owned that house?"

"Yeah, I can, because why would you question it?" A thought struck me. "You know who'd be a good fit for you?"

"Who?"

"Tim."

"Yeah?"

"Yeah."

We hugged and Carla said, "Now let's party!"

We rejoined the others and sang and waltzed our way into the last day of our hugely successful bonding trip.

Dominic had been one hundred per cent right about everything – I never thought I'd see the day.

The last day in Lahinch opened up with a beautiful blue sky and we took a quiet walk on the beach and had an authentic fresh seafood lunch before we hit the road. I felt fantastic.

"I'll go back in the car with Dominic," Anita offered. "I want to try and pin down that date for him and dad to meet."

"Sure." I was half-sorry as I wanted to see what he had to say about the trip.

We all packed up and swore we'd be back again soon. We thanked the owners who had been so welcoming, lighting the fire for us each morning and keeping it going when we were out. The fresh home-made brown bread and bottle of wine on arrival. The spotless, fresh-smelling bed linen, the Christmas tree. They knew their stuff.

Carla and I chatted on the drive home and it felt great to have her back in my life. Properly. As we were on the last lap of the journey her mobile rang – she only ever spoke on hands-free while driving so she hit the receive button. It was James. (I really had to stop texting when I was driving, never mind talking on the phone without hands-free. I was truly ashamed I did this and made up my mind on the spot never to do it again.)

"Sweetie," his posh accent filled the little car completely, "when are you home? I need some TLC badly."

"Oh, baby, I'll be home in about half an hour," Carla gushed, to my astonishment and alarm. "Would you like me to stop off at Superquinn and get some of those salmon steaks you love and do a nice salad with them for you? I mean, I've been driving for over four hours but I should be able to drive out of my way and do that for you?"

Okay, now I got what she was at. Phew!

"Yeah, do that, that'd be nice," he said. "And is that shower of yours fixed yet? It's getting totally ridiculous at this stage – why is it all taking so long?"

"I've no idea, pet." Her face was hard as nails but her words sounded incredibly soft.

"Also, did you manage to look at those holiday brochures?" (He said 'brooooo-shares') "I know I have to pay you back as soon as I get my first instalment for the new book – but don't worry, it won't be long."

She looked at me. I looked at her.

"Also, sweetie, I think I'll stay at yours over the Christmas holidays if that's okay. I need a change of scenery for inspiration, I'm totally blocked."

"See you back there," she managed and hit call-ended.

We were both quiet for a few seconds.

"Seriously, how do you do that?" I asked then. "Keep it all in like that? It's just so cool!"

"It's just my personality, I imagine. I want to scream and shout and cry but I know in a few months I'll be so happy I kept my cool and composure. It's important to me."

"Do you want me to get out of the way?"

"Oh no!" she said. "I want you there for this. I need you there."

She had called Gordon that morning on my phone (in China!). And he had filled her in on how long James had been working for him. It wasn't that she didn't believe me but I actually wanted her to hear it from Gordon's own mouth – it was the least I could do.

When we pulled into the house in Ranelagh half an hour later, he was sitting against the hall door.

"I'll get the bags," he offered as Carla stepped out of the Mini and popped the boot. He went straight behind the car, not attempting to kiss or hug her. "Where are the Superquinn bags?" His head popped up and he look confused as he stuck his head back inside the boot and pushed our cases from side to side.

"Oh, I didn't go to Superquinn, I suddenly remembered I had something in the fridge that's just perfect for you."

It was so noticeable now that he still hadn't made any attempt to kiss this beautiful creature.

"Oh seriously? What is it? I mean, I was looking forward to the salmon steaks, Carla."

He slumped away from the boot as I now dragged both the bags out.

The back of the house reminded me of Paul instantly and a silent dread fell over me. I dropped the bags on the kitchen floor. Carla still had her coat on and was opening the fridge and from behind her I could see she was removing the solution she used to wash her new boobs with. It was a dark green colour, sticky, and smelled awful, like gone-off cabbage. She gently wrestled the large container out and removed the lid.

James was lazing in front of the TV, the dreaded Sky Sports Plus droning on in the background, telling us more about Wayne Rooney and how much money he was making, like any of us gave a shit. Another despicable excuse for a man.

I closed the fridge door for her as she held tight to the container and began her final journey into James' life.

He didn't even look up as she tipped every last bit of the rotten solution over his big head. He screamed. "What on God's earth are you doing, Carla! Have you like lost your tiny mind?"

"Oh James, that is just my little way of saying goodbye to a sticky, foul-smelling, complete fake chapter of my life. Now kindly get your lazy arse out of my house and never come back." She still wasn't shouting.

He didn't even ask why. He took his coat off the floor where he had dropped it and trudged his way out the back. He closed the door gently behind him.

"My beautiful couch!" She was on her knees, tea towel in hand now, mopping up the solution.

I filled a basin with water and together we cleaned up the mess.

"He didn't even ask me why," she said as she wrung the cloth out.

"He knew," I offered.

"Yeah, but he didn't even want to try and save it."

I could feel her tears were coming and I knew she didn't want them to, or want me to see them.

"I'm running out to the shops to get a few bits. Get unpacked, showered and into your jammies. We can watch the repeat of *X Factor* and relax. I'll make us a nice dinner. I'll do a big spaghetti bolognese and get some garlic naan bread to dip in it."

She smiled at me and I left quickly. I left her to get it all out, on her own, in private, because I knew that was the way she wanted it.

11

Work was so much better over the next few weeks. We were all getting on really well. Even Dominic had calmed down and I now understood him better. I even had admiration for him now, for what he had achieved in his life, and he was a wonderful father and a good husband really. Debbie said he was a "changed man" although I wouldn't quite go that far. (It was only a couple of days in Lahinch, not a month up the Amazon.) He told Debbie the weekend had been better than any therapy. He didn't know the half of it.

Carla had called Paul to offer him his job back when we got back into work. I could see from her face that his response was filled with expletives. He had rather unkindly told her what she could do with herself (go fuck herself) and her job (go fuck her job). She said she didn't blame him really as she had been out of line.

I had called him after that and he told me he was working in Belfast for the next few weeks so he wouldn't be around. There was no chatty conversation or even a space to make an arrangement for next time. He just said, "I'll call you whenever

I'm back down in Dublin, okay?" and that was that. So much for a declaration of love. Or even interest. I couldn't stand this game-playing. That all meant I couldn't call him before he called me, right? My new boyfriend was slipping through my fingers like quicksand. I was disappointed but more than anything I felt rather numb. It was like I had been dragged through a hedge with the guy. I had gone from adoring him to hating him in a few short weeks. Were we dating? I honestly hadn't a clue. He wasn't one for sending text messages, didn't trust them, he said. So I put it into my heart that he was genuinely busy, I was busy and Christmas would sort out our relationship one way or the other. I still fancied him so that meant something to me at least. Every night he was in my dreams.

Anita was a different woman – warm, focused, healthier-looking and not half as pushy as she had been. She was in truth now a proper team player. She was happier at home too. Her husband was out of town on business and she was relaxed. Not watching the door every night for him to come home. "It's almost better that we know he's away. We can lock the door at six o'clock and it's just us," she said over tea one morning in the kitchen (Carla had her on the green tea now, I just couldn't hack it). "I mean, I'm not wondering where he is all the time, will he come home for dinner etc."

"Sounds to me like you're all better off without him." Carla dipped her green-tea bag up and down. Anita sighed. "I'm sure you're right Carla, but with kids involved it's just not that easy."

"Will he stay home for Christmas?" I asked her.

"Oh God, yeah, he will, he has to – it would really break the kids' hearts if he didn't. Katie is only three, remember, and she needs her daddy. Stevie is still a baby at heart but he's starting to realise that Superdaddy isn't quite Superdaddy after all."

I dipped my Twix into my Lyons tea, they dunked their green-tea bags.

Gordon was still in China and I hadn't told anyone about his job offer yet. I needed more information, I realised after we got back from Lahinch. I mean, where would my office be based? Salary? Hours? I need to sit him down and talk to him. I knew Dominic wouldn't sack the others now – he had been pushing us to our limits there but I also knew they would all miss me if I went and I would miss them. Did I want to leave?

Carla had also mentioned she might sell the house in Ranelagh now – she was turned off it after James and then Paul. She had other builders in who were with a big firm and had finished Paul's work in no time with lots of manpower. The property was fantastic now but, with the current market in the state it was in, she had already lost big money on it and I knew she was worried. My advice to her was to rent it to a family, try to cover her mortgage and then some in order to rent somewhere cheaper with me. She was of the same mind. I was planning on looking at some apartments with her after Christmas. So it was all work and today I was settling the wonderful Mrs Kilroy into her new home.

"I'd better dash," I said to Anita.

"Good luck," she said.

I dashed into town, down O'Connell Street and did a U-turn back around to Cleary's Department Store where I was to pick Mrs Kilroy and one of her nieces up and take them to Inchicore. There they were under the clock like we planned and I pulled into a bus lane, flicked on my hazards and hopped out.

"Take your time now!" I held the car door open for Mrs Kilroy as she slowly manoeuvred her old body out. She had a grey headscarf over her new perm and an old, grey, ankle-length macintosh. Her niece took her large walking-frame from the boot and put it in front of her.

"Ma!" Mick Kilroy rushed out of the house and gave her a big hug.

"Ah, there ya are, son!" She gummy-smacked her lips (her false teeth were only slipped in when she was on a night out). "Have ya the kettle on? I'm only gaspin' for a cuppa tea. I've never put an X on so many pages in me life!"

Her Irish accent was still thick despite all those years in London. "Sure I only ever mixed with Irish friends there really," she'd told me when I'd asked her about it. Some words had a twang while others remained completely Dublin.

Now she slowly made her way into the house in Inchicore that she now owned and would undoubtedly spend the rest of her days in.

"Thanks, Mia!" Mick squeezed my arm. "That was a great price. Come in and have a cuppa tea with us."

"Sure, Mick." I locked the car and we went inside.

Welcome Home, Granny banners were displayed on the walls of the little house and what seemed like one hundred grandchildren and great-grandchildren clapped as she entered.

"Get away outta that, will ye!" she said as she eased herself into an orthopaedic chair.

I sat beside her and was immediately handed a cup of tea and a plate of biscuits.

"Leave my teabag in the cup!" she called. "It's all I ever dreamed of, you know, Mina," (she just couldn't say Mia but I didn't mind in the slightest) "coming back to Inchicore. Silly dream to have, you're probably thinking?"

"No, not at all," I answered honestly as I saw all these faces staring lovingly at this wonderful lady. I could imagine them in and out of the house at all hours of the day and her never being lonely. "Fambly," she said, mispronouncing the word, and she slurped her tea noisily. "It's all that matters, you know, Mina."

I nodded. Family. I hadn't seen my own mother in ages. I had to get around there after work. I finished my tea and waved goodbye to one big happy family.

"Come back and see me, Mina!" Mrs Kilroy gripped my hand with her arthritic one as I left.

"I will," I told her and I meant it.

As I drove back to the office I listened to some Take That and thought happy thoughts.

Everyone was in powering work mode today.

"How did it go?" Anita asked as I took my seat.

"Oh great – she's so happy, Mick's happy!"

"Coffee?" Carla asked.

"No, thanks, I'm all drunk out." I plonked down and clicked on the property overlooking Sandymount Green that I had my eye on for Peadar and Damien. It was a beautiful old two-bed recently refurbished, small, with a stunning view over the green and surrounded by shops and restaurants. I thought the location was good for Damien – Dart stop and regular bus services plus a lot of the local folk walked or cycled into town.

"So will you come to this bootcamp with me, Mia?" Carla was laying a terrifying-looking brochure on my desk.

Boot camp? I was on red alert. I didn't like the sound of this.

"It'll be great. It's two nights a week and it's fabulous for fitness. My surgeon says it's fine for me to do now until my scheduled operation to remove this silicone next year."

"Oh Carla, I don't know really. It's not very bright at nights any more, is it?" Clutching at straws here, I knew that myself.

"There are floodlights," she came back without skipping a beat.

"It's outdoors?" I almost didn't recognise my own voice.

"Yes, it's in a football ground in Ballsbridge. Come on, it'll be great to be all fit and toned for Christmas and the big office Christmas party!"

We both laughed at that one.

I picked up the brochure: *Military Style Fitness Techniques* and *REAL MILITARY INSTRUCTORS* jumped out at me in green and black colours.

"This will be great for us!" she enthused. "The fresh air, the heart pumping – ah, I can't wait!"

I knew she wasn't going to give up. "Oh, okay, sign me up! What night is it?" I threw the offending brochure into my drawer.

"Tuesdays and Thursdays."

"*EastEnders* nights!" I buried my head in my hands.

Carla was unmoved.

The office was silent after a while with only the whirring of the printer or the tapping of keyboards. I stared at the little house in Sandymount on my screen. I slipped my feet out of my shoes under my desk and wriggled my toes, then slid out the drawer and broke off a massive bit of Curly Wurly. As I chewed it with my head down (which is not as easy as it sounds), my mobile rang. Why was it every bloody time I tried to enjoy a piece of chocolate I had to speak? It was like the Gods of Secret Chocolate-Eating were bearing down on me.

"Where on earth have you been? I could be dead for all you care!" It was my furious mother.

"Oh, Mam, I had to go away last minute on a work thing. I was actually planning on popping over to see you tonight."

"But the butcher isn't here yet!" My mother was probably the only person in the world I knew who had her meat delivered *daily* by her local butcher. The poor man had to stand there as she opened each pale-blue striped plastic bag tied with red tape and scrutinised each pork chop, each sausage, each rasher, rib, you name it. Then she'd ask the poor unfortunate red-faced butcher if he thought he was pulling the wool over her eyes. She was actually in a 'meat club', if you can believe this. She paid money weekly into the club so at Christmas the turkey and ham were already paid off. "Oh, Mam, I don't want dinner."

"Nonsense! I'll ring him now. He's supposed to deliver a nice piece of brisket and sure I'll boil a cabbage and throw on a few potatoes, it's the least I can do if you're coming for dinner. Where is he at this time of day at all at all?"

"Grand, fine, see you at six-ish so." I hung up.

I rang up Mr Nolan who was selling the house in Sandymount and chatted with him for a while about realistic selling prices. He was selling for his parents, an older couple who had moved into a retirement home. He seemed a decent sort of man. The boys were in the Canaries for a fortnight but I was pretty sure we could still be in with a chance. Properties notoriously stayed on the market until after Christmas at this time of the year.

"You will not believe this!" Carla was over again and Anita and I looked up from our desks. "James has just texted me." She was reading from her phone while shaking her head, blonde hair bouncing all over the place. "He is saying he takes it the holiday is off. 'I need to know,' he says, 'because another friend can take me to his apartment in the south of France if we're not still going.'"

I laughed out loud.

"Is he for real?" Anita asked her. "Wow, what a grabber he is!"

"Oh, does anyone fancy a few drinks tonight in the Palace – I know I do." Carla ran her hands through her hair now to tame it.

"I can't." Anita shook her head.

It was tough on her. She was always rushing from pillar to post – her life was like a wall chart of constant planning. She had a lady who came in to mind Katie during the day (a neighbour who gave her a good deal) and Stevie was doing his Leaving Cert. He was to answer all his questions into a Dictaphone as he had lost the finger from his right hand and couldn't write properly again yet. It could take months for him to learn how to hold a pen and write clearly. The poor guy, I thought sadly, what an awful thing to happen to him. He wanted to take a year out and travel and Anita thought this was a good idea. I admired her.

"Well, yeah," I answered Carla, "but I have to go to my mam's for dinner. I could meet you later? Call for you around nine o'clock and head there together?"

"No, no – sure Tim will be on so I can stroll down and have a drink, sit up at the bar with him."

I worked hard for the rest of the afternoon and had lots of viewing lined up with Anita for the rest of the week. I wearily pulled on my coat at five o'clock and headed home for a bit of brisket.

Samantha was on the couch when I arrived.

"How's you?" she asked without really wanting to know the answer.

"Grand," I replied without really looking over at her.

"Fifteen minutes!" Mam yelled at me just as I reached the door of the kitchen.

"Hello, Mammy." I puckered my lips and she offered me a cheek.

I plonked beside Samantha and said, "So how's Niall keeping?"

"Oh, he's brilliant." She turned to me and hugged the cushion. (I hated cushion-huggers. I didn't trust them.) "Oh

Mia, I've never been happier but I do need to talk to you about something."

She dropped her comfort-cushion, jumped up and pulled the sliding door over on Mam. Then she came back and sat very close to me on the couch.

"Well, the thing is," she went on really quietly, "he wants me to move in with him – well, with him and his dad. His dad owns the house and will under no circumstances hear of us paying rent, so we can save there and get our own home." She was obviously delighted as her smile spread across her face and, to be honest, she was usually pretty expressionless.

"Right," I said. "Great if that's what you want." Why was this such a secret? I would have thought she'd have shared this with her best friend Mam by now?

"But, you see, well, the thing is, you will have to move back in with Mam. She's not getting any younger and she needs the company."

"*Over my dead body!*" I all but yelled and she shushed me quickly.

"Why not? Sure you could be living here rent-free, Mam is terrific company, and you have no reasons not to."

"I do have reasons! My reason is I am an *adult,* an *adult*, and I don't want to live with my mammy, end of story, Samantha. Don't you dare bring it up either, okay?" I couldn't believe this.

"Well, I was going to tell her tonight I was moving out so that's the way it is."

She got up, fixed the cushion and went to open the sliding door again. (What Mam was making of the sliding-door action I couldn't imagine. Too busy to notice hopefully.)

I stared at the brass ornaments on the fireplace, polished within an inch of their lives. There was just no way I was moving back in here, no way whatsoever.

"It's up!" shouted Chef Ramsay from the kitchen and we went in to take our positions at the table.

We always sat in the same seats. I wondered what would happen if I sat in Mam's place?

It was brisket. Don't ask me what brisket is and don't tell me if you know. I ate it, I ate the cabbage, I ate the potatoes, I drank the sherry.

"So, Mam," Samantha said as she heaped butter onto her potatoes and not a pick in the world on her, "Niall has asked me to move in with him and I have accepted."

It was like déjà vu of the last meal. What would she tell us at the next one? That she saw Dad every Sunday for a Happy Meal with a strawberry milkshake?

"Oh, love," Mam put her fork down, "that's great." She didn't look like she meant it.

"Are you sure, Mam?" Samantha asked her.

"Well, no, I mean yes, I mean I'll miss you so much, pet, but you have a great career going and a steady boyfriend so I suppose I'll just have to accept it. In a way I knew it was coming."

Wow, I thought, she hasn't taken it too badly at all.

"When will you go?" Mam asked, ladling the butter on top herself now. She, however, did have a pick on her.

"Oh, not until after Christmas. I'll go then." Samantha looked sad now.

"Grand so."

I tried to make conversation as we finished the meal. I told them about the team-building weekend. Samantha was, in fairness to her, very enthusiastic about it all and Mam thought it was one of those yokes that was a waste of time and money. For gobshites. Like gyms, she informed us. Apparently they were for gobshites too. Why spend money to go into a place and step up and down on a step when you can run up and down the stairs? Or what was the point in getting on one of them fancy running machines? Sure who wanted to run and not get anywhere? It just didn't make any sense. Run to the shop, buy a loaf of bread.

"Yes, Mam," I agreed. Sometimes she did make good sense.

I cleared the table and stacked the dishwasher while Mam and Samantha went to sit down in the living room.

The 'good dishwasher' was a recent addition to the house – she hadn't believed in dishwashers either until Mrs Cooke next door got one and suddenly it was a must-have. I had taken her to Power City to buy one.

"How does it know which?"

The saleswoman plastered a smile on her face. "Which?"

"Which spoon, for instance, needs a better scrubbing than another spoon? Say I used one to scrape a pot of chocolate and another to stir me tea?" Mam leaned on the aforementioned dishwasher.

"Well, madam, it washes all at the same intensity," the confused girl replied.

"Sure, that's a waste! Is there no one with, say, two compartments that you can put really clean spoons in one and really manky spoons in the other?"

"No, madam, not as far as I am aware." The girl smiled, not knowing what was coming next.

Mam pulled herself up straight.

"I'd like to speak with the manager, please."

Oh no! I sat on the edge of a Hi-Fi table. Were they still called Hi-Fi's?

"Mam!" I pleaded with her.

She did this all the time. If she didn't like the answer she got, she asked to speak to the manager. One time I took her to

Blackrock Market and she asked the woman on her own stall, selling old teapots, to speak with the manager.

So in Power City the manager left his busy post and told her the same thing as the assistant did. We settled on the cheapest one.

Now I made her a cup of tea, cut her a large slice of flaky apple-tart and brought it all in on a tray.

"Do you want some?" I mumbled at Samantha as flaky pastry fell from my mouth.

She shook her head and stood up. "I have to go upstairs and call Niall so you'll probably be gone by the time I get back down."

"She's on that phone to him for hours," Mam said, with flaky pastry falling from her mouth (I see where I got it from) as Sam pounded up the stairs. "A bit of cream on there." She nodded at the plate and pushed it back at me.

I returned to the kitchen and blobbed a massive lump of cream on the side. It looked delicious so I stuck my finger in and had a taste.

I went back to the living room and delivered the plate to Mam.

"Okay, I'm going so," I said. "I'm meeting Carla at the Palace for a – work meeting."

Mam looked as put out as I expected she would. I went into the hall, grabbed my coat and returned to say goodbye.

"Sure time enough after Christmas so," Mam said.

"Time enough for what?" I was checking my purse to see if I needed to stop at the Drink Link on the way.

"Time enough for you to move in here after Christmas." There was a dollop of cream hanging off her chin.

I dropped my purse on the ground, and all the coins hit the floor, scattering around the room. This could not be happening to me. I had to nip this in the bud right now.

"Mam, I'm not moving back in here." I moved nearer to her.

"What?" She looked at me and then back at the TV, cream still hanging on for dear life. "I missed what he said now with ya dropping all them coins!" She pointed to Noel Edmonds on *Deal or No Deal*. "The Banker's in some mood today!"

Ah God, I couldn't do this now. I just did not need this. The guilt was going to fucking haunt me but I knew I couldn't move back in there. I was a horrible daughter and that was fact, but horrible I had to stay for my own sanity.

"Let's talk when you're not so busy." I scrambled around the floor for the coins and stuffed them back in the purse.

Outside, I jumped into the car and blasted the heating. December was just here and it was freezing! "I am not moving back in there!" I told my car. "Not in a hundred million years. I do not care. I cannot do that!" I turned the engine over as my phone rang. "Yes?" I answered without looking at the screen, just getting it on the last ring.

"Hi, Mia, it's me, Paul."

I turned off the engine.

"Oh hi, how's all up north, mate?" I really came out with some weird stuff.

"Up north is good, yeah." He sighed hard and he sounded, well, lonely.

Oh my God, was he about to open up? This was something to grab onto. "Have you any mates up there?" Not too bad, Mia! I curled my toes up, praying not to say something really stupid.

"I was wondering if you'd like to come up and visit me? If you weren't too busy, that is?"

I shut my eyes tight and blew out three silent, short, raspy breaths. "Paul, I think that would be really nice." Good girl, I smiled to myself.

"Great!" He sounded really happy. "So, I looked at the train times and one leaves Connolly at six o'clock on Friday evening. Do you think there's any way you could make that?"

"Friday, yeah, sure!"

"Great, well, I'll pick you up from the train but, when you get off, go down the escalator to the car park below because it's too hard to pull up outside Belfast Central. The house I'm in is only ten minutes away so we can pick up a Chinese and a bottle or two?"

"Or three!" I laughed.

"Huh, what?" he asked.

I hit the steering wheel hard.

"Mia? You okay? Three what?"

"Three-ball!" I now added to the mess.

"Three-ball?" His voice was high. "You want a three-ball?"

I looked at my face, now flaming red, in the rear-view illuminated by the street lamp.

"No, sorry, Paul, I was trying to be funny about the wine, you said two bottles so I said three. I'm not really sure why I said three-ball after that, but I know for a fact I don't want a three-ball."

He was sniggering now. "Grand so – I wouldn't have known who to call!"

We both laughed.

"See you Friday!" I said.

"Yeah, see you then."

I hung up.

The old excitement returned instantly. My palms were sweating. What would I wear? Was it the one night or two? I wish I had started that bloody boot camp last month, I thought, as I felt the muffin top I now clearly had. "Bad desk with hidden chocolate!" I said as I looked over my shoulder and reversed out of the driveway.

I parked at the Palace on the street directly outside the window and put enough money in to cover me until the following morning. I was going to have a few.

Carla was propping up the bar, looking stunning. Her blonde hair was in a bun on the top of her head – now the reason for this, I knew, was that she hadn't washed it – however, to everyone else it looked as though she had just had it done in the hairdresser's. It was function-perfect. She was wearing a short pink skirt with this tight black polo neck and high black boots.

"Mwah!" we air-kissed.

"You look amazing," I told her.

"Do I? Thanks, I'm scruffy as a dog though, I didn't even shower!" She was sipping a glass of wine.

"How's Tim?" I saluted down the bar to him, clicking my heels together, and he laughed, his floppy blond hair in need of a cut now.

"So how was the dinner?" she laughed.

"Oh, have I a story for you!" As I sipped a cool pint, I filled her in on Samantha's co-habiting news and then my mother's request and then Paul's phone call and the weekend ahead. I was actually breathless by the time I'd finished.

"Wow, you couldn't possibly live in harmony with your mam, could you?"

I shook my head.

"But I'm delighted for Samantha, I think she's a sweet girl – and Paul, wow, that's serious, right?"

"Well, I dunno, do I, but you know what, Carla? I'm going to find out just where I stand with this guy once and for all. If it's going nowhere I don't want to do one-night stands any more – not that I have anything against one-night stands as such – it's just I want more now or nothing at all. Must be my age, I guess." I applied some Rose Vaseline to my winter-chapped lips. Offered some to Carla who looked shocked and then repulsed so I replaced the lid.

Tim put a bowl of mixed nuts in front of us.

"Is this a new thing?" I asked, overly excited and my mouth already full. Carla didn't touch them.

"Yeah, management's decision. They sent me to Musgraves today to buy bags and bags of them – apparently it's what all the pubs are doing now in the recession."

"What, putting nuts out so people can just eat them and not have any dinner?"

I thought it was a reasonable question but Tim and Carla fell about laughing and slapping each other's arms – more of an excuse to touch each other, I thought as I chewed, but anyway.

"No, it's the fact that the nuts are salty, causing a thirst," said Carla, "so therefore they make you drink more." She looked at Tim and he nodded.

"Whatever! Another pint so, I'm gasping after them nuts!" I said as I threw another big handful into my mouth.

We chatted for the rest of the night and Tim, I observed, was clearly absolutely besotted with Carla. As he served each customer he glanced over at her, every opportunity he had he spoke to her. He actually couldn't take his eyes off her to be honest and he hung on every word she said. I knew that she wouldn't jump into another relationship for a while but I could tell that she did like him and was enjoying the attention. James had never given her any attention, he was always criticising her and it had definitely damaged her confidence. Tim was just what she needed, a really nice guy to flatter her and treat her like a princess.

"I need to go clothes-shopping before Friday and I'm broke," I said as we finished our drinks to hit the road.

"You can borrow whatever you like of mine," she said as she pulled on her woolly pink cashmere cardigan.

I laughed in her face. "Carla, seriously?"

She shrugged her shoulders and we called it a night.

Back home we made tea and toast and carried it to our respective rooms.

"Thanks, Mia!" Carla smiled at me as she balanced her plate on top of her tea and opened her door.

"For what?" I asked, my mouth already full.

"For being such a good friend to me." She closed her door behind her with her bottom.

I sat on my bed and munched away while trying to work out what to take with me on Friday. I had to pack for two nights just in case he expected me for the whole weekend. I needed a good waxing too – I must book that in tomorrow. I leaned over, dropping toast crumbs on my duvet, to make a note. I'd go to Dundrum shopping centre after work and buy two new outfits, put them onto the bulging credit cards. They would have to go there – I had no spare cash! I hadn't a clue what I should look for. Well, no, I did, I thought as I braved a Gok Wan look in the mirror. I winced. Oh, it was jelly-like! It was wobbling when I moved. I stood there and shook in front of the mirror. Everything moving. Boobs, belly, thighs, all shaking their stuff! Okay, I needed something to suck me in. I didn't have to choose style, colour or any of that – once it sucked me in that was all that mattered. Some nice, very elasticated underwear to . . .

Oh! My hand flew to my mouth. I ran to my bag, grabbed for my diary and flicked back the pages . . . oh no, no, no, please no! I counted with my finger. Phew! I slammed it shut. My period wasn't due till the following weekend. What a nightmare that would have been! Men obviously never thought about those kinds of things when they invited women on dirty weekends away. Well, why would they? But that could have been a bit of a passion-killer – although our lovely James loved to have sex with Carla during her period – personally, I thought that was absolutely sick!

I slathered on the Elizabeth Arden eight-hour cream that Carla had generously lent me – she was so generous with her stuff. It absolutely stank and was so gooey my face stuck to my pillow but, boy, did it work! I settled down for a good night's sleep, feeling calm and contented.

We'd sold two houses by Thursday evening and Anita really closed the second deal. Both were bargains, to be honest – a four-bed in Rathfarnham that had been six hundred thousand but the lucky couple got it for three hundred and fifty thousand, and a small two-bed in Rialto for buttons too. Dominic was thrilled and I didn't feel bad leaving work early on Thursday evening and heading over to Dundrum.

It really was a shopping centre like no other. Obviously no one had told the shop or the shoppers that we were actually in the middle of a very bad recession. It was all Brown Thomas bags and extra-large smoothies. The glamour of the women was just astonishing, I thought, as I sat on a comfy leather bench to drink my low-fat Starbucks latte. It was full-on glamour. How women shopped in six-inch stilettos was beyond me. I looked around at the magnificent Christmas decorations. Truly beautiful and not a tacky bauble in sight. The centre had every shop a girl could wish for, from Alwear to River Island to Top Shop and Miss Selfridge. They didn't call it Miss Selfridge for no reason. 'Miss' as in eleven to twelve-year-olds because no *Mrs* would ever fit into their clothes – it was like me trying to fit into the children's section at Gap. I knew this, so avoided it like the plague it was.

I drained the low-fat although still creamy-tasting latte and headed for Marks & Spencer's. I knew what was right for me and all those other shops just were not.

Over to Lingerie first where I decided to get measured after being offered the free service by the delightful older sales assistant. It was slightly embarrassing but I did it and she made me feel very comfortable.

"Okay, so you're a good 38DD," she said, smiling at me. "Pop into the fitting room and let me bring you some bras to try on."

I stared at my puppies in the mirror. I had been wearing a 36D for years. She came back with some of the prettiest bras I had even seen, and lo and behold they looked great on me. They pulled my boobs right up and seemed to give me a longer body, and more tummy area – not that this was necessarily good but you know what I mean.

"I think that one is great on you." The sales lady was back and peeped over the door. It was a black bra with pink lace trim and little pink flowers.

"Yeah," I said, "I really like it."

"There are pants to match," she offered.

I glanced at her name badge. "Hilda, I think you and me both know the pretty knickers won't do me any favours. Could you kindly bring me some black Lycra sucky-in pants in a generous sixteen?" Hilda laughed and off she toddled. It would be actually easier to exercise and eat less than go through all this, I thought, as six-foot models came and went in see-through negligées and bras that wouldn't hold my loose change.

"Nice, Lorcon?"

I was shocked as one girl paraded out of the cubicle to her waiting boyfriend who actually finished what he was doing on his Blackberry before he looked up and nodded his approval. I pulled my head back into the fitting room as good old Hilda came back with a variety of suck-in pants and I settled for a pair she had found with a pink trim! Genius woman. They came up to my boobs but, by God, they were good! I thanked Hilda and paid for my stuff. Was I supposed to tip her? I really didn't know. I knew I was supposed to tip the hairdresser and the girl or guy who washed my hair but was I supposed to tip the beautician I was now going into to rip the hair off my bikini line? That one I didn't know either.

I had decided to shave my own underarms and legs but my bikini line needed to be tackled by a professional. Whenever I shaved there it looked as though I had hacked it with a Stanley knife. I always came out in red blotches and red lumps. Not a job I'd be crazy about, I thought, as I gave my name and took a seat in the sweet-smelling salon.

"Mia Doyle?" asked the girl now standing in front of me in a pink uniform.

"Yes." I stuck out my hand to shake hers but she didn't seem to notice and I dropped it again just as quick.

She led the way efficiently as I followed her into the treatment room. I took off my trousers and pants and put on the paper knickers while she was heating the wax. She made some small talk as she applied the hot wax with the wooden spoon to the area. Some pipe music chimed away in the background.

"Have you ever considered electrolysis?" she asked.

"Not really." I shifted my weight on the hard bed.

"You should. You're extremely hairy and they're very dark hairs. It would be really suitable for you." *Rip!*

"*Ouch!*" I actually said the word 'ouch'.

"Okay?" she asked in surprise as though I was the first person ever to yelp in pain during the waxing process.

"Fine." I decided to keep quiet now and gritted my teeth for the rest of the horrible ordeal.

"Is there anything else you would like to have taken care of today?" she asked eventually as she rubbed some cold witch hazel into my bloodied bikini area and I wiped the tears from my eyes.

"Like what?" I had to ask.

"Well, any other treatment – eyebrow-waxing maybe?"

"No, no more waxing," I whimpered and cowered away as I pulled up my pants. I must remember to tackle my own brows tonight, I thought.

"The doctor is also in this evening and actually has some free periods," she mentioned as she cleaned down her work area.

"Doctor? Doctor for what?" I said as I buttoned my jeans gently.

"The Botox doctor. She's amazing and, like I said, we've had a few cancellations due to the weather out there." She smiled and took her eyes right up to my forehead where her gaze rested for a minute too long.

I tried to remove my frown. "Do you think I need Botox?"

"Well, it's a very personal choice, I think. I mean, I get it done, but I had a constant frown-line in my forehead that always drove me nuts. You have some furrows here and here and here and here." With that she dragged her hand firstly over my forehead, then across my left eye, then across my right eye, then down both sides of my cheeks. "But nothing a bit of baby Botox couldn't sort out for you."

I looked at her forehead and sure enough it didn't move. "Frown," I asked her.

"You want me to frown?"

"Yeah, please. Imagine I had just told you your dog had died in a horrible road accident – imagine the local vegetable man ran over him in his delivery van – how would you react?"

She looked over her shoulder and then back at me – why did people keep doing this?

"Well, okay," she said and indeed her eyes did look droopy and sad but that was it, nothing else moved. I would never have guessed she was deeply upset.

"Brilliant," I said as I got my credit card out, "but not for me, thanks, anyway."

"Sure," she beamed. "Well, you can pay Sasha G at the till – and hope to see you again soon. Enjoy your holiday."

"Eh, my holiday? Yeah, I will, thanks!" I called after her as I paid Sasha G who was trying to sell me some spectacular wonder cream from behind her on the shelf.

I just kept on shaking my head and left the shop. I actually needed a holiday after all that.

Back to M&S for the battle of the outfits. I rummaged for ages and finally settled on three outfits to take to the dressing rooms. A black wraparound dress with a little silver trim on it – a flowy crimson skirt that came to just below the knee with a crossover white top that should look great with my new DD bra – and the last was my favourite but I knew it was a long shot. It had looked so amazing on the mannequin. I'd stood staring at it for ages before finally deciding to seek its components out on the shop floor. It was an above-the-knee light-denim skirt with gold buttons down the side, an army khaki-green shirt complete with epaulettes, thick green khaki tights and knee-high black suede boots. It was a look I really liked.

I stood in the huge queue and waited my turn patiently.

The sales assistant handed me a number on a stick and I found the free dressing room right down the back and pulled the curtain closed.

The black dress was good on and I was happy to see my

reflection was okay. The dress clung to my waist yet had enough excess material to drop kindly over my tummy. The magic knickers were working a treat, I thought, as I turned from side to side and saw no unwanted bulges. It was a possibility. The skirt wouldn't close on me so I didn't even bother to try on the top.

Now for my dream outfit. I said a silent prayer as I pulled the light-denim skirt up and it went over my thighs. Phase one, I told it quietly. I swirled it to the side and with bated breath put my index finger and thumb on the zipper. "Work with me here!" I told the zip. Slowly, very slowly, I eased it up and joy of joy it made it all the way! Super! I opened the buttons on the khaki shirt and eased my arms in. They went in okay. Now for the pesky buttons. It was the chest area that was the danger zone but this must have been my lucky day as the buttons closed with room to spare and I clenched my fist in the air. Victory! I did a little light dance on the spot. I'm sure this dressing-room saw more upset than happiness so I was glad for it too. Bending to put the khaki tights on was not so easy but I did it and then pulled on the suede boots easily before I stood upright to look at my reflection.

I was over the moon. It was the type of look I loved, a look that said 'thrown-together' (as though any outfit really thrown together could look that good!). It said casual yet dressy, it was bang up-to-date and I just loved it! I didn't even look at the price tags because that wasn't important to me. Once it fitted, that was all that mattered. Some day I wanted to open a shop called "If It Fits . . . Just Buy It!" It was somewhere *I* would shop. I looked again. I would wear this after work so this was the sight Paul would see when he picked me up from the train. I changed and made my way to the till, handing back the other two outfits to the girl on my way.

"May I have your loyalty card?" the girl asked and I shook my head. Loyalty cards, I just didn't see the point in them.

"That will be one hundred and sixty-nine euro, please," she said as she folded expertly.

Eeek! It was pricey and I didn't usually treat myself like that but it was worth every penny to me right then. I couldn't wait to show Carla.

The smells coming from all the different food areas was just too much after all that, so I gave in and sat down in Fargo's where I ordered a lasagne and chips with a Diet Coke and it was delicious. I dipped my chips into the tomato sauce as I studied the fashions on the big screen and watched the world go by. Was there anything in the world quite as satisfying as a successful shopping trip, I wondered as I sipped my Coke? I could hardly wait for tomorrow now.

12

The rain sleeted down the window as the train pulled into Belfast Central and I folded up my magazine. I got up. I loved trains. I pulled down my bag and took my seat again. So I was to go down the escalator, he said. I pulled out my Elizabeth Arden foundation compact and checked my reflection. All good. I slipped an Airwaves into my mouth. I felt like I was on some kind of adventure and in some way I was. I made my way off the train, down the platform and down the escalator and there it was – the white van. Paul's white van. And there with the paper spread out over the steering wheel was Paul (well, when I say 'paper' it was the *Sun*).

"Sweaty palms are back," I whispered to myself as I crossed over, magazine over my head, and tapped on the window.

He jumped then opened the door quickly. "Jeez, hey, you're early?" He looked at his watch.

"Don't think so," I said. "We were due in at eight twenty-two – pretty bang on time, I'd say."

He jumped out, put his arms around me and drew me in

against him. I nestled my head in his shoulder and breathed him in. It was still one of the sexiest smells I had ever smelled.

He took my bag. "Quick, hop in out of the rain, my lady," he said with a pretend bow.

We settled into our seats and he drove off.

"So you enjoying it up here?" I was much more comfortable now. I held onto my seat belt.

"It's a great city, you know. The people are so warm and so bloody funny! I really like it."

I gazed out the window at everyone rushing around. Friday night was a busy night in Belfast city.

We pulled into a cul de sac after a short time and Paul turned into a very regular redbrick at the end of it.

"Attic conversion," he said by way of explanation. There were rows of felt and wood carefully lined up at the side of the house. Once inside he put on some lamps and drew the curtains.

"It's cute." I dropped my bag and sat down.

"Love your shirt, Mia," he said as he returned from the kitchen, holding a bottle of wine and a can of Heineken. He weighed them both.

"Wine, please, and thanks for the shirt compliment but it's ancient – just threw it on before work this morning – sure it's grand, it'll do." Ah, I'd always wanted to say that. It felt great.

He poured me a large glass and handed me the wine. His huge body dwarfed me as he sat beside me.

"So, Mia, I think I owe you a bit of an explanation about what's going on with me."

He eased open the can of Heineken. The hissing sound filled the room and the strong beer scent filled my nostrils.

"If you want – I mean, I'm not asking." I wasn't. It was suddenly all very serious and I suddenly didn't want to know.

Once again I was feeling uncomfortable. I was like a rising temperature with this guy.

"Okay, well, it's like this. I'm married but separated. It's all very complicated right now so I have been under a lot of pressure. I like you, I really do, Mia, but I can't offer you much right now. I can't offer you what I think you might want." His eyes gazed into mine and he looked very calm and relaxed.

I should have guessed, I realised. "How long were you married?" I asked and, although I wasn't shocked, I was put out.

"Ah, it doesn't matter, does it? What is time anyway?" He was shifting on his seat now.

"I don't know what I want from you, Paul, to be honest. I really like you too but we've had some very dodgy moments together and we barely know each other . . . so . . ." I raised my glass and tipped it off the side of his can of Heineken. "So let's take this really slowly, let's just have fun and know where we both stand. I wasn't thinking marriage but I was wondering if we were seeing each other, like were we . . . oh God, I can't think of another word and, yes, I watch too much US TV . . . exclusive?"

He didn't speak.

"Really, Paul, that's all I need to know right now. I am sorry your marriage didn't work out, I really am, it must be so tough. One of my friends is going through what I consider a marriage breakdown and she is gutted over it. I mean no one goes into marriage lightly, do they? Well, she did it because she was pregnant, but you know."

"My wife was pregnant too," he nodded at me. "I was forced into marrying her really. Her father was a complete bully and threatened to do all sorts to me and to my family if I didn't do the right thing by her. We didn't even know each other. I was only seventeen, a virgin, hadn't a clue." He took a long drink.

"You were married at seventeen?"

"Yeah. She was seventeen too – teen bride – I mean, don't get me wrong, Mia, she does –" he corrected himself, "*did* all she could to make me happy and, believe me, I tried. Then when my son was born I just fell in love with him at first sight so I tried to make it work. But my wife and me – there was no chemistry there whatsoever. We were just going through the motions."

He had a son?

He couldn't stop talking now. "But her father was always breathing down my neck, watching my every move. When I set up my own company, work took me away for weeks on end and, apart from missing my son like crazy, it was great. I felt so free."

"So when did you separate?" I asked quietly.

"Ah Mia, years ago, weeks ago, months ago – she's determined not to let me go. I mean, I have sat her down and told her I am not happy but she keeps saying we can work it out." There was a ring at the door and I jumped out of my skin.

"Oh shit, the Chinese, I forgot! I took the liberty of ordering their meal deal for two – bit tacky, I know, but hey, that's me!" He dragged himself up and I went to my bag to find my purse

"Please," he said, "this is on me."

I took a deep breath after he left the room. I sort of felt relieved, as I had known all along there was something wrong – all that flying off the handle, the snappiness – there had to be baggage. At least he had opened up to me. I mean, I'd rather he wasn't separated with a son but he was and that was that. At my age it wasn't unusual to meet a man with baggage. Not that I considered kids 'baggage' but that was the word everyone used, wasn't it?

Chatting openly with him like this should have been all I wanted, but I felt uneasy.

I stood up to shake the feeling. I looked around. The house had very old carpet and very old furniture. I listened to Paul making small talk with the delivery man. The place was slightly musty. All done in greens and browns. It badly needed a facelift. I ran my finger over the top of the mantelpiece and it was covered in dust. I sat back down and fixed my ever-decreasing skirt. It wasn't made for sitting on a low couch in, that was for sure – especially not in elasticated knickers that came halfway down my thighs.

I wondered what his ex-wife was thinking now? What she would say if she knew he was here in Belfast with another woman? I wondered how long ago he moved out of the family home? He had a seventeen-year-old son – wow, that was crazy! Just like Anita, I thought, as I fixed the cushion behind my back. Just like Anita, I said again. "Anita." The name formed on my lips this time.

"Here we go, fit for a king!" He had silver containers stacked on top of each other and he was hopping them up and down. Obviously boiling hot.

"Oh shit, sorry!" I jumped up and helped him with half of the hot load.

He opened the door to the kitchen and I gasped. He had the most romantic table laid out. A red linen tablecloth with six small red candles in a circle in the middle of the table, six red roses in a crystal vase, a wine bucket with a bottle of Moët, two champagne glasses, plates, red napkins and silver cutlery.

"Oh Paul! That's so gorgeous! Thank you for doing this for me."

I carefully laid the food cartons on the countertop. I leaned over and we kissed fully on the lips. I pulled away but he dropped his cartons beside mine, not quite so carefully, and pulled me back.

We stared into each other's eyes before we locked lips in full-on passion. He pulled roughly at my khaki shirt, sending two buttons pinging off, but I didn't care. He unzipped my skirt and it fell to the ground, leaving my hold-it-in in full view. I pulled his T-shirt over his head and unbuttoned his jeans, our lips never leaving each other's which I was glad about as he didn't actually see the knickers. I decided to take this matter into my own hands right now – I pulled my own knickers down and kicked them away – hopefully far away.

He groaned. "Mia, you're so filthy!" He lifted me then into his strong arms and sat me bare-arsed on the freezing countertop before he entered me quickly and passionately. He was now at my neck as he thrust away, eating my earlobe and moaning.

I sighed deeply, my breath fierce on his face. "Oh Paul, do you have a condom?" I had to stop him.

"Oh shit! I'm so sorry, Mia!" He withdrew. "Hang on."

He bent down, picked up his jeans and removed his wallet while I obediently sat on the counter knickerless but with a pretty bra on and sucking in for dear life. He removed a condom and handed it to me to open.

"Will you put it on?" he asked as his mouth found mine again, rough and hard, his stubble cutting into my face.

"Sure."

I tore at the small packet and took out the rubbery matter. I slid off the counter, reached for his very erect penis and tried my best to be sexy while trying to get an elephant into a mousehole. I just couldn't do it. I was starting to sweat, the smell of rubber now engulfing my nostrils. He took over and rolled it down in one easy swoop. The pressure was off me and I was going to enjoy myself now. He lifted me onto the counter again and entered me. I kissed him hard and we had mad passionate amazing sex for the next – oh, six minutes! When he came he flopped his head onto my shoulder and then dropped his head onto my lap. I rubbed his head as our breathing slowed down.

I had enjoyed it intensely but it was all over a bit too quickly for me.

"Sorry," he said, "I couldn't stop myself."

"Don't be stupid! It was, well, fantastic!" I told him and actually I wasn't lying. It *was* fantastic – quick, but fantastic none the less.

We dressed and I was really grateful that I could pull my skirt up first and then sneak the knickers up underneath. However, my casual, dressy shirt was ruined and I hadn't the heart to search the floor for the buttons even though every inch of my being really wanted to.

"I'm just popping upstairs to change my shirt."

"Oh fuck, I wrecked it, didn't I?" He was tying the laces on his Adidas red-and-white runners.

"Not at all!"

I collected my bag from the front room and ran up the stairs and into the room straight ahead. I ran the brush through my hair and put on my old favourite Karen Millen top. He'd seen it before but I was one hundred per cent sure that he didn't remember. I was also bursting to pee. The downstairs loo was practically in the kitchen and I usually peed really loudly so I popped into the upstairs one and peed freely. Normally I considered it rude or nosy to use an upstairs toilet in a stranger's house – I don't know why, something my mother had engrained into my head, I supposed. When we were younger none of our friends were ever allowed up the sacred stairs.

"I have *The Hangover* on DVD if you fancy watching that after dinner?" he shouted up.

"Sure!" I shouted back down. Why did people insist on talking to me while I was on the toilet?

We ate the reheated-in-the-microwave Chinese food (never good) at the beautiful table and drank champagne and laughed. It was a really nice meal, with sweet and sour, spicy, black-bean dishes all thrown into the mix and the Moët as always made me giggle. I tried to eat a little slower as most of my food was gobbled up before his plate was even half-empty. It was a fun and relaxing meal.

When we moved in to watch the DVD, we laughed hard as the gang in the film tried to piece together the events of the night before. Been there, boys, I thought. *Bridesmaids* was still way better though.

"So, Mia, how come you haven't been snapped up yet?" he murmured into my ear.

I looked up and the light caught his dark eyes.

"Dunno, really, Paul. You know, time-old story – I just haven't met the right guy." I snapped my fingers and he laughed.

"And what kind of guy is that?"

"Well, honestly, just someone who is kind and loyal and truthful. Someone who I fall in love with. I have never had a 'type' really."

"So money isn't important to you then?"

"God no, never! Money doesn't come into it at all with me," I answered honestly.

"But you chose a profession that's very money-oriented." He spooned a chicken ball into his mouth.

"It wasn't about money and quick riches – property, that is

– when I got into it. It was honestly only about a roof over your head. Then the Celtic Tiger hit and everyone was borrowing fistfuls of money for houses even Simon Cowell could barely afford. So for me it was just a job out of school – that's it."

"But surely that's not the case with Carla. I mean, she's in it for the money, right? The sporty Mini, the house in Ranelagh, the posh boyfriend from Killiney. The attitude. She thinks she has it all, that one."

"You really don't like her, do you, Paul?" I put my glass down hard on the small coffee table.

"Oh, don't start!" He waved his napkin at me. "I know that temper of yours! A nice harmless conversation will turn into a blazing row and I'll be chasing you down the Falls Road!"

I linked my hands together. "I am a very calm person, Paul, but I don't like my friends being insulted, that's all. Carla just happens to be my best friend."

"Really?" He was genuinely surprised.

"Why do you say it like that?" I asked.

"She just seems so fake, I dunno, so not like you. You're so down-to-earth – opposites attract, I suppose."

"You don't know her at all, Paul. I mean, you only ever did business together and who is ever honest in business, eh?" He could really rile me, I thought, as I sat upright now, grabbed my glass off the table and gulped the champagne down.

"Okay, okay, sorry, touchy subject." He moved away from me.

"And for your information she has split with James who turned out to be an incredible tosspot!"

He laughed at this.

"So, tell me about *your* best friend if he's so, so incredibly faultless and wonderful. Is it one of those idiots you were with in the Palace with sambuca all over their hands?" I challenged him. "This faultless Wonder of the World!" I poured more champagne into my glass now and it fizzed over the edge as I gulped it down. "This super friend of all friends that doesn't have any faults, Mr Perfect Friend!"

His eyes clouded over and he looked sad, then he looked straight at me. "Honestly, Mia, my best friend in the whole world is my son." He smiled. "He's everything to me, but he's in no way perfect . . . any more."

"What do you mean 'any more'?" I asked.

"Well, he *was* perfect but his stupid fucking mother bought him a Claddagh Ring for his Debs, and he jumped off a dumper and pulled his fucking finger off."

"What? What?" I jumped up and knocked my glass off the table. "*What, Paul, what?*"

"What the fuck?" He looked at me and grabbed the glass off the ground as I was about to trample on it.

I thought I was going to throw up. "No, surely, Paul – no way!"

"Sit down, will ya, what's wrong? Is it the finger?"

"No, Paul, seriously, I need a glass of water." I could feel my paleness.

He ran to the sink and handed me a glass of cold water. I gulped it down.

"Paul, is your wife's name Anita?" I could not believe I was asking him this.

He stared hard at me, confusion darting all over his face now. "Yeah," he said.

"I know her. She's my friend," I croaked before tears ran down my face. I collapsed onto the couch now, skirt up around my backside and it all ran through my mind like a freight train. What Anita had said about her husband, what kind of a man he was, what I was doing to them, to the kids, the affair . . . I thought I was going to have a panic attack. What a stupid eejit you are, I repeated over and over in my head.

"How do you mean she's your fucking friend?" He was on his knees now, leaning on the table in front of me, his eyes wide with shock.

Separated, my arse, I thought as I saw the panic rise in him.

"I work with Anita," I managed to say. I felt sick to the pit of my stomach.

"What do you mean you work with her? Are you gone mental? Anita sells encyclopaedias! *You* work in an auctioneer's!"

"No!" I shouted now. "She *used* to sell them alright but now she works with me, and Carla, and you have a three-year-old daughter called Katie too, don't you?"

Now it was his turn to hyperventilate. He went a whiter shade of pale. "Oh shit!" He pulled himself up, the body slow and bent.

I was having an affair with Anita's husband. I knew I was a bit slow on the uptake at times but how had I missed that one? I had just had sex with Anita's husband. For the second time. How on God's green earth had I not seen this?

"She can't know this!" I said suddenly. "It would kill her."

"It's not the first time," he muttered meekly.

"But I bet it's the fucking first time her so-called friend had shagged her husband, don't you?" Anita's face came into my mind now, on the horse in Lahinch, full of hope. "And what are you playing at anyway?" I shouted at him now. "You aren't separated at all, are you, Paul? You're still living at home, she said. She said," I was remembering quick and fast, "she said you don't give her reliable child support and you have had an affair before, you big brave man!" I spat the words at him and went to leave the room but he blocked me off at the door, eyes blazing, and now for the first time I was scared.

"Don't presume that all she says is true! There are always two sides to every story. I already told you I'm not in love with her, I haven't been for years and years but she won't let me go! She didn't even tell me she had a new job, for fuck's sake!"

"Oh, bullshit!" I yelled in his face. I couldn't help myself. "She can't keep you there! You're a grown man! You're just too afraid to leave her, admit it – you want your cake and want to eat it, or to fuck it I should say! Are you still having sex with her?"

I wanted to go but the thought of setting off home was daunting – I was in a strange city and I didn't navigate strange cities well at this hour of the night. The rain was still beating down outside.

I ran up the stairs to shut myself away into a bedroom until the morning but he followed me.

"You *knew* there was something in my past – you must have!" he yelled.

I swung around at the top of the stairs. "But it's *not* in your past, that's the point!" I shouted in his face.

"Whatever! But, I mean, you never asked me any questions, you just went along with everything, and I thought that you must have decided to just go with the flow."

"Go with the flow?" I stared at him.

We were both silent now standing at the top of the stairs. What if he throws me down and kills me? What if this is all too much and he needs to kill me so I won't tell his wife? No one knows where I am. I took my voice back down.

"Okay, Paul, I'm freaking out here and my mind is running away with me. What are we going to do?"

"What is there to do, Mia? We have to just forget it, okay?" He put his hand on my shoulder and gripped it tightly.

I looked into his eyes. "Forget what? Us? Or forget that this ever happened?" I didn't even know what I was asking any more. I was delirious. I tried to think straight but couldn't.

"Listen to me." He put his hands on either side of my face now. It wasn't in an affectionate way by any means. "I'm in a bit of a bind here now, love. I don't know how to get out of it. I have responsibilities to my kids, especially now after Stevie's accident. I'm not evil and I'm not a prick. I just don't know what to do any more. But one thing's for sure, you can't tell her, Mia." He thought hard for a few seconds before the tears came into his eyes and dropped down his cheek. He rubbed them away.

I didn't believe them. "Okay, Paul. It's okay." I didn't know if I meant it but all I could see was this man in panic. It was completely and utterly unsettling. And here I was, the brazen mistress.

He sobbed louder now. "It's been so tough, what with Stevie's accident, then that bitch kicking me off the job when we had no VHI. I do give her money, I do pay the bills when I have it, but I have to sort my head out so I need my own space. She said she understood that. I need my own place." He was studying me intently to see if I was buying this performance.

I thought again of Anita and how she'd die if she knew what was happening right now, if she heard him speak those words. Less than two months ago I didn't know either of these people, I was fine, I was getting along and now I was right bang-slap in the middle of their marriage. Only you, Mia, I thought, only you!

I stood there for ages as his sobbing slowed down and we were silent.

He was petrified I would tell her yet I didn't know why – after all, he'd done it all before.

After what felt like ages he pulled himself together and went into the bathroom. I heard him blow his nose and then he came out.

"This wasn't exactly the night I had planned." He had a wry smile.

"I can't stay with you – in the same room, I mean, I just can't."

He nodded. "Do you want me to take you to a hotel?"

"No, I'll just crash in a spare room if that's okay? I think we should both go to bed, Paul. I don't know what else to say to you."

"Are you going to tell her?"

I couldn't make out if it was fear or just interest behind the tone of his voice. I shrugged my shoulders.

"So is this it? Is it over between us, Mia?" He opened the door for me and I went into the room with the small single bed.

"In your flat in Rathmines," I turned to him, "you had a picture of you and a woman on the Eiffel Tower – was that her?"

"Yeah, that was her thirtieth."

"It has to be over, I mean, how can it not be?"

He shrugged his shoulders.

"You're not in love with me, are you?" I questioned him, knowing quite well what his answer would be.

"I think I am, you know, but I think it's for the best if we call it quits." He stood in the open door.

I knew if he could have run down the stairs, out the door and all the way home to Anita and his kids right now, he would have.

This couldn't have happened to a nicer guy, I thought, as I said, "I can't handle this right now" and closed the door in his face.

I flopped onto the bed and pulled off my boots. I really wanted to ring Carla but I always did that when something big happened to me – I always blabbed and blabbed and more often than not I wished I had slept on it. This was my problem and she had been through enough lately. Paul was Anita's husband, he was the father of two children, a father to Anita's two children. He had a family. Even with all the things she had told us about him, she hadn't made him sound so awful, and he was awful, wasn't he? Or was he just not in a happy marriage? Just like Dad, I thought, and my mouth fell open. I had always cursed women like me, women who allowed themselves to carry on affairs with married men. Women who wrecked people's lives. But I hadn't known. Had Angela known Dad was married or had she simply fallen in love with him and then he told her? I didn't even know if I was ever in love with Paul but I knew he was never in love with me, so how had I been so thick?

I got into bed and pulled the duvet up over my head. It didn't smell so good. I was itchy. I was parched but couldn't risk him talking to me again. I closed my eyes and begged for sleep to come. My skin stung from the tears that had fallen onto my mass of make-up. My mind was spinning at a hundred miles an hour. I honestly didn't know what to do for the best. I wasn't trying to protect my feelings but I was trying to protect poor Anita and I didn't know the best way to do that. A tear slid down my face. She didn't deserve any of this. I just wished I was transported out of here. What kind of person was I? I shouldn't be here after what I just found out, I knew that. I eventually fell into a fitful sleep.

I awoke early and had to go downstairs for a drink. My tongue was stuck to the roof of my mouth. I had no idea of the address where I was so I couldn't even call a taxi. I could walk out onto the road and hail one, I thought. I hadn't made up my mind what to do next. Paul was still in bed. I put the kettle on and dug the train timetable out of my bag. There was one at lunchtime that I wanted to be on. I made a cup of tea after I found the dregs of a bottle of milk and a cup and teabag. I sat at the table waiting for him to wake up. I wondered how many women he'd had in this house? I shivered as I remembered him being inside me for those seconds without protection.

It was bitterly cold so I went up to wake him. I had decided I needed to speak with him before I left.

He was out for the count. No problems sleeping there, I noticed.

"Paul!" I shook him. "I need to go. Shall I get a taxi or can you drop me to the train station, please?"

"What? Oh, what time is it?"

"Midday."

He stretched his bare arms up over his head and they knocked against the wooden headboard. "Yeah, sure, hang on." He reached for my hand and I pulled it away.

"I'll be downstairs," I said and left.

A while later I could hear his van keys jangling as he stood at the front door.

"Are you ready?" Then a big yawn.

"Yeah." I grabbed my bag and we went out to the van.

"So did you come up with any answers? What are you going to do?" he asked as we headed out onto the main road, wipers working overtime as the rain pelted off the windscreen.

"I don't know, I'm still not sure. I don't think I can tell her though." I rubbed the condensation from the inside of the window.

"You don't *think* so?" he sniffed. "Listen, I need to know

for definite if you're going to tell her or not." He stared straight ahead.

"I don't know, Paul, I haven't a clue what I'm going to do."

"Okay, have it your way, but as far as I'm concerned this never happened."

I was truly lost for words as he almost broke every red light and I clung onto my seat in sheer fright. He pulled up outside the station, braking sharply.

"I can't park here so you have to hop out quick," he told me and I obeyed.

He drove away immediately and I stood there watching the tail of the white van disappear. The van that had once excited me repulsed me now.

Inside the station I plonked down in the small restaurant and I bought a full Irish breakfast – microwaved but I didn't care. I asked for extra toast and wolfed it all down with tea before the gate opened for my platform. I handed my ticket to the guy and headed down to Platform 2 where the train was ready and waiting.

Saturday was busy and the train was full. I listened to a group of excited Belfast teenagers heading to Dublin to the O2 to see JLS. Ah, the simple life! I envied them. How was I going to go into work on Monday? How could I face Anita? I had to tell Carla, I really had to talk to someone. I needed advice. But I knew exactly what Carla would say. Tell Anita. Tell Anita. Tell Anita. And I just knew I couldn't. I wasn't ready for that yet. So I had to keep this awful secret to myself for the time being. I'd never hear from him again. I knew that much. Come on, Mia, I whispered to myself, think about what you two had. Nothing. It was never real. How has he ever shown you that he liked you? He's had sex twice with you. Oh well, then it must be love! You idiot. There were no other signs. The trip to Glendalough? He knew it was a hotel job once he got you there, thicko. Okay then, the romantic table last night, he didn't have to do that. Seduction, thicko. It was a horrible feeling in the pit of my stomach.

I must pull myself together. I had a really busy few weeks ahead in the run-up to Christmas and I had people relying on me like Peadar and Damien – and Gordon, I needed to make a decision on Gordon too.

"Head down, Mia," I whispered to myself as I opened my *OK* magazine and read about everyone else's fecked-up lives. Aha, I wasn't the only one, I said to Kerry Katona.

I bought a coffee from the trolley and gazed out the window. What would this Christmas be like? I hadn't given Mam's words about moving in with her a serious thought. I really hadn't, it just wasn't an option. But I got an ache in my chest every time I thought of her turning out the living-room light and heading up that staircase on her own to bed. God, I didn't want to end up lonely – or lonely and bitter, that was even worse. I sipped the foul-tasting coffee again. Then the thought struck me like a hurley stick to the head. Buy A House. But I had no money. Neither had anyone else. If I could work my butt off and make loads of commission, I could get a little house somewhere in Meath or in Kildare and it would be mine. It was time I had my own place, time I looked after myself, time Mia Doyle was independent.

"Aahhhh, Mia, what are ya like?" I stopped. I had spoken out loud without realising and the group of girls all burst out laughing.

I knew what I would do. I would let things settle for a while. I would write a letter to Anita immediately, as soon as I got in the door, explaining it all, how I didn't have a clue, how I felt like the worst soul alive, how I just couldn't face hurting her more, how I had thought I was probably in love with Paul but how I was now feeling. I would put it away in my drawer along with that day's newspaper until I had made a decision.

13

I put my head right down (literally) for the next two weeks before the Christmas break. I was quiet as a mouse and couldn't bear to look at Anita. She kept enquiring if I was alright, that I seemed distant, had she done something to offend me? Ha! Had she done something to offend me? Give me a laugh.

I was so guilt-ridden I felt physically sick and couldn't eat.

I felt guilty but I also felt abused.

But there's never an ill wind and all that – I was in the mood to cut through all bullshit and that gave me the guts to deal with the Mam-and-Samantha problem. I called a family meeting. I told them in no uncertain terms that I was not moving back home but that obviously I was worried about Mam so what could we do?

I suggested getting someone in to do some home help and Mam nearly flipped the lid. "I am not a cripple!" she shouted at me.

"I don't think you can say 'cripple' any more," I told her so she wouldn't say it in public and embarrass herself.

"Why won't you move in?" Samantha started at me again.

"Because I can't, I have a life, I work late nights, I go out, I need my own space. I'm an adult for God's sake. I just don't want to live at home."

"But Mam's great, she doesn't ask any questions."

"No, because you are the Golden Child, you do no wrong – you get up, go to work, come home, eat your dinner and go to bed. I'm not like that. I'm all over the place, Samantha. Sometimes I go out for a few drinks, things like that, I come home drunk and I bring home take-away food."

Mam's eyes rolled to heaven now and she blessed herself, twice. "Them Chineses will be the death of you late at night!"

"Listen!" I finally threw my hands into the air. "I am *not* moving in and *that* is *that*!"

I slammed the door as I left.

To make things worse at the office, Dominic and Debbie had their heads down doing an audit on the books, and Carla was away – so it really was just myself and Anita.

Carla was in Westport on a five-house sale – five new builds, detached, in a cul de sac, which could not be moved until she took them on. Carla was in negotiations with a well-known health spa nearby to buy the properties and let them out as extra accommodation. Carla also had a deal with a local department store to supply cosy bathrobes, slippers, candles, bath salts etc for the "pamper houses" as she had now christened them.

"Are you looking forward to our Christmas party?" Anita asked as we headed off to show a house in Malahide.

I was grateful for the bad weather because it meant I couldn't take my eyes off the road. It had been sleeting for a week now and it suited my mood.

I eased the gears into fourth and said, "Yeah, I'm sure it will be nice."

Dominic had organised Kris Kringle (naturally I got Anita) in the office with champagne, followed by drinks at the Four Seasons in Ballsbridge in the Ice Bar.

Anita was very excited about this. "The Ice Bar!" she had squealed in delight. "How posh!"

But the best bit was it was bring-a-partner if you wanted. Carla had not surprisingly asked Tim and I knew what was coming next.

"So are you inviting anyone special?" asked Anita now. "That boyfriend you were telling us about in Lahinch?" She laughed quietly.

"No, Anita, I don't really think so." I had to ask but the words lodged in my throat. "Are you?" I managed.

"Well," I could feel her eyes burrow into me as we turned onto the Clontarf Road to awful traffic, "you won't believe this but I have a feeling all is going to be okay with my husband. He's been like a different man recently – attentive, at home all the time, fantastic with the kids – he even took Katie to Imaginosity on his own and they came home delighted with themselves." She cleared her throat. "He seems, I dunno, different since he came back from his job up north. It's like he's had a change of heart, like he missed us – he even bought me flowers. Oh Mia, it's all I want, really it is. I know I'm pathetic but I have one life and it's only a happy life when I have him. I think we were meant to be, I really do."

I beeped loudly as a man in a BMW jeep cut in front of me. "Asshole!" I yelled, raising a finger. Anything to break this conversation up right now.

"Mia, are you okay?" She was trying to mouth an apology to the furious driver.

"Sorry, yeah, fine. I just know that Gary and Mandy O'Donoghue are sticklers for time." They were lawyers and they billed by the hour.

"So, what do you think then? About my husband?" She wasn't going to drop it.

"That's great, really great." 'Please, please, please say no more,' I chanted over and over in my head.

"So is he coming to the Christmas party with you?" The words were out before my brain registered them. This time I did look at her. I could tell the answer before the terrible words left her mouth. Her eyes said it all.

"Yes. He is."

What the fuck? What was going on here? What was he playing at? I hadn't heard a single word from him since I left Belfast over two weeks ago. Nothing. In love with me, my arse! What was he playing at here?

"He's gorgeous, you know!" she went on. "I mean, you wouldn't believe it looking at me that I had a gorgeous husband."

I realised I had driven, well, inched along in the traffic, with no recollection of it whatsoever.

"You know, the way you and Carla fall all over that Don Draper from *Mad Men*, especially you trying to lick the screen that night like Carla told me – hilarious! Well, I think he looks a bit like him!"

I made a noise, a sort of gurgle in the back of my throat. We pulled in at a stunning five-bed detached in Malahide. I'd had it on my books for over three months but just knew there was a couple out there who would bite, so I kept on at the owners to give me more time before I dropped the price. Time was running out for me as they were getting desperate to sell.

They were waiting – impatiently as I expected. I shook their hands as did Anita and I let us into the oak white pebble-dashed house.

It was still on at one million euro and it was worth every

penny. I had been here several times over the last few months but it never ceased to take my breath away. It wasn't Shrewsbury Road but it was a magnificent house. The property had three storeys and was two thousand seven hundred square feet. Of the five bedrooms two of them were en-suite and the master bedroom was fitted with a walk-in wardrobe. Every human comfort had been catered for with no expense spared. The living room was all walnut wooden floors with a polished stone fireplace and a gas log fire. The sunroom was complete with tiled floors, ceiling speakers and double doors out to the patio area. The kitchen-cum-breakfast area had Mirari wall and floor units, black granite worktops and my favourite Kuppers Bush appliances including an American-style fridge (oh, I so wanted one of those fridges one day!). This house was bright and inviting and it really offered the ultimate in space and practicality.

Anita was on fire today, I thought, as she removed her coat to reveal a lovely turquoise polo-necked dress. She hadn't removed her coat in the office that morning as we were running late so I hadn't noticed. Her figure was amazing in the dress. She was smiley and open as she walked the couple around this three-storey executive home.

"See," she gestured all around her, "it's designed to take full advantage of sunshine and light. Spectacular, isn't it?" She paused and took a long deep breath, as though she was breathing in the house. The way you would take in a perfect day at the beach, with bright cloudless blue skies and still blue waters. "Gary, Mandy, you can both rest assured that not only will you get a quality home built to exacting and high standards but you will also be located in one of Dublin's premier residential areas." She paused. "Coffee?"

It had been her idea to buy a small kettle, cups, coffee, tea and biscuits for our viewings. This way we didn't use any of the client's belongings yet could offer that homely cuppa.

They accepted and wandered around, muttering to each other, while we made it.

When we were all armed with cups and bickies, they told us they really liked the house . . . but . . .

"Listen, girls, they have to come down on the price." Mark blew into the hot liquid.

"They can't budge." I crossed my arms and stood firm as I felt Anita eye me closely. Oh don't do this, I thought, don't undermine me here.

"Mia, perhaps we could put another call in?"

Sweet Jesus, was she for real? I was livid. "Em, right. We can but try. Anita – let's go and discuss strategy." I smiled at her through gritted teeth.

We removed ourselves to the hall, shutting the door behind us.

"I know what you're going to say," Anita said, wringing her fingers together. "It's just, Mia, I've been on this case all week and I've studied this market so closely while you were on the Sandymount House. Did you know there are now two other houses within a hundred yards of this, fresh on the market with Sactt Auctioneers and they are up for nine-hundred-thousand euros?"

"What?"

"Seriously, I mean it. I think if we can close this at nine today the clients will be delirious."

I leaned back against the wall. Suddenly I didn't care again. This was always my problem. I went through weeks of giving it all and then one day the grind was just too much and I packed it all in. Same old Mia.

"Go on then," I suggested and she started to walk away.

"No, wait, hang on!" I pulled her back. "Stay here, give me one last shot and then it's all yours."

She nodded.

I strolled back into the living room. I wasn't a shark, but this house was worth way over a million and I owed it to my clients to get this for them. This was my job after all. It was one part of my life I could try and do right. Gary and Mandy were smiling.

"So?" he asked. "Did they drop?"

"Listen, guys, not great news, I'm afraid. I just got off the phone with my clients and they have an offer on the table for one million – so I'm afraid that's that."

I unplugged the kettle and started to roll the flex. This couple could well afford it.

"Oh, Gary!" Mandy was visually upset.

Bingo! I said to myself. B.I.N.G.O.

"Well, hang on there, Mia," said Gary. "I mean, we have looked at the house three times – we're very interested." He had his arm around Mandy in her mink jacket (whether or not it was fake or real I honestly couldn't tell).

"Oh I know, Mark," I said, "and with your little girl in the local crèche and both your offices in Malahide village it was perfect for you guys." Putting the cups away now as slowly as I could.

"Wait." He was beside me. "Ring them back, offer them one point one million euro but I want it off the market right now."

"I will indeed, Mr O'Donoghue. If you'll excuse me for another moment, please?"

I strutted back out into the hall, closing the door behind me.

Anita was smiling. "Well, fireball?"

And I laughed now too.

I made a pretend call and then the two of us joined the new owners of The Oaks in the living room.

I dropped Anita back at the office at the end of the day.

"I'm meeting Peadar and Damien now in The Front Lounge to show them some brochures so I'll say bye-bye for today."

I was relieved to be away from her and I wanted to call Paul as soon as humanly possible while she was still in work. As I drove into town I dialled his number. "*The person you are calling may have their mobile powered off.*" Hmmm, he usually had a voice-message service.

So he went back to her. I flicked the windscreen wipers on as the day darkened. Was this guy for real? I had to get him before the Christmas party, that was for sure. I put on some music until I hit town.

The boys were in a quiet corner under the Christmas tree when I joined them with the brochures. They both were wearing green shirts and black trousers.

"Are you two blending in with the decorations?" I laughed as I sat back in the large black sofa.

"Hey," Damien said and I immediately knew something was wrong.

"Hey," I said back as I saw him take Peadar's hand.

"Have you found us anywhere yet, Mia?" Damien asked rather breathlessly.

"Damien, the poor woman! Would you give her a second to chillax!" Peadar laughed.

He picked up his huge glass of red wine and took a long gulp. I noticed his hand was shaking.

"Well, yeah, I have a great property in Sandymount I think you'd both love." I passed the brochure to Damien.

"Is it in our price bracket?" He hadn't even looked at the picture.

"Damien . . ." Peadar rubbed his thumb over the other man's hand.

The waiter came over and I ordered a latte.

"What's up, guys?" I asked then.

They looked at each other.

"It's just, Mia, that I'm not so well, you see." Peadar sat forward now. "I haven't been very well for a while really but . . . well, I'm not going to get any better, ever, let's put it that way." He forced a big bright smile.

"Why? What's the matter with you?" I was never one for decorum.

He cleared his throat. "I have cancer." He suddenly seemed very pale under the tanned skin.

"Oh Peadar!" I exhaled.

Damien leaned forward now and picked up his coffee cup.

"Yeah, Mia, I'm afraid I do, like it or lump it," Peadar laughed. "I have to face it. So that's why Damien's a bit over-eager to get us our place. You see, I'm refusing chemo or any hospital care so my angel here has agreed to take a leave of absence to care for me."

Jesus, I couldn't speak.

"So, Mia, we really need you to help us as quickly as possible," Damien said.

"What kind of cancer?" Again my mouth didn't think before I spoke.

"'Colon' one word. Or –" he put on a posh voice now and raised his glass, "colorectal cancer if you want to use the correct terminology. Colorectal cancer can be detected and diagnosed using a combination of tests, including a faecal occult blood test, a colonoscopy, virtual colonoscopy and/or a barium

X-ray of the colon." He laughed, obviously repeating what he knew only too well now, but the laugh was caught in his throat. "You see, Mia, my colorectal cancer has gone beyond the okay stage and has spread outside the colon. Treatment may require a combination of surgery, chemotherapy, and radiation therapy. I have been there before, I have seen that all before – I nursed my own grandfather and then my father through the same cancer. My father took every medical treatment available and there is no way I am going through that, for it all to end up the same way in the end." He drank long and hard.

"There is wonderfully successful treatment, with a fantastic success rate he can have but he won't!" Damien suddenly blurted out, sounding quite angry now, his voice shaking.

"We have been over and over this, Dames." Peadar stared hard at Damien and Damien closed his eyes and after a few seconds nodded his head.

My latte arrived and I picked it up with a visibly shaking hand.

"Peadar and I are okay, Mia, you know we really are." Damien put his hand on my shoulder. "I have to respect his decision. I have talked to him until I am blue in the face but, as the weeks have gone by, he won't budge, and I may be wasting precious time." He folded his hands together. "Okay, Mission for Mia: we need to sort our home as soon as possible. We need some special features now for our new home. I want enough space downstairs for a bed for Peadar if I have to move him downstairs," he paused, "long term. And I want a view of a park or other green area upstairs and downstairs for him." He nodded now at Peadar who nodded back. "I'm sorry Mia, this isn't pleasant for you but you are our friend, right?"

"Yes, of course, totally – it goes without saying that I'll do whatever I can, and that also goes for after I get you the house of your dreams. I'd like to be around to help in any way I can."

"See, I told you!" Peadar smacked Damien playfully on the knee. "She's a keeper. I knew my pudding would get her in the end!"

We went through my bunch of brochures, some way out of their price range that I had brought for a laugh, and then some they could afford. It was the Sandymount house I hoped they would love and they did. They fell in love with it as soon as they saw the pictures – the small redbrick two-up two-down, snuggled between a chemist's and an organic food shop and facing onto Sandymount Green. Its downstairs had been a hardware shop run by a delightful old couple for over forty years, but it was all revamped now and I loved it.

"When can we see it?" Peadar asked.

I lifted my bag and dangled a set of keys in front of them.

"Mia, it's after six – you don't have to do this now," said Damien.

"I would like to," I said.

We finished our drinks and made our way to my car and on down to Sandymount. It was such a miserable evening and the rain was pelting down as I parked in front of the house. The smell of freshly cooking chips from the nearby Borzas Chipper wafted through the air and I loved it. It was comforting. We opened the door to Number 141 and closed the horrible night out. I flicked on the switch. They had kept the really old switches and I thought they were fantastic.

A very small hallway led into a nice-sized living room with a white door closing off the small but neat kitchen. There was also a downstairs toilet, which had once been an outhouse and was now cleverly covered and attached to the back of the house. The small winding stairway led up to the two upstairs bedrooms. The front bedroom was what we all wanted to see and I opened the door slowly. The view almost took my breath away as I had never been there at night. The view of the park was even better than by day. It was subtly lit and silhouetted in the frame of the window. It reminded me of olden times, of years gone by. You could see the passersby so clearly but if you looked closely you could also see the white angry waves of the sea in the background.

"Perfect!" Damien clapped his hands as Peadar fell onto the bed.

"It is, isn't it?" he said as he stared up and out of the window.

And it was. It just was. A sense of peace fell over the room. I can't explain it, it was special.

"Who fancies a bag of chips?" Peadar piped up and we all agreed.

"First, though, Mia, can we get it, do you think?"

"I guarantee I'll do everything in my 'Mia Power'," I quoted with my fingers here, "to get this house for you, no matter what. You have to trust me on this. In fact, I am so confident that tomorrow I'll even book Jack, who works with us, to bring his van to your apartment to move all your stuff out as soon as we get the go-ahead."

"Are you serious?" Peadar asked as he jumped off the bed, suddenly full of life again.

What was I saying here? I looked down at the real fireplace that was in perfect working order and then back up at the guys.

"What about the price, you loon?" Damien asked me. "The paperwork and all the hidden fees, the solicitors and all that shit?"

"Oh we'll do that, Damien, stop fretting. You have five

hundred thousand, right? I know that. I'll make that work, believe me. All you need to do now is to concentrate on making your new home 'home'."

We got into a group hug and then I went with Damien to get three bags of chips and two smoked cod. Peadar's appetite didn't stretch to the fish. We bought some freshly baked organic bread and got milk, teabags and sugar. We sat at the kitchen table and had the most delicious fish-and-chip butties and sweet tea and I hoped to God I had made them a promise I could keep.

14

"Then he just clicked the top of his Gold Mont Blanc and signed!" Carla was back and delighted with herself in her sleek black business suit, hair scraped back into a bun, with silver earrings, as I sat curled up on the couch in my Penney's pyjamas eating a pick 'n' mix.

"Delighted for you," I smiled at her and stuffed a refresher into my mouth. The cheap fizz made my face contort wildly.

"Pretty!" Carla pulled a face at me and removed her jacket. "So how was the rest of your week?" She was zipping down her boots now and rubbing her feet.

"Oh, you know, mental." I chewed.

"Really? Open-a-bottle mental?" She nodded at the kitchen.

"Oh, yes, please, my little friend!" I swallowed, closed the enormous bag and followed her barefoot into the kitchen.

"By the way, my surgery is scheduled for January tenth, thanks goodness," she told me as she opened a bottle of red, the cork popping out easily.

"That's great!" I reached for two glasses and we headed back inside.

The heating was on full blast as it was so cold out.

I was genuinely delighted she was taking that stuff out of her body. I was all for reconstructive surgery and, believe it or not, I wasn't even against boob jobs per se, if it was really right for that person, but I had always knows it was not right for Carla. It wasn't her.

"Tim's going to come with me so you'll be spared this time." She poured the wine.

"Oohhh, like that, is it?" I tucked my feet under me and pulled the cuddly fleece blanket around my shoulders.

Carla nodded. "Yeah, it is. I mean, we've had a kiss, that's it, but we've been having amazing talks for ages now and, you know what, Mia, he's so normal. He's so nice and kind and giving. It's going to pan out slowly, this one, but I really do like him."

"Cheers!" We clinked glasses.

"And well done on the close!" I added.

"The close!" she echoed.

"As for Tim, I think he's a great guy, Carla, and great for you, I really do."

She was beaming now. At last my old Carla was returning. How did women change so much when the wrong guy came along and how come everyone could see it except themselves?

"Has James been in touch?" I asked.

Her blonde hair flew around her face as she shook her bun loose, like something from a shampoo advert. "No, not a word. I was wondering, while I was away, did Gordon throw him out?"

"No, Gordon's still away in China."

"Ask him when he gets back, will you?"

"I'll be sure to ask."

"So Shrewsbury Road is being held off on?"

"Yes, I'm expecting him back at the end of the week though." I paused. "Carla, you know I don't feel right about having taken Gordon's business away from you."

"Don't worry, Mia, I honestly don't mind."

Carla tied her hair back now in a low ponytail. "So what else is up, Mee Mee?"

"Ah, you know, this and that." I told her about Mam wanting me to move in still. Then I told her about Peadar and Damien and she listened with tears prickling in her eyes.

"Oh, Mia, that's so so sad, the poor guy!" She was rubbing my knee. "But, Mia, you can't promise them the house. They may not be able to get it. From what I understand from you they have five hundred thousand, but it's on the market for well over five."

"That's right." I squirmed in my seat.

"What's the vendors' story? Do they have another property they're in right now or what?"

"No, well, yeah, it's a funny one really. I got it all through word of mouth. Basically there was an old couple, the Nolans, who owned it and have moved into sheltered accommodation in the new Marley complex. Their son did the place up over the summer. I've been in touch with him and he told me some guy has bought it off him but he said that this guy plans to put it straight back on the market."

"Mia!" Carla stared hard at me. "What! You don't even know if it's for sale?"

"Oh Carla, I do, it is. John Nolan still has it on Clovers books so this sale hasn't gone through yet. I just need to get this guy's number so I can find out exactly what he wants for it!" I was starting to sweat now, gulping, thinking about what I had done. "Fuck." I put my head in my hand. "Help me here, Carla, please!"

"Okay, just let me sleep on it and I'll see what I can come up with. Is there no other property around cheaper that would do?"

"No, no, no, there's just not and we don't have the time to mess about here. I was googling Peadar's illness and it's impossible to gauge how long he can survive without medicine."

"Listen, you've promised them this house, Mia, you know you can't do that," Carla told me in no uncertain terms. "You have to tell them you overstepped the mark. They'll understand you did it out of kindness and that you honestly said what you did in good faith."

"I can't, Carla. Look, I am in charge of the viewings for the Nolans until a 'Sold' sign goes up. It's almost Christmas. No one will want to view over Christmas, Carla, you know what the business is like – it will give me more time to see what I can do. I have to get this house for them."

Carla shook her head. "Mia, face it – you're clutching at straws."

"I felt so moved by their situation, Carla. I felt the house was just meant for them."

We sat back in silence as Carla digested my latest crisis.

"That is just so tragic, Mia, but why won't he even try conventional medicine?"

"He nursed his own grandfather and then father through the same cancer and his father took every medical treatment available. Peadar said never, ever would he go through that."

"But surely he should try if there's any chance at all?"

I could understand Carla's disbelief. "Well, that was Damien's first reaction too. Anyway, Carla, it's his decision and he's so incredibly brave and charming and just so loving. He just adores living."

"He sounds amazing," she nodded in agreement.

"He is."

"So," she asked after a while, "are you bringing the elusive PeePeePeePaul to the Christmas party?"

I wasn't expecting it and was caught off guard so I stammered. "N-n-no."

She knew me well enough to realise that when I stammered something was up.

"What now?" she asked.

"Ah, nothing. I mean it's gone, it just sort of fizzled out." I avoided eye contact with her.

"Really? I thought you really liked each other. Sorry I didn't ask before but I didn't want to be pressuring you to talk about it. I know you – if you wanted to talk about him you would. Did he do something bad to you?"

"No, no, he didn't, he just, well, he just stopped calling, I suppose."

"Okay so, take Gordon to the Christmas party."

She smiled and I actually spat my drink onto the sofa. She mopped it up with a tissue. (Carla always had tissues, not old snotty crumpled tissues but new ones in the packet.)

"Gordon? Are you mental?" I laughed at her now.

"Just a thought," she said as she pulled some of my blanket around her and switched on the TV.

Phew! I closed my eyes, conversation over.

I sipped my wine and sat staring at the faces of the cast of *The Wire* but didn't hear a word. I had so much spinning around my mind right now. I was a wreck.

"Okay, listen, Mr Nolan, we have five hundred thousand on the table now if we can do this before Christmas and close the deal." My hand hovered over the page with pen in place to write down whatever he said next in case I forgot.

He laughed. "Ah listen, Mia, this guy wants it. He's meeting me tomorrow. It's a done deal, I'm afraid, so there's no way. No can do. Sure I have his offer in for the asking price of five twenty-five." The figures jumped out at me: five twenty-five. They simply didn't have that money. "I'll come back to you if anything happens." He hung up.

I pulled my coat on. I was running now to meet Gordon in the Shelbourne to finalise the Shrewsbury house and to discuss his job offer.

Carla looked up from her computer. "Well?"

I shook my head and she winced.

"See you all later!" I called over my shoulder and closed the door.

The rain had stopped and the sky was bright blue but bitterly cold. I liked this kind of weather. The type where you could wrap up all the bits of your body that you hated and no one thought you were hiding anything. Even skinny people had to wrap up their toned arms and shapely legs in the cold because if they didn't then they looked ridiculous. Winter really was the larger ladies good, good friend. I couldn't ever live in Oz or LA where it was bikini weather all the time, I couldn't even imagine the amount of work that would go into that.

I drove into town and parked in Setanta and strolled up to the Shelbourne. I was excited about seeing Gordon but had so much on my mind with the Sandymount house I was a bit all over the place. He was sitting in the seasonally decorated Saddle Room sipping black coffee with some papers in front of him.

"Howdy!" I dropped into the bench in front of him.

"Howdy to you, too!" He smiled at me.

I had forgotten just how handsome he was. Dressed today in a navy shirt, open to the neck and black suit trousers. He was simply – sorry, there was no other word for it – dashing. He had that three-day-old dark shadow-stubble that I loved.

"So, long time no see. Shrewsbury first – what do I need to sign?"

I opened my bag and pushed page after page in front of him. I wondered if his pen was a Gold Mont Blanc but as I had no idea what one looked like I couldn't tell.

"That's that! Congratulations!" I shook his hand and he laughed quietly. A back-of-the-throat kind of laugh. Husky. Dirty.

"Coffee?"

I nodded and he poured me a cup.

"So, Mia, the job offer. Can we now discuss?"

"Yeah, listen, I am so flattered but I suppose I'm nervous. I mean, where would I be based, what's the salary, is there a contract etc etc?"

"Well, you'd be based in my office in Shrewsbury Road. I was thinking of sixty thousand for the first year. You'd be in sole charge of my properties here in Dublin, London, and in the US. I'll give you a one-year contract to start."

I didn't know what to say. I drank a gulp of coffee. "Wow, Gordon, that's some offer," I managed.

"So, do you accept?"

"I really don't know. I know this sounds mental but right now I have a shitload of stuff going on in my life and in my work that I can't just walk away from. Believe you me, I would love to, I really would, Gordon. I would love to take your offer and run – but I've always sort of been running, you know, hiding from my responsibilities, and now I need to face them."

"Two bottles of Heineken when you're ready, please," he asked a passing waitress and, yes, she looked at him and her eyes popped out of her head.

I smiled at her. I didn't blame her.

He tidied up all the papers and put them away as the Heineken came and I accepted mine on its little white doily and drank long and hard.

"So what's up?" He looked up at me with his eyes so caring I felt my shoulders slump and suddenly felt very vulnerable.

"Oh, Gordon!" I dropped my head into my hands then looked back up into his eyes. "I'm a fuck-up, I really am. Don't employ me. Ever." It was out before I even thought about what I was saying.

He didn't react, just sipped his beer. "Why?"

Oh, the way he sipped that beer! If only I was in advertising, I would make Heineken gazillions with him in the advert, I knew that much.

"Oh, if I told you everything that is spinning around inside my wooden head right now, you would run a mile, Mr McHale."

"I wouldn't, I won't," he said and looked as though he meant it.

"You will." I nodded my head. Why was I doing this with him? It was very unprofessional and I had never done anything like this before in my life and I had met many a sexy millionaire at this game.

"Try me," he said.

I knew he was going to say that. I took another long drink and stared into his wonderful deep eyes. I was actually going to do this. I stood on my own toe hard under the table to give myself the chance to come to. Nothing changed.

"Okay, so how's about this for some heavy shit." I pulled a bobbin from my wrist and twisted my hair in a pile on top of my head. I removed my suit jacket. I was ready. "Number one. I have been having an affair with the husband of Anita, a girl I work with in the office in Clovers. More than that, she is a friend, a friend who has been confiding in me about her marriage breakdown. I didn't know she was married to him but there you go. Number two. My elderly mother who was abandoned by our father years ago when he ran off with another woman, wants me to move back home with her and I know for a fact that she's a nervous wreck on her own in the house. When Dad first left she was petrified of turning out the last light at night and I think she still is. Number three – last but not least. I have promised a property to a terminally ill friend and now I can't close the deal. Just little things like that, you know yourself." I let out a sigh which I realised was of total relief, having unburdened myself of all that.

He did look shocked, there's no point in saying he didn't. He rolled up his sleeves, deep in thought. He carefully folded them over and over until they were above his elbows.

"Did you tell the girl yet? Anita, is it?"

I nodded and then shook my head, both at the same time. "No, I didn't tell her – yet – I mean, I hope I will – oh, I really don't know because I can't seem to get it clear in my own head what to do for the best. You are the one and only person I've told."

"Okay, it sure sounds complicated, Mia. Is it still going on?"

"Oh God no, he's a total arsehole! I don't know what I ever saw in him, I honestly don't, I haven't a clue. I haven't seen him since we figured the whole sordid thing out. But you know what? She's bringing him to our Christmas party next week so that will be –" I raised my two thumbs in the air, "loadsa fun."

"Why haven't you called this prick to sort it?" He raised his voice slightly now.

"Oh, I have tried, Gordon. His phone's disconnected or something."

He looked down for a few minutes and then said, "Hmmm . . . and this house for your friend, who's ill, where is it?"

"Sandymount, on for five twenty-five and my friends only have five and I have told them it's theirs and they are almost in the process of moving in as we speak. Well, when I say '*on*' for five twenty-five, the owners, the Nolans, have agreed to sell to someone and the deal's being done tomorrow." I raised the green bottle to my lips.

His eyes widened. "Mia Doyle, what house is it in Sandymount?"

"I know, I know. It's 141, on the green there, beautiful. So do you still want to give me a job?" I laughed awkwardly.

"Well, that's a bit of a scatter of stuff alright but you can work it out, big girl like you!"

I never liked being called a big girl. I knew he meant I was an older girl but *big* was a word I always hated. "I'm sure I will, Gordon, one way or the other." I smirked at him, suddenly feeling heavy-shouldered again.

We were both silent for a few minutes and I listened to the women behind us recounting a wedding they had been to at the weekend. The things they were saying about the poor bride! From the horrendous dress to the slutty make-up to the cold awful food! Wow, I thought, with friends like that who'd need enemies?

"I can't help you out on the friend situation," Gordon broke into my thoughts, "or tell you what to do, and I can't advise you on your mother for that matter but I can sure as hell help you with the Sandymount house."

"How?" I asked.

"Well, I'm the other bidder!" he said and began to laugh.

My mouth fell open. "Oh shit, really, Gordon, really, are you? Oh, you see, Peadar is terminally ill and it is their dream home and –"

He raised his hand. "I'll speak to Nolan again now and close this for you." He took his phone out of his pocket.

"But how? We only have five and you've put five twenty-five down!"

"Buy it off me. I'll sell it back to you today for five." He winked at me, the sexiest wink in the world. I was truly gobsmacked. "What? You'd do that for me?"

"Nolan, Gordon McHale here."

I sat back as he negotiated the deal, got the property off the market, the sign down and arranged for the papers to be couriered to the Shelbourne.

"Why would you do this? Why would you lose twenty-five thousand euro for me?"

"Because," he said, "it's a good deed, it's a nice thing to do, it's the right thing to do. I am a nice guy, Mia."

I jumped out of my seat, ran around to him and flung my arms around him. "Oh, shit, you are a nice guy! Oh shit, shit, shit, I can't believe this! Are you sure? You won't back out on me? I don't think I could handle that!" The sense of relief I felt was euphoric.

"No, I won't, you have my word. Let him move in there now. It's his home as far as I am concerned."

"He has a partner – Damien. He's gay."

"I guessed," he said laconically. "When you said his partner's name was Damien you really didn't need to add the 'he's gay' bit!"

It felt like the biggest weight in the world had been lifted off my shoulders. Anita and my mam would no doubt climb back up there in a matter of minutes and add their weight but right now it was one less thing on my mind.

"Are you hungry?" he asked as he picked up the menu that stood in its little silver holder.

It was now after six and I was suddenly starving. "Yes, are you?"

We ordered two fresh scampi and chips and bottle of red wine that Gordon picked and I couldn't pronounce. Several people came over to shake his hand while we ate.

"Who are they?" I asked through a mouthful of lemony fish.

"Just people I know vaguely." He smiled. He poured me another glass of the most velvety warm red wine I had ever tasted.

"White wine with fish surely?" I tipped the bottle of red with my knife.

He shook his head. "Not always, not this fish. The home-made parsley sauce is heavy and the red wine cuts it better than white in my opinion, but sorry, I really should have asked – if you prefer white I can get you that."

"No, I love it, and you did ask and I said whatever you wanted. I never understand what wine goes with what food. I mean, to me unfortunately it's still just wine, it's there to be drunk and the food is there to be eaten. I don't really have that in me – that whole wine-education thing. Don't get me wrong, I adore a nice bottle of wine, but I'm just not good at all that smelling and tasting stuff. I have tried!"

He nodded and stuck his nose back into the glass.

"I mean there, what exactly are you getting from that wine now?" I asked as I stuck my nose into my glass too, well, as much of it as would fit – it wasn't exactly a button nose!

Suddenly he looked different, younger. "Well, you know, you taste through smell." He was rolling the glass around in the palms of his hand now. "So I like to find what I can smell from the wine, see?"

"Well, yeah, I get it. It's just I find it hard to pinpoint a specific smell. If I look at the back of the bottle and it says, I dunno, apricots and red berries or whatever, then of course I can smell them!"

He smiled at me now, a big beaming smile. No one had ever smiled at me like that.

"Okay, Mia, so smell and tell me the first thing that comes into your mind. Take a good deep smell."

Oh for the love of God, why did I start all this? I smelled.

"So?" he asked.

"Wine," was all I could offer. "It just smells like wine to me, Gordon."

He burst out laughing now. "Mia, don't you get a hint of smoked grass?"

"Smoked grass, are you mental?" I smelled again "Well, okay, now that you've said smoked grass I can smell smoked grass. But it's just like when someone tells you not to think of an elephant all you can do is think of an elephant. Honestly, Gordon, I would never have come up with smoked grass in a million years."

He smelled again, obviously delighted with his little game. "What about blackcurrants? Surely you can smell the blackcurrants?"

I obliged but again shook my head.

"Okay." He put his glass down. "It's not for everyone, agreed?"

"Agreed!" I laughed now.

"Have you ever seen *Sideways*?" He began to eat again.

"No." I didn't ask what it was about.

"Oh, we should watch that sometime." He reached for the salt and, as he shook way too much onto his fish, I kept replaying his last sentence over and over in my mind.

After dinner he asked me if I would like to go to the Renaissance Private Members Club for an "after-dinner" drink. I said yes. Naturally.

I had put the call in to Peadar and Damien to say the deal was signed, sealed and delivered, and they were more than thrilled. I loved this man standing holding the door open for me right now, I envied Mrs McHale like I had never envied another woman in my entire life. But we were friends now, Gordon and I. He was larger than life yet so soft and gentle and, yes, so so sexy. We strolled down to the private club and I didn't care that I wasn't dressed up. Gordon was like my Dolce & Gabanna dress and Jimmy Choo shoes. He was greeted at the door like a friend by the bouncer and warmly received and, as we made our way up the very dark stairs, he took my hand to lead the way. It was like being shot through the heart by a bolt of lightning. If I thought Paul had stirred sexual emotions in me by having sex, this hand-holding was way off the radar. It must be true what they say, that women's libido goes up with age because I was like a puppy in heat.

We were seated by the incredibly beautiful red-haired hostess and Gordon ordered another bottle of red.

"Are you trying to get me pissed, Mr McHale?" I asked as I let my hair loose and ran my fingers through it.

The lighting was so subdued, it was fantastic. I loved it. I probably even looked good in it.

"I want you to come and work for me, Mia." He leaned in close to me and I could smell what I now recognised as Joop aftershave. I wondered how come I could recognise the smell of an aftershave at one hundred paces but couldn't tell one wine from the next?

"I know you do and I think I do too but, you know, Gordon, I have to be honest – I'm not all that career-orientated." The wine was loosening my tongue now. "I mean, I love the business but it's a job to me really, you know?"

"That's what it should be, Mia, a job and not a life."

He sat back now as the waitress poured a drop of wine into his glass and he repeated the whole routine thing, and smiled at her as she melted into the thick red carpet.

"Is it a life for you?" I asked after she had left.

"Yeah," he sighed. "It is, I suppose, unfortunately, but I'm working on it."

"So, do you have kids?"

"No, no kids, Mia."

"Does Mrs McHale think you work too much?"

He smiled now at the mention of her name and again I was so jealous of her.

"Oh, she does, she worries about me something fierce – she never stops worrying about me."

"Do you not get to spend that much time together then?"

"Ah, we do, I suppose. In fact, we'll be spending a nice quiet Christmas here in Dublin together."

"That's nice." I tried to smile.

We chatted more about business and life and we laughed and laughed and he really was great company. So easy to be around, so easy to chat with. He actually must have found me interesting because whenever I spoke he listened intently, and whenever I cracked a joke he roared laughing. He agreed to give me until after Christmas to sort out "my issues" (as he called them) and make a decision on the job.

"Why do you still want me after all I've said tonight?" I slurred my words as he more or less carried me down the dark stairs at three o'clock in the morning. I had never known a night to go by so quickly in my entire life.

"I don't know, Mia. It's a hunch, I suppose – it's a strong feeling I have about you."

"Right," I slurred.

He hailed one of the hundreds of empty taxis, opened the door and put me in.

He leaned over to do up my seatbelt for me as I gave the address, our faces inches apart.

"Well, goodnight, Gordon." I managed to slow down my words to get them out and I thought they sounded okay.

"Goodnight, Mia." He stood back and closed the door and I could see he was laughing hard as we pulled away.

15

My head was bursting. I couldn't get up.

"Mia, it's after eight!" Carla called up the stairs. "I have to go ahead!"

"Yeah, go make an excuse for me, will you? Please say I have food poisoning, okay?" I rasped.

"Okay!" She slammed the door.

Did she really have to do that? Oh, why did I get myself into these messes? What had I said to Gordon last night? I honestly couldn't remember much after we got to that private club. I pulled the pillow over my head. But he had saved my life, I remembered that much – he had bailed me out of the Sandymount house mess and I could never thank him enough for that. One thing for sure, I had told the guy way too much for him to ever be able to employ me. I wasn't dedicated enough and he needed someone who was truly ambitious. He needed Carla. I shut my eyes tight. I would have to get up soon and look for tablets.

I rolled out onto my hands and knees. Crawling, I stopped in front of the mirror. I stopped and looked long and hard.

Yesterday's make-up was well and truly gone. This wasn't a good sign. At what part of the night had it all disappeared? I hadn't even bothered to nip to the loo and retouch it. Now there wasn't a panda eye in sight which means I mustn't have had a screed of make-up left on my eyes by the end of the night or morning or whatever that period of time was on the twenty-four-hour clock when I collapsed into bed.

I was still in my top and my pants – at least I had got the trousers off. I took slow baby-steps all the way down to the kitchen, head pumping, and got some painkillers with water.

Then I heard my phone ringing in my bag. I scurried to find the bag's contents sprayed across the kitchen table. I was all ready to make retching noises if the caller was Dominic. I flipped it open and saw it was Gordon.

"Whadda'ya want?" I croaked as I made it to the couch and collapsed.

"Oh my head!" he groaned.

I heard his duvet rustle as he turned. I half-laughed but it hurt too much. He really was becoming more and more human every time I encountered him. I bet he looked perfect – bit of stubble and dry mouth but sexy as fuck.

"Oh, are you not going to work either?" he whispered.

"No way," I said. "I am dying here, Gordon."

He laughed. "Ah stop, it hurts to laugh. I don't do wine sessions really – well, a glass or two with dinner – but we had four bottles."

"Four!" I shut my eyes tight. That was it! This hangover was here for the day. If I thought it was just a bottle each I could convince myself that I had given enough time to the hangover and shoo it away, but now that I knew how much we really had drunk, not a chance. It was like when you had a really late night and were wrecked the next day but you thought you got in at two in the morning – you are getting through the day until someone tells you that you actually got in at five in the morning. That's it. You feel a million times worse.

"Yeah, four, I just checked my visa bill."

"Oh shit, did I not even pay for one of them?" I cringed.

"Oh, you wanted to, you put up a fair fight, shoving euros in my shirt pocket, then my trousers' pockets. But I wouldn't let you."

I dropped my jaw – his trousers' pockets, oh Mother of God! I took a deep breath. "Gordon, is this the first time you've had a hangover in years?"

There was silence for a few seconds. "Yes, Mia, it is. I actually can't remember the last time. I think it was when I was best man at my friend Michael's wedding in Cannes two years ago. I'm too busy for hangovers. It's not that I don't like them, I actually do. They're a great self-inflicted way of doing nothing all day. I simply don't have the time in my life for them."

"Oh well, this is my last one, I mean it." I tucked my phone under my ear, padded into the front room and flicked on the TV. I collapsed onto the couch and pulled the blanket over me. Jeremy Kyle was on.

"What's going on in the background?" he asked now.

"Oh, hangover TV," I told him. "Do you have a TV in your bedroom there?"

"How did you know I was still in bed?" I could almost see him looking over his shoulder before he said, "Well, yes, I do, as a matter of fact."

"Good. Okay, so turn on TV3. 'Am I really the father of your baby or is it my brother's?' is today's theme." I settled back for a good screaming match. God bless TV3 and their genius daytime programming.

"How utterly charming," he said but I heard the TV come to life in the background.

We laughed and cringed and informed each other of our states over the next hour. We laughed at our unfortunate aches and pains but secretly were both enjoying this day at home. When my battery beeped, he asked me to plug in my phone. I obliged and trudged over to the nearest socket to do so.

"I'm opening my fridge," I informed him.

"Oh, great idea, hang on until I go down," he said.

It was five minutes later when he spoke again.

"Sorry, kitchen further away from the bedroom than I thought – I don't go in there much."

"Ha, Mrs McHale must love that!" I managed. "She not around then today?"

"No," he said very cheerily. "She's actually still in the South of France."

Good for her, I mouthed as I closed the empty fridge and opened the cupboard. Ah, great! Beans. He located the same and we both made our beans on toast in our separate kitchens and sat down to eat them on our couches.

It was four hours later when we hung up.

How bizarre, I thought as I finally hit the shower. That had been almost like chatting with Carla. So easy, such fun, no sweaty palms or awkward silences – it had been so lovely.

"Mrs McHale," I said into the steamed-up mirror as I rubbed it, "you are one lucky cow."

I was starving after the beans and toast so I made some tinned chicken soup, covered it in black pepper and opened some files at the kitchen table.

As I glanced around the kitchen I suddenly thought of Paul. Funny, I hadn't thought about him in almost two days. Was he petrified that I was going to tell Anita? He had obviously made up his mind to go back to her. I had no doubt he had changed his phone number but it was a stupid thing to do. I mean, he needed me on his side to keep my mouth shut.

I blew on the spoon a few times then put the hot peppery mouthful into my mouth. I looked all around the kitchen. It seemed a bit alien to me now, like I couldn't understand the initial excitement I had when walking into it and seeing him there. It felt like another life yet was only a matter of weeks. I was glad he had gone back to her, I suddenly realised. I was glad a family had a second chance of staying together. He had done the right thing as far as I was concerned. We never got that chance – Dad never decided that he had done the wrong thing by leaving us for Angela, ever. In fact, I'd say he thought it was the best decision he ever made in his whole life. He tried to keep in contact very half-heartedly and it broke Mam's heart when he called and we were chatting to him on the phone. Laughing out of fear with him, laughing to stop the tears from flooding out of me, and then it all became too much for me and I stopped coming downstairs when the phone rang and so eventually did Samantha.

I blew on my spoon again. I had known all along something was up with Paul. I knew that deep down. I'm not saying for a second that I knew he was married, but I knew there were questions I needed to ask him but I was so desperate I just didn't. I was afraid if I opened my mouth he'd be gone. I was enjoying having a boyfriend, I was enjoying the excitement and the chance of a good sex life. But I deserved more than that.

I looked up at the new kitchen again. Why did I sell myself so cheaply? Surely I was worth more? I had people who loved me so I knew I was a good person. I shook my head. Quite apart from the atrocity that he turned out to be married to Anita, he had never treated me well. When I looked back on the few dates we'd had, it was all about sex. Not even very good sex. Let's face it, I couldn't remember a thing about the first time and the last time hadn't exactly been earth-shattering. Why had I convinced myself that I really liked the guy? Because that's what you wanted, I told myself. You wanted to like him. We never talked. I had talked more to Gordon, and yes he was another married man, but we spoke, we communicated, we clicked, we made each other laugh. I didn't think Paul made me laugh once – well, maybe once, but I couldn't remember it. Was this all to do with Dad leaving? Did I purposely go out and seek married men to destroy families, like mine had been destroyed?

I laughed now and dropped my spoon into the empty bowl. "No, Mia," I said out loud to the empty space, "that's not your style at all."

I washed up the dishes and thought about work. Tomorrow we were decorating the office for Christmas and it would be all talk about the Christmas party. I couldn't handle it. I'd been trying to get as many appointments out of the office and apart from Anita as I could. There were a couple of nearby viewings that she could hop on a bus to, and I could take some far-out viewings. She was taking driving lessons courtesy of Dominic and in fairness to her she took a bus to any viewing that she was handling on her own. She wasn't lazy. I didn't think she thought that I was lazy any more either.

The hangover had abated somewhat and I was bored now. I picked up the sweeping brush and swept the kitchen floor. I liked to sweep, it was the one and only part of housework that I actually enjoyed.

I opened the fridge to look for hangover nibbles and then closed it tight. This was what happened to me, I would graze there all day like a prize cow if I could.

So I decided I would go shopping. My bank balance had come up since my last visit to Dundrum and I had presents to buy, so why not do it today? I'd have to go far from the office so I decided to head out to Liffey Valley. We didn't do gifts, Mam, myself or Samantha, but maybe I would buy Mam something small.

I took a couple of CD's off the shelf and headed for the warmth of my beloved Ford Ka. As I sped along the M50 I sang along to U2, hangover seemingly gone now. I always thought it was a miracle that you could be so in bits one minute and then it was all cleared up the next. I drove all the way with no lights against me and parked easily. I sauntered around the centre, marvelling at the glamour but it was not as "totally loike" as Dundrum was. Dundrum was Posh Spice and Liffey Valley was Mel B. Different types of glamour. Totally different spices.

I needed something for the dreaded Christmas party. I wanted a black dress – a few sparkles would do. I checked out all the windows before I saw a dress I liked in Dunnes. It was plain black with sequins and a halter neck in the Savida section. I took it to the changing room along with a three-quarter black cardigan. I tried it on in a sixteen and joy of all joys, can you guess what happened? Elated, I literally screamed out of the dressing room to anyone who could hear me, "It is too big! It's too big! This dress is too big on me! Do you have a size fourteen, please?"

The sales lady gave me a funny look but obliged and went off to get me a size fourteen. She knocked on my dressing-room door with it and it slid over my head and fitted perfectly. It emphasised my shoulders which were good, I liked my shoulders. It was loose around my middle and fell flowing to just above the knee. I bought it. Job done.

I bought a bottle of Lucozade and sipped it as I looked for a gift for Mam. A girl tried to spray perfume on me as I walked past, either because she didn't like how I smelt or because she wanted me to buy it, I wasn't sure. Her face was unreadable. Emotionless. Zombie-like. Maybe she had a hangover too, I thought, and suddenly felt immense pity for her. Could you imagine spraying perfume all day with a stinking hangover? I shivered. I saw a beautiful framed portrait of a woman in

Debenhams. It caught my eye. It actually reminded me of Mam years ago. I couldn't put my finger on it but I bought it and had it wrapped and all. I loved a place that offered a free wrapping service. It always looked so much nicer than when I wrapped things myself. Plus I just liked free services no matter what they were.

My mobile rang and I, as usual, dropped my bag on the shop floor to rummage for it, getting it on the last ring.

"Hello?" It was Peadar. "So we're all in! Ding-dong!"

I threw everything back into my bag and backed myself into a quiet corner as the girl was tying a gold ribbon on the wrapping.

"Oh great, how are you feeling?"

"Ah, I'm okay, love. I'm . . ." he paused, "I'm making a super dinner and I was hoping you would join us? If you aren't doing anything else?"

"No, that would be lovely," I said.

"Great. Eight bells. And are you allergic to anything?"

"No, just drink, I'm afraid. I'm suffering today so I'll be off the booze. Can I bring anything?"

"Absolutely nothing, honestly. Okay, love, see ya later so!"

I was starting to feel a bit rough again. Time to go, I thought, as I bundled the wrapped picture under my arm and headed for the parking machine.

Carla was all snippy with me when she got home.

"I covered for you but you should have called Dominic," she said as she viciously stirred her fresh wholewheat pasta around in the pot of bubbling water. She was so healthy-looking after her brisk walk home from work in that cold.

"I know, sorry." I rubbed her shoulders. "How was it?"

"Oh fine – well, I ended up having to drive Anita to your viewing in Clonskeagh which I could have done without and as it turned out the guy never showed so it was a complete and utter waste of our time."

"Ah, some people!" was all I could manage.

She looked at me sympathetically now. "Oh Mia, are you alright? Where were you last night? With Paul?" She pulled the pot off the cooker.

"No," I shook my head, "not with Paul. I ended up drinking with Gordon McHale."

"Gordon?" Her beautiful unlined eyes popped out of their sockets. "I didn't even know Gordon drank," she mused.

"Ah, he doesn't really, I think I kind of led him astray."

"Hmmm?" She was smiling now.

"Oh, don't be ridiculous, Carla, not like that! Anyway, let's talk when I get home, can we? I won't be late? I am running out to dinner with Peadar and Damien. They are getting sorted at the house and want to eat there but I won't be on the vino so I'm driving. I won't be too late, so see you when I get home?"

She pulled me into a great bear-hug. "Sure!"

I pulled away, not trusting my emotions, put on my coat and headed for Sandymount.

"Oh!" was all I could say when Peadar opened the door. Glass in hand as always, but he looked terribly thin and pale.

"Oh?" he repeated after me, sniffing. "'Oh, you look fab, Peadar'?" he finished for me.

I smiled. "Yeah, you do look fab – it's just I thought the glass was for me and I could puke at the moment!"

I wiped my feet on the Welcome mat and handed him the bottle of wine I'd brought for him. "How lovely!" he said.

I walked in ahead of him and he gently closed the door behind us. It looked like a different house. It even felt different. It was so warm and all their furniture for the apartment they so loved had somehow miraculously fitted it. Their sofa took up most of the back wall of the living room and their pictures hung from every available space. Peadar had been busy, too busy it seemed, and it showed.

"Damien's a bit behind, as usual," he grinned and took my coat as I surveyed the room. "So what do you think?"

"It's unbelievable," I told him honestly and accepted a glass of sparkling Pellegrino water with lemon.

"Come on upstairs!" He walked ahead and I noticed his jeans were hanging down off his bum.

The crackling open fire welcomed me as he opened the bedroom door. He had taken away the blinds and the park light zoomed into the room. The double bed was decked out in a crimson bedspread and loads of matching cushions. He had a small table with three stools in the corner and again a picture hung from every space on the wall.

"Oh, wow, this is so beautiful!" I held out my hands to welcome the heat. It was the warmest feel to a room I had even known. There was so much life in it, from the roaring fire, to the life in pictures on the walls, to the real people going about their business outside.

"Isn't it though!" He was thrilled.

"How are you feeling?" I had to ask.

"I'm okay, Mia. I'm doing okay. I mean, I know I did too much during the move but it was worth it. I needed to do this while my strength was good so I'm really pleased. I can enjoy it now."

I took his hand. "You've done an incredible job. I absolutely love it."

"Thank you." He squeezed my hand tightly. "I don't know what magic wand you waved to get us this house at that price but you did it and I'll never forget it. When I am gone I want you to be around for Damien. He doesn't have anyone, Mia, just me. His family all relocated down to Cork a few years ago and he doesn't speak with his parents or his brothers much any more. I mean, they accept him and us – it's just they've grown apart. Promise me that, will you?"

He looked into my eyes and I nodded fiercely. "I promise." I could feel a massive lump in my throat.

He put an arm around my waist and squeezed me.

"Hey, lay off the love handles!" I playfully slapped him away.

"That's my girl! No, come on, it's such a lovely evening and I have a fab dinner on the go if I do say so myself."

True to his word, when Damien came home and had oohed and aahed at all the finishing touches to the house, we sat down in the small kitchen and had the most divine spaghetti bolognese – you know, the one where the sauce is almost soupy it's so gooey and extra tomatoey – all organic ingredients, he told us, from Simon next door. His illness wasn't mentioned again and I think they both preferred it that way.

"Simon," Peadar remarked as he shook bucket-loads of Parmesan on my dish, "is quite the hottie."

He winked at me as Damien said, "Excuse me?"

"Well, I'm just saying that he's hot and single and you'd better be on your best behaviour, Damien, what with him next door all day stroking those organic cucumbers and me on my own in here."

"Peadar!" Damien and I shouted in unison as he fell into fits of laugher and Damien's face broke into a massive smile.

After dinner we 'retired' (Peadar's word not mine) to the couch to watch *Will & Grace* and we all laughed hard at Jack and Karen and Co. I couldn't believe it when I glanced at the clock on my phone and it was almost ten o'clock. Carla would be waiting up for me.

I said my goodbyes and hand in hand they walked me to the door.

"When will we see you next?" Peadar asked.

"I don't know actually, guys, I have a lot on with work and family and Christmas but why don't I call you guys next week and make a plan?"

"Great, because we want to have you over for a Christmas night, whatever night you're free. We have our book club here in two weeks and then some other friends coming over from Brighton. So let's chat?"

"Yeah, and I want to have you both to my house. Carla can't wait to meet you but I have to warn you it will be take-away food!"

Peadar squealed. "Oh no! Let me make something here and bring it over – something like a lasagne – and I'm sure even you can pop a few baked potatoes into the oven, Mia?"

"Okay – deal," I agreed and I kissed them both goodbye.

They waved me off and I made my way up the road to my car. I beeped the alarm and its flashing lights lit up the dark night.

"*Boo!*"

I jumped out of my skin and screamed in my man's voice.

There stood Gordon. In a black leather jacket and jeans.

"Fucking hell, Gordon, you scared the living daylights out of me!" I faked a faint and he faked catching me (I didn't let all my weight collapse on the poor unfortunate, of course) and we both laughed as our breaths rose on the cold air.

"What are you doing here?" I asked.

"Well, I was passing and I thought I'd stop by to take a last look at the house that lost me so much dosh. Is everything okay with your friend?" He narrowed his eyes.

"Oh yeah, he, well, he's as good as can be expected. They had me to dinner. And you know what, when this market goes up again you will feel even worse!" I grinned.

He thrust his hands deep into his jeans pockets. "They obviously really like you, Mia Doyle."

I loved how he said my name. What was it when someone you really liked said your name? It always sounded different, sexier, more intimate. "Ah, you know, I guess I just have what it takes!" I batted my eyelids. "How's your head?"

He shook it. "That was one rough day."

"So where are you off to now?"

"Home, I guess. You?"

"Yeah, home too, I guess. You and your smoky blackberries or whatever the heck they were!"

"So did you hear any more from what's his face? Em, Paul, wasn't it?"

"Oh no, don't expect to at this stage."

"Well, you were giving him some bashing last night, said you were going to get him today. In fact, you said you were going to 'stick it to the slimeball'!" He was trying not to laugh.

"Oh no! Was I on my soap box?" I couldn't remember any of that conversation. "Sorry, Gordon."

"Nah, that's fine, I happen to agree with you. He needs a good thumping. It's men like that that give us perfect ones a bad name."

I laughed. "Shit, it's cold! Must go."

He took his car keys out and a loud beep-beep was heard almost directly behind me. I looked around to see a sleek black BMW.

"New Beemer?" I asked.

"Nah, have a few cars, Mia – the joys of being rich, I suppose. Them's the perks, as they say. Funny thing is, I haven't a clue about cars, never really cared much for them."

I laughed. "Well, the Ford Ka is just a cover for me." I beeped mine again. "Don't want people to realise how much I'm really worth!"

We both laughed.

"So, I'd better go, I guess," he said. "It's a great house, Mia, I love it. You did well for them."

He opened the door of his car and I opened mine.

"Gordon?" I said suddenly. "I think Carla would be better for the job than me." I hadn't planned on saying that or expected the reaction his face showed.

"Oh, okay." He leaned on the frame of the car door. "Can I ask why?"

"Oh look, Sandymount House is still open – do you want to grab a late coffee and chat for half an hour?" Carla would probably be in bed by now anyway so our chat about Paul would have to wait. Anyway, I wasn't sure I was ready to tell her all yet.

"Great," he said and we both beeped again.

"And stay away from her!" I joked to the BMW and pointed to my Ford Ka. "She's not interested in the likes of you!"

Gordon laughed hard again. He really did seem to think I was funny.

I was wearing jeans and a green polo-neck jumper (that matched my eyes) with my hair in a ponytail. As I sat in front of the fire at the back of the pub, I caught a glimpse of myself in the old-fashioned mirror. Hey, I looked okay!

Gordon arrived back with two coffees and a plate of bickies. "Don't you just love old-fashioned public houses?" he smirked as he unwrapped the black paper and took a bite off the bickie.

"I do actually, I really do. I can't stand those new posey pubs. That's why I always go to the Palace. It's just a proper pub – it does exactly what it says on the tin. It even smells like a pub is supposed to smell." I sipped my coffee, thought about taking it back as it was only lukewarm, then thought that might seem stupid after all I'd just said about old-fashioned pubs. "Anyway, look, about the job – it's not that I don't really appreciate your offer but I just don't think that kind of high-powered job is really me, I suppose."

"So what are you?" He shook the packet of sugar roughly (lucky sugar, I thought), tore the paper off and poured the sugar into his cup. Then he repeated the exercise.

"Two? Really?" I asked and he nodded. I had sugar envy. "You know what, Gordon, I haven't a clue what I am. I probably haven't much left to tell you about myself after last night anyway. I don't know why I'm telling you all of this but here goes. I suppose I want what every woman on the wrong side of thirty wants – a husband, a family, a career I'd love and a wonderfully fulfilled life – but is that ever going to happen for me? Who knows, right? So I suppose what I'm saying is, and this is a terribly un-PC thing for me to say, if the right man came along I might just want to have children and not work outside the home at all. I quite fancy the idea of bringing up a family." I paused. Wow, I had never admitted that to myself before! Ever. I honestly didn't know I even felt like that. I felt myself blush all over now. Emily Pankhurst would be pelting me with rotten tomatoes (she'd never have wasted fresh ones – well, she probably wouldn't even have been allowed in the pub but you know what I mean).

"Hmmm, I see." He looked confused.

"But why can't I do both, I suppose you're thinking? Well –"

"No, I wasn't thinking anything of the sort. Jeez, Mia, it's a free world. It's a free choice if you have the opportunity to make it. If it's not a matter of financial urgency and you want to stay home and raise a family, that's okay. In fact, I think it's great – and that doesn't mean for one second I think women should stay at home, but I agree they should have the choice and not feel like second-class citizens if they do choose to. Actually, I dislike the term 'stay home' because as far as I can see so-called 'stay-home' mothers are never actually *in* with their kids."

"Is it okay though, Gordon? I mean really, is it?"

"Yeah," he said.

"So look at me – does it look like I'm anywhere close to nabbing a rich husband who will be more than happy to let me stay at home and bring up our family while he goes out to make the money?" I looked into his eyes and realised for the first time that, apart from Carla, there were very few people in the world whose gaze I could hold without wanting to look away. But Gordon was one.

"I think it's important to aim for what you really want in life," he told me.

He took off his jacket now and wouldn't you know he was wearing a tight black V-neck T-shirt. Wouldn't you just know it? This was too much for my fragile head to take it. It looked as though he had just taken the T-shirt out of the packet. The bulging arms, the tanned skin . . . there was something wrong with me and my suppressed sexual appetite lately, I realised. He was so naturally gorgeous. God had truly blessed him. Lucky sod. He didn't seem to notice my drooling or my eyes on sticks, so that was good.

I managed to put my tongue away before he looked back at me and said, "It's not a job for a lifetime I am offering either, you know. I've had lots of great staff come and go over the years but I've made sure to value everything each and every one of them brought to my company."

"I know, but if I leave Clovers I suppose I leave my comfort blanket." My cup rattled as I found the saucer. I suppose it was because I couldn't take my eyes from him for one second to look down at the table.

"Well, if Anita finds out about you and her husband you might not have any choice?" He raised his perfectly groomed eyebrows.

"Oh stop, Gordon, will you!" I slapped him on his upper arm. Hard. It felt good.

He opened another bickie and I finished my coffee.

"So it's a no then, is it?" he asked and I knew it was for the final time. He was a businessman, after all, not a recruitment-company manager.

"To be honest, as I said, I think Carla would be much better at it than me, and I want the best for you because you have been so incredibly great to me. I owe you that."

"Okay." He coughed and covered his mouth, then looked at his watch. Rolex, I wondered? "I'd better get going, I have to catch a flight at six a.m."

"Oh right, yeah." I pulled on my coat, reluctant to leave the pub.

"Have I just made a huge mistake?" I asked him as we made our way towards the exit and walked slowly to our cars.

"Nah, I don't think so."

We stopped.

"I think you need to be honest with yourself in this life and that's what you have done." He leaned in and kissed me on the cheek. My face tingled. "But don't say anything to Carla yet. I need to think about it before I decide if I want to offer it to her. Okay?"

"Sure," I said. "So where are you going tomorrow anyway?"

"I'm going to LA."

"To LA!" I pretended to cry.

"Yeah, I'm looking at Madonna's house."

"Nooo!" I said, my eyes wide open.

"No, not really!" he laughed. "I have to go to a wedding, would you believe – a three-day trip to LA – head-wrecking."

"Oh poor unfortunate Gordon! Bold LA, making you go there to the beautiful sunshine and fantastic restaurants! How will you survive it, eh?" I beeped first this time. "Ha, beat ya! Eat that, BMW!" I folded myself as daintily as I could into my car.

"Funny girl!" He closed the door for me and I turned on the engine and rolled down the window. "Automatic." I pointed at the window and clicked my tongue.

"Stylish," he said and pulled the collar of his black leather jacket up. "Actually, Mia, you could do me one favour when I get back."

I was serious now. "Sure, Gordon, anything."

"Well, Mrs McHale is back in Dublin for the next week and I was hoping you could come to the house in Killiney to meet her and have a bite to eat? She loves to entertain, you see and I know the two of you will get on like a house on fire."

I plastered a fake smile on my face. "Brill, yep, that's ace. Lovely, really lovely, super. When?"

He was trying hard not to laugh, I could see that. 'Super' might have been a word too much. He knew I didn't want to have a stiff meal with him and his wife. But, after everything he had done for me, I'd walk on hot coals if he asked me to. "I'll call you when I get back from LA, okay?"

"Great, I'm looking forward to it!" I revved the Ka and he walked away.

16

"A little to the left, Dom!" A cheery Anita with those awful Christmas-tree earrings that light up called to a poor dangling Dominic.

He was on top of our not-so-steady stepladder trying to hang our angel.

"There! Perfect!" She clapped her hands. "Don't you think, Mia?"

She was so cheerful since Paul had gone back to her and I decided there and then, on that very spot, not to tell her about our affair. I just didn't see the point. Sure it would ease my conscience but it wasn't about me – it was about her. The marriage was clearly working again, and telling her might wreck that.

She hummed to Wham's "Last Christmas" on the CD in the background as Dominic stepped down.

"Wow, I was getting dizzy up there!" he said as he broke into a very loud chorus of "Dizzy, my head is spinning" and fell around the office. Carla and Anita were laughing. Debbie and I were not. Poor Debbie, I thought. All the years she must have had to laugh and laugh over and over and over again until one day it was all too much so she stopped but he didn't notice. We caught eyes and she threw hers up to heaven but smiled before going back into her office and shutting the glass door.

"I'm not really feeling Christmassy at all," Carla said from her desk. Dressed in green three-quarter-length combats and a tight red jumper, she looked like Santa's Little Helper!

"So is everyone set for the big party?" Dominic had stopped dancing and actually looked a little dizzy now.

How I would love to get out of this party!

"Can't wait!" Anita said before rushing over to answer the ringing phone. "Good afternoon, Clovers Auctioneers, Anita speaking, how may I help you?" she said professionally as though she had worked here all her life. Dressed today in a smart short navy skirt, navy shirt and silver blazer, with her hair tied back and subtle make-up, she was the part. She was good at the job, I had to hand it to her. She loved it. She had calmed down so much on viewings and was quite easygoing at this point.

"So what happened to you last night?" Carla perched her perfect tush on the side of my desk.

She had left before me this morning to go for a swim before work. A swim. Can you believe that? Who does that?

Before I had the chance to answer, she continued, "Just as well you didn't come back." She pulled the tight red sweater down and Dominic's eyes were out on stalks. He wasn't so much a pervert, I decided now, as a boy. He actually couldn't help himself.

"Tim came over."

"Ohh?" I swung my seat around. Now she had my full attention. "And?"

"Toilet," she whispered and we got up.

Inside, she turned to face me and flicked her blonde mane. "Oh Mia, wow!" She pushed back the door of the cubicle and plonked herself on the closed toilet-seat. "Five times!" She fanned her face with a piece of toilet paper.

"Five times what?" I asked, leaning against the door.

"Mia! We did it five times last night, can you believe that? He is incredible. I mean, it was just straightforward sex, well, apart from the kitchen sink."

"Urgh!" I made a face. I was impressed though.

"Oh Mia, it was just the best night of my life and afterwards he just held me and held me and told me that he loved me and that he wanted us to be boyfriend and girlfriend and that he would do anything to protect me. He was just yummy!"

I was thrilled. Absolutely thrilled. I thought it was a perfect match. I hugged her and told her so. Timmy boy, I thought, I never thought you'd be a five-times-a-nighter.

"So what's happening with Paul?" she asked now as we flushed the toilet although neither of us went.

"Oh, it's over, gone, finished."

"Oh, I'm sorry, Mia, you really liked him, didn't you?"

I shook my head, probably a little too violently. "You know what, Carla?" I looked into her eyes. "I actually didn't. It was all about sex, or rather the impression I had of what he'd be like at sex. I *wanted* to fancy someone. And he never really liked me, I know that now."

"Ah, how can you say that? He did! He came looking for your number and all, remember?" She bowed her head. "Is this all because of me, because I acted like a total immature bitch and fired him?"

And for the first time I dealt with the fact that Carla would know who he was at the Christmas party. I had been pushing this to the back of my mind. How could I have been so incredibly thick? My heart started to race and sweaty palms were wiped. What was I going to do now?

"Mia, are you okay?"

I was shaking now. What a complete idiot I was. I knew by the concerned look on Carla's face I'd have to explain myself.

"Oh Carla, he's married," I whispered now.

Her face fell. "Oh, I'm so sorry, hun."

"To Anita," I whispered.

I watched her facial expression change from one of pity to one of confusion to one of complete and utter shock. She pointed to the door.

I nodded.

"Does she know?"

"Don't be ridiculous! Do you think she'd be fucking hanging Christmas decorations if she knew!" I hissed.

Carla was speechless. I poked her.

"This isn't good, oh my God, Mia, how? I mean? Shit, it does add up, doesn't it? I mean all the stuff she said about him and the job and all – but when and how did you find out?"

I filled her in as she actually bit one of her nails, something she hadn't done in years.

"You have to tell her!"

"I knew you'd say that – and that's probably the very reason why I haven't told you before!" I stared at her and she didn't fight back. She actually seemed convinced that it was the right thing to do.

The door opened suddenly and Anita came in. "Eh, hello? Are you guys okay?"

"Grand," Carla opened the door and smiled, "just my time of the month – a bit crampy." She rubbed her washboard.

"Okay, it's a Tim on the phone for you, Carla. I have pain-killers in my desk if you want one?"

"No, I'm okay, thanks, Anita, and I'll be there in just a second. Thanks, hun."

Anita left, the door swinging shut behind her, and we stood looking at each other in the mirror.

"Do you think she heard us?" I asked, panicking.

"Mia, we were whispering so low I could barely hear us! So he's just going to come to the Christmas party as brazen as hell?" She shook her head.

"I guess so." I shrugged my shoulders.

"Don't you think she deserves to know? I mean, if it was me I'd want to know, but I suppose I'm not married and I don't have kids and if he's gone back to her and it's all as hunky-dory as she says it is, then what good would it do?" Carla had talked herself out of her own argument in the space of a sentence, albeit a long one.

"You know what, Carla, I'm going to ask my mam's advice on this." For the first time since Dad had walked out I was going to approach a subject that mattered to me with my mother.

"What are you doing here?" She looked up from *Deal or No Deal* and pushed her feet into her brown slippers.

"A very good evening to you too, Mam. Where's Samantha?"

"Ah sure, she's in Niall's. She's never home any more. After Christmas is right!" she sniffed as she got up. "I have a mince stew in the pot I can heat up."

I noticed she took longer to stand than I remembered. "No, Mam, I don't want food. I want to talk to you." I sat on the arm of the couch. I liked the arm of the couch, probably because when we were younger we were never allowed to sit on it.

"Oh, what have you done now then?" She sat again.

I took a long deep breath. "Mam, I have had an affair with a married man."

She didn't react.

"I didn't know he was married and, yes, typical of clumsy me, he's married to a girl I work with."

She was very still.

"I wanted to know what I should do. I mean, I need advice. Do I tell her or do I spare her feelings?"

She hit mute on the bearded creature that was Noel Edmunds (thank God).

"Does he want her back?" she said in a low tone.

"Oh, he's gone back to her, they have two kids, but I just don't know what to do."

"Do you love him?"

"No." I shook my head.

"Does she love him?"

"Yes," I nodded.

She patted the side of her chair and I perched on the edge. "You know, Mia, I loved your father so much – I still love him, I suppose – but when he met Angela he fell completely in love with her. He loved her more than he had ever loved me and he told me that." She put her hand on mine now. My eyes pricked with tears. "So if you're looking for my advice, I'd say leave well enough alone. It sounds to me like he's trying to make a go of it this time and I think they should be given the chance."

"She knows he's had an affair before though, Mam, and she still wants him. Would she not be better off without him? He's an absolute asshole!"

Now Mam shrugged her shoulders. "Sure none of us know what goes on behind closed doors. If this man has any morals at all he's put all that behind him, if not then she's a grown woman and only she can make this decision. What's it going to prove to her if you tell her? I know when Margie told me she was at that funeral and she was sure she saw your dad and that Angela leave together after being huddled in a corner all night, I didn't believe her. I called her a filthy liar even after he didn't come home that night or for weeks after." I squeezed her hand tight. "And you know, Mia, my biggest regret is not encouraging you and Samantha to keep up your relationship with him. I was wrong and I feel awful about that every day of my sorry life."

"No, Mam, don't. We decided that, not you."

"Ah, sure yis didn't – I did it, I know that. I was glad when yis didn't want to see him any more, I was glad he was being punished." She stood up now and went into the kitchen. "Tea?" I followed her. The kitchen was dark and cold. I flicked on the main fluorescent light and it flicked three times before it came on.

"Mam, why don't you have the heating on?"

"Ah, I stick it on about half an hour before I head up to bed."

We were both silent for a few moments.

"You know, Mam, you're still a young woman. You aren't sixty-one till next year. There's so much life left in you, so much you can do."

"I'm not independent, Mia, I never have been. I'm not like you. I can't."

The kettle hummed.

"Yes, you can! I mean, why don't you sell this place? It's too big and it needs too much doing to it." I looked around the drab kitchen. "I really think you should sell and get a nice small apartment for yourself. Somewhere near the sea, you love the sea. It's so safe, apartment living – there are lots of people all around you. You could join a course or go back to work – anything!"

She took one foot out of her slipper and pulled her tights down over her toes. "Ah, I'm too old! I can't change my ways now, Mia!"

"No, Mam, you're wrong, you're not too old!" I implored her.

"Listen, Mia, I know you don't want to move back in here with me. I know that you have your own life to live, I know that. I'm not trying to pry but you are the wrong side of thirty and I'd dearly love for you to be married and have kids."

"Jesus, Mam!" I exploded. "Do you not think I want that too? What do you want me to do? I can't kidnap a man on the street and tie him to my leg and drag him into a church! I can't do it. I am trying, Jesus, I am – that's probably the very reason I didn't question Paul enough because I hoped against hope he could be the one and I could finally make you happy and proud of me for the first time since Dad left us!" I was out of breath.

"Me, he left me, not you," she corrected me.

"No, me too, Mam. He left us all. He could have tried harder to keep in touch." I banged the counter with my fist and she stared long and hard at me.

"Oh, I'm sorry," she said. "I thought I'd put you off marriage for life. I mean, I'm sure you have offers all the time? The only reason I'm always harping on at you is that I thought you hated the idea of marriage because mine was such a disaster."

"Are you serious? No! I want to be married but, well, I've never had an offer, okay?"

She opened the press and flung two teabags into the pot (she never made tea in cups) and she waited. Why was there always time for tea? She shuffled to the fridge and got the milk.

"It's advice I wanted, Mam, not another lecture! Okay, maybe lecture is a bit strong but you've been on my back for, oh, well, the best of thirty-odd years." I wasn't angry any more.

"Okay, sorry, love. Advice? Should you tell this woman you had an affair with her husband? No, is my advice. Walk away, leave them alone to get on with it. That's up to him, not you." She poured the boiling water into the pot.

"But I work with her every day – she's a friend."

"Then be a friend to her – stay out of her private life." She stirred the pot and then poured us each a cup.

I picked up my cup and sipped the boiling tea, the only noise coming from the humming of the fluorescent light above. Mam lifted her cup and made her way to the door.

"Let's go in and sit in the warmth, love."

I followed.

Gordon said tell her, Carla said tell her but then said the opposite, and now Mam said no. I was none the wiser but I was wiser about Mam. I watched her drink her tea, her small hand wrapped around the warmth of the cup, and suddenly my heart melted for her. I couldn't leave her rotting in this house like this and I couldn't move in here either.

"So, Mam, I have made my mind up for you. This house is going on the market. Let's get you set up with a new place and a new start in life for the New Year."

She was eerily quiet. Did I have her?

"Okay?" I pushed.

She looked all around her, sipped her tea and then said quietly, "Yeah, okay, Mia, let's do it." We smiled at each other and then we clinked cups.

I slipped the black dress over my head and tied it behind my neck. I was going to the office Christmas party whether I liked it or not. I had to. I had to grace it with my presence and get closure on it. The rain pelted hard against my window as I heard Carla sing *"Tis the season to be jolly, tra la la la la la la la la!"* at the top of her voice from the newly plumbed shower. I pulled on my red high heels and looked in the mirror. "Not bad, Miss Doyle!" I turned to check out the rear of the woman in the mirror. "Not bad at all!" I plastered the make-up on, I needed it tonight, and glossed over my bright red MAC lipstick with shaking hands.

"Oh, be over soon, night!" I implored.

"*Wowee!*" Carla whistled as she stood with her shower cap on (hair done in hairdresser's earlier) and towel (could be a tea towel) wrapped around her beautiful flawless skin. "You look incredible!" She paused. "Are you going to be okay?"

"Yes, fine, don't worry about me. Well, I'm going to give him the look of all looks when Anita's back is turned just so I feel better. You get dressed and I'll open a bottle downstairs."

"Okay, cool. Tim will be here in fifteen minutes so can you let him in?"

"Sure." I flicked off my light, threw my lippy into my bag with my Elizabeth Arden compact and went down. The Christmas tree's white and red lights twinkled brightly at me and I sat down gazing at it. It was a perfect tree.

I had to get through this night one way or the other. I had absolutely no idea how it was going to pan out and I couldn't understand how Paul hadn't called me once to discuss. He was either mad or blind. Or why he couldn't have made up an excuse? Maybe he would pull a sickie at the last minute, I thought hopefully, not for the first time.

It had been a busy last day in work before our Christmas break and I had found some great apartments for Mam to look at after the holidays. She was excited now and was busy fussing over the couples and families who came to view our house. Samantha too was delighted and had even invited Mam and me to Niall's house to join them all for Christmas dinner. After much discussion over corned beef and cabbage, Mam and I had agreed.

The doorbell brought me back and I opened it to welcome an incredibly handsome Tim. Dressed in a smart black suit with a bright blue scarf, he sauntered in.

"Hey there, Mia!" He kissed me on the cheek. "You look fantastic!"

"Oh thank you, my dear, and may I return the compliment?"

He hit a pretend tennis ball back to me and I rustled his floppy blond hair.

"You always know the right things to say!" I said.

I offered him a drink but he declined – he was driving us there in my car. I poured myself a large glass of cold white wine and grinned at him.

"So?" I winked now. "All well in Timmyland, I gather?"

He blushed. "Yes, thank you. Now drink your wine, woman, stop your messin' and let me check the football results, will you, before we go."

I handed him the TV controls and sipped my chilled white wine. It tasted great. I smelled it. Nothing came to mind. I stuck my nose right in and sniffed hard, so hard that I sucked a drop up my nose and made my eyes water.

"*Da-da!*"

Carla was at the door and I'm not sure who fancied her more, me or Tim. Dressed in a skin-tight short red dress with sheer black tights and silver high heels, with a black and silver choker necklace and her blonde curls tumbling all around her, she looked like Cameron Diaz in *Mask*.

"Wow!" Tim nearly jumped out of his skin. He kissed her on the mouth very softly. "You look so bloody good, Carla – you're stunning!"

"Yeah, not bad!" I laughed as I handed her some wine.

"Oh thanks, guys! I'm looking forward to a good night out. I can't remember the last time I got all dressed up like this and actually felt good about myself."

Wasn't life funny, I thought, as Tim helped her on with her coat and I unplugged the Christmas-tree lights. To every other woman on the planet she had it all, she was stunning, yet she hadn't felt that way.

"You okay?" Carla whispered as we both squeezed into the back of my car.

"Do I smell?" Tim asked as he reversed out.

"No," said Carla. "It's just I'll be with you all night and I want to sit beside Mia now."

He laughed and we chatted en route while Carla held my hand in the back seat.

As we parked she leaned towards me and said, "Anytime you want to leave just tell me, okay?"

I pulled her back. "What if it all comes out and Anita knows you lied to her? You hate liars, you know that, and I don't want to make a liar of you."

"Oh, I'm not lying, Mia. If she asks me, I'll tell her, if she doesn't then it's none of my business." She raised her eyebrows to me.

"That's fair enough," I whispered back as we entered the office.

Debbie and Dominic were there. My desk was laden with mince pies, nuts, plastic cups, napkins and Carla's desk housed bottle after bottle of wine and beer.

"The twins did the shopping," Debbie explained as Dominic kindly helped me with my coat and Tim took Carla's.

"Wowwowow!" Dominic said. "Don't the pair of ye scrub up well? Nearly as good as my wife." He fished a pretend sponge from my bag and began pouring some kind of shower gel onto the imaginary sponge and rubbing himself all over.

"Enough!" Debbie caught him by the hand. "Enough, love. Relax, have a drink. You've had a hard year of it – it's time to just relax."

He stopped and then picked up a mince pie and began to chew it slowly.

"Some music, I think?" Debbie said and pressed play on the small CD player. The Pogue's "Fairytale of New York" bellowed out.

I reached for a plastic cup and filled it with red wine.

"What time are we leaving for the Ice Bar?" Carla asked Debbie who was dressed in a long gold halter-neck and looked great.

She was munching on a handful of nuts. "Ah, around ten if that's okay with you lot?"

We all nodded. I could feel the door opening before it did. Then I felt the breeze wash over me and I knew he was in the room.

"Hey all!" Anita called out and I turned around slowly.

She stood there hand in hand with Paul. Both smiling. Both looking happy. Both wearing long black coats.

"Welcome, welcome!" Dominic said and helped Anita with her coat. She was wearing a cocktail dress – it was dark-green and silver and she looked beautiful. Her hair was curled and pinned up at the sides. He was wearing jeans with a black shirt and black suit jacket.

"So everyone, this is Paul, my husband!" Anita began and Tim was the first to step forward and shake his hand.

"Tim Hughes. But haven't we met before? You look very familiar."

Paul shook his head. "Don't think so, mate."

I'd overlooked that one. So had Carla. Jesus, was I suffering from some form of amnesia?

"Paul, this is Dominic," said Anita, and they shook hands. "This is Carla," shaking of hands and he never flinched, "Debbie," same, "And finally Mia!"

I held out my hand and he took it and squeezed it hard and for longer than anyone else's. "Great to meet you all! I've heard so much about you lately."

"Drink, Paul?" Debbie offered.

"Please, Debbie, if it's handy." He removed his suit jacket.

My skin was actually crawling. Literally crawling. I wanted to run out the door.

"Mia, you look stunning!" Anita said as she stood close to me. "So does Carla – that colour is amazing on her. So is that the lovely Tim then?" She twirled her wedding ring which had now reappeared on her wedding finger.

"Yeah, that's him alright." I gulped my drink. I was so aware of Paul's presence in the room. "Okay, everyone's here now so we'd like a bit of hush," Dominic said. "Debbie and I would just like to thank you girls for all the hard work you have put into Clovers this year. You all adapted brilliantly to the necessary changes and we recently welcomed the wonderful Anita with open arms. We couldn't be happier with how the business is going, as other businesses are crumpling during these crippling times. It's you girls have kept us afloat with your charm, talent and determination. So we got you all a little something to say thank you."

Debbie handed Dominic three gold envelopes and he handed one to each of us. We all opened them at the same time. It was a luxury weekend break at the Powerscourt Springs with three treatments, two breakfasts and two evening meals.

"Thank you so much, this is fantastic!" Anita gushed and Carla glanced at me.

"Brilliant!" I gushed in turn.

"Thank you both!" said Carla.

This was all I needed – a girly weekend away! I couldn't go on it, that was for sure. It was one thing dealing with Anita in the office, but a social weekend was out.

Tim and Paul were chatting about Manchester United and Carla and Anita were hugging Debbie and Dominic.

I poured another generous cup of wine and looked over at

Paula and Tim again. Paul didn't seem remotely stressed or put out. I saw him make some wild gesture to Tim and Tim laughed. It was a golf swing, I think. I licked my lips which were completely dry.

How on earth could someone behave like this? *Well, you're doing the same*, the little voice inside my head drilled at me. I'm doing it to protect Anita. *Well, maybe so is he.*

"Shut up," I said but as usual I said it out loud and Anita turned to me.

"What? Who are you talking to?"

"Oh, no one! I think I need some air."

"But it's lashing out there!"

"Oh well, yeah, I know, but I need to make a private call so I'll sit in my car."

I opened the office door and ran for the quiet of my car. I slammed the door and leaned my head back against the cold seat. I just wanted to start the engine and get the hell out of there. This was the most awful situation. I didn't fancy him any more in the slightest and I realised then that he was actually creepy. I realised that I had never fancied him at all. I closed my eyes and recalled that the first morning Carla had introduced him to me I didn't bat an eyelid. I hadn't felt any chemistry. We had shared the space of the tiny kitchen and made polite small talk but there had never been anything more until that night I had come home totally depressed by still being single and on the wrong side of thirty, downed gone-off wine, and then he'd appeared. I had just wanted a man, I realised. I just wanted to be normal and have a boyfriend. I knew he was using me but I was using him too. Then I made myself believe I was falling in love with him.

There was a loud knock and the window nearly came in on me. I screamed.

"Open the door!" Paul snarled.

"Fuck off!" I shouted and he pulled and pulled at the handle.

My temper suddenly raged so I opened the door and he got in. I turned on him. "What the fuck do you want, you total knob?"

"I want to tell you that I'm sorry. Okay, listen, I never meant to hurt you, it was all a bit of a joke and then I realised you were falling for me" He was playing Mr Nice Guy.

"Oh, save it, Paul!" I stared back at the office. "I really don't care."

"So are you or your cronies in there going to tell her?"

I looked at him and saw through him. He was petrified. He knew that this could be the final straw for Anita and she could finally leave him.

"Answer me this, Paul, why do you do it? Why do you treat her like that?"

"I don't know." He looked out the window at the rain.

"But do you love her?"

"Of course I love her!" he shouted at me.

"So why do what you did and say all the stuff you said – if you love her?"

"Because, Mia, wake up – I wanted to have sex with you. That was all. I never wanted to lose my family over this." He threw his hand at me as though I was a piece of dirt.

I felt sick. "And the others? All the other affairs?"

"All the others? There was just one before you. But I'm going to counselling now, so I'm sorting it all out. It won't help her, you know – if you tell her, I mean."

"Paul, please get out of my car."

He moved to go but stopped, hand on the door handle. "Mia?"

"What?"

"I really did like you but I did just think it was a fling, you know. I never meant to hurt you."

I glared at him now. "Oh, you didn't hurt me, Paul, you really didn't – you only hurt yourself."

"What's that supposed to mean? Is that a threat?"

"You are a liar and a cheat and you don't care about anyone except yourself!" I knew my voice was raised now.

"Oh, is that so? Well, Little Miss Slutty, I couldn't give a shite what a vile bag like you thinks, okay?" He was shouting in my face now.

"See, you're crazy. You're hot and cold, saying one thing one minute and the complete opposite the next!" I couldn't help it but I raised my hand and slapped him hard right across the face.

As I braced myself for what might come back, time stood still.

Nothing happened.

The rain pelted off the roof of the car and slid down the windscreen. I chewed the inside of my lip until it was raw.

"Get out of my car," I mumbled as I watched the rain fall.

"No," he said back, his head now in his hands. "We need to sort this. It's uncomfortable in there. You're acting so suspiciously, Mia. You've got to pull yourself together."

For some reason I started to hum. I think it was that U2 song about Bono's dad, can't be sure.

He groaned louder now and ran his hands through his short black hair. I noticed the hair on the back of his hands, thicker and coarser than I had ever noticed before. Spider-like. And I hated spiders. He was completely alien to me here and now. A complete stranger.

"Stop humming, for fuck's sake! Do you know what a mess we're in here? If you can't sort yourself out, why don't you go home? You're acting like a child in there!"

"I have nothing to say to you." I chewed my lip again.

Then I saw her standing there in front of the car, my mobile phone in her hand. In the rain, just staring at us. I grabbed for the door handle and opened it as she turned and ran into the dark. I got out.

"Where are you going? What are you going to say to her?" He looked at me like I was crazy. A look of scorn and revulsion.

I was crazy, I supposed, and I was certainly revolting. The rain felt good. Cold and hard, like I was getting the beating I so truly deserved.

He jumped out now too, slammed the car door shut and ran into the night after her.

"Please, love!" he shouted on the wind. "We need to talk, I need to explain . . ." His voice trailed off.

I ran back to the building and stood inside the open door, staring out into the rain, wondering what the fuck I should do. I stood there for ages but they didn't come back. I needed to see Carla. I went back to the 'party'.

17

"Mia! You're soaked through!" Carla rushed towards me, alarm written all over her face.

"I know."

"Where are the other two?"

"Outside somewhere," I said quietly. "He followed me out to my car."

"Oh no!" Carla whispered, raising her hand to her mouth. "I hadn't noticed. I thought you were on a call and they were in Debbie's office."

"She saw us and ran off. He's gone after her – it's up to him to tell her now."

Carla took my big cold, wet hands into her small warm ones and gently rubbed them. We stood there, just looking at each other. There was nothing else to say.

"I know, Mia." Anita's voice broke the silence.

She stood there like a drowned rat with her rat of a husband by her side.

"I didn't know he was married, Anita, least of all to you." Debbie handed me a towel and I wiped my face with it, all fear and fight gone from me now. "I honestly didn't."

"She didn't," Carla said.

"You knew too?" Anita narrowed her eyes. Paul stood behind her, coward that he was.

"He started the work on my house, Anita," said Carla, "and he never said he was married."

"It's okay, Carla," I hushed her.

"He said it's over now," said Anita, her eyes boring into mine. "Is it?"

"Yes, it's totally over. It was never really there to begin with. I mean, it was a few times but I hadn't a clue he was married. Had I known, you must believe me, there is no way I would go out with a married man. Still less with one married to my friend."

Debbie handed Anita another towel.

The office was silent as the CD finished and no one dared to change it.

"It's just unbelievable," Anita whispered. "This is just not happening to me again!"

"Listen, Anita, it's not your fault." I approached her. She could scream, hit me, kick me, whatever, I didn't care any more. I didn't care that now Dominic and Debbie knew, because what could I do?

"It must be my fault!" She had rubbed all her eye make-up off with the towel and her face was a black mess. "I mean, why does he keep doing it to me? This is the last time. Never, never, again!" Her breath was raspy but she wasn't crying.

Paul put his hand on her arm. "I love you, you know that, you are my life, I adore those kids. It will never happen again, never again."

She turned to face him. "Can you love the kids and do this to them?" she asked quietly. "Can you really? Dominic, could you do this to Debbie and the boys? Could you risk it all for some flings here and there?"

Dominic stuck his chin out and bravely shook his head. "No way."

"Could you, Tim?" She turned on poor Tim now. "Could you risk losing Carla for a one-night stand?"

"No, Anita, no, I couldn't."

"See, Paul? None of these decent men would do that but yet you do it time and time again."

"Hey, this is only the second time! The other one was ages ago!"

I honestly nearly laughed. He was unbelievable. There were only two he had been caught out on. I had absolutely no belief that he hadn't had dozens.

"It's over," Anita said. She started to nod her head, slowly at first but then faster and faster. "Yes, Paul, it's over, it's really over."

His face fell. "Ah, come on, what do you mean? Over *her*?" He spat the word *her*.

"*She* – her name is Mia – happens to be my friend."

He laughed now. "Well, with friends like that, Anita –"

"She didn't know, Paul!" Carla snapped. "We didn't even know you were married!"

"Shut up, fake titties!" he yelled at her and Tim stepped forward.

"Watch your mouth, okay?"

"Well, Paul," said Anita, "you have managed to bring me to the lowest ebb I could ever be at! I hope you're proud of yourself, I really do." She threw the towel in, literally. It landed at his feet. "Go, please, go far far away from us! We don't need you. I can't do this to the kids any more and I can't do it to myself."

"Are you sure this is what you want? Because it's not what I want," he grovelled.

I got the feeling that if this was in the privacy of their own home he would have grovelled and grovelled and worn her down and she might have given him another chance. But not here, not on her turf, she was stronger here.

"Get out now, it's over." She walked away towards the toilet and I followed her.

"Happy?" Paul called after me.

"I couldn't be happier!" I gave him a huge bright smile over my shoulder.

"Music!" Dominic hissed at poor open-mouthed Debbie as I disappeared in the toilet door.

My fake smile evaporated as I stepped inside. Anita stood there, confronting me.

"I don't know what to say, I really don't." Tears were forming in my eyes now. "I'm so very sorry."

She handed me some toilet roll, if you can believe that.

"Oh, it's not your fault, Mia. I totally believe that you didn't know – sure weren't you just about to tell me all about this hot and cold kind of boyfriend when we were in Lahinch? Remember, when the American lads knocked on our door?"

"Oh! I was, wasn't I?" I remembered suddenly with enormous relief.

"I thought of that out there and knew you were telling the truth."

She blew her nose and then I blew mine.

"Are you okay?" It was all I could ask.

"You know what, I am. I have to be. I am moving on. I know he meant it there that he'd changed, but he meant it before as well, and he was as nice as pie to us for six months or so and then turned nasty again."

"Wow, he really does have a split personality, doesn't he?"

"You better believe it! He can be so charming and then the devil himself the next minute."

"How will Stevie and Katie take it?"

"I don't know," she said, "but I am their mother. I need to protect them from this ever happening again. Believe it or not, Mia, Paul is a good dad. He does love them in his own way, so I'll make sure he stays in their lives, but I just won't be there waiting any more."

"I have been eaten alive over this, I really have," I sighed. "I've asked everyone's advice. I wrote you a letter the day I found out, then I decided it would do more harm than good if I interfered. I felt that maybe now it was all behind him and you could all move on. My dad left us, you know, and we never got over it . . . but we cut him off."

"Ah, families all have their issues, don't they?" She turned to the mirror. "Oh great, look at my face!" She ran water on some tissue and scrubbed at her eye make-up.

There was a knock on the door. "Can I come in?" It was Carla.

"Yeah!" we both called in unison.

"Sorry, hun!" Carla hugged Anita who forced a smile.

"Has he gone?"

"Yeah. Will he go back to the house?"

"Oh, you must be joking! He can't handle hassle of any kind. He'll head straight to the pub, probably pick up a girl, and head back to his flat in Rathmines."

"Should I ask Tim to fly back to ours and grab some clothes and wipes etc?" Carla asked us. Only Carla could think like that. We looked at one other.

"It's probably a stupid question but can you forgive me?" I asked Anita. "I mean, can we get over this?"

"Yeah, we can, we will." She smiled at me and I smiled back. "Do that, will you, Carla? Get some stuff for us because I say 'Ice Bar, here we come!'" Anita pulled the clips from her hair and shook it free.

"Wow, I really admire you, Anita," Carla said as she opened the door.

"You do?" Anita asked, fear and relief written on her face.

"Oh, big-time!" Carla said as she closed the door behind her.

The Ice Bar was rocking as we sauntered up. It was illuminated in low blue lighting and had an incredible Christmas icy feel. Carla had done her best but my party wardrobe wasn't great. I was wearing my Karen Millen hide-a-multitude top (oh, ironies of ironies, and I wasn't telling Anita that one!) and black trousers with the red heels. Carla had given Anita a coral-coloured silky top and grey skinny jeans and she looked really hot.

I squeezed up to the bar and ordered a round as Dominic shoved his credit card at me. "Use it!" he yelled. "Is everything okay now?"

"Yeah, I think so, thanks, Dominic!"

I loved the fact that neither he nor Debbie had asked any questions. They had sat tight until we sorted ourselves out and, now that they perceived we had, they were ready to party with us. I admired the way they had dealt with a very sensitive situation.

The Ice Bar was belting out Christmas tunes and the massive tree was beautifully decorated in subtle greens and reds. It was alive. I saw a table open up and shouted over the din at Carla to grab it – she was on it quicker than Linford Christie.

"Is that Rosanna Davidson?" Anita asked as I handed her back a Mojito. She nodded in the direction of Ireland's Number one drag queen. I'd seen him on Brendan O'Connor's *Saturday Night Show*.

"No!" I laughed and thought the drag queen would be pleased. "That's a man, Anita!"

"That's a *man*?" she shouted back in my ear and I had to stick my finger in it to stop the ringing.

"Well, as far as I am aware women don't have balls, do they?" I pointed to his skintight white faux-leather leggings that left nothing to the imagination and she sipped her drink heavily and we took our seats.

"I can't believe we're sitting here like this after all that." I looked at her.

"I know," she nodded, "but onwards and upwards, hey?"

"Exactly," I said and sipped my own Mojito.

I leaned back and relaxed for the first time in weeks. Thank God that was all over with. Thank God that guy was out of my life. Thank God I hadn't ruined Anita's life – he had ruined that part for her a long time ago. I was relieved Peadar and Damien were at least in a home they loved but I couldn't think about what was around the corner for them. I was relieved that Mam had agreed to move on with her life at last. I was also planning with Carla's help to get Mam a makeover. We were going to book her into Peter Marks (none of them new-fangled hairdressers' with stupid names like Cowboys and Indians, she had warned me) for a brand-new style and then we were going to get the personal shopper in Brown Thomas to help her with a whole new look. I knew she'd love it. She really was a good-looking woman, she just didn't see it any more.

Tim and Carla were kissing under the mistletoe and they really did make a spectacular couple. I watched Dominic's drooping eyes go up and down and then from side to side, rolling around in his head. The cold window frame held him up until Debbie finally gave in and said she was taking him home.

"Are you mad, woman?" he chastised her. "I'm off to The Pink after this!" He hiccupped now, right on cue. "Merry Christmas, everyone, and see you all in the New Year!"

Debbie kissed us all and I hugged her tightly. She managed to do her job, be a colleague and wife to Dominic and be a mother and she never moaned. Ever.

"We might take off too but only if you don't mind?" Carla whispered into my ear.

"No, go for it!"

I waved them goodbye and got more drinks for Anita and myself. I still had Dominic's credit card but I didn't use it. He'd paid for enough already. We spent the rest of the night crying and laughing and then hugging in the corner and later we ordered from the sushi bar just because everyone else was doing so.

In a horrible way I was glad about what had happened with Paul because she deserved so much better.

"I'll never marry again, that's for sure," she told me, as she popped a salmon teriyaki into her mouth.

"Ah, don't say that, you might again, one day." I dipped my sweet shrimp into my soy sauce.

"Nah, not interested, honestly. I'm not just saying that – oh, I want to date big-time – but I won't marry again."

I believed her. I put a smidgen of wasabi on my crab and avocado roll and immediately regretted it as my mouth burst into flames. I did it every time – when would I learn? I had to drink a full glass of water before I could speak again.

"Could we call it a night?" Anita suddenly asked. "The food has knocked me out, I'm afraid. I can't do both – I can either drink or eat but not mix the two. I couldn't get another drink down me now in a million years."

I completely agreed and we gathered our stuff and left.

"So what will happen tomorrow?" I asked as I put her into the first taxi that came after we had waited forty minutes.

"Well, I'm going to go down to my parents in Wexford with the kids to have a nice family Christmas." She put on her seat belt.

"Will Paul come down?"

"I'll invite him to see the kids but that's it. I'm going to divorce him in the New Year." She pushed her hair from her eyes.

"Here, love, this isn't a confessional box – are ya closing the door or wha'?" the taxi driver shouted back at her and she closed the door.

Ah, nothing quite like the Christmas spirit, I thought as I stood there waving her off. I couldn't wait for my bed. There was not a taxi light on anywhere so I started to walk. I should have called one from the hotel, I supposed, but it had been a few years since I had any trouble getting a taxi in the city. Ranelagh wasn't too far and I felt like the air. I gripped my bag under my arm and headed for home.

As I got to the lights on Donnybrook Road, a car pulled up beside me.

"Get in!"

I jumped as I saw Paul edge closer to the kerb.

"Go away, Paul!" My heart was racing now and I clutched my mobile in my coat pocket. The streets were empty. It was that in-between time. Clubs were still open, people not heading home yet.

Taxis raced by. I kept walking. He followed.

"Mia, for Christ's sake just get in! I need to talk to you!"

"Have you been following me all night?" I was trembling and stopped dead on the path.

"I was waiting for Anita but you never left her side and bundled her into that taxi so I didn't get a chance." He stopped the car now and put on his hazards.

Cars flew by and no one looked out their window at us even once. Everyone was too busy and too used to seeing drunken fights during this Christmas party night.

He got out. I shivered.

"Sorry," he said now.

"It's okay, Paul. Listen, it's over and done with as far as I'm concerned, okay?"

"Well, you haven't just lost your wife and kids, have you?" He pulled the sleeve of the jumper he was wearing over his hands.

"No," I answered.

"But I have."

"Look, Paul, I never wanted any of this to happen. You have to take responsibility for your own actions here." Still no passers-by.

"I have, I mean I did. I was truly sorry. I made my decision. I went back to her, I did, for life." He looked at the ground. "You need to tell her it was all you, that you chased me from the very beginning, that you said you'd kill yourself if I didn't see you again, that I was trying to tell you I had a wife I loved."

I put my hand up, mobile clutched in it. "Absolutely no way!"

"You have to do something, you fat cunt!" He edged into my face now and I burst into tears. He stared at me and then all around him. "Right, I know I have major anger issues, I lash out whenever I feel threatened, always have done, but I didn't mean that, I just said it to hurt you. Anyway, let me have my say."

I didn't say a word. I just stood there shivering.

"After I dropped you to the train station," he went on, "I went straight back and attacked the extension – I was sawing through wood in seconds – and then I stopped and just sat on the floor wondering what the hell I was doing. If I didn't love Anita at all, then how come I thought about her all the time? How come I couldn't get her out of my head? You see, I hated her for trapping me by getting pregnant but I didn't hate her for making me a husband and a father – I just felt I deserved some of the fun that all my mates were having. The slagging I got all the time – 'Ah, poor Paul, what an eejit getting himself into that mess! Who'd have thought little ole Anita would out so soon. Any chance of a go on her, mate?' Then as the years went by I just didn't take the marriage seriously, I was angry I hadn't been able to go on lads' holidays, to travel Australia like I'd planned to do since I was a kid. I had a map on my bedroom wall with pins in all the places I was going to see. I always dreamed of going to college and studying something, anything – I had a good brain, ya know."

When he paused for breath, I jumped in. "I believe you, Paul," there was no way I was angering this guy, "but I honestly don't know what you want me to do now, I can't do what you want."

Some car did slow down now and an older gentleman peered out.

"Talk to her?"

"What?"

"Talk to her, please."

Was this guy for real?

"You won't though, will you, Mia, because you don't think she should take me back, do you?"

I wondered if there was another tirade coming. "Paul," I said, "here's what I'd do if I were you. I would find someone to talk to, talk through all these things, then maybe get the family to come and listen and talk. I can't say if Anita will ever take you back as a husband but there is certainly no reason why you can't still be a fantastic father to your two children – that's what family is all about."

He wiped his nose with the back of his hand. We stood in silence, my breath fast and heavy and his slow and short.

"I'm sorry for all the stuff I said to you, okay?" He turned and got back into his car.

I put out my hand to hail a taxi. Miraculously one stopped.

"Ranelagh, please!" and I gave my address.

"Ah, Jesus, love, you could have walked there!" the driver said as he indicated to pass Paul's car.

"Do They Know It's Christmas" played out on the radio as I looked back and Paul was just sitting there, staring straight ahead. I turned around and let out a sigh of relief. I had been scared, no doubt about that. He was pretty messed up. But I felt quite happy with my advice. I had been honest and it was true. Anita wouldn't take him back but I knew she would keep him in her life for the sake of the children and I knew one Christmas she would have the good grace to have him around for dinner with all the family.

Carla and Tim were snuggled up on the couch watching *It's A Wonderful Life* (I'm not making that up) when I got in. I flung off my red shoes and collapsed beside them, whether I was wanted or not.

"There's tea in the pot." Tim grossly touched the pot with his socked toe.

"Na – thanks."

Carla pressed pause. I was imposing. "I'm sure you'd like to talk?"

"Na," I said again, "I am totally and utterly all talked out." I stood and lifted my shoes by their straps. "Night, guys."

18

As always the run up to Christmas took over everyone's lives. Grafton Street twinkled and people twirled their way up and down the street (more so that they wouldn't bump into others than from any merriment). I enjoyed the time away from the office and stuffy buildings and tried to sleep and eat well. I even went to two of the boot camps with Carla which left me near-dead but at the same time made me step away from the pizzas at night and go for tuna salad instead. After all that hard work.

Carla and Tim had decided to book a last-minute to Lanzarote before Christmas and off they went. They were both such free spirits, no responsibilities or ties really. I had dropped them to the airport and hugged them both tightly as people turned their heads to see if maybe this gorgeous couple might be famous. I imagined what they were both going to look like with a tan (yeah, you got it) as I sped away before I was towed.

Dublin airport was a total maze to me. I would need a map

the next time I was going anywhere. Note to self, give myself plenty of time. When would I get away again? Not next year, that was for sure – I didn't have the spare cash. Carla had decided to stay in Ranelagh after all. Well, now that Tim was moving in, she could afford it. They had both got on their knees in protest when I said I should go and give them their space.

"No! Please!" Tim begged. "If only to help Carla keep the house and get the mortgage down! Come on, Mia, at least until you really want to go?"

So I agreed I would stay for now. I honestly believed they both wanted me to stay there and I was happy to be on the same lower rent.

Back home, I flopped on the couch and flicked on *Xposé*, my favourite TV3 show that I never got time to watch these days. The clothes for the season were stunning and I lay back to enjoy the collection from Irish designer Synan O'Mahony. If ever I get married, I told Karen Koster, he is making my wedding dress.

My phone rang and for once it was there in front of me on the table. No scrambling around. I was relaxed. I checked the caller ID. It was Gordon and I sat up delighted.

"Well, hey there, dude!" I drawled in my best LA accent.

He burst out laughing. "Well, hey to you too, baaaabe!"

"How's it going?" I muted the TV but still kept one eye on the clothes (I never got that Sky+ thingy – it was all too much for me).

"It was, well, you know, hectic and I kind of ended up buying a place there!"

"What?" I almost screamed. "To rent or to love?"

"Oh, to – I dunno yet really. It's small but it's in the Hills and it's stunning, Mia, truly breathtaking. I'd rent it for weeks at a time but I actually think I'd use it too. Anyway, I'll tell you about it later and I have loads of photos. Any news with you?"

"Oh Gordon, Gordon, Gordon, where do I begin?"

"What?" Another phone rang for him.

"Go on, get that," I suggested.

"No, I want to know if you're okay?"

I filled him in on the whole Christmas party saga and he was a great listener.

"I'm glad," he said at the end, sounding really happy. "I'm glad she knows, you know. It's for the best, out in the open. You both deserve better. Anyway, listen, tomorrow night for dinner, is that okay?"

I shut my eyes. I wasn't in the mood for making polite conversation. "Yeah, sure. What time?"

"I'll pick you up say seven thirty?"

I gave him my address and we hung up. I was sure his wife had little or no interest in meeting me. I mean, I wasn't taking the job so what was the point? So we could all be friends? I pressed mute and watched the rest of *Xposé*, tempted to eat the ham and mushroom pizza that belonged to Tim in the freezer.

Then I glanced at the clock. Boot camp was at seven – I'd go. I'd actually go on my own without Carla nagging me. I dragged on my tracksuit and made my way over there. (I had to look in the hall mirror as I opened the door to make sure I was still me.) It felt good, I had to admit, running it all out of you. I liked to sweat as it felt like it was really burning calories. Pilates or yoga just didn't do it for me. I ran and jumped and skipped and gave him twenty and was puffed and exhilarated by the end of it. It was unreal how much more energy I had. If I had stayed on the couch at home and eaten that pizza, I'd be crawling up to bed by ten o'clock. I drank more water and thanked Sergeant Major. I wasn't his favourite, I knew that.

I jogged back to the car, absolutely delighted with myself.

I relaxed all the next day and cleaned the house. It was never really messy but I knew Carla would appreciate it. She had called earlier and they were having a fantastic time.

"I miss you," she told me.

"I miss you too," I replied. I wasn't jealous, I was thrilled for her. I used to think that I hated James because he took up so much of her time, but I was glad to prove myself wrong.

By six o'clock I was ready to jump into the shower to get ready for the dinner at Gordon's. I wondered what was appropriate to wear as I left some coconut leave-in conditioner in my hair and opened my wardrobe. I decided on a pair of blue jeans, a pair of neat plum-coloured ankle boots I had forgotten I owned and a white shoestring crocheted top that I found hanging at the back of my wardrobe. I had tried to squeeze into a few bits from Carla's wardrobe last night and wasn't surprised when nothing fitted. Why did I do that to myself?

I washed out the conditioner and listened to some classic Barry Manilow – "*Oh Mandy!*" I sang into my hairbrush as I applied my make-up. I had arranged to meet Anita tomorrow for coffee before she went to see her parents in Wexford. She had sounded okay, a little down but that was to be expected. We were working through it.

At seven I was all ready to go and I looked nice. I threw in Carla's Newbridge silver hoop earrings and that was that. I sat watching the Christmas-tree lights flash on and off until I was slightly hypnotised.

Gordon knocked at exactly seven thirty. I pulled on my coat and opened the door.

"All set?" he asked.

Yes, he was tanned and so healthy-looking. He had his black leather jacket on and jeans . . . and runners! Gordon in runners?

"What are you laughing at?" He looked down at his runners.

"Is this like, the new, like, LA you?" I couldn't stop myself from laughing.

"I'll have you know, Miss Doyle, that I always dress like this at weekends."

I closed the door as he extended his arm in the direction of the Silver Merc and I slid in. The heated seat welcomed my bum and the pale cream leather smelled like new.

"Nice wheels," I said, rubbing the heated seat under my bum as we hit the road.

"So are you hungry? We've been slaving in the kitchen all day."

"Oh, you're joking – not for me, I hope?"

"Well, there are a few others joining us."

Ah, for Christ's sake! I stared out the window. "Does Mrs McHale not have caterers?"

"No." He shook his head. "Evie does it all herself."

Good for her, I thought for the second time in as many weeks.

We drove with a seemingly noiseless engine along the coast road until we reached The Tindles at Killiney. It was a stunning white house set on the cliff's edge, giving it an amazing view. A small driveway with three other parked cars there. There was the Black BMW, a Silver Audi and two other cars which I couldn't make out. The house looked like something from a Jane Austen book, decorated for the season. It was literally Christmas personified. The huge green wreath on the red door stood out as he slipped the key in the lock. The windows with several small individual panes were decorated with holly and stencils and falling snow. It was beautiful from outside but when he opened the door I gasped. An elegant hallway welcomed us, with a huge dark-oak winding staircase and a glittering chandelier above.

"Can I take your coat?" he said.

I slid it off and he hung it over the banister. I'd never have done that, I'd have put it away somewhere – how could you ruin the look of such a banister? He threw his leather jacket on top of mine now. Lucky coat, I thought.

He was staring at me.

"What?" I asked.

"You look so nice," he said. "Come on in here and let's have a drink."

We entered the room to the left which had a roaring open fire with red and green candles decorating the mantel above it. There was a small chrome bar.

"Wine? Beer?" he asked as he got behind it.

"Wine, please." I sat on the white couch and put my bag on the wooden floor, partially covered in what was probably a million-euro rug.

"Where's Evie?" I asked now.

"Oh, she's still getting ready, she takes forever. You women! I'll get her –"

"No! Leave her! I know what it like getting ready, it's a nightmare."

He poured three glasses of red wine. "Well, you really do look beautiful," he complimented me again, softly this time, as he handed me the glass. His white T-shirt, so sharp against his tanned face and arms. A recent tighter haircut making him look younger.

He stood in front of the fireplace. "I love my heat," he offered.

"Indeed," I replied and he laughed.

"What?" I laughed now. "Why are you always laughing at me?"

"Because you're funny." He smelled his wine.

"Funny how?" I asked, now sounding more like Joe Pesci in *Goodfellas* than a sexy femme fatale.

He sat beside me now, still sniffing, so I sniffed too.

"Well, I love the way you think," he said. "We're very, very alike. I find it hard to laugh when I'm with other people – but with you –" he shrugged his shoulders, "it's just very easy all the time." He smiled and I smiled back.

No wonder he wanted me to work with him! I relaxed him.

I sniffed my wine. "Gordon! You won't bloody believe this but I can smell apricots off this wine!"

He jumped up. "Oh yeah? You can? Brilliant! So can I!" He was literally ecstatic.

"Okay, calm down! It's not that exciting!" I said as he laughed again.

"Sorry, I got a bit carried away!"

He sat again and we sipped and sniffed for a while.

"So . . . did you kick James out?" I finally remembered to ask.

"Oh God, yeah, and I took great pleasure in it, the little creep. You know, he'd been using my personal belongings including my cars? I flung him out on his arse. Has Carla seen him since?"

"No." I thought I heard a noise upstairs.

"Evie must be ready," he smiled. "Actually, here's Denise and Seán now!" he added as two headlights beamed into the room, blinding us both.

"Not much parking space out there, though, is there?" I grinned.

He got up and rubbed my head, then went to open the door.

He ushered an elderly couple in and introduced them to

me. I wondered if they were they Evie's parents? They seemed very normal nice people, apparently not all that well-to-do, and good fun. Denise, with a close-cropped, very blonde hairdo and pearls, wore a navy trouser suit. Seán, a bald man with glasses, wore a black suit and spotted dickey bow. Wow, the dress code was all over the place!

"So where is the lady of the manor?" Denise asked as Gordon gave her a can of Heineken, believe it or not. I was expecting sherry or Pimm's.

"On her way, I believe," said Gordon. "Shall we go into the dining room so she can sneak into the kitchen en route to check her din-dins?"

"Lovely," Seán said, pushing his glasses back up his nose.

The dark navy carpet was like sponge under my feet. I wanted to take off my boots and let my bare feet sink into it. The dining room was, well, a proper dining room. Silver candlesticks and Waterford crystal but with Christmas crackers on every plate. Good for Evie, I thought. I relaxed as the smells wafted in and was surprised when Gordon sat beside me with Denise and Seán opposite us. There was one place set at the head of the table. Wow, she rules the roost, I thought.

"Sorry I'm late," came a voice as the swinging doors between the kitchen and the dining room opened and there stood Evie McHale.

"Evie, dear!" cried Denise as she and Seán jumped up and kissed her on both cheeks.

"And you must be Mia?" She made her way over to me.

I couldn't move. I was rooted to the chair. Was this a joke? What was going on here? I stared at Evie and then at Gordon and then at Evie and then at Gordon again. His face was expressionless. He stood.

"Mia, I would like you to meet my mother, Evie McHale."

I stood slowly, realising what he had done to me here. He

was laughing now into his napkin. "Pleased to meet you, Mrs McHale!" I offered my limp hand.

"Oh, Evie please! Gordon has told me so much about you and aren't you a stunning girl altogether! Please sit, the filo prawns are just warming and I made a divine chilli dip, if I do say so myself. So is everyone alright for a drink? I hope Gordon is being a good host?"

She fussed around the condiments on the table as I sat again slowly. Gordon was still laughing, shaking in his seat now. Denise and Seán were looking at him but Evie didn't seem to mind her son's unusual behaviour and left to busy herself in the kitchen.

I leaned towards him without looking at him. "You asshole," I muttered. "You absolute asshole!"

He had tears running down his face now which he was desperately trying to rub away before Denise and Seán saw them. "Sorry, bit of a private joke," he explained to them. They laughed good-naturedly and began chatting to each other again.

"Why?" I asked.

He shrugged and wiped his face again with the back of his hand. "Cos it's funny," he answered as Evie returned with the prawns plus chilli dip.

Which was more shocking to me, I wondered as I gulped some water. That at first I thought he was married to a seventy-year-old woman or that I now realised he wasn't married at all? So he was single. Gordon McHale was single. My heart started to race and I was short of breath.

"So, Mia, Gordon tells me you're a bit of a whizz kid with selling houses?" Evie said. "Tell him to sell this one, will you? It's way too big and I'm not here very often any more – and I am terrified of all this recession talk, I worry for him." She unfolded her red-and-green-linen-with-little-gold-stars napkin and placed it onto her lap. Before I could answer she was off again. "Was Gordon telling you he bought me the most beautiful place in Falcarragh in Donegal? It's far from all this he was reared. We had a very modest house in Firhouse. Gordon's dad worked all his life in Miley's bicycle shop so I don't know where all this entrepreneur property-developer-man stuff came from." She looked very fondly at her son. "Are you an only child?" I asked and he nodded.

"Oh yes, Mia, he's my Golden Gordon!"

Now it was time for me to laugh.

"We tried and tried to have more but it just never happened. My ovaries, you see, they –"

Gordon stopped her mid-sentence by coughing loudly first and then lifting his hand in the air. "Yes, thank you, okay, Mam! We really don't need to hear about your ovaries over dinner!"

Everyone laughed and so did Evie.

Denise asked after Evie's plants in Donegal and the two women struck up a conversation. Seán asked Gordon about the market and I was thrilled to sit back, eat the delicious food and hear Gordon's opinion on it all. He was fascinating. He knew all there was to know about the property market here and abroad. He was lucky. The properties he had were all holding their own, all in fantastic locations, and although he would never see the crazy money from the sales of them that he would have during the Celtic Tiger, he didn't seem to mind. "I'm getting by nicely," he told Seán. "I was lucky though." He let out a low whistle. "I had sold well just before the crash and paid off the mortgages on this, some other houses and a few apartments, so I was able to buy Shrewsbury. I could never have bought it during the boom, no one could, and it just wasn't worth that money anyway. It was my dream house as a kid. I always loved it. I used to play the board game Monopoly at a friend's house and this was the property that was top notch. I bought it whenever I could – in fact I went into the horrors when someone landed on it before me." He laughed now and I stared at him. "I had to go and check it out. It was standing on the road where my love of houses developed. I put myself through college doing puncture repairs at my dad's shop and then started by borrowing a stupid sum from the bank that they threw at me and doing up an old house at night on the old airport road. I sold it for five times what I bought it for to an airline pilot, paid back the bank and I was off. I was lucky – it was great timing for me. I'm also lucky now, in the recession, that although the house prices are falling, people are starting to rent more for long-term periods and that's what I am now. I'm a landlord." He looked at me and our eyes connected.

"Your dad would be proud," Seán winked at Gordon.

"I know." Gordon picked up his wine.

"Mia," said Evie, "would you like turkey with all the trimmings for dinner or vegetable curry?"

"Oh, turkey all the way please, Evie."

"Denise and Seán, I know I don't have to ask – and you, Boo-boo?" She tickled Gordon under the chin and he blushed. No doubt at his mother's very public use of what must be his childhood nickname.

"Mam, seriously stop – turkey too!" he laughed.

"Oh, Boo-boo, Boo-boo, like turkey?" I asked in all seriousness and he grinned at me playfully. I wanted to tickle him under the chin.

The conversation turned to politics. I was never all that comfortable in those sort of discussions lately. There was just too much going on in Ireland and it was draining, so I discreetly pushed my chair back, put my napkin beside my glass and made my way into the kitchen. Evie had a green apron on now and was lifting the turkey from the oven.

"Can I help, Evie? It's a lot for one person to do."

"Oh hello, dear, aren't you very thoughtful! But, honestly, I love doing it. I just need to let this bird rest for a few minutes – everything else is ready to serve."

The kitchen was just unreal. An Aga in the corner, an old-fashioned massive wooden family dinner table, pine presses and a sliding door that looked out over the lights of Dublin. It was tiled in grey and black.

"Actually, Mia," she pushed a bowl towards me, "could you give these strawberries a wash? You can use that colander. I just want a few to go on top of the ice cream with the brandy pudding later."

I was more than happy to oblige and set about washing them carefully.

I noticed she was sipping a glass of water.

"Don't you drink?" I asked her.

"Ah, I do, but after all this is done." She sipped her water, then lowered her voice and said, "He's a great boy, you know. Does everything for me, he's wonderful – but I worry about him, he works too hard."

I didn't know if I should answer so I pretended there was a particularly dirty strawberry I was working on.

She was spooning the vegetables into serving-dishes. "Ever since his father passed on, he's felt like he owes it to me to be here for me all the time. That's one of the reasons I moved to Donegal, to try and give him more independence down here. He's my life, you know." She was beside me now, choosing the best strawberries out of the colander and putting them in a bowl.

"I bet. He's a really great guy." I shook the colander and put it down on the draining-board.

"So are you two dating then?" she quizzed me as she poured gravy into a sauce-boat.

"Oh no, no, we're just work mates – well, no, we're friends, I suppose."

"He talks a lot about you though he never talks about anyone."

"Well, if he does, it's because I was involved in his biggest ever purchase – his dream, like he just said."

"Hmmm," she said.

She transferred the turkey to a large oval serving-dish and began to skilfully slice one of the breasts. It was like watching an artist at work.

Then, removing her apron, she went to the swing-doors and called Gordon to come and carry in the turkey.

She took two huge gold trays and filled each with covered serving-dishes. "Shall we, dear?" She lifted one tray and I lifted the other as she opened the swinging doors with her hip and we re-entered the dining room.

The meal was amazing. I was eating myself backwards with all these fantastic meals while never cooking a morsel. What did that say about me? My strawberries were perfect although Gordon's eyes opened extra wide when Evie said I'd helped with dessert and he pretended to approach it with exaggerated caution.

After dinner we adjourned to the lounge and I couldn't speak I was so full.

I excused myself to fix my make-up, grabbed my bag and went out to the hall toilet. As I sat on the toilet to pee, I flicked open my phone. I had three missed calls. That was never good. I didn't recognise the number either as it wasn't inputted into my phone. I hit my message minder.

Received at seven forty-nine p.m.

"Mia, it's Damien. Peadar's taken a turn and they're insisting on taking him in. I don't know what to do! Can you call me back on this number as soon as you get this, thanks."

Received at eight fifteen p.m.

"Mia, they're taking him to St Vincent's Hospital. I tried, I

really tried, but they talked me into it. They told me he will die in the next few hours if he doesn't get medical treatment and that I don't have the right to make that decision. I'm just not strong enough. I'm going to go with him in the ambulance . . . sorry . . ." the message trailed off.

Received at nine p.m.

"It's me again, oh, where are you please? He has pneumonia. They have him on all sorts of stuff but he doesn't look good, he really doesn't. I'm meeting with the doctors now but they want to speak to his next of kin – oh, please come, Mia!"

I jumped up and threw the phone into my bag. Flushed the loo and ran back into the room. "Gordon! I have to go!"

He jumped up. "What's wrong?" He clanked his glass down on the table and came to me, putting both hands on my shaking ones.

"It's my friend Peadar – he's taken a bad turn, he's in hospital."

"Let me drive you."

"Oh, I'll get a taxi – we've all been drinking and I don't want to drag you from the party."

"Okay, let me call one and I'll come with you."

He left to call the taxi and Evie kindly put her arm around me as I apologised. She led me to a chair and sat me down gently, taking the seat beside me.

"Some things are more important than silly dinner parties, dear."

I was so grateful for her understanding and kindness.

Meanwhile my mind raced. What did Damien exactly mean by a turn? What kind of turn? I also knew how much Peadar did not want to be in hospital. He hated the places. Ever since he had watched his own father die in a hospital, he had been traumatised. No one would believe my life right now, I thought, as Evie handed me a tissue even though I wasn't crying. There had been years of nothing much – work, weekends of snogs and hangovers, worrying about getting old and barren. Worrying about being a spinster. Then the drama tumbled upon me as though I had been saving it all up for a special occasion. *Boom!* But it was my life and it was all happening to me right now. I would almost prefer the dull life. Almost.

Oh, why hadn't I called to see them last night? I could have. I sent Damien a text to say I was on the way.

I saw the taxi sign light up the driveway. I thanked Evie, said goodbye to the others, and we left. Gordon was quiet and so was I. Just before we reached St Vincent's he put his hand on my knee and he left it there until he had to take it away to get his wallet before we got out.

19

In A&E Damien was cradling a white plastic cup and watching the TV3 news. He jumped up when saw us.

"Hi!" I grabbed him into a hug, forgetting to introduce Gordon. My mouth was so dry I took his cup and drank the freezing cold coffee.

"Gordon." Gordon extended his hand.

"Damien."

They shook. He sat and so did we.

"He's not good, Mia, his lungs – and he's not responding so well yet and all I want to do is to take him home because he hates hospitals and he'd hate being here but what option did I have?"

"How did it happen so suddenly?"

"Oh, he's been hiding it so well! 'This little cold,' he kept saying. You know, I found out he's been on sun-beds every day to keep his colour up, he's been wearing four T-shirts under that bloody dressing-gown at a time and throwing most of his food away. I went shopping and he was not well at all when I left, his breathing was really shallow and hard. He laughed it off, saying he'd a hangover plus the cold, so I went. When I got back he was in bed and Jesus, Mia, I thought he was dead. He was semi-conscious and his breathing was unreal and I did the only thing I could do – I called the ambulance – against his wishes."

God, I felt awful for this poor man. "What else could you do, Damien?" I whispered.

"I should have nursed him at home the way he wanted it. It's just, well, it wasn't how I pictured the ending – I thought it would be slow and gradual, not like this. I never thought he could get some infection like this."

"It very often happens like that," Gordon said quietly. "When the immune system is weak, the body is vulnerable to infection."

"They said I could go in but I said I was waiting for a friend."

"Do you need to call his family?" I asked.

"I have done."

"Are they coming now?"

"Yes," he managed and then removed a tissue from his pocket and blew his nose.

There was no more to say on the subject so I took off my coat and said, "Come on, let's go through."

Gordon took my coat from me, prised my bag off my shoulder and sat down. "I'll be here," was all he said.

I linked Damien's arm and we pushed open the green plastic doors and stood at the empty nurses' station. Monitors beeped behind closed curtains and people whispered.

"Where is he?" I whispered and Damien pointed to a cubicle where I could see numerous pairs of feet under the curtain.

"Yes," a small friendly-faced nurse asked.

"We're with Peadar O'Driscoll," Damien offered.

"I see." She came out from behind the desk. "One moment, please."

The smell and the tension was making me feel sick as a grey-haired doctor in green scrubs approached us.

"Hi, this way if you don't mind."

We followed and he sat on a bench at the end of the corridor.

"Now, Peadar is suffering from one of the most common pulmonary complications affecting cancer patients – pneumonia." He paused. "It is a potentially life-threatening inflammation of both lungs. Basically, Peadar's cancer is progressing and both his cancer and the therapies can weaken the immune system in ways that make cancer patients especially susceptible to all bacteria, fungi and viruses."

Damien was so still.

"What I recommend now is to remove a small piece of lung tissue – a process known as a transbronchial biopsy – for microscopic examination and cultures, and prescribe medication to combat fungal and viral organisms that might be responsible for the patient's symptoms."

"Is he going to die?" I blurted out.

This time the doctor paused for ages. "I can't say. He isn't taking the medical treatment for his cancer which was strongly recommended to him. I understand his fears, I have read his notes, but in my opinion he's crazy. I have many, many patients who respond miraculously to this type of treatment for colon cancer. I know his feelings but, as I say, there is so much we can do to help – if he would allow us." The doctor stood now, shaking his head. "I have to go. We're hoping to get him into theatre in a few hours. Will the rest of his family be here by then?"

We both nodded.

"It's not what he wanted," Damien dropped his head in his hands, "but we didn't really seem to have the time to get to this stage of the conversation. Yes, I said I'd nurse him, but honestly, Mia, I thought that was when there was no hope left at all. I thought it would be way down the line and we didn't discuss this kind of sudden crisis. What do you think?" His white face stared at me. He was in turmoil.

"I think you did the right thing. I mean, in any case, you had no choice – I'm sure it would be manslaughter or something if you didn't call for medical assistance in such a case."

We walked back outside to Gordon.

"Oh, Gordon, you poor man! You can go – seriously!" I said. "You should get back to your mother."

"No, I'm staying if that's okay with you, Damien?" he said.

Damien nodded and then stood again. "I should call his mother again. Give her an update."

Damien took his mobile call outside and I lay my head naturally on Gordon shoulder. "Thanks for being such a great friend," I whispered.

My head was pounding now with the drink and the shock. Gordon rubbed my head.

"You know what, Gordon," I sat up, "what's this all about really? I don't know, I really don't. Are you religious?"

"I don't know," he answered. "Sometimes, I think."

"It makes me realise all the time we waste and all the moaning we do, and this bloody recession is getting everyone down and depressed, and for what? Life is so short. We should love every day. I know it's easy to realise it when you are in this kind of position but you know what I mean?"

He nodded.

"You do it, you appreciate it all, don't you?" I asked.

"Well, yeah, I appreciate it, but it doesn't mean I'm happy." He looked down.

"Gordon McHale not happy? Why? How?"

"I suppose I want more."

I laughed. "More? That's a true businessman for you!"

"No," he raised his voice, "not business, not money, not material things."

"So you aren't happy at all?" I stared at him.

"Not really. Not fulfilled, I suppose is a better way of putting it." He stared back.

"They'll be here in an hour." Damien was back. "His mam and brother. They'll need to sign some things."

I could see how much this fact hurt him. They were not a married couple so he had no say as far as the law was concerned.

He sat down next to me.

"Damien," said Gordon, "don't you think if he pulls through this he should get the treatment?"

"I always said he should, I always begged him, I've researched it to the bare bones and, yes, a lot of people respond but a lot don't – it's a chance one takes."

"But surely worth taking?" Gordon said.

"Yes, I think so. Let's see what happens next, shall we?"

Eventually Mrs O'Driscoll and Keith, his brother, arrived. Both really nice quiet people who had faced cancer in their family before. Now again it loomed and they were clearly terrified. The paperwork was signed and after some hours, Doctor Compton, who we had spoken to earlier, told us the procedure was completed and Peadar was now in ICU in recovery. He said they had to make sure he remained unconscious for the next twenty-four hours and in isolation, so we should all go home.

Damien broke down and Gordon put his arm around him and insisted on us all coming home with him to Killiney. There was plenty of food left over and plenty of rooms for us all and we could all go to the hospital together in the morning. I could see the look of pure relief on all the faces and I squeezed Gordon's shoulder.

I called everyone on the way home and Gordon told Evie

what was happening. I called my mam, Carla, Samantha and even Anita. I realised how small my little world was.

By the time I was brushing my teeth in the en-suite bathroom I was utterly exhausted. I looked in the mirror. My eyeliner was down my face, my teeth stained red from the wine earlier and I even had 'wine cracks' at the sides of my mouth. I scrubbed at them now. What must the doctor have thought?

A knock came to the bedroom door and I jumped. It was Gordon. Dressed in white boxer shorts and a black T-shirt with *Genesis* on it.

"Just checking you're okay?" he whispered.

"Yes," I said, "and thanks for my Genesis T-shirt – a bit of a collector, I see?" I pointed to my shirt and then his.

"Yes, well, Phil Collins really."

"Phil Collins?" I gasped.

"Yeah, *Face Value* was one of the greatest albums of all time."

"Shut up, nerd!" I said as he came in and I gently shut the door behind him.

I sat on the bed. He sat beside me.

"Phew, it's tough on Damien, isn't it?" he said, rubbing his eyes, "and he's such a nice bloke."

"Yeah, it's tough alright, poor man."

Before I knew what I was doing I lay my head on his shoulder. My heart was suddenly in my mouth. I'm sure he could hear it pounding. We were both very still. I heard his breath become heavier and then I lifted my head and looked into his eyes. He didn't budge, his beautiful eyes very serious. He pushed my hair out of my face, then he held my face in his hands.

The silence spoke volumes to us both.

His breath was warm now on my face and I could smell his mouthwash.

"I don't want to do this when you're so vulnerable," he said, "but I am absolutely mad crazy about you, Mia."

A jolt of surprise – shock really – ran through my body. But I believed him. I don't know why or how but I didn't feel like he had lost his mind, I didn't think he was trying to get a quick ride, I totally believed that he was mad about me. Isn't that mad, I thought, as I stared back at him.

"I think you are the most open, honest, funny, intelligent and sexy woman I have ever met." (You should get out more, was the sentence that ran through my head now.)

He put his arm gently around me and we lay back on the bed. I moved myself quickly and lay fully on top of him. I could feel his heart beating in his chest. I leaned in closer and put my lips on his. Softly. He moved gently, slipping his tongue in and out until I couldn't take it any more and kissed him back with such passion he was probably groaning with pain and not pleasure. We ripped the Genesis T-shirts off each other and he rolled over on top of me. He bent his head and kissed my breasts and I thought I was going to yell. (I literally had to clamp my hand over my mouth.) Then weirdly, the faces of the lounge girl in Kiely's bar, the girl in the Shelbourne and the bullies in school ran through my mind with me singing na-na-na-na-na at them. I shot back to reality when he was removing my knickers with his left hand while still caressing me with his right. I should say "condom", I knew, but I didn't. I reefed down his boxers and took him in my hand as he groaned. He entered me after what felt like an eternity with me literally pushing him inside me and it was the most incredible, slow wonderful sex I had ever had in my entire life. I was completely in love with every part of this man. It was exhilarating to know he felt the same and I knew he did. With his wonderful face gazing down into mine, I knew that this was a life-changing moment for me. He wasn't like the others, not that the others had really been all that bad except for Paul, who obviously had his own major issues. Gordon McHale was meant for me. I just knew it.

As we lay there panting side by side post-sex, I kept my right hand firmly on his ass. Then he leaned up on one elbow and said, "I've been waiting for that for so long." He kissed me again and again softly.

"Why didn't you say?" I reluctantly removed my hand from his bottom and pulled the covers up to my neck now. I wasn't that comfortable with my body yet.

"Because you were all over the place, seeing that bloke, and I wanted to wait for you. I knew the minute I saw you on the landing, taking in Shrewsbury. I wanted you. I don't feel like that very often so it was a fantastic feeling. To fancy someone like crazy. I loved it."

"Is that why you offered me the job, you dirty hound?"

He laughed. "Well, yes and no, really."

I pinched his nipple (not because I cared about the job but because I now could pinch Gordon McHale's bare nipple if I wanted to). "Okay, Gordon. I am believing you. I'm not full of angst or nervous around you, I'm just mad about you really, I suppose, I always have been even when I thought you were married, but then after that I just envied your mother when I think about it."

We both laughed like kids and I knew Peadar would approve.

"Do you think Peadar will make it?" I asked as I pressed rewind in my head and put my arm on his shoulder.

"I hope so, Mia, I really do, but I haven't a clue. But if he needs money for anything, private care, whatever, I can help."

"You're wonderful! We'll see."

We lay in silence, stroking each other, holding each other

tightly and I was glad that this moment of pure joy was tinged with some sorrow because otherwise it would be just all too good to be true.

We all sat at the nurses' station at seven the next evening. I had watched the clock all day and it had ticked by so, so slowly. It seemed so strange that the hospital was decorated for Christmas.

"Doctor Compton will be down after he has been in with Peadar – he's just doing his rounds," a nurse told us.

Gordon and I held hands and Damien gave me a wry smile. I reached out and took his hand too. Evie had made us all a massive fry-up but most of it had been left on the plates. Mrs O'Driscoll and Keith were silent.

Then we saw the doctor approach, his face unreadable until he got to us and broke into a smile.

"Well, it seems he had a good night, he's fully conscious and has responded beautifully to the medication. And, he has agreed, in principal, though he needs to talk with Damien, to starting treatment for the cancer as soon as he can."

"*Fucking yay!*" I jumped up and punched the air. Then sat back down red from top to toe, mortified.

Gordon was hugging Damien and Keith was hugging his mother.

"Can I see him now?" Mrs O'Driscoll asked.

"Of course," Doctor Compton said, "It's supposed to be one at a time, I'm afraid, and only for a few minutes each. Obviously Damien is eager to get in to see him too so the two of you can go down together on this occasion but keep the visit short, won't you?"

I wanted to hug this doctor, with his wonderful sense of what was right.

"Is that okay, Dolores?" Damien asked and she nodded and they followed the doctor down the long corridor to ICU.

"Isn't that brilliant?" I asked this specimen beside me. I was beginning to feel woozy, now the realisation was kicking in. He was my boyfriend. No doubt about that. The chap couldn't keep his wandering hands off me. He kissed me now and two nurses nearly fell over their medicine trolleys. Keep walking, ladies, I silently told them, he's all mine!

"I'm thrilled," he said and he genuinely was.

"Gordon, I suddenly realised, where are all your phones?"

"I switched them all off." He looked a little pale.

"No, don't be silly, go home now and sort your business." I kissed him hard and, yes, more nurses drooled.

"If you're sure? I do have a lot of stuff to sort out but I'm staying here if you need me."

"I'm sure you should go," I said and kissed him again.

I was already dialling Carla as he walked briskly out through the hospital doors.

"*Whhhhhhhhhhhhhatttttttttttttttt!?*" She screeched so loud I had to hold the phone away from my ear. "Oh, I am so thrilled for you! Wow, he's just such a nice guy! Great for you, Mia!"

I filled her in as Mrs O'Driscoll and Keith reappeared and told me Peadar would like to see me now. She was sobbing but it wasn't disconcerting.

I rang off and made my way to ICU. Damien was in the corner, speaking to a nurse, and he winked at me. I peeped around the door. Lifting an oxygen mask off his white face, Peadar managed in a very strange voice to say, "Well, hello, Miss World," and we laughed.

I sat by the bed and shook my head at him. "The minute I score a great bloke you have to go and take a turn!"

He smiled with watery eyes.

"I know you can't really talk, so don't," I said and crossed my legs, "but, look here, Doctor Compton thinks that you could actually be around for a good few more years if you stop playing silly beggars."

A tear rolled down his face now and he licked it when it hit his mouth.

"And you're not in heaven yet, Peadar, so you can't actually turn your tears to wine."

He laughed out loud now and coughed and coughed and wheezed and I jumped up and screamed for the nurse and the bugger laughed more.

"Now, now, stop this! He can't have any excitement!" She tutted hard at me and ushered me out of the room.

I looked back just in time to catch him blowing me a kiss. I leaned against the door of ICU and roared laughing.

20

"Okay, is everyone sitting down?" Samantha said. In her cute yellow polo-neck and black suede skirt she looked rather like a bee. I'd actually chosen it for her as a gift for Christmas.

A hush came around the huge glass table in my new home, Number 2 Shrewsbury Road. I still couldn't quite believe it. The house was like an unbelievable dream. I had copied Evie's style and decorated it in dark reds and dark greens with white fairy-lights twinkling on the massive tree, and draped red fairy-lights over our picture frames. The table was laid to match.

Instead of a formal starter I had laid out little bowls of nibbles around the table for people to pick at. Small chicken pieces wrapped in bacon, salmon and cream cheese on tiny squares of brown bread and good old-fashioned sausage rolls.

Samantha was the self-appointed turkey-carver, you see. Knife held aloft. Steam rose from the turkey and the smell was mouth-watering.

I glanced around the table. Gordon beside me, then Carla and Tim, then Damien and Peadar (Peadar in a wheelchair which he hated, so we had wrapped it in red tinsel and had battery-operated fairy-lights on it), then Niall beside Samantha. Mam and Niall's dad Mr Byrne were side by side (and by all appearances getting on like a house on fire). I saw Mam pat her newly styled hair to see if it was still there. Evie sat on the other side of Mr Byrne who was clearly delighted with the company of the two older women.

Mam adored her new look. Not only adored it but it had actually given her a new lease of life. On the same shopping trip where I bought Samantha's clothes, we had brought Mam into town and into Peter Marks on Grafton Street. We chatted with Zita the stylist, made an appointment for two hours later, and then went for coffee. Then we went and met the personal shopper for Brown Thomas, Fiona, at the information desk, and she was unbelievable. Gordon had insisted on treating us all to our Christmas outfits and he wanted me to spend a good amount on Mam's new look. I thanked him as I slipped his gold card into my purse. That great day was something I thought money couldn't really buy us but somehow it had – here we were, the three of us, shopping together, having fun, even laughing. It was like *Pretty Woman* for near-pensioners as Mam twirled in and out, pushing back the soft brown heavy velvet curtains, to show us her outfits. I had to hand it to Fiona (who honestly, though, looked more like a straight school principal than fashion guru in a green pencil skirt and shirt and dark-rimmed glasses). We settled on two outfits much to Mam's outrage. "I'm not spending Gordon's hard-earned money on two outfits!" But I did. The first was a trouser suit in navy, tailored, with a three-buttoned jacket. We bought a white silk shirt to go with it and kitten-heeled boots. The second outfit, which she was wearing today, was a soft cerise pink wraparound top with a white singlet under it, a black linen to-the-knee skirt, sheer barely black tights and black knee-high leather boots. She kept the latter on, that day in town. So childlike, I noticed, as she skipped from the store swinging her bags.

We dropped her back to Peter Marks and when we went back to collect her later, I almost, just almost, walked past her. There, sitting in the window, waiting for her two daughters was a stylish older woman. Her newly cropped hair was highlighted in golds and browns and was shaped into her head, with soft layers – it took years off her.

Sitting here today, Mam was of sunny disposition and happy. It didn't do her any harm, I must admit, that I had fallen for a millionaire property developer who was helping us get her settled in her new apartment where (this is true, would you believe) Peadar and Damien had lived after Gordon had the racist homophobic bullies kicked out.

Samantha and Niall seemed very happy and I thought that he was actually a very nice guy, a little bit too dull for me but hey, he didn't want to marry me – but he definitely wanted to marry my sister.

Peadar had been on treatment and, although it was tough going, he wasn't looking too bad at all. He'd had long discussions with Doctor Compton and the other doctors, then with Damien and his family regarding what to do next. He decided to meet again with Doctor Compton in January, when he was fully recovered from the pneumonia, and then choose an option. He would probably go ahead with a treatment in a clinical trial. It was a research study in TCD to help improve current treatments and obtain information on new treatments for patients with cancer. He was an inspiration to me. It was hard going for him but at the end of the day he was still here with us and, sick as he was, he was still able to mill the wine I noticed as Damien scolded him.

The doorbell rang just as Samantha had achieved some hush.

"Oopps, hang on, sis!" (I cringed at that one myself.) I pushed back my seat and walked through the great big hall and opened the heavy door.

"Hi." There stood Paul.

"What?" It took me at least thirty seconds and a struggling Anita laden down with Katie and gifts to realise it was Stevie, Paul's son.

"So sorry we're late but the drive up from Wexford took longer than we thought and Mam and Dad were fussing over us, weren't they, Stevie love?"

"Oh, I'm thrilled you made it!" I led them in and took their coats.

"Oh wow, Mia!" Anita said. "Seriously, I loved this house the day I saw it. I never could have sold it as you did that day, I was too busy rhyming off boring facts, but you were right at the heart of this house. It was meant to be."

I hung up the coats in the closet.

"How are you?" I asked as Stevie lifted Katie up to see my crib.

"You know what, I'm absolutely great. I feel fantastic and in control and just happy to know what direction my life is going in. I saw Paul – last night he came by, we had a drink, he cried, I didn't, I kissed him goodbye on the cheek and wished him a Happy Christmas and, you know what, Mia, I actually meant it!" She smiled and I hugged her tight.

"Let's eat so!" I led them into the dining room and they sat at the end of the table.

"Okay," Samantha tried again, "we don't want this fabulous

turkey to go cold, so I just wanted to wish my sister and Gordon every happiness in their new home!"

"Here, here!" Carla was tipsy already. She and Gordon had at last met and she had agreed to leave Clovers and go work for him and she was over the moon. It was a perfect job for her and the extra wage would help her so much with the house repayments. "I have never seen Mia more content and it makes me so happy!" She raised her champagne glass and we all stood.

"Ehem!" I cleared my throat. "Unaccustomed as I am to public speaking . . ." a few giggles but Gordon laughed hard (you had to love the man, he really got me), "it's been a complete whirlwind of a year, never mind the last few months. It's totally unreal to me that I'm standing here today around a table in this house with all the people I love here with me. How did this happen?" I scratched my head, looking at Gordon, and I suddenly realised I had everyone's full attention. "Anyway there have been a lot of lessons for me to learn about myself and about all of you and I suppose most of you have learned lessons about me?" I looked at my mam. "I think, when my dad left us I tried to block love out, especially with you, Mam, and you, Sam, as it was too close to home. I was afraid of being hurt by you guys too. But I've learned it's not about old loves, it's not about the past, and that it's impossible to love or be loved if you can't just be yourself. Whatever that may be! So I dumped my baggage, shredded it all. With all these lessons learned about myself and the people I surround myself with, Love and I are finally able to get on together and I am so comfortable with being me. I thank you all, and I love you all."

I sat down, a bit red in the face now but happy and yeah, okay, more than a bit tipsy too. Carla had tears in her eyes and blew me a kiss.

"Merry Christmas, everyone, and let's enjoy this day!" Evie said.

I wasn't wearing Spanx knickers so for once I could breathe, I wasn't uncomfortable in my own skin, I didn't feel too big or too useless. I felt 'Wow, what a lucky girl I am!' and I was. Lucky. I raised my glass and sniffed at my wine.

Gordon rose to his feet. "So, finally, as I am the man of the house –"

"The turkey will be dead cold!" Samantha protested.

"The turkey can always be reheated – it's never hot enough anyway!"

The table all laughed.

"As man of the house, I would like to just say a few words. Firstly, welcome to my new extended family. I am slightly jealous of you all, that you have had Mia in your lives for longer than I have, but I intend to address that issue. I know what she's like – she likes fairytales, she loves a happy ending . . ."

My brain was starting to slow down and suddenly I couldn't keep up. Everyone was reacting in slow motion. Facial expressions slowed down to a freeze-frame pause. Now he was reaching into his trousers' pocket with a bit of a struggle.

In slow motion I saw Carla's eyes open wide, I saw Tim guffaw, I saw Damien squeeze Peadar's arm and I saw my mother's hand rise to her mouth. Was I having a funny turn? "Mia?" Gordon spoke my name.

"What!" I shouted at him.

He was in front of me now. Then he was gone. I looked down and he was on one knee. I could hear nothing. Nothing. It was as though I was under water. It was a deafness that I couldn't shake.

Then his mouth opened and he spoke. "Mia Doyle, I can't put into words how happy I feel when I am with you, or how much I adore you and all I can do is tell you that I couldn't imagine the rest of my life without you by my side, every single day."

I was panting now. He opened the black shiny box very slowly and a single diamond sparkled up at me.

"Will you marry me, Mia?"

I heard that alright.